The Faultline

A novel by
John McLellan

D1425021

John McLellan has written many things in his life, as a student, as a manager, as a trustee, and as a management consultant, but this is his first novel.

He has worked in logistics, film and television, including with the BBC, and more recently as an equality, diversity and inclusion adviser to the NHS. He graduated from Swansea University in the late seventies with an honours degree in Geology and undertakes voluntary geology fieldwork guiding on the Jurassic Coast and elsewhere.

He is also now a writer living in Bristol, UK, with his partner David.

He still collects rocks!

The Faultline, first published in 2022 by Twelve Acre Publishing, via John McLellan and Whitehall Printing. This edition published July 2023.

Gratitude is given to Dave Cousins of The Strawbs for the use of two quotes and to the estate of J L Carr for one quote. Both of these people have had far more impact on me than I realised until writing this book.

Thanks also to the publication: Wester Ross and Lochalsh – 40 Coast and Country Walks, by Paul and Helen Webster (worth getting when you visit the area), for the quote in part two.

Paperback ISBN: 978-0-9555902-3-8

During the Covid-19 crisis, the author had the privilege of working in Southmead Hospital, Bristol, as a Frontline NHS Volunteer. The role involved many long, quiet walks around a very large hospital and it was in these circumstances that much of the shape and content of this book evolved. A donation has been made to the hospital charity from sales of this novel.

#faultlinenovel   email: faultlinenovel@gmail.com   Find The Faultline on Facebook

To Dave, who puts up with so much.

A few quotes from readers of the first edition.

'It's wistful, reflective, thought-provoking, romantic, actually that's a pretty good reflection of the landscape you've set it in too'
(IT, Scotland)

'I felt like a child on Christmas morning when the package arrived. It is such a beautiful novel'
(RMcE, Scotland)

'What a great novel The Faultline is!'
(TC, Netherlands)

'It's one of the most moving books I've ever read'
(MS, Poland)

'I also gave my 89 year old Dad The Faultline to read and he couldn't put it down'
(LF, Scotland)

'…a beautiful and marvellous novel, I could relate to so much'.
(CV, England)

'I finished your book last night, loved it, very insightful and warm and so many bits that had me turning the pages faster.'
(SB, England)

'I think it's one of the most affecting books I've ever read! And I've read a lot of books!'
(CR, Scotland)

'Your book was the perfect book for me to read after my journey to the Highlands'
(GL, Italy)

*'It is warm, lovely and I have rec~
so wish you u
(LS, ~

*'Just finished your book with a very u
relationships with others is wh
(PH, Scot~

D1425134

Foreword

None of the characters in this novel are real people, and any resemblance to anyone living or dead is coincidental. All the characters are hybrid assemblages of memory and imagination.

The geology, landscape and wildlife, however, are portrayed as realistically and accurately as I can manage. Their contributions to the beauty and wonder of the North West Highlands of Scotland are enduring.

John McLellan
4th November 2021

Part One

Kinlochewe, 1977

"The mind seemed to grow giddy by looking so far into the abyss of time…how much farther reason may go than imagination may venture to follow"

John Playfair, pioneer geologist, 1822

"From mountains high I gained strength for my soul"

From 'Lay Down' written by Dave Cousins, The Strawbs. 1973

Peter's field notebook sketch map:

FIELD NOTEBOOK   30 JULY 1977

CONCLUSION OF MAPPING. SKETCH-MAP OF LOCATIONS!

LOCHANS FADA

SLIOCH

PATH

CADH A GHOBHAINN

(STEVE'S AREA)

GLEANN BIANASDAIL

LOCH MAREE

MEALLAN GHOBHAR

TOGAIRLOCH

SINGLE TRACK ROADS

FIELD STN

KINLOCH RIVER

KINLOCHEWE

GLEN DOCHARTY

R. GRUDIE

Mtn TRAIL

GLAS-LEITRE FOREST

PUB

TO ACHNASHEEN

"SUE ROCK"

BODY TRAIL

CAMPSITE

DRUIM GRUDAIDH

OLD RUINS

VIEW POINT

QUARTZITE PLATEAU

MEALL A'GHUBHAIS

SCREES

BEINN EIGHE

CORRIE MHIC FHEAR-CHAIR

(GRAHAM'S AREA)

TO TORRIDON

LIME HUT

DRUMLINS

CHAPTER 1

The day started far too early for Peter. At two-thirty in the morning he was half-dreaming, half-sleeping, drowsily coming round into consciousness. He was convinced there was someone in his tent, talking closely in his ear. Then, another one the other side. They were hard, older men's voices. Harsh, Scottish brogue. He fully woke-up with a start and sat-up. There was no one in his tent. The voices were outside.

It was just confusing, adjusting to camping, he decided, realising it was just another late finish in the pub for the oil rig workers. Was this to be a performance every night, he wondered. He might need to move to another part of the campsite. There were about a dozen men, billeted in a bunkhouse down the road a little. The quarter-mile walk to the bunk house from the pub, passed along the road close to all the tents on that corner of the site. This was the second time on the trot he had this late night, early morning ritual.

As he leant back, he realised it was already getting quite light. Even this early! He mulled a moment – the year's longest day in a few days' time. He had never been so far north in June before this and the sheer amount of daylight had been a real surprise.

It was difficult getting back to sleep, but he managed to drop-off for a while. Then the men's coach called for them about six. It was a rickety old bus and the engine turning-over made a heavy and loud rattle and rumble. Peter lay awake for the second time, just letting his mind wander over all that was happening up here in the far north-west. In a way, he thought, it was related to what he was doing; or at least there was some sort of connection.

It was a new phenomenon apparently, just started this year. After years of geological exploration, North Sea oil production platforms were being constructed at Loch Kishorn, forty miles down the road from here, for the next phase of oil production. The hundreds of workers involved were billetted all over the region, wherever there was cheap and ready accommodation. They all got paid handsomely, according to the gossip in the pub anyway. As far as Peter could see a lot of it went on booze and fags.

He tried to doze a little more. The bright mid-June early morning light was warming his tent. He drifted off half day-dreaming, images of walking, a distant horizon never getting closer.

It was the sound of other campers stirring that had finally compelled him to get up. He had forgotten how much sound you could hear under canvas. People coughing, tent zips being slowly opened, or briskly unzipped, people trying to be quiet but making noise doing it anyway. Gas and primus burners igniting, clanking pots on camping stoves. Whispers and bits of conversation being carried across by the air between the tents.

Getting out of his sleeping bag, he felt bathed in the peaceful glow of sunlight through orange fabric, putting him so near to the rest of the world around him and yet removed from it. The canvas enclosure both accentuated and separated the proximity of others. After a few days on his own, he had already come to view the little tent as a kind of private sanctuary.

He was grateful for a bright start today though. After a bit of dithering around the last couple of days, Peter felt determined. Today was definitely to be a much more organised approach to the task of producing his map and he needed to stop prevaricating and get on with it.

Fortunately, he was early to the washing block. Nobody else was around. No queue. Nobody at all in fact, and the wash-basin cubicles free for him to choose. In the mirror he noticed his hair was getting longer and more lank. No time to wash it today though. On the way out he filled his water bottle and the kettle from the tap on the corner of the block, surveying, at a rough count, about a dozen tents of varying styles. Some small ridge tents and others, larger frame-tents of various sizes and shapes, plus a few touring caravans.

Back at his own tent, he sorted himself out. While boiling-up water for tea, he ate his usual bowl of cereal, with a lot of sugar and milk. He had decided this was a relatively cheap way of getting in a lot of energy, which he was concerned about, but didn't cost much either. Balancing calorie intake and money outflow was already becoming a daily preoccupation. He already felt thinner than normal.

He packed his rucksack and made sure he had all the maps in the case for the day's work. It was too much faff, but it was hard to know what to leave out. He was a few days into a new experience and didn't want to be putting effort into getting around his mapping area, only to find he had left a note book behind, or a spare pencil was needed, or something vital forgotten.

This had felt like a big mountain day and he thought he ought to wear tough breeches but they felt too heavy and it seemed it might be too warm. If the weather changed, too bad, he thought, as he settled on shorts. Hoping it would stay fair enough, even at three thousand feet up.

Graham must have heard him and half-heartedly shouted a weary good morning and good luck from his tent. Peter wondered if his friend was also going to get out onto the hills today. Knowing he was finding it equally hard to settle into the work aspect of the trip. It hadn't helped, as Graham freely admitted himself, that he had been given a chunk of Moroccan Gold by his brother before coming away. Peter thought he seemed content, so far, to while away a fair bit of time just enjoying it.

Peter's mind wandered to the previous day, also bright and sunny, and a good day to be out doing their work, but lost to other things. It had instead been a day exploring the village, going to the tiny site café, walking up the road to see what was there, and generally wasting time, he reflected, on any other pretext.

He and Graham had spent an hour or two chatting over joints, about politics, philosophy and anything else that seemed relevant at the time, going down the pub later and then trying to sleep. He felt bad about it now. Everyone local was saying it was really unusual to have such a settled spell of good weather up here.

Once packed and boots on, Peter looked-up and across the campsite. The roadside part of the campsite might have the problem of occasional night-time drunken noises, but he thought the view outwards and upwards more than made-up for it. The main feature looking from here was the bulk of Meall a Ghiubhais, the mountain that topped and dominated his geological mapping area. Right now, he could see it was completely clear of cloud and looked dramatic and enticing. That was just what he needed for motivation.

He walked out and past Steve's caravan, with no sign of Steve. Peter felt he was ticking-off the plus points of the day. He liked Steve, but didn't want a conversation this time. Not only would it delay him but Peter also feared Steve would be chucking-in geological comments which would all be well intended but would have the effect of making him feel less confident about the fieldwork ahead.

But now he saw he wouldn't get past Julie, who was outside the campsite reception hut. He could see she was already in shorts too, getting herself organised around the café part of the site reception hut that she was managing with her friend. She leant against the corner of the small wooden building. Her long curly hair, distinctively reddish in the morning light. She tried to waylay Peter with the offer of a tea, one hand holding aloft a china mug, the other hand on her hip. She looked very cheerful, with a big smile accentuated by her large round-rim glasses.

Peter liked Julie's sense of fun and slight flirtiness. She was always breezy and friendly, studying at Swansea but doing the summer job of helping run her Uncle Ben's campsite and looking after the tiny tea room with Sue. They had arrived just a few days before Peter and would be similarly spending a lot of their summer in the small Highland village.

He thought they had seemed pleased when he and then Graham arrived and had first gone in to say hello. They said they hadn't really expected other students to be here much, let alone for several weeks, like Peter. Seven weeks in fact, he thought, also realising he was now already nearing the end of the first of those.

'You're up and about bright and early today?' Julie said, 'You look geared-up for something.'

'Yeah, I've loads to do and feel I've been wasting the good weather really.' Peter knew he sounded a bit clipped but hoped it would be sufficient.

She gave Peter a look that said she thought he was a bit daft, cocking her head to one side and raising her eyebrows. 'Wasting good weather? I think we should all enjoy it while we can'.

'I know Julie, that's true I suppose, but I've miles to cover and really haven't done much. Anyway, its work isn't it! I am here to do something.' Peter had slowed down on the approach to the hut and now stopped.

'Well' she said. 'You seemed to do a lot before this weekend, when your lecturer fella was up here. You went out a couple of very long days then didn't you? Can't you just write down whatever he said!? Those guys just want you to repeat what they have told you anyway.' She was giving him a cheeky grin.

'If only!' Peter laughed. He wished it was simpler. He took a piece of paper out of his map case. 'Anyway, look, it's good I've seen you. This is the note of where I'll be today. Will you give it to your uncle please?' He thought he still sounded hurried, but hopefully a bit friendlier.

'Sure.' She folded and put the note into her back pocket. 'But won't you have a cuppa with me to get you going?', and she was already starting to go to the café doorway.

'No. Honestly' Peter said. 'Stop it, will you?' He smiled at her. 'I really have a shed load of stuff to do and I really am going to do it. Today. Anyway, I spent a fair bit of time here yesterday.' He also started to move, away from the hut.

'You did, and that's why it would be nice for you to stop again. What are you actually going to do anyway?' she asked, giving up on the tea offer now but not the chance to chat.

Turning and pointing at the hills and mountain opposite, Peter said 'OK, I'll point it out. I'm going up to that first shoulder of the hills, that's about eighteen hundred feet up. From there I go straight over that big mountain, Meall a Ghiubhais, only I can't really, as I would fall off the other side as it's all cliffs. So, I have to go round it.' He indicated a half-circle in the air. 'Then I'm coming back round the same mountain from the other end, and then eventually back down here.'

'Well!' she said. 'Rather you than me. It looks a fair old way'.

'About fourteen miles I reckon.' Said Peter. 'Yeah, it is a fair old way, as you say.

'You'd better get going then', she smiled a really genuine smile, 'see you when you're back. Maybe another day off tomorrow though, eh?'

'Hmm, maybe. Listen – don't forget that note. It's going to be lonely up there for me today and…'

'Yes, I know, said Julie, filling-in the sentence. '…if anything were to happen, the note would let us know where you were.' And she smiled at him.

'Exactly Julie! Ta.' He thought he really liked the use of the word us.

Walking down the road to the start of the access path onto the mountain, Peter was just mulling over the campsite life. He felt he could already be getting into a bit of a routine. He just needed to make sure the bulk of the day was on fieldwork, and then making the other things fit in, like going over to the village shop, going down the pub in the evening, and going to the café. He admitted to himself that the two girls were a nice distraction, but they, and the café itself, were not what he had expected. In all, there were now five students on the campsite, all of them around twenty years old, as it turned out, and he had initially imagined it would just be himself and Graham.

Most of the time, he thought, the two girls seemed bored. Julie's Uncle, Ben, the campsite owner and warden had said the site and the little cafe would get busier as the summer holiday season got underway. Right now though, Peter thought that Graham and he had become the sole object of attention some mornings, and it seemed as if Julie and Sue went out of their way to waylay them as much as possible. In just a few days they had already been served teas, pies, pizzas, chips and anything else the microwave and deep-fat fryer could produce, and at a price Julie hoped wouldn't be noticed by her uncle.

So, it felt good to be walking and Peter purposefully strode out. The mile to the Pony Track path seemed to go quickly. This was the third time he had been up this way - an old stalkers path apparently, but now a useful way into the Nature Reserve.

Peter noticed for the first time the number of small trees planted by the path and he wondered if these were seedling trees of the Old Caledonian Forest that he'd read about. There was an eight-foot fence around this area and a tall gate across the path – all to keep out the red deer he had been told, though he didn't really understand. Once through the gate, the path started to steepen and he felt the sense of space opening up around him as he steadily gained height. So much landscape, so many glimpses of big Scottish mountains, going on for miles in all directions. He felt eager and fit and attempted to keep-up a good stride.

There was a stream to cross which he knew was fed from a spring rising just over the bluff, so he took a drink. It was about here he had decided to start following a line across the Nature Reserve – the central part of his mapping area. He checked the map and could see where he was exactly. Peter thought the Ordnance Survey guys had done a brilliant job making these six-inch maps so accurate. But, John Mackenzie from the Reserve had disillusioned him by telling him they were compiled by aerial survey. Either way, he was grateful as he could pinpoint exactly this spot on the pony track and that exact rock outcrop in front of him.

He would follow a line, a transect, firstly up towards the main peak, then deviating round the end of the mountain, and back to the line on the other side, as he had described to Julie.

The sun rose in the sky and even at nine-thirty in the morning he realised it was going to be bearing down on him and he was conscious there was no shade on the open expanse of mountainside. When he had been planning the fieldwork he hadn't really thought of hot sun being an issue in North West Scotland, but had put in a pair of shorts and sunglasses, as they were pretty lightweight, and was grateful now. They had pretty much been an afterthought.

Peter thought about the discussion he'd had in the pub soon after he arrived. It was the Reserve Warden who had said that this weather was unusual, remarkable even, and sunnier here than the already infamous, nationwide, drought of the previous year. He seemed to know everything about the place and Peter had made a mental note to ask about him about anything odd or unusual he encountered, as long as he didn't feel stupid doing it. The warden had said that working and walking quietly around the nature reserve on your own was the best way to experience it and gave the best chance to see wildlife. These were also things he just hadn't anticipated about the project.

The first part of the transect went well. With about a half-mile to finish, he stopped at a view point for a bite to eat and the first cigarette of the day, giving a wave to a couple of walkers a few hundred yards away on the nearby Mountain Trail. The rocky expanse he was walking over was essentially a plateau of hard, crystalline quartzite. Too much of it really for his purposes. Too much rock exposure, it was hard for him to know what to include on his map and what to leave out.

The geology was not as straightforward as it had first looked either, which made it worse. The apparently undifferentiated quartzite as he had at first assumed, and discussed with his supervisor just three days ago, made-up the whole plateau. It was on close examination though that the rocky expanse was revealed as actually being densely folded and fractured. Features that he would need to record and map in detail and then hopefully make sense of later.

He was finding nearly every outcrop had some significance and the six-inch scale map included all of them – hundreds of rocky hillocks scattered over a huge area. Peter thought he was unprepared for this too and wished he had made this discovery while he could have spoken about it with someone who knew what they were talking about. He felt a bit daunted. There was about twenty five square miles to map in total and he could see his initial rough plan for covering it over the remaining six weeks was made irrelevant by the detailed work now needed here.

Anyway, he was hungry, needed a sit down and a think. He needed to feel sure of his navigation, especially that he could get to the far side of the hill and back today, before he set-off. The next few miles were trackless and he felt he would be on his own until he got back to this point again in a few hours.

He wolfed down some oatcakes, cheese and peanuts. He thought of an older friend, now living in the Lakes and in the mountain rescue, who had advised him, more like insisted, salted peanuts were a good thing to eat in the wilds especially when working-up a sweat. "Salt and protein Pete, that's what you need", he remembered.

Peter wondered if he was always going to be hungry, especially doing the fieldwork – it was more tiring and energy consuming than he had imagined. He didn't really have enough cash for the amount of food he wanted to have, let alone the cigarettes and pints down the pub! The thought of weeks of compromises made him feel unhappy.

Moving on to pass the summit of the Mountain Trail itself he came across the couple that he had waved at, just finished eating and one of them lighting a cigarette. They had a brief chat together, all admiring the views and the weather. Peter thought they sounded Glaswegian, but he wasn't sure. They wanted to know more of what Peter was doing and the man offered him a smoke.

'Go on', the man said, 'I can see you want one. Perhaps you can just tell us what all these rocks are for a minute?'

Peter felt pleased to be able to tell them something about the rocks but it was his second cigarette in fifteen minutes and it instantly made him light-headed and a bit giddy. A bit nauseous even. He tried to hide it.

'You're kidding surely?' said the man at the end of Peter's brief description. 'Two billion years old? Two billion! I can't get my head round it. Well, good luck to you making sense of it.'

They exchanged friendly waves as Peter went on. He was sure he could see the man still shaking his head in disbelief.

This part of the mountain was the only place he had so far seen anyone else on any of the days up here. The nature reserve's waymarked trail reached this place as its highest point and there was a marker stone and a rudimentary orientation table. It was pretty much in the middle of his mapping area, had a good view and was well chosen by the Nature Reserve. It was fantastic to just look around. No other sign of habitation or human activity of any type and a wild and rocky landscape in all directions and at all levels of horizon.

The quartzite plateau looked glassy in places, in the sun, back the way he had come, across to the east. A rolling area of rock, bounded by the higher ridges and screes of Beinn Eighe and what Peter thought of as 'his mountain' behind him. The summit of his mapping area had a Gaelic name he wasn't sure he had mastered and was easier to describe to others as 'my mountain' to distinguish from other mountains seen from the village hidden far below.

He had followed a two mile straight line so far, after slogging-up three miles of the pony track in the morning sun. It was too daunting to go straight up the mountainside now to continue the line. Following it down the other side looked impossible, with a band of steep cliffs to negotiate. So, he had decided to draw the roughly east-west transect line on the map and do it in two parts. From this point he now had to go round the northern end of the mountain to resume the line on the other side.

At first he was on ground already experienced with his supervisor a few days earlier. It had been cloudy and a bit drizzly then but today the shade of the northern cliffs provided some shelter from the sun as he continued to gain height. There was a lochan up here and then, higher up and on a further two hundred yards, a second one where the smallish pool of water looked really inviting. Something for another time, Peter thought, hoping it might stay warm enough for a swim one day. It was a sheltered and hidden spot, with a smaller cliff to its north, obscuring the view of it until you walked right up to its edge.

To the north, Slioch now commanded the view, its gigantic bulk suddenly thrusting straight up from Loch Maree below. The steep sided upper half of the mountain all sandstone, sitting on the lower part of crystalline gneiss. On a day like today, with the broad water of Loch Maree below, the image looked something akin to pictures he had seen of Canada or the Rockies.

To the west stretched a vast plain of rocks, lochans and smaller steeply carved hills. All of it an intense mixture of dark red, greys and shades of blue, stretching towards the sea. It was hard to see where the land ended exactly and the distant haze shimmered where Peter thought the coast must be.

As he now came round the western side of the mountain, he was on new ground, at the far corner of his mapping area, back on the transect line and very much alone. He had been right not to come up and over the mountain. The slopes down from the summit ended in two lines of cliffs above him, both pretty difficult to climb down. The lower line of cliffs to his left dropped vertically onto the rock pavement which he was now walking up, just a few yards wide. This feature itself formed the top of another band of cliffs dropping away to his right.

Peter felt a little disorientated and more than a bit overwhelmed. The landscape around him was enormous and it had a look that, as a climber and walker, he could maybe have revelled in, but everything he saw also spoke of geology on a big scale. And that, he considered, was intimidating. Mainly he felt daunted by just the practical task of trying to make sense of it all. Fundamentally, he felt he would never get it all mapped. It had taken hours to get here, to this remote point, so how often would he be able to do that? And how could he get up these cliffs or even make an assessment of them?

He hadn't expected to find himself on what was essentially a sloping platform of rock. Here, the maroon shades of the Torridonian sandstone rocks piled layer upon layer rising above him, hundreds of feet thick, to form a dark, brooding mountain which sat on the brighter, white quartzite of the platform where he was standing.

This was all wrong, he knew. It shouldn't be like this geologically, as the quartzite in this part of the world would normally sit on the sandstone, the other way around. But it was this way here, on this mountain, and that was one of the reasons why he was studying it. And at this point, he was walking along the boundary of the two rocks – where a tectonic thrust had pushed the older red rocks over the younger white ones. He felt pleased with himself for at least having this rudimentary assessment running through his mind as he walked along.

And then he saw something odd. There was something that just couldn't be a geological feature, but was still within the rock formation. A glint of sunlight reflected from something that looked metallic, not just another bit of quartzite. Whatever it is, it's caught in the sandstone up there thought Peter. He thought it might be a beer can or something like that, thrown away by someone. But what would that be doing here? Peter wondered how many people had ever been just here, let alone littering the place.

Whatever it was, it lay about fifteen feet off the ground, Peter assessed, when he reached the point directly below it. Maybe something had blown there, but that seemed unlikely too. He decided he needed to check it out. This would involve a bit of a scramble but nothing he couldn't imagine reversing safely to get back down. The rock was fractured and jointed and there was a distinct, weathered vertical gap he could use to lean into and brace his legs while his hands found holds to pull himself up.

Not for the first time this day, however, he was reminded that he was on his own. What he considered to be his self-preservation part of his brain switched-on.

There had been little discussion of safety issues in advance, by either himself or his supervisor, and Peter felt complicit in that. He had shrugged off any consideration of what-ifs, or fears, with a youthful confidence in his knowledge of walking and climbing. Only his friend Graham, back at the campsite, had brought him down to earth. He had taken Peter aside just a day or two back, in the pub, and told him that whatever belief in himself he may have, he was still young and inexperienced with the scale of the mountains here, and that being alone made a big difference. "Remember to remember you are on your own" he had said.

Thinking of it now, Peter felt touched by his friend's concern and he thought of him too, maybe also alone in the wilds right at that minute, if he had managed to get out of his tent. He could be on the wild land to the south-east. They could be close to each other, only a few miles away maybe, as the crow flies, but more like hundreds of miles in effect.

Once actually climbing on the rock, Peter discovered the angle felt decidedly vertical but the brief and short ascent was straightforward, stepping-up on large blocks of rock. Most of the gaps in the rock were vegetated with mosses, lichens and other small plants. There were also some small insects and it made Peter think that so far he had encountered few midges, totally unlike his previous Highland trip to Glen Coe a year earlier.

He hoped that midge-free conditions would continue, although he knew it was unlikely. The Nature Reserve folk said the dry and sunny conditions right now were keeping them away, but he knew he needed to watch-out for the first rainy day to come.

But right now, in the one large horizontal rock crack to his right Peter could see there was indeed something made of metal. It seemed duller here than it had appeared with the sun on it and was pretty nondescript in close-up. It seemed like a smooth, slightly pitted lump of aluminium – a bit like, he thought, the colour and texture of old saucepans.

Stretching across, he could put his hand on it, realising straight away it was not only hard and solid, but also firmly locked into the sandstone strata. To reach further to the right meant stepping onto a bulging rock that would potentially put him off-balance.

Although the short ascent to here was easy and Peter was sure about reversing down, he knew a fall would break something for sure.

Looking along the cleft containing the metal though, Peter saw something like another piece further along – about six feet away from him. It occurred to him then that this all might be just one, long object. A length of aluminium, wedged in the rock, partially hidden by the vegetation, possibly six feet long? He felt flummoxed and also aware now that he was suddenly starting to feel a bit wobbly standing on a thin ledge. The balanced position he was in was causing the muscle of one leg to twitch and tremble.

Descending back to the ground took a bit of thought after all. He felt more pushed out by the rock going down, worsened by the need to lean out a bit to see where his feet were going. Pushing-up on the sandstone to climb up had been ok. But going down, Peter could feel his weight causing his hands to slide over the rounded sandstone holds. Back on the ground, Peter saw it was now half past two. He would need to get going if he was to avoid any concern back at the campsite, and if he didn't want to be too tired to eat anything properly.

The quickest way now would be to go round the southern end of the mountain, keeping at this contour level if possible, then doing a diagonal descent across the eastern screes, onto the main quartzite plateau again and then back down the pony track to the village. Slightly panicked by the realisation he was only just over half-way on the day's distance, Peter quickly ate half a Mars Bar and drank some water. This settled him enough to remember to make some notes in his book, draw a quick sketch of the broad geological features and finally remember to get out his camera and take a couple of photos.

Then he set-off. The going was steeper and scarier than his reading of the map suggested. He went with some speed and found that once he had started he knew it was easier to just keep going than to turn round and try and reverse the route. He found it exhilarating. Even so, he had to fight the desire to stop, especially when the cliff loomed above him and the steepness of the scree below him combined to give him a sharp feeling of vulnerability.

There was no sign of any other person, nor anything man-made, within his entire field of view. What there was, included the ridges and summits of the Beinn Eighe range, filling most of the panorama ahead. Behind and above him, there was just a wall of rock and below a fan of steep scree under his feet and tumbling down hundreds of feet. He had to navigate a line between the two and then a descending line across a mile of scree to the level area below. There was no path, nor any indication anyone had been this way recently.

He felt relieved to eventually find himself back on what now felt like reassuring, familiar ground. He made a bee-line for the nearest point on the pony track path that eventually led down to the village of Kinlochewe. It was up and down progress, over and around many small hillocks and craggy outcrops of rock. Once on the Track itself, he headed down the relatively well-defined path, leading ultimately to the village and campsite.

He got into the campsite nearing seven, made sure Ben, the campsite boss, knew he was ok, and then started going slowly over towards his tent; weariness suddenly making him feel like he had lead in his boots. Sue appeared from the washroom block as he was about to pass it. Her long hair darker and straighter than Julie's, but equally striking, Peter thought. She immediately smiled at him.

'Did it go ok then?' she asked.

'Yeah, thanks. Really tired now though.' He hoped he was returning her smile.

'Yeah, I can hear that in your voice but you look fine. Well you've been out there for hours, hope you found some good rocks.' She smiled and then added, 'or whatever it was you hoped to find out today.' She put her hand to her mouth. 'Oops, sorry, I didn't mean that to sound dismissive Pete.'

Peter thought she had a really nice way of speaking, a bit London sounding, like him. He wanted to carry on the conversation, suddenly feeling a bit less tired and wanting to share something about the day with her.

'Its fine Sue, rocks aren't everybody's thing! But, actually, I found this weird object up there. Don't know what to make of it. Some metal, sort-of embedded in a cliff.'

'Bits of deer fence or something?' Sue suggested, thinking of one of her own memories of walking in Scottish mountains.

'No, it really is on a cliff face. Vertical, near-enough.'

'A bit of metal on a cliff face? I don't know Pete, is it something to do with electricity or telephones?'

'Yeah – good thoughts Sue, but there's nothing else around. Nothing like that once you're off the road down here. Oh, I don't know either. The annoying thing is I will have to go all the way, right over there' he pointed back at the bulky mountain over his shoulder '…again to have another look!'

Sue laughed. 'Well don't worry, you don't have to go right now at least. Maybe Graham will make you a cup of something. Jules has got my tea ready I know, so I'd better carry on.' She started off towards the caravan she shared with Julie, but turned and added. 'See you down the pub in a bit maybe?'

'That's for certain!' Not for the first time, he couldn't help noticing and admiring her looks. Feeling cheered-up, Peter strode over to his part of the site. Graham was in his tent already, brewing some tea in the canopy of the fly-sheet, sitting in the doorway of the inner tent. They had been lucky, and pleased, to get the two pitches close enough together, but also separated enough, by a hedge of juniper saplings. It was ideal really; they didn't want to be on top of each other. As Peter approached, he gave a friendly hello wave.

'How's it going Pete? That was a long day after all then!?'

'Yeah, it was. Best part of eleven hours. I'm absolutely knackered Graham. Can you spare some of that water do you think?'

'No worries – I'm already making you one! I saw you being waylaid by Sue and thought you would be a bit weary. Not with her, just with your day up there', said Graham, nodding towards the mountain where Peter had just been. 'That's a really big mountain back in Wales, but one of many here isn't it!?'

'I really like it, even if I still can't say its name!' And Peter dropped his rucksack to the ground and sat on the flat rock that they had found and put there for the purpose. Graham passed him a lit cigarette, without asking, and poured the water onto the tea-bag in Peter's mug.

'Thanks Graham. Do you feel like going over the pub soon? I need some chips and a pint. Something quick and easy. And cheap.' Peter thought how nice it was, right now, like this, to have a friend here and how miserable it would have been to be here on his own as had seemed likely at one stage.

Their friendship had already developed up in a few days up here, hundreds of miles from home. They hadn't been so familiar in term time but often found themselves in the same group, chatting or meeting in the coffee bar or refectory. Now though, they felt closer – reliant on each other really, Peter thought.

Peter had been surprised when Graham wanted to map in the same geographical area too. It had put them in a similar position really, and that had made each of them feel less out of it. Coming up here had really been the least-cost fieldwork project option versus other choices, that otherwise involved heading-off abroad. Peter thought he and Graham probably felt there was no alternative in reality and had made the best decision they could.

But here and now, Peter was just glad of Graham's company. Comfortable with each other, and no forced chatter. Stubbing out the cigarette and downing the tea, he said to Graham, 'I just need to go over the wash block. I have to be a bit cleaner, or I'll get thrown out of the pub'.

'Doubt it Pete. Think anything goes in there and that lot off the rig don't exactly smell like cut flowers most evenings!'

Chapter 2

The pub visit that evening, already becoming a nightly event, had been good. Peter felt both replenished and sleepy by the time he tucked himself into his sleeping bag. It had been good to chat about the day's work with the others. In the end, all three of them had tucked into chips and beer. Jock, the barman, had indicated them to the waitress as 'those three young English lads'. And Peter thought they were a bit alike, except Graham was a bit stockier and Steve had shorter, cleaner hair.

He and Graham had agreed with each other that Steve was the bright one amongst them – keen and enthusiastic about geology and able to talk and sound like a lecturer, even though he was only at the end of his second year. But Steve, over the course of a couple of pints denied this and made light of his interest and knowledge, trying to shrug it off. Peter and Graham weren't convinced.

Steve had said that he thought that Peter's mapping area was not only extensive, but clearly had a lot of exposure. He had been able to see that from his own mapping area on the hillside directly opposite, on the other side of Glen Docherty. Steve had said how, today, Peter's mapping area had actually shone in the sun at times, when viewed from his territory to the north. 'It's all your quartzite exposure', he had stated, 'looks actually shiny at times with that sun on it'.

Talking about this, Steve had gone on to suggest to Peter that all the intense folding and fracturing he had described in the quartzite might be what he called an imbricate zone, caused by the Moine Thrust pushing over the rocks which now constitute Meall a Ghiubhais. Neither Peter or Graham were sure they understood what Steve was saying but both thought it sounded good.

Steve's view was that the thrust effectively caused the quartzite to move westwards, and it had done this by splitting layers that then slid over each other and stacking, rather like a stack of cards pushed over. Peter hadn't felt like exploring this in the pub but knew he would need to speak with Steve further about it sometime. It was an area of knowledge new to him.

Peter turned over in his sleeping bag and settled on the cushion of jumpers, T-shirts and socks that made-up his pillow. He felt cosy in here. It was a tiny space, but it was just his and he liked it that way.

He thought more about the evening's conversations. Both the other guys had been interested in his discovery of the aluminium strips of metal in the rocks. They had speculated about old mineral workings as a possibility, or thought it was maybe some GPO or electricity work, the same thoughts as Sue.

Peter was really grateful they had been interested and even more pleased when both of them had said they would be happy to come and have a look. Both the other students had got to a similar point as Peter, they said, having explored their areas broadly and now poised to get stuck into detail. They had both said a break and a look at someone else's rocks would be good. Peter felt this might be true of Steve but doubted Graham had actually done very much yet, but he was chuffed with his interest anyway.

So, amazingly, Graham had agreed to be called early the next day, so they could go on a repeat of this day's walk for Peter, but going directly to 'the aluminium' and then straight back home to the campsite. They would call for Steve on the way and Peter had no doubts he would be ready and waiting.

He started to drift-off, thinking mostly of the scenery he had seen today. His head was full of images of rocks, cliffs, mountains, that amazing view of the distant sea. It was peaceful. He turned over and then his mind moved to images from the pub as he went in and out of sleep. People playing darts, the crowded feeling when the oil workers came in. The friendly chats with people he hardly knew.

Images of these people drinking, coming and going. An image of Sue came to his mind, seeing her in her jeans and T-shirt. Light-blue denim, snugly fitting, and the shirt with the runes from Led Zeppelin's fourth album running across her chest. He was thinking he really liked that look and that it suited her. He felt a sense of contentment settling as sleep finally overtook him.

In the morning, the three students got away on another fine day. No Julie this morning and they, in fact, had to post their route note through the letter-box of the reception cabin. Peter wondered if it was a day-off for either or both of the girls, or whether they were expected to work every day. It was possibly just that they passed at a moment when everyone was doing something else and thinking that, he felt a pang of disappointment.

On the way up the path the air felt very still, just a light breeze across their feet, at ground level. Peter smelt the warmth of the ground rising – an earthy, musty smell that he thought was something to do with the red deer, but he wasn't sure.

Graham was unusually chatty, asking about Peter's mountain, the Nature Reserve and chatting a bit about Julie and Sue.

'So, what's the mountain called again?'

'Meal a yoovaysh is how it sounds I think. Something like that. It's spelt Meall a Ghiubhais.' He spelt it out to the other two. 'And it means hill of the pine tree or something. A lot of the hills around here have a Meall or a Meallan in their names, I was told anyway, and you can see on the map. I don't really know any Gaelic though.'

'It might be in your blood Pete, your old man being Scottish.' Suggested Graham. 'So, this was the first nature reserve in Britain, you said.'

'Yep, apparently. It's called Beinn Eighe National Nature Reserve, even though it seems a good part of Beinn Eighe isn't in it.'

'It's good to walk and talk, but could we slow down a tad? It'll make me breathless!'

'That's all the fags Graham!' said Steve.

'Talking of which, it might be time for a break soon Pete'. Muttered Graham, ignoring Steve.

'We can slow down a bit but there's a way to go, and it levels off soon. A bit anyway' said Peter. We can have a fag soon, ok? Once we have got onto the flatter area. Call it deferred gratification.'

'What's that then?' Steve asked.

'You know' pitched in Graham…'when you have to wait for something, it supposedly is better, gives you a greater reward. Sort-of thing Pete picks-up talking to other students at uni when he should be in the lab doing the geology practicals.'

Now it was Peter's turn to ignore the conversation. Really though he was enjoying the walk and the bit of banter was fun. They walked on over steepening ground and conversation ebbed for a bit.

'And you think Julie fancies you, do you.' Graham suddenly asked, out of the blue, as the ground levelled-off again.

'What!? Where did that come from Graham?' Replied Peter.

'I don't know – just the way conversation went last night I suppose.'

'I didn't actually say that Graham. What I said was Julie is a bit flirty at times, even early in the morning like yesterday. Maybe she's like that with everyone. I don't know. I like her.' Peter paused. 'It's nice the way they try and look after us, don't you reckon?'

'Yes it is.' Said Steve. 'I don't think they have enough to do but I expect the campsite gets much busier soon, with the school summer holidays. I like them too.'

'Well, you'll have to join the queue behind Pete then!' said Graham. Then he abruptly stopped and was clearly listening to something. The other two tuned-in to the distinctive call of a bird they could now hear. A mournful whistling sort-of call, Peter thought. Graham was a keen bird watcher and he suddenly said 'Golden Plover. Look. There.' pointing away to the left.

They all stood still as the plover was walking up the ground parallel to their route, many yards off, but close enough to see one wing held to its side. Graham explained the bird was probably trying to steer us away from a nest nearby.

'There can't be many people use this path or it wouldn't have settled here. This might happen every time you come up here Pete.' Graham went on to explain about the plover's behaviour. Peter and Steve were quiet. Peter was remembering the Easter field trip a few months back, where Graham had been the referral point in the group, for all questions ornithological. Steve just thought this was a side to Graham he hadn't encountered before, tending to think Graham wasn't deeply interested in very much and now feeling guilty about that.

Peter thought of what Graham had just said and felt it would be a nice thing if he was joined by plovers every day. While Steve left the path for a couple of minutes, he mentioned to Graham about the eagles again and also the strange encounter with a black bee. Coming here, he hadn't thought about wildlife but now he could see the Warden had been right and there was more around here than many other places he had walked or climbed. Or on his own most days he was perhaps just being more observant.

They moved more quickly across the plateau bit and up to the cairned viewpoint. Graham and Steve were amazed by the remoteness, wildness and the quiet. Peter found he was now seeing it afresh too, through their eyes and felt quite awe-struck again too. None of them felt like saying much, just quietly absorbing the landscape. They just enjoyed a cigarette, even Steve, while Peter quietly pointed out the mountains and features he knew, and had recently discovered.

When they moved off, Peter felt he was on familiar ground, although it was only the second time he had contoured around the mountain. He felt a bit guilty for not checking first everyone was ok with the terrain, but he had felt all three of them were in the same position really - having to find their way around remote country and being fit enough and sensible enough to manage wild terrain. Each had to trust their own judgement and Peter assumed they were all ok with doing that.

Steve asked what Peter and Graham had been saying a little way back, when he had stopped for a minute or two, about a bee and eagles. Peter described how he had been on this part of the mountain the day before when he looked up from the map at one point when he suddenly heard a quiet but deep buzzing near his head. A black bumblebee had arrived from nowhere and droned around.

Peter demonstrated how he had literally stumbled backwards as the bee seemed to zoom in towards his head, and he had never seen one like this and wondered if it was some local variety. 'It seemed astonishingly big, shiny in the light and seemed to hang in the air in a most peculiar way. It also moved very slowly, droning all the time.' Peter said he thought the iridescence and the way it could hang in the air had given it a surreal look in this highland landscape.

Steve listened very carefully to this and said 'That's a good description Pete, I can visualise it from what you said. You should ask the warden about it'. Peter felt as if he had been given marks out of ten, hopefully scoring quite well.

'Yeah, maybe. About the eagles though, I have seen one every day so far, which I didn't expect at all! I'd never seen one before, except maybe a speck in the distance. Brilliant really'

'Wow' said Steve. 'Well my area is just across the valley so maybe I should keep a look out too?'

'Yeah, definitely'; said Graham. 'These distances are nothing to an eagle – it could just soar across both your mapping territories in no time.'

'They nest up high on the north end of my mountain, above us.'

Explained Peter. ' The Warden told me how the Nature Reserve monitored the eagles and how their presence was "their pride and joy". Egg collectors could never get to the nest where it was perched on a sandstone ledge high up the corrie cliff – too steep and too loose to ascend. Something like that.' Peter suddenly felt embarrassed talking about something he felt he really knew little about.

Graham took over. 'When Pete was up here a few days ago with Doc Griffiths, our supervisor, they saw four eagles at once. Four! Allegedly!'

'Yeah, Graham's not sure about that are you?' said Peter. 'I know it sound unlikely, but we were up there on the summit having lunch and looking down, when four eagles, we think, floated out and along the line of the mountain, only a couple of hundred feet below us! We thought it looked like a family outing.'

'It's just a bit early for two eagles to have been reared and fledged' said Graham. 'But given it was the Doc, as well as you, you obviously saw something.'

'Oh. Thanks mate' said Peter. 'Thanks for your confidence!' all three of them laughed. 'I agree though, if the Doc hadn't been here I'd think I had been day-dreaming.'

'I will ask the Warden' continued Peter 'about both those things, but I didn't want to sound like a prat if it's really too soon in the year for what we saw or something.'

'You should ask him Pete!' suggested Steve. 'Especially about the bee thing. He's not going to bite your head off is he?'

As they came round the north end of the mountain and started to contour towards the western cliffs, they all exclaimed at once, as they saw a herd of red deer around the broad pool of water that Peter said was Loch Bhanamhoir. The deer had seen them too, or heard them, and moved off as a group, northwards and quickly went out of view among the rocks. They chatted about it and all agreed that red deer were the one wildlife thing they had seen and had in common, and were encountering often. They all felt it was something very special.

Peter took a slightly different route to the day before, missing the two hidden lochans. When they at last got to the cliff with the aluminium object, the morning had gone. This meant the sun had come round the south end of the mountain and was starting to light-up the cliff in front of them. Similar to the day before, Peter thought.

To see something through another's eyes he mulled, as Steve rattled off a series of immediate observations. He was enthusiastic and did genuinely seem fascinated by what he saw. He summarised it so easily too.

'Your mountain Pete is basically a thrust outlier of the main Moine Thrust, but you know that already. A klippe is the technical word. It's caused all that quartzite we walked over to be imbricated as the thrust has passed over. What you have on this far side of the mountain is fantastic though. You can see just from the rock colour variation above - billion year old red sandstone sitting on a wedge of two billion year-old grey gneiss, and all of that sitting on another band of sandstone, sitting on top of five hundred million year old white, whiteish anyway, quartzite. This sloping shelf we're walking up is a result of the sandstone being eroded differentially to the quartzite.' The other two exchanged a look. There was nothing to argue about, so Peter didn't. And neither did Graham.

'There it is!' said Peter. 'You can see something sort-of shiny just there.' Pointing enthusiastically. Pleased that it really was there and that he found it again so easily. The other two squinted.

'I thought when you said shiny, you meant like gleaming.' Said Graham sceptically.

'In fact it is more sort-of like a dull shine, if you know what I mean'. Said Peter.

'We need to take a look Pete. It's vertical! How do we get closer?'

asked Steve, sizing-up the wall of rock in front of him.

'The whole cliff is a bit steep, but we only need to go up fifteen feet or so, as you can see. Just a few steps up really.' Peter said, noticing the other two looked more reticent. 'Look, I'll go up and then you can have a go if you feel like it?'

Second time around, Peter found he got up the blocks of sandstone quite swiftly. He leant out across and touched the metal and tapped it, but it just sounded dull, no different to the rock really. He had expected a hollow ring maybe but could see now for certain that the metal looked as if it was welded onto the cliff, rather than hanging onto it. He looked down at Graham and Steve. 'Did you hear that?' he shouted. 'Not very convincing was it. Why don't you come up and take a look? I'll drop down, out of the way.' And Peter reversed the short climb back to the ground.

After some hesitation, Graham clambered up. Peter leant into the rock below him and stretched up his arm to reach Graham's feet. Reassured by this, Graham also managed to get to a position where he leant across and touched the metal.

'Well it is metal. Don't know what it is though. Like you said last night, it runs along that groove for several feet. I don't feel terribly steady here, how do I get back down? I've lost sight of my feet.'

Peter talked through the first reverse moves and then guided Graham's right foot with his hand to the next cleft down, and with a little more encouragement they were both together on the ground again within a minute. Graham just jumped down the last three feet and almost toppled backwards, so Peter had to grab hold of him. Then Peter also felt out of balance and had to immediately lean in towards the cliff for a few seconds holding Graham while he recovered his balance. Peter noticed it felt peculiarly comforting to be hugging him like that.

'OK, you can let me go now'. Graham said, turning to give Peter a questioning look. 'Did you think I was going to topple backwards over the cliff below?'

Peter found himself blush a bit for some reason. 'Just wanted to make sure you were safe Graham.' He knew he was feeling a bit self-conscious but wasn't sure why. 'Anyway, we're fine now.'

Peter wondered if Steve was ok clambering up. But he also guessed Steve would do anything within reason to get a closer look at something interesting and, sure enough, he went up the line very slowly and a bit awkwardly, but determinedly. Although they were focusing on the metallic outcrop, Steve actually surprised Graham and Peter by saying that he thought the short ascent route, the vertical cleft, was a fault. In his view there were probably a line of short faults along here triggered by the thrusting action above.

'The faults are at right-angle to the plane of the thrust.' Steve explained, hanging onto a protruding part of the cliff. 'Look guys, if you look at this layer of sandstone here where my right hand is, it's about as far as I can stretch. You can see it has a line of red pebbles in it, mostly small but it's quite a compact layer. And here by my left foot…' he said, pointing down, '…the same tiny pebbles. I noticed it just now as I passed it - you can see the same line running along northwards – back along the path we came up. So, the fault has fractured and dropped the rocks about six feet or more to the north.'

Peter and Graham looked at each other again and both felt a bit like they were back at school. Except Steve was so not showing-off. He was just really pleased to be discovering things. Peter thought he couldn't help being caught-up with Steve's enthusiasm. Touching the metal, just as the other two had done, Steve also said he thought it was really weird. He hung about there for a while before climbing down, again very slowly, but without needing any help.

When on the ground Steve started examining the rocks at waist height to his left, to the north. 'Here', he said. 'I think this is the same layer of sandstone as the outcrop of metal six feet further up

– it's got the same characteristics and here, crikey! Look here in this cleft is another piece of that metal.'

They all stood back to take in the discovery. So, here was a large cliff with at least one supposed fault in it, with some metal in the strata, either side of the fault and seemingly moved by it. The faultline had displaced the layers of sandstone by about six feet. And it was as if the peculiar metal had been moved too.

They speculated about it and the weird thought of the metal being geologically ancient. 'Was there a seven hundred million year old alien survey ship, or something, that wrecked here and that was later moved by the fault?' Graham joked. And yet, that was what it could look like at first impression. They all laughed at the idea.

They continued chatting about it, half jokily and half seriously. It was a really odd thing. The fault had clearly split the sandstone layer and the distinctive line of tiny, dark red pebbles could be traced on both sides of the fault. But the metal, aluminium or whatever it was, had the appearance of also having been moved. But there was no way this was possible – there just wasn't any metallic aluminium anywhere when the sandstone had been deposited, nor when the thrusting and faulting had occurred.

They talked about the possibility of a plane wreck though, and that it just so happened that parts of it had ended-up in two places. Maybe there were more bits scattered over the rock face – that would be a good thing to know and would shed more light. They'd looked around a bit but Peter thought he needed to do more of that another time, if at all.

For this was two whole days now walking to the furthest part of his area and he wondered again how often he could come here. He ought to redo his plan really, a rough assessment of how he could use the next five to six weeks to cover the geography effectively. The good weather likely wouldn't last and that needed to be factored-in too.

Between them, they decided the best thing to do was talk to the Warden, John Mackenzie. And yes, they could all see this would potentially mean yet another foray into this part of the landscape, for Peter at least. If the Warden was in the pub that night, then Peter would speak with him. Maybe the three of them would try and collar him early on.

Graham said he had heard of planes wrecked on hillsides and mountains and wondered if it was something like that. Peter wondered why he hadn't thought of that more, as he had seen crashed aircraft wreckage before. But that had been a tangled clutter on the ground below a cliff on Ben Loyal, a hundred miles further north. It hadn't been embedded in the rock as it appeared here.

They were then all quiet for a bit, lost in their own thoughts. Peter found himself feeling grateful being here with two friends. 'Thanks for coming up here you two. It's a whole day out for you both.' he said. The other two just nodded, shrugged. Peter asked them what they thought of the whole area.

'You've got a real task on your hands Pete.' Graham offered straight away. 'Look, when we were coming up this morning, that whole area to the east is my mapping area. It's tussocky heather and long walks, but I don't have anything like the amount of rock outcrops you do, and I don't have a bloody great mountain in the middle like this.'

Steve agreed and thought Peter needed to be systematic or he would never get around the whole area. He thought there was a complexity of geology that would require a lot of field rock identifications and measurements.

Peter thought they were probably right. Part of the issue was the ruggedness, it just took a lot of effort to get into and around his territory, even before stopping and starting repeatedly to note all the geological features. Thinking this, he decided they needed to move on.

Peter felt that the way back from here round the north end of the mountain might be a bit too much of a scramble for them as a group, so he suggested they head-off mostly back down the way they had come. It was easier than they had expected, partly because Peter took a way through slightly higher ground. They were soon back at the hidden lochan under the eagles' cliff that Peter had admired the day before. This time the sun, by chance, was right on it.

Without really much discussion they all agreed it did look inviting and headed down the fifty feet or so of scree and grass to the edge of the lochan. It had a little beach of weathered sand and the peat had been eroded to create an obvious place to sit. Peter knew he would have to go in the water and was surprised and a bit disappointed when Graham just sat down on the peat edge and lit-up, while Steve just sat next to him.

'I meant inviting…meaning as a place for a dip! Don't you fancy going in guys?' Asked Peter. 'Don't you think it would be good? We don't have to stay long. Just in and out really?'

'Are you going to Pete? I haven't come prepared. Nothing to wear and I don't have a towel.' Said Graham. Steve just said 'yeah, me too'.

'Last week when I was with the climbing club lads, we did the same thing.' Said Peter, hoping to be encouraging. 'We just stripped-off and jumped in. Well two of us did, and the others didn't. They carried on down to the hut. I just used my T-shirt to dry-off.' He also told them it had been a similar day and that he had worried about getting cold but with no wind and the sun it had been ok. He had a jumper in his ruck-sack today and he could put that on if needs be.

Peter knew that since school he hadn't bothered about taking clothes off with others. Doing a lot of cross-country running and swimming meant lots of times in changing rooms and it always seemed quicker and easier to Peter to just get on with it. He couldn't stand wriggling around with a towel round his waist trying to slip in and out of clothes without exposing himself. But the previous week's dip into a mountain stream was the first time he had done that, although he had day-dreamed about it often. And it had felt great.

Graham didn't react much but Peter thought he was looking relaxed, just sitting quietly, enjoying the place and the moment. Peter decided to go for it before his courage dissipated. He took-off his boots and socks, which felt a relief straight away. Once he had pulled his T-shirt over his head, he saw Graham was starting to do his boots too. 'You've persuaded me Pete but I bet its cold.'

'Of course it's cold' said Steve. 'I'll miss on this thanks.'

'Come on' said Peter, 'we can just be in and out and it will feel great, even if it freezes our nuts off.' He had the rest of his clothes off and walked-in up to his knees. The lochan was less than a hundred feet across, quite circular really. Up close the water looked less inviting – a murky brown, but that was just the peat colouring the water. He cupped a handful and it appeared quite clear in his hand. It was cold, but not as bad as he expected. Graham now coming in behind him was going on about it being perishing. A word that brought out his Welshness, Peter thought.

With the level now up to his knees, Peter turned and sat down. Leant back and then plunged his head under. He could feel a tightness across his chest and he sat up with a jolt, gasping. Then laughing and spluttering at the same time. It literally took his breath away but the coldness did make him see things more clearly too – everything looked much brighter all of a sudden.

Graham had got as far as his knees now and was holding his arms across his chest, making a point of shivering, Peter thought, as if trying to protect himself from something bad about to happen. He was lean, not as thin as Peter, but both of them quite musclely. A bit unfair, Peter considered, that Graham had no apparent interest in his physical well-being but looked in good shape anyway.

Graham was noticeably more hirsute too, which Peter also viewed a little enviously! Peter liked the way Graham's hair crawled smartly up to his navel, and then up a thinner line to his chest and a light fanning-out of hair across there too. His own body hair had yet to do any of that, and now he sometimes wondered if it ever would.

Peter leant back, getting more used to the water and resting on his elbows so that all of him was submerged save his head. A loud splash, some more gasping and a few swearwords and curses and then Graham was almost beside him, similarly leant back on his arms.

'Great isn't it!?' Peter said encouragingly.

'You reckon Pete! I'm not doing this again in a hurry. It's absolutely, bloody perishing man.'

'Come on, it's good. Don't you reckon you can see more clearly once you've immersed? We're here in the sun and nearly a thousand feet of cliff above us, no one around. Well, except Steve over there. We may see an eagle shortly for Christ's sake. What's not to like?' And Peter thought he really meant that. 'And it gives us a decent wash as well. Better than a stand-up rub down by a wash basin I reckon.'

'Very true mate. Very true. It does save washing at those sodding basins. But I'm starting to go numb and will have to get out in a minute I reckon.'

'Come on Steve', shouted Peter. But Steve just shook his head and stayed sitting on the rock, watching them. 'you don't know what you're missing!'

'Ignore him Steve', shouted Graham, 'you're better off as you are.'

They waited a couple of minutes. Graham looked to Peter as if he was struggling to stay put, maybe to make a point and not wanting to give-up first. Peter just wanted to stay in, enjoying the feel of the soft water all over and around him. But in the end, he recognised he was becoming chilled too and eventually made the first move. Graham quickly jumped-up to follow.

Getting out of the cold water made the air seem very much warmer. Back on the beach, by Steve, Peter grabbed his T-shirt and gave himself a dry. It wasn't much, but would have to do. He stretched the shirt between his hands and did a rub across his back a few times. Then dabbed at his front, stretched the now damp shirt again to pull around his legs and attempt to dry his feet. It felt great. He felt the sun on his abdomen and could feel the drying of his front was starting to arouse him, which made him feel self-conscious again.

Graham noticed too. 'Oi man –put it away will you!'

'It's just the sun Graham, sorry, it just happened.' Peter felt himself flush, but carried on looking at Graham who had turned his back towards him. He thought of Graham falling backwards into him back at the faultline. Turning back the other way and feeling a bit unsure of himself, Peter found Steve was just watching him. Peter just gave him a sheepish grin and finished getting dressed.

The two swimmers decided to pass the rest of the walk back to Kinlochewe, just in their boots and shorts, wet T-shirts hanging off their sacks to dry. Steve said he admired them for going in. Peter thought that was an odd expression but for the first time realised that Steve was maybe a bit shy. Always plunging into talking about geology was probably a way of masking this, Peter decided. He thought Steve would have liked to get in the water but couldn't bring himself to do it.

As if he had been reading Peter's mind, Steve launched into a description of the rocks around them as they all headed off to continue the descent back to the village. He thought the large boulders on this shoulder of the mountain were a mix of erratics left by glaciers but mostly parts of collapses of the cliff above.

He made the three of them stop by one ten-foot rock that he said was solid, granitic gneiss with one side of it in the form of mylonite – a crushed mineral layer from the thrust contact itself, Steve clarified. Peter hoped that he would have realised that himself, but mostly thought it was just helpful to have someone else's observations – doing some of his work for him.

After Peter and Graham had extolled the virtues of swimming in the lochan, and the three of them had ran-out of geological talk, or at least two of them had, the conversation on the descent turned to women.

Graham started it, out-of-the-blue again, when he asked about Peter's girlfriend, Penny. He wanted to be reminded how long they had been together and Peter explained that it had really been on and off for a year and a half. Peter explained that he really liked her company and saw her as his girlfriend but she had pushed him away a couple of times and had sometimes seen her old boyfriend, Gordon, from before uni and had also gone off with another guy a couple of times. Part of the way through explaining all this, Peter wished he hadn't started as it all made him feel fed-up. As usual, he also started thinking again how the direction of the relationship was probably down to him.

'Do you think you love her though?' continued Graham.

Peter sighed and hunched his shoulders. 'I think so', he said. The truth was he had said "I love you" several times to Penny but she had yet to say it back to him. 'I'm really fond of her but then she goes off. It leaves me wondering where I stand. But I miss her when we're not together.' He tried to distract himself by looking out at the landscape. 'Don't know why I said all that. It's boring isn't it!'

That stopped the conversation for a bit. They continued walking, passing through the plateau-like area and starting to descend more steeply onto the pony track again. They halted and had a good look at the cliffs and mountains opposite, on the other side of the glen, at

Steve's mapping area. Steve, who had been silent for a while, became quite animated, seeing more the longer he looked and taking a few minutes to draw a sketch and make some notes in his field book.

Setting-off again, Peter decided to flip the conversation. He didn't know previously, but learned now that Graham had a girlfriend at school and she lived back in the same small town, near Carmarthen. She hoped to marry Graham and he saw her whenever he went back, but he didn't know if he loved her nor if he felt the same about possible marriage.

Graham went on to explain there was just an assumption in his home town that couples would form in their late teens and just go on to get married at some point. Often, Graham said, when the woman became pregnant. There hadn't been anyone else for him so far and he wasn't that bothered about it most of the time while at uni. He didn't think he had what Peter and Penny had, or seemed to have.

'But then you're not settled really, you two, are you?' Graham said back to Peter. 'It's not like it's all one way, is it?' Peter didn't answer, so Graham carried on, 'At the Easter field trip you and Clare got very smoochy and you snogged most of the time in the minibus on the way home, I seem to remember.'

'Oh, no, that's just not true!' exclaimed Peter. 'We didn't. I mean, well, we did…well we didn't do anything other than a bit of a kiss and cuddle. What happened there was all that you saw. Nothing else.' He paused, wondering if he wanted to carry-on with this now. 'Look, Penny had been playing up to this other guy and Clare was interested in me on that trip and we became smoochy I suppose.'

'So you didn't …?' Graham let his voice tail off.

'No!' But Peter knew he probably would have done, had she wanted to. Or, more likely, he thought, he would have failed in the attempt. But he also hadn't wanted to upset Penny and was pleased Clare saved him from that really. It had been comforting with Clare but neither of them continued with it after the Easter break. Peter thought now, that maybe it had been a way of trying to get out of feeling a love for someone that wasn't being returned. Talking about it in the open air, half-way up an ancient mountain, with two friends, he was no longer sure what he thought.

Then, Peter went on to explain, hoping the other two weren't bored, that he had told Penny about it – about Clare and the smooching. He had been thinking it was maybe what adults did, he was honest about it but Penny's reaction was to go into a sulk. They shared a house together, but not usually the same bedroom. They did share food and meals but this time Penny had up-ended the food Peter had just got cooked for them both, into the waste bin. Then she had got in her old car and driven off. No explanation later where she had been that night. It had left him perplexed and sad.

'It left me thinking she didn't want me as a lover but didn't want anyone else to have me either. It made me confused and then we were into revision and exams, and now I'm up here.' Peter said, to near silence from the other two. He wasn't sure they were still listening, walking down the track three abreast.

Then Graham simply draped his arm around Peter's shoulder and, seeing that, Steve did the same thing on the other side. Peter felt touched by this but at the same time he felt uncomfortable as the centre of attention. After a moment, he said 'Oh fuck it anyway. Bollocks to it.' And he put his arms momentarily across the shoulders of the other two for a few yards until they all pulled-away from each other as the path narrowed going over a bluff.

'What about you Steve?' Peter asked. 'You're being very quiet. Is there anyone back home or at uni?'

Steve shrugged and sighed and Peter thought the gesture was like a copy of his own. Graham and Peter stayed quiet, wondering if Steve was going to divulge any information or not. After a moment, Steve explained that there wasn't really anyone. He had a girlfriend of sorts at school, in the sixth form. They used to listen to music together a lot – Strawbs, Steeleye Span and stuff apparently. It had never really become a big thing, he explained, and then she had gone off to a different university and they had stayed as friends, seeing each other between terms and now she had got involved with a guy in the university, so that was that.

'Did you screw then?' asked Graham. Peter thought Graham was being deliberately direct just for the hell of it, and teasing Steve. But Steve didn't seem to notice and answered straightaway anyway.

'Sort-of a couple of times.' Said Steve. Peter found himself being amazed, partly that he was answering at all, and partly with the actual response. 'We spent an afternoon together a couple of times in her parents' house when they were away. She doesn't have any brothers or sisters. I'm not sure either of us knew what we were doing, to be honest'.

'Fair play Steve' said Graham 'you are being honest there man. I shouldn't have put you on the spot.' Then, after a pause, 'I wonder if it's all worth it really.'.

Peter wondered what the 'it' was that Graham meant, did he literally mean sex itself or the effort of a girlfriend? He didn't know what to ask, so Graham's comment was left enigmatically hanging in the air.

They passed the point where the golden plover had been and were all amazed that the bird returned, adopting the same behaviour, just as Graham had predicted. Once past it, they were now starting to descend more steeply towards Kinlochewe, although it still looked small and distant. They paused to take in the scenery again, which had changed, while they had been talking, so that the mountains now all seemed to loom up around them, more massively and extensively.

'And what then if Sue, or Julie, at the campsite café invited you into the caravan then?' Graham asked, after a bit, not wanting to finish the discussion they had been having.

'Who me?' blurted Steve.

'No. Well, it could be. But I was thinking of Pete, as the girls are interested in him I reckon.'

'No' replied Steve 'I think they are interested in you too Graham'.

'Well, not that I had noticed. Still, go on Pete – what about Sue?'

'Come off it Graham, we hardly know them. They have been friendly, made us tea, fed us. That's a long way from being invited into their caravan for rumpy-pumpy, isn't it?' Peter said, light-heartedly. All three of them laughed a bit.

'Yeah you're right, but what if Sue, say, wanted to be cuddly like you said about Clare last Easter, or wanted a kiss and cuddle the same way?' persisted Graham.

'Well it's not going to happen is it. Julie's always there and …'

'See!' exclaimed Graham 'It is Sue you fancy then, a bit. You've considered it obviously. You see! You're blushing now.' Graham stopped and playfully pinched the side of Peter's face, which was turning red.

'Invite Sue to your tent then.' Graham continued, 'She likes the odd ciggie but never has her own. You could invite her over. You know you want to.' Graham continued.

'Sod off Graham. Leave off! How do you know what I want or don't want?' Peter wasn't really cross though and enjoyed the joshing. He also knew he wasn't being completely honest. It was Julie who had been overtly friendly and chatty and he had warmed to her but as the week had gone on, he had found himself noticing Sue more too. He knew he liked the look of her and liked the idea of her coming over to his tent, now Graham had planted the idea in his mind.

But what if she wanted to stay with him. What if she wanted him to sleep with her. He was a bit unsure of the prospect now he thought more about it, remembering other one-off opportunities that never really worked for him. It was different with Penny, when they did actually do anything, but that had taken a long time to settle down too. He felt embarrassed thinking about it. Graham seemed to pick-up on this and changed the subject.

They spent the last part of the walk back chatting about school, what they had liked and disliked. How different it had been getting to University. The experience of living at home while studying, for Steve, and the differences being away from home, for Graham and Peter.

At the campsite it was Sue who met them coming back. She was in the process of taking some food from the village shop into the café fridge for the next day. Peter thought of the talk they had been having on the way down from the hills. He found it was a bit like seeing her afresh and he liked the feeling it provoked in him.

Sue had on a light blue T-shirt, one of those with sleeves that looked rolled into the shoulder, and dark blue, faded, denim shorts that he hadn't seen before. 'If you boys would like a tea, I can do it for you. We're closed really, but for you three it would not be a problem.' She said cheerfully. 'It's been quiet here today and Julie and I have been sitting out in the sun, as you can see.' She meant the two deckchairs outside the tea room door, but Peter thought she might as easily have meant the sun tan on her legs. 'If not though, see you over the pub I suppose?'

They all enthusiastically took the offer of tea though. It was a cheerful moment, the tea refreshing the three guys who shared the story of the day. Julie came over and joined-in and Peter thought the two young women were genuinely interested in the strange discovery, but also the birdlife, the deer, the swim in the lochan. Peter noticed they had been a little coy about describing the latter.

As they were chatting, Julie dropped-in a surprise by saying a fourth geology student had turned up. 'He. Because it is a he. Honestly, do women not do geology or something? He is from

Newcastle. That's where he lives and that's his university too.' Julie looked at the three of them but held her look on Peter a bit longer, making him feel he had to speak.

'That's crazy! I don't know why we keep turning-up like this. There are women though Julie. Graham, wouldn't you say about half of our year are women? They're just not here.'

'Where are they then?' Sue asked.

'The Maritime Alps!' Peter and Graham said in unison. 'Neither of us…' Graham flicked his thumb back and forth between him and Peter '… could afford to go there but that's where nearly all the others are.' This made everyone go a bit quiet for a minute.

'Well, I chose to come here' said Steve, with the implication that he could have gone abroad. 'And I I'm pleased I did.'

'Yeah, I agree Steve.' Said Peter. 'I don't think there was a choice, because of the money, but the Easter field trips up this way, bit further up in Sutherland, made me want to come back here.'

'There's quite a group down in the Alps,' said Graham, 'including all the female geologists! Drinking wine and eating fondue, I expect!' His accent making him sound particularly laconic.

'Bet they don't have tea like this though, eh?' Said Julie. And she collected-up the now empty mugs with a flourish. 'And anyway, we're pleased they're all there and you're all here, aren't we Sue? Now get out you lot, you all really need a tidy-up before you come down the pub too. Go on, bugger off and get yourselves sorted.'

CHAPTER 3

Later, Peter left Graham smoking half a joint in his tent and got down the pub early. Steve had spotted him and run out from his caravan to join him.

He launched straight into his news, half breathlessly from running over to Peter. 'The new guy's called Nick. He's in that big frame tent over there and he's coming down the pub later too. I guess you're wanting to catch Mr MacKenzie. I hoped I could join in?'

And John MacKenzie was there, but in the front bar. This was the posh bit of the pub, for hotel residents only it said, but evidently it was for significant locals too. Peter felt annoyed at himself for feeling a little intimidated going in there, but the big bearded bar man, Jock, who was usually in the rougher public bar, gestured him in. Peter told him he wanted to speak with John MacKenzie and the Warden, hearing his name, broke-off from a chat and came over. As usual, Peter found himself thinking that the Warden had that weather-beaten appearance of someone who spent his entire life working outside.

He had a noticeably lilting accent which Peter had learned was typical of the far north-west. 'How are you two getting on? I saw three of you going up the track this morning. I was working on the new seed propagation area by there. Are you doing a bit of working together now then?'

'We're fine thanks John.' Said Peter, still feeling a bit awkward using the Warden's first name, even though he had been told to do that. 'We're not working together, no, but Steve and Graham came out with me today to help check-out something I found. There's two things I could do with your opinion about please, when you have a moment.' The Warden looked intrigued and seemed to study the two students more closely, as he nodded. Peter took that as an ok, and elaborated on his discoveries.

'The first is a huge black bumble bee. Slow moving and a real drone to its buzzing, seems to hang in the air and also seems to follow me about.' And without pausing, and ignoring Steve, who was wanting to jump in. 'Plus, has there ever been an airplane crash up on Meall a Ghiubhais?' He hoped he had said yoovaysh correctly. 'Maybe a wartime thing or a light aircraft?'

'Ahh' said John MacKenzie. 'The bee! Very good you spotted it! It is a black Mediterranean bumble bee and we've no bloody idea at all how it's turned-up here, but strange things get blown in sometimes and we think this warm air from the south has somehow drawn it up here. We had to look it up. It's a long way to the Med from here.' He paused to take a sup from his pint. 'But no, I don't know of any plane crashes on your mountain.' Peter noticed that when the warden spoke, he had a manner of speaking quite loudly without any sense of being overheard nor bothering if he was.

Steve couldn't wait to get in on the conversation, excited about facts as ever. 'This plane is what we all went up to see.' He went on to explain to the Warden how Peter had made this strange discovery, where it was, what it looked like and why it seemed really odd. Peter thought it saved him the trouble really, and he didn't mind.

John MacKenzie confessed that that the discovery point was the far corner of the Reserve as well as the end-point of Peter's mapping area, and he didn't get over there that often himself. 'By the time you get there, from here, you feel it's time to turn round and come back, near enough, as you've found I should think.' Looking at Peter for confirmation. Peter nodded.

'I do have a faster way there though, two ways actually, but you need a Land Rover. Anyway, that all sounds pretty strange. You might be onto something though.' Pause for another sup. 'There is an airplane wreck on Beinn Eighe, in the big corrie, beneath the Triple Buttress cliffs, if you know where I mean. Think you…' looking at Peter '…were there a couple of weeks ago weren't you?'

Peter felt chuffed at this. When he had first arrived on the mapping area, he had been to the Warden's house to introduce himself. There had been an exchange of letters between the University and the Nature Reserve and it was a requirement for Peter to do that. But he hadn't expected the Warden to remember his rather garrulous explanation of the mountaineering trip leading into his geology work and particularly his account of going up Beinn Eighe via that very corrie.

'Yeah. There was a mention of the plane wreckage in the mountaineering hut log book, you know, the Ling Hut, down towards Torridon?' The warden nodded. 'We didn't see any bits of plane when we went through the Corrie though.'

'Bit of history for you two then. Come and look at this.' And John Mackenzie indicated they should follow him as he led them all from the bar.

They went into the quiet residents' lounge. In here there were half a dozen really old looking leather armchairs and a big heavy and bulky sofa seemingly covered in tapestry or something. One older man was in there asleep, head back, mouth open, gentle low-level snoring coming-out. On a table by the door they had come in by, was a long wood-framed glass case with a huge fish in it. A salmon Peter assumed. There was another filling the deep window sill, looking out onto the road. There were several sets of deer antlers on the higher bits of two walls – hard to count as the points were all so overlapping and jumbled-up.

But they had been taken to the third wall, surrounding the large fireplace. On this wall were various framed black and white photos, each a foot or two square. Peter and Steve could see that they were mostly of groups of people, all men, with dead deer at their feet, holding dead fish or in one case a large assemblage of ropes and climbing gear.

But two photos were different, young men, in leather jackets with furry collars and close-fitting caps and ear muffs on some of them. Peter thought they reminded him of guys you saw in films like The Dambusters or 633 Squadron. At least, that's the image that came to mind. And it was these two photos that John MacKenzie addressed.

'This first one is part of the American flight crew of an aircraft that crashed near Gairloch, just after the war ended. Tragic really. They had survived the war and were heading home but their plane encountered cloud and they unfortunately clipped the top of Slioch. They reckon the pilot was trying to ditch in the sea by Gairloch, but it came down just short and they all were killed. Mostly around your age. Some a little older'.

Peter felt taken aback and could see Steve react in the same way. He found himself feeling moved by the story, but more by the way the Warden had expressed it. The matter of fact tone made the story more shocking really. 'Were you living here then' he asked.

'Aye. But I had just become a teenager at the war's end. I don't remember hearing anything about the crash until years later, even though you can now easily see the wreckage. There's a huge, bent propeller sticking out of a watery bog up there. Silvery cylinders scattered about too, bits of metal fuselage here and there. A party of Americans came over, put up a memorial plaque. There were photos in the local paper. Not sure how this one ended-up here.'

'I bet it all felt a long way away from the war, right up here didn't it?' asked Steve.

'Quite the opposite'. The warden cleared his throat. 'There was a lot going on up here then. More than you would know or maybe more than you will ever know.'

'Really!' said Peter. ' I've heard of something up in Orkney but assumed round here you would have all been well out of it?'

'Nobody talked about it then and not a lot since. We were all told not to tell anyone anything. It was drilled into us. We stuck to it and most still do! What I can tell you is there was a huge naval presence up here. Really huge. For most of the war!'

Peter and Steve were all ears.

'Lots of ships, naval and otherwise, going up and down. Planes a lot of the time too. Seemed like most days to me, as a nipper. We were cut-off from the rest of the country. You couldn't get out and nobody could get in.' Peter and Steve were wide-eyed now. 'Honestly. The whole of the north-west of Scotland was cordoned-off. Folks who were adults then, still living here now, will never talk about it. Never.'

The Warden than pointed at the second photo of a smaller group. 'This one's the crew from the Lancaster Bomber that crashed on Triple Buttress, going the other way to the American one, also after the war ended. There's less said about it. No memorial up there or anything. Again, I don't rightly know what this photo is doing here. I guess some previous owners of the hotel had these, for whatever reason.' He let the two students stare into the photo. Peter noticed the names of the crew were written underneath the Beinn Eighe plane, hand-written it seemed, in very faded ink script.

They left the snoring guest and returned to the lounge bar. Anticipating something, as if by telepathy, Jock had lined-up three pints for them. 'On me' said the Warden.

They propped up the end of the small bar, and Peter still felt a bit awkward being here, in scruffy jeans and a pretty worn jumper. Steve asked if it was possible if the plane on Beinn Eighe might have hit Peter's mountain, part of it detached before it hit the Corrie – the bit they've found maybe. Steve explained that Peter reckoned you could strike a straight line from that corner of Meall a Ghiubhais, pronunciation not yet corrected, across just a couple of miles to the Corrie.

'Maybe I'll come and have a look with you.' More of a statement than a question, from the Warden.

Steve laughed. 'You've got to go up there again after all Pete. You'll wear your legs out before you get the rest of your map done.'

Peter thought it was no joke but was pleased with the interest. He felt grown-up, adult, taken seriously, at the idea of John MacKenzie coming up there with him. Anyway, they agreed for a couple of days' time, quite an early start but with the offer of a Land Rover pickup from the campsite he couldn't argue.

Leaving the Warden chatting to another local, Steve and Peter went back into the public bar. Peter was grateful his offer of buying a return round had been politely refused. 'You need to save your money lads' the Warden had kindly said, with a wink and a smile.

So, it was earlier in the bar than they would usually arrive. Easy to get a seat for a change and even easier to get in a game of darts without the risk of an off-course arrow going into someone. Jock even joined-in for a few throws, when the few people in the bar were all served and preoccupied. But, as the evening went on Peter looked around, and felt sorry not to see Julie and Sue coming in, nor Graham. He wondered if his smoking buddy had maybe got a bit stoned and stayed in his tent.

At some point, the Newcastle student Nick did come in, noticeably tall and slender, with black hair that seemed to sit on his head like a beret. He quickly eased into the company of Peter and Steve, helped by the flow of beer. Steve, who was a couple of pints ahead of where he would normally be this time of the evening, suggested they maybe get a bottle of whisky as a carry-out and take it back to his caravan. They had seen others doing this – the oil platform workers mostly.

It was four pounds a bottle and Peter couldn't help hesitating. As it was, Steve flashed a fiver and said they could sort-out money later. The bottle was wrapped in a paper bag and, feeling like a group of real boozers, the three of them strode off back to the campsite. Steve, clearly with wind in his sails Peter thought, seemed to have lost some of his shyness and sauntered over to Graham's tent, woke him up and persuaded him to come over. Graham looked a bit dishevelled but perhaps more sleepy than anything else.

Steve's tiny caravan had an odd assortment of crockery and glasses, but a couple of short tumblers and two wine glasses were quickly lined up on the Formica table that had the dual purpose of being the support for Steve's bed that folded down from the wall at night. Steve poured a careful measure of whisky into each glass, using the first as a measure for the others. Very precise, equal measures Peter noticed.

With the exception of Graham, they had each had at least four pints of beer in the bar. They decided the whisky could do for a couple of nights, thinking they would be a bit drunk if they finished the whole lot. They talked about rocks initially, weaving in stories of how and why they went to Leeds University in the case of Steve, Bristol in the cases of Graham and Peter, and Newcastle for Nick. It had been a simple case of the one nearest to home for Nick and Steve. Graham and Peter's choice had been influenced by the positive experiences of friends from the year above at school and from the recommendation of teachers.

They all agreed that each other's university had a good reputation for geology and they shared an awareness of good research relations between lecturers in each place. Steve was more knowledgeable than the others about this and Nick commented that he seemed to know of the entire faculty in each place and what projects they were all working on.

They shared the fact that, for each of them, geology had been a natural choice. Steve had loved the subject at A level, having initially been uncertain of it alongside his interest in more defined sciences. Nick had approached the subject similarly but had also really enjoyed school field trips to the Northumbrian coast and further afield. Peter and Graham had also loved the field-trips, although not just for the geology, and additionally Peter had collected rocks and fossils since he was a young boy, on holidays to the seaside and other places. They had all done well at A level and S level, getting the same marks of B2, except Steve who had achieved A1. By the time they discussed this, none of the other three were surprised at Steve's grade.

As the talk went on and drifted away from geology, they learned some surprising things about each other. Steve actually took piano lessons and had reached a high grade. Nick came from a large family of three brothers and one sister, who had mostly taken camping holidays for years, which is why he had a large frame tent. Graham had been interested in ornithology as far back as he could remember. Peter had been on walking and climbing trips since he became a teenager and had been President of the Climbing Club at Uni for the last year.

Peter thought everyone's story was interesting but Steve's was particularly revealing. Thinking of what Steve had said, Peter built a picture in his mind of him at home with his parents. He thought that he had never lived anywhere big enough to accommodate a piano, even an upright one, let alone the sort Steve had described. And it sounded like it had a room all of its own too.

It seemed to Peter that Steve was the most different of the four of them. Not only was he really good at geology, conscientious about his work, and tenacious at fieldwork, he was the one of them that had a car! He also had a rented caravan, not a tent. He lived at home with his Mum and Dad and just sounded well-off compared to him and Graham.

Piano lessons fitted with rest of the facts. His private music teacher was called Timothy and was a bit theatrical and flamboyant, according to Steve, whatever that meant. Peter thought he would normally be a bit dismissive of all this but found he couldn't be critical in this instance, as Steve was just so very animated talking about it and clearly got a lot of pleasure out of playing the piano.

Provoked by Steve, shyness now dislodged by alcohol, they sang some songs. It was mostly bits of pop songs to start with, parts of rugby songs then, led by Nick. At some point Nick found himself singing a folk song – Wild Rover, with all of them joining in the chorus. This then led into Whisky in the Jar, Black Velvet Band, Moved Through the Fair and others. Peter was surprised to find himself in the position of knowing quite a few, once they had started. Mostly picked-up in climbers' bars but also at his Uni's Folk Club. There was some joshing about Steve going to get a keyboard somewhere to help them all.

They were surprised and disappointed to find they had cleared most of the whisky bottle. By the time they were down to the last inch or two, the subject came round, once again, to women. There was a bit of a repeat of the day's conversation on the hill, principally for Nick's benefit, who wanted to know, in his own words, "all the gory details". By which he meant he wanted to know who had laid whom, what was it like, what did they do exactly, and more.

Nick rather confidently, but unconvincingly Peter thought, gave the impression of being a bit of a lad, with an intimate knowledge of quite a lot of women at Uni, and at school, but not interested in getting a relationship. "Just getting a screw" was his main stated interest.

So, Peter was still the one, as it turned-out, with a current serious girlfriend although he hadn't offered-up all the discussion he had provided to Graham and Steve earlier. The way the discussion went made Peter appear older and more 'settled', according to Nick. He was the one who used the word: serious. This was all very different to how Peter actually felt.

Things took a more boisterous turn on the last refills of their glasses, and the talk turned to Julie and Sue. Nick was lewd from the outset. Graham and Peter gave a knowing look to each other.

Graham took a sideways glance at Nick and made a roll of the eyes for Peter's benefit, who nodded in silent agreement. When Nick started to describe in some detail what he had observed of the two women when he arrived that day, Graham suddenly turned to him, speaking quietly but firmly.

'Come on, you can't say stuff like that. You don't know them. You haven't been here a day yet. They're not here for you to lust and leer at!' This brought the conversation to a halt. 'And they've been really nice with us'.

It came over as proprietorial a bit, but mostly it struck Peter that Graham really did have a very adult view of women. More so than he did himself, in fact. Feeling pretty drunk, Peter knew that at one level he was simply physically attracted to them. He wouldn't express it as crudely as Nick, but nonetheless the desire was there. On the other hand, as Graham had said, the girls had just been friendly and nice. He thought for a moment about how they might feel if they had overheard the discussion. Disappointed, he imagined.

In trying to be quiet, leaving the caravan at one in the morning, arms draped across each other's shoulders, they were actually being quite noisy. There had been a long farewell process, it seemed to Peter, actually getting-up off the seating, trying to clear the cigarette smoke for Steve's benefit and saying goodbye to him, as if they wouldn't be seeing each other in a few hours.

Nick went off in one direction after several no-hard-feelings goodnight pats on the back. The remaining two then became aware of the night-time silence across the site. In a whispered conversation with Graham on the way back to their tents, Peter felt the need to confess to desperately wanting to be in bed with Sue right now. He wanted a cuddle and snog as much as anything else. Graham's arm pressed tighter into Peter's shoulder and Peter liked the feel of that. Graham didn't really say much but commented on how the attitude of guys like Nick this evening, sometimes got under his skin. Peter wondered if it was because he had a sister a couple of years younger than him.

Somehow Peter found himself leaning very heavily into Graham by the time they were in front of his tent. The hundred yards or so from Steve's caravan had seemed like a long walk and Peter felt they had done a lot of talking today. He was just feeling very at ease in Graham's company and was leaning into him solidly now, not just for stability but also, he found, for comfort.

'Well, we had better get some sleep I suppose.' Said Graham, trying to disentangle himself from Peter.

'Aww Graham, I was just enjoying that. Thank you for being a good mate.'

'Think you might be a bit pissed Pete. Don't be soppy. Come on, time for bed.'

Without knowing he was going to say it, Peter found himself saying: 'Graham, can I come in there with you?'

'What! You want to come into my tent?'

'Yeah. Can I? We can just carry on having a chat like this?'

Graham had now separated himself from Peter and they stood facing each other, again suddenly aware of their conversation in the middle of the campsite in the middle of the night, surrounded by other tents. Were people asleep? Was anyone awake and listening? Their voices dropped to hushed whispers.

'What are you saying Pete? What do you want?'

'Oh, I don't know Graham. I was enjoying our chat. I liked your arm on my shoulders. Can't we carry on with that in your tent? Maybe a chat and maybe a hug.'

'Think you might be better off with some water and some sleep Pete.'

But Peter looked at Graham square on, putting one hand on each of his shoulders and speaking very slowly, and still in whispers.

'Graham, please can I come in your tent with you, just for a while?'

'No Pete, come on, time to go back to your own tent don't you think?'

'Please Graham. I won't be a nuisance; we can just put arms round each other like we've just been doing. Have a chat. A hug. Please.'

'Peter. Where's this coming from? What are you doing man? Come on' he said gently, 'we have had a nice evening and a nice chat, but you need to go back to your own tent now. Just over there. Go on, shoo.'

'Please Graham. Come on, Please.' Whispered Peter, now lowering his head, not able to keep looking at Graham. He could hear the pleading in his voice and thought it was like someone else speaking, not him.

'Peter' Said Graham, still friendly, but much more firmly. 'Sorry to have to spell this out for you, but. You. Are. Not. Coming into my tent. OK?' And he gently and slowly took Peter's arms down and turned him towards his tent. 'Just get into your tent, drink some water and have a good sleep. See you in the morning.'

Peter moved across slowly and reluctantly, still feeling like he was observing a scene in his life, rather than participating in it. He put the feeling down to the whisky and the beer.

He was aware Graham was gently pushing him through the tent flap and inner zip doorway. Somehow, before he knew it, Peter found himself alone and in his sleeping bag, without remembering actually taking-off his trainers and clothes. But then gulping down a bottle-full of water brought about a clarity and reality. God, he thought, had he really just asked Graham to get into his tent with him? What was he trying to do?

His mind clearing a bit, he thought of the conversation as a bit of a sequence. It had started with talk about girlfriends, and he had spoken of Penny. Then they had gone onto Sue and Julie. Some of that had been a bit dirty-minded, in Steve's caravan, but that was Nick mostly, wasn't it? He couldn't be clear what he had said himself. Hoped it wasn't anything too embarrassing.

Then they had been out in the fresh night air and he had felt giddy. The walk back with Graham had taken ages. He had told Graham that he fancied sleeping with Sue. Graham hadn't said anything to that. He had just felt really good making that confession, admitting it to Graham and feeling close to him as a result. But where had that other stuff come from? He felt embarrassed with himself when he heard in his head, the plea he had made to Graham to get in his tent. Had he actually wanted to cuddle Graham, like he had cuddled girls. Like he wanted to do with Sue?

The water was reviving more than his awareness. He thought that maybe he needed to feel himself, that would shake-off all these thoughts. He moved his hand down inside his sleeping bag. A mixture of images came to mind but as he laid back and his head settled into the make-shift pillow, he could feel the effect of the whisky sweep over him, euphoric for a moment but then everything was swimmy and he was asleep in seconds.

When he awoke several hours later, he felt he hadn't moved. His legs and back felt stiff. His mouth parched and his head muzzy. He looked at this watch and realised he had slept through all the noises of the night without interruption. His mind started to replay the previous evening and mostly he felt himself wanting to squirm with embarrassment.

Chapter 4

With a breeze blowing through the open window just above her head, Sue found herself feeling wide awake. It was five in the morning. The angle of light through the flimsy curtains was just too strong. It never seemed to bother Julie though, she thought, looking over, past the kitchenette and to the small door beyond. Now she was awake though, she knew she would need to get up.

Going outside she found it was that curious mixture of cold and warm air as she moved in and out of light and shadow on the way across to the site's washroom block. There was no one else around, very peaceful, just lots of birdsong. Each tree and bush seemed to have its own throng.

She had worried a little that their caravan being so close to the site entrance and main facilities, would be noisy. But, so far it had been unbelievably quiet, even compared to home. People tended to go out around nine in the morning and back again at four or five, those that returned to the site, those who were not moving on elsewhere. New people would turn-up at the same sort of time, with occasional stragglers now and then up until about seven in the evening.

No one inside, so she was in and out again really quickly. If only it was always like that she mulled. The guys have it easy, but there definitely were not enough facilities for women and she hated queuing. At least she and Julie could wash in private in their caravan.

And they had access to a shower! There were none on the site. Julie's uncle was really nice but wouldn't want her going in to his house for a shower this early, she would have to wait a while. Or maybe just skip it until later, or tomorrow. A week and half and she had already changed her usual habits. She was thinking about this as she got back into bed, hoping to snooze a bit longer.

She didn't consider herself very big, five foot six and everyone called her slim, but the caravan beds were pretty tiny. In the daytime, there was a couch each side of the table, but at night these could become beds. She found she liked alternating from one side to the other on different nights. Julie had explained to her some complicated mechanism of collapsing the table, and effectively creating a larger bed. But it was just too much faff and she was happy to make do. Better than camping and she didn't mind the feeling of roughing it a little anyway.

The alarm went off at seven and she was pleased to realise she had drifted off into a second sleep after all. Feeling properly awake, she went over and made a tea, and, as usual, took a mug into Julie, to wake her. Julie never, ever, heard the alarm. Julie was an owl, she thought. 'And I'm a lark', Sue said under her breath.

She shook Julie, who was on the bottom bed of a bunk, not much wider than her own couch bed but looking more like a proper bed. They had thought it best to have their own space in the caravan. Julie liked to read until late for instance – Sue could wake seemingly at any time in the night and see the light under Julie's door.

'Here you go Jules. Lovely mug of tea for you.'

'Aw, thanks pet.' Julie said, sleepily, coming round from a dreamy world. She sat-up, ran her hand through her dark, flowing, curly hair, gave herself a little shake. Took a sip.

'Don't know how you can do that! Drink it so hot.'

'That's what my Mum's always saying, but Dad's the same.' Julie took a bigger swig. 'Cast iron mouths and stomachs, apparently! What's it like outside?'

'Good! I went over the road at five and it was warmish even then.'

'Five! You're mad you are. What on earth are you doing up at five?' Julie shook her head and rolled her eyes.

'It's actually quite nice at that time, well with this weather it is. Gorgeous light Jules. Anyway, I did doze-off again if it makes you feel better.'

'Did you go across in just that T-shirt?'

'Yes, why not? It wasn't cold or anything.'

'Sue, honestly, it's not exactly long is it? It doesn't leave much to the imagination!' Julie shook her head again, but smiling at her friend. 'Right, well I'd better get myself into gear and go get a shower.' 'Unless you're going first?'

'I'm skipping it this morning. Can't be bothered. I'll just have a quick wash here and catch-up on some reading.'

'Ooo you mucky thing. You suit yourself – but remember I have to share this space with you.' Said Julie, pretending to be shocked. She winked at Sue, glancing at the main window shelf. 'Well you have that pile of books to get through I suppose.'

'You can talk Jules, I was just thinking how you seem to always be reading into the early hours. I hope it's not all course prep for next year?'

No, but, well, a little bit of it is. I can't just pick it up at the start of term like you.' Now it was Sue's turn just to give a smile back.

Sue was quite happy to drop into the world of Hesse for a bit. Ten minutes later she was sat at the big caravan window looking out on the world, mug of tea to hand and Steppenwolf on her lap. What she looked at, across the road, was Julie's uncle and aunt's house, Glen View, and the post office shop to the right of that. She noticed the blackbird was on top of the phone box, singing. There were quite a few trees in view and she liked seeing all the birdlife this time of day. This morning it was chaffinches feeding right across the road; never many cars to bother them.

It was very different to home, thought Sue, thinking of her Mum right now probably getting tea for herself and Dad, probably worrying about me, wondering if I'm ok. She made a mental note to call later. The phone box could get busy, but Julie's uncle let her use their house phone, as long as she kept it quick.

Keeping it quick meant just enough time for her Mum to ask if she's eating enough; sleeping well; enjoying herself; getting on with Julie; not working too hard; getting showers; washing her knickers ok?... And enough time for her to reply, Mum I've only been away a fortnight! Bit less even! I'm fine, everything's fine. I'm enjoying myself...'

She watched Julie go over to the house and then stuck her nose into the book for a few pages. When she noticed Julie coming back from Glen View she knew it would be around seven forty-five. Time to get dressed and to get the tea room open.

The cafe had been an innovation of Julie's uncle and aunt a couple of summers back, but had become too much for them to run as well as the main tasks of running the campsite and also helping-out at the village shop.

Julie had been roped-in the previous summer to help, for a few weeks. This year, Julie had offered to bring her best friend and here they were. Sue thought that she had been made very welcome right from the outset. "Call me Ben", her uncle had said, and "call me Pam", her aunt had said too.

Julie came in. 'That's better, I feel more alive again now.'

'You say that every morning Julie.'

'Well at least some of us have a shower every morning!'

'It doesn't do to wash all the oils off the skin all the time. According to my Mum anyway.'

'Hmm, That's as may be.' said Julie 'Anyway, Uncle Ben says some of the people who checked in yesterday specifically asked about opening times. Sounds like they might be in at first thing - eightish.'

'Better get our skates on then, eh?'

Sue saw it as her role to make sure they always made the opening times and were never late. It felt a privilege to be here and it's one of the things she felt she could do to show she was taking the role seriously. They were provided with all the food they wanted from the shop and got a few pounds each week in addition. Sharing the caravan was free, and all-in-all Sue felt she had landed on her feet for the summer.

Setting up the little tea room at the end of the reception cabin, really didn't take very long. There were two tables for two and two for four. She needed to make sure milk was in the fridge, but there always was as they had always remembered, so far, to get it from the shop each afternoon late. She would fill the two kettles and get them going. Get the bread and bacon out of the fridge.

She didn't know who these campers would be, but everyone so far had been very friendly. Julie's uncle had said the site was still quiet and wouldn't really get busier until the school holidays in July. So, the second half of June, right now, was a good chance to work-out the job.

It was easy really. Sue just served mugs of tea, cooked quite a few bacon sarnies and some cakes. People tended to come in for a bit of breakfast. Maybe a mid-morning coffee or two. Lunchtime, some others would call in, passers-by, day-trippers. They had a microwave and a deep fat fryer. Basically they could do frozen pizzas or pies and chips for two people at a time. It had worked fine so far. The afternoon was mostly teas and shortbread until they stopped at sometime between five and six.

The days were quite long, on paper, but so far there had been plenty of breaks during the day. They had found a couple of deckchairs in Ben and Pam's garage and just sat outside between customers if it was dry. Dressed in as little as they could get away with in the sun and warmth, or in jeans and sweaters on the cooler, greyer days.

Sue hadn't known what to expect about the campers generally. She thought there might be couples or maybe friends walking and climbing. People like herself maybe, probably a bit older. And all that had been true. There had been quite a few retired folks too, they would usually be the ones who arrived with caravans. Julie's uncle only had half-a-dozen spaces for them, otherwise it was tents.

She thought about the mountains around and wistfully thought about getting up some of them soon. They were going to have Sundays as days off, or that was the idea so far. If it got busy, they might do short shifts on their own, but they would have to see how it goes. As it got busier, they might take days off in turn, rather than together. It was a case of suck it and see.

One day the Warden of the nearby Nature Reserve, Mr MacKenzie, had called in. He was quite a pal of Julie's uncle, and she thought it was sweet he had just popped in to introduce himself. As it happened, he did also stop for a tea in the end. Julie had been busy with something and Sue found herself asking the Warden about all the mountains around, of which he was incredibly knowledgeable. She told him of her love for mountain walking and he had said she must make the most of her time up here, extolling the virtues of some walks to places she mostly would never be able to pronounce or remember.

Sue knew Mr MacKenzie had some sort of relationship with the work of the geology students on the campsite. This was the one group of people she hadn't expected to encounter. Both herself and Julie were surprised when the first turned-up to stay in one of the other static caravans. This guy, called Steve, had a beaten-up old VW and had driven up from Leeds where he was at Uni doing geology. They hadn't seen much of him yet, but he had been around nearly as long as them. He seemed very earnest, Sue thought. He would say hi and so on but they hadn't had much conversation yet and Sue had decided he was just a bit shy.

Then two more had turned-up, separately, but both from Bristol Uni. According to Julie's uncle yet one more was to arrive today — from the north-east or somewhere, with a frame tent.

Of the Bristol pair, one was a guy called Peter, but everyone seemed to immediately call him Pete. She wondered why that was, until she thought about it and then couldn't remember the last time anyone called her Susan. Except perhaps her Mum when she really wanted to be listened to.

Pete, it emerged, lived near Reading somewhere. The other one was called Graham, and he was from South Wales somewhere, not so far from her and Jules' own University town. They seemed like good friends but didn't seem as dedicated to study as Steve though.

Pete had arrived first, on his own or somebody dropped him off. He had been climbing first for a few days apparently. He had that climber look about him, a bit wiry and always in rolled-up shirt-sleeves. She felt envious about the climbing. Graham had turned-up a couple of days later, about the same size as his friend she thought, bit stronger build, dark and wavy hair to Peter's fair and straight. More slouched, or maybe just more chilled-out. His parents has brought him, all the way from Wales. They hadn't hung around though and had soon gone off.

These two students had become noticeably motivated early on when a lecturer turned-up from their university, to get them set-up with their projects. She wasn't quite sure what it involved, but when she did see Pete going out, he seemed loaded down with paraphernalia, maps, Perspex boards, note books, rucksack. The warm sunny weather though seemed to have led to both of them hanging around more since the lecturer went away.

Sue thought she and Julie had taken advantage of that a bit. It was Julie started it. She had said, "those two boys both look like they need feeding-up" and "I bet they're more interesting company than the other campers". Julie had also suggested giving them some stuff on the cheap, partly to see how much they could keep them hanging around. And so far, it seemed to have worked. They had enjoyed their company for bacon sarnies and all the rest of it for about three times she thought.

Yesterday, Julie had been talking to her while they were sitting outside the tea room on the deckchairs, getting some sun. Julie had said she liked both of them but thought Pete was more dishy. Sue had heard this sort of thing before with her friend and knew she would be pestering and, no doubt, chatting-up Peter.

The two guys had explained they were going to be here for seven weeks in total. Sue was pleased that they would be around for so long. It meant that they would be around until early August and it wouldn't be that long after that before she and Julie would be winding down to go back home themselves.

In the same conversation, she and Julie had discussed what it might be like living seven weeks in a small tent, which is all the two guys had. They had decided that keeping yourselves and your clothes clean would be the main hassle. Sue had asked whether they might offer them showers at Glen View one day or maybe use of the washing machine that Pam had in the outhouse, but Julie had poured cold water on the idea, saying her Aunt and Uncle wouldn't want to set a precedent or something.

So, back to work this morning, it was a youngish couple who came into the tea room first. They were from Gorebridge, somewhere south of Edinburgh they said. They were chatty and just wanted some tea and a lot of toast, to save doing their own breakfast. Apparently they wanted a good start before walking out of the village and down to Loch Maree and up the big mountain Slioch. Sue knew this was about the easiest one to pronounce but didn't know much else about it. They had a little chat and the couple were enthusiastic.

The way these two people described it though, Slioch sounded like a serious undertaking. A long walk from Kinlochewe to the base of the mountain and, after that, a sustained slog up more than three thousand feet to the summit. About twelve miles in total, they said.

As this couple were thinking of leaving, Pete came in.

'Hello. So, you're off on the hill again today then?' Sue hoped she didn't sound like she was making a point!

'Yeah. It needs doing. Graham and I have been hanging around too much. He's still asleep though I think. Didn't get a reply anyway when I left.'

'What can I get you then?'

'Nothing actually.' Said Peter. Sue felt disappointed, hoped not to show it. 'I need to crack on up there. I'm trying to get into the swing of it. Maybe a bit more of a recce today and a big day tomorrow…or maybe the day after.'

Sue thought about the idea of getting up and out onto the hills every day. She knew what Peter meant. Sometimes she had been on climbing trips and had ended-up festering around a hut or a campsite instead of getting out on the mountain.

'Well, try and finish in time to get in here before we close eh?'

'Oh, that would be nice. Thanks Sue.' And she loved the smile he gave her. Genuine and warm. She thought he was right at that point, sounding like an adult but still looking boyish too. Sue watched him head off towards the gate, where he was intercepted by Julie. She must have seen him and was probably having the same chat as me, Sue thought.

Julie was upbeat coming into the tea hut. 'Just had a wee chat with Pete. I saw him here when I came out of Glen View.'

'Well you wouldn't have wanted to miss-out on a wee chat would you' Said Sue teasingly. Both of them finding the occasional Scottish word creeping into their speech.

'No, that's true. He really wouldn't stop though, this time. Ah well, maybe we'll see him later. Or if not, it's my turn to catch him tomorrow morning, ok? Make sure you remember!' Sue smiled and nodded.

Making and serving breakfast for the early-bird campers, Sue found herself away with her own thoughts. Quite a few people came in and out, for a change, and not being able to chat much with Julie meant her mind was free to wander. She thought that the work and life this summer would likely settle into a pattern most days. She felt happy with that prospect but thought she would need to put an effort into doing her own thing, or routine would take over.

Between serving people, Sue made a little list in her head. She didn't need to go to the pub every night, even if that seemed what the geology students were doing. She couldn't afford it and she didn't want to put on any weight. In that vein, she decided she should do a little walk each evening, after work, on her own, with Julie or maybe invite one of the guys? There were three ways in and out of Kinlochewe, east, west and south, and she determined exploring all of them in turn, would be her starting point.

'You look happy' said Julie, interrupting her daydream.

'Yeah, you know what? I feel happy too!'

CHAPTER 5

Everything was a bit slow for the guys on the campsite after the whisky drinking night. By the time Peter and Graham emerged, separately, from their tents, the sun was well up and other campers had gone out for the day. They quietly shared mugs of tea and, after a couple of discarded attempts, a cigarette. Peter was still feeling embarrassed remembering the previous night, but said nothing to Graham about their chat, and was pleased Graham didn't seem to be acting any differently towards him.

Wandering over to the other side of the campsite together they discovered Steve had a bad hangover and hadn't got up or been out. This was a significant departure from the normal run of things, Peter felt, and wasn't surprised to hear Steve suggest he was going to make an afternoon foray "so as not to lose all the opportunity". Peter thought it was too late to get onto the mountain and gave into the idea of just drinking tea and reading a book. *Seven Years in Tibet* was his current one – it felt like an implausible story but apparently true. Good escapist stuff anyway and he thought an afternoon reading that and dozing would set him right again.

By late morning the three of them were ensconced in the tea room. Seemingly to the delight of Julie and Sue, who only had dribs and drabs of other customers coming and going. In the end, they were all together there for a couple of hours. More tea was followed by small pizzas, and then some cake. According to the two women most of the stuff was past its sell-by date and needing finishing-up. Peter didn't know if that was true or not and didn't really care; he just liked the feeling of being really full-up for once, making him content and giving him the feeling he could have happily stayed there all afternoon.

The three of them talked with Sue and Julie about the previous evening and night, missing out some of the discussion, but sharing some of their stories. Nick was a bit of a longer subject of discussion as he wasn't there and had somehow been the one person who had managed to get out and about that day. This was according to Sue who had spotted him much earlier.

Eventually, Steve made a bit of an announcement about feeling better and proposed making good use of the unintentional day-off. He explained that with the day on Peter's mountain, and now this day, he was unlikely to be around in the day ever again before the end of his field work. "Ever!" It seemed to Peter that Steve felt a real need to say this – some sort of public statement. As if speaking out loud his intention would make it happen.

Steve then said he thought a trip to the village of Torridon would be good, to the public showers there. Ben had told him about it apparently. Sue and Julie exchanged a quick look about that, but said nothing. He offered to take anyone interested in his car. Peter thought this was very polite, not to exclude the girls even though it would be impractical, and unnecessary, for them. But he jumped at the offer, as did Graham.

It was ten miles down the road. A tortuous and slow single-track road with passing places every few hundred yards. It would take a half-hour or more. The idea had immediate appeal though, as all of them were fed-up with stand-up wash-downs.

'Thanks Steve' Sue said, speaking for herself and Julie. 'It sounds like an adventure. It'd be good to join you too, but Jules and I need to clear-up here anyway. What am I saying! We might actually have other customers too.'

'Yeah, ones who actually pay' said Julie, laughing.

'Come back and tell us all about it down the pub later.' said Sue.

'What are you saying Sue!' Julie asked, deliberately sounding shocked. 'Gosh, everything up here is a novelty to you isn't it!? They're just going for a shower – what do you want them to tell you!?'

They all joined in a bit of banter then of what they might be able to say about their trip. It was all good humoured and put the three guys in a good mood for the drive down the road.

On the drive towards the gate, Nick was coming back up the road on foot. It turned-out he had been woken by the surprising level of light on his first day and had got up and about, despite a bit of a hangover, and made a start at figuring-out his project, he said. He had been round to the base of Slioch and back. It had been further than expected, he said, and quite hard work despite being mostly level. Steve invited him to join in, and Nick ran to his tent to grab a towel, needing no further encouragement.

Steve turned-out to be a very safe driver, as Peter had expected. They all joined in the game of spotting any other vehicle coming towards them in the distance, so Steve could pull-in to a passing place before they met. The road was slightly familiar to Peter, having hitched lifts up and down it during the climbing meet before he started the geology work proper. It was wild land all around and, because of the stop-start in the passing places, seemed to take a lot more time than anyone expected.

Nick was the more garrulous of the four, taking up most of the journey time mostly with talk about himself. Steve somehow managed to concentrate on the road as well at Nick's conversation. Peter thought he and Graham were just happy to look out at the scenery and do the car-spotting.

As they had already learned, Nick lived and went to university in his hometown of Newcastle. He had lived there all his life and that explained his broad Geordie accent. It turned out his elder brother had done geography and was now a teacher. Peter got the impression that Nick admired this brother, just from the way he spoke. He talked about his brother's footballing talent, playing and getting tickets for games, going to matches together, living with their Mum and Dad still. Nick's brother apparently had a different girlfriend every week and Nick made it sound as if that's what he tried to do too. Steve did a good job of keeping this information flowing via a litany of questions from the driver's seat. Until at one point, the landscape opened up abruptly.

'Wow, look at that!' Graham pointed wildly to his left. 'Pull over can you Steve?'

They got out on a piece of ground, not a passing place as such, but a spot created by many cars doing just what they had done. It was obviously a good place to get a photo of what they were now staring at. In amongst the flanks of mountain to the south of the road, there was a distinct small valley that broadened out onto a level flood plain with a lochan. The valley itself was seemingly filled with dozens of small, rounded hillocks. The whole vista had a distinctly lumpy look with these grassy mounds scattered around, some merging into one another.

'I stayed down there last week'.

They all looked at Peter. 'It's a drumlin field. When I came up here, we stayed at that hut you can just make out – that building a mile or so over towards the drumlins a bit.'

'There's two buildings' Nick said, 'Do you mean the one by the lake?'

'It's not much of a lochan but that's actually the smaller building and is something to do with fishing and the estate. The further one is the Ling Hut – owned and run by a Scottish climbing club. That's where I was a couple of weeks ago.'

Graham became the guide, interrupting Peter and, for once, trumping Steve's knowledge. 'I know what we are looking at, and it's a superb example I reckon. We did drumlins at school. Not like that lot but there's some on Gower and up in Snowdonia. It's moraine, if you all remember, rock debris dumped by a retreating glacier. The melt water from the mountains has rushed through the moraine eroding it into that hummocky appearance. But, it's fantastic, they run all the way up that little valley don't they?'

'They tail-off a bit as you get further up' said Peter. 'Three of us went up there from the hut. There's pictures of them in the hut and a bit of explanation. People come from all over to see them apparently.'

'Who Pete? People who love drumlins?' Graham being drole.

'Ha bloody ha,' said Peter. 'Yes, people like us I suppose. Like you anyway – you're the font of all knowledge on them by the sound of it! Students. I don't know, tourists maybe. Like you said, people interested in drumlins I suppose.' They all laughed.

They took a vote and decided not to go to the drumlins just then. It had been fifty-fifty but Steve had casting vote as driver. He really must have been in day-off mode, Peter thought as they continued down the road instead of going exploring.

Ten minutes later, it was three o'clock in the afternoon when they finally arrived in the tiny strung-out village of Torridon. At the entry to the village was the public convenience. Like most public buildings around there, it was white-washed, pebble dashed walls and a slate roof. Not much bigger than a large garden shed. Divided into two halves, the part marked Gentlemen managed to cram in urinals just big enough for two, two toilet cubicles and one shower. The showers were 10p a time and they wondered if the hot water would last four showers in succession.

So, they decided to double-up, a trick Nick had learned on a field-trip somewhere apparently. The basis for sharing was determined as north and south of the country. So Steve and Nick would go together. Graham and Peter as the other pair. A coin toss-up by Steve, the driver leading everything now it seemed to Peter, meant he and Graham would go second.

It was all a little embarrassing in such a confined space. It might have been easier for some of them to wait outside but they all stayed cramped in the little building. Nick was fooling around a bit, making jokes about their bodies mostly. Young adults reverting to adolescence with the sudden nakedness Peter thought, although he joined in as much as anyone, teenage embarrassment resurfacing. Once Nick and Steve were back-to-back in the shower, they started singing the song 'Bare Necessities'. Nick showing off, Peter decided, and Steve covering his shyness. They seemed to know all the words and it became a spontaneous singalong as they all joined in, laughing and singing.

The water came out cold at first, causing gasps and shouting that became louder as the water quickly went very hot and the building soon filled-up with steam. Shampoo served for both hair and body for everyone and came out of a metal swivel bottle in the shower. A dark green gunk smelling a bit of pine trees and disinfectant. The notice said the shower would run for five minutes and Peter found himself doing the countdown as the two wet guys rinsed off.

Then it was his turn. He had managed to do the countdown at the same time as taking off his clothes. He was wearing light blue, cotton briefs and had found himself half-studying what the others were wearing. Steve was in white y-fronts at the same point, which Peter thought was normal, Graham had worn similar style pants to his own and Nick had a pair of larger ones like Steve's but string woven apart from a panel at the front and back. It all reminded Peter of a scene from his Mum's Littlewoods catalogues a few years back. An early source of pubescent inspiration scouring the women's underwear section – but also the men's he remembered now.

Dried-off and feeling fluffier, the boys went back to the car, still good humoured and joshing with each other across the road to the waiting car. Steve suggested they do it as a weekly event and he would relent a bit on his earlier stated commitment to devoting all remaining time to his mapping. Nick, newly aware of the need to do washes at a basin, moaned about the absence of a campsite shower, a bit helplessly Peter thought. Nick was also wondering how he would get any clothes washed without machines. Peter thought his Mum probably did everything for him back in Newcastle – maybe even scrubbed his back he pondered dismissively.

On the return drive the car radio picked up a signal intermittently through the long valley, past the looming bulk of Liathach and then the Beinn Eighe range, but nearing Kinlochewe someone was singing a song with the lyric *two, four, six, eight motorway*. Or that's what Peter thought he heard. Steve surprised him, and Graham, by telling them both it was a group called The Tom Robinson Band, that he really liked, and the record was currently shooting up the charts.

Peter had never heard of them. They sounded a bit punk and he wasn't sure he liked it. He still felt happily stuck with prog rock. Punk seemed like a complete departure from what he knew he liked and he was taking time to accept it. There was a chat in the car and Graham shared Peter's position, or even older stuff like Curved Air and Jethro Tull, but Nick and Steve seemed very knowledgeable and keen on the new wave of music.

Getting bored with the discussion after a few more minutes, Graham said the best thing he had heard in a long while was their singing in the shower back down the road. That quickly led to a repeat singing of the song by all four of them. Swinging into the campsite gate, Ben looked up in surprise as he heard the strikingly odd sound and words *"…bare necessities, those simple bare necessities, forget about your worries and your strife, yeah man, those bare necessities, that's why a bear can rest at ease, with just the bare necessities of life."*

Chapter 6

It rained that night and this incoming change to the weather was slow moving. The drifting cloud in the morning was accompanied by drifts of midges. Peter had brought bits of mosquito coil to burn in the doorway of his tent, but worried what the pyrethrum would do to him after an older cousin had told him it was used to exterminate pest infestations. That cousin was a public health inspector and the information troubled Peter. It kept the microscopic insects at bay though.

Graham shouted across that they would just have to smoke more. Adjusting to the newly changed situation Peter noticed that for anyone heading to the facility block, the journey had become a sprint, usually with head covered by a shirt or jumper. Or people just running with arms flapping wildly.

Out of the valley though, Peter knew, or at least hoped, the slopes of the hills and mountains had enough breeze to keep the midges away most of the time. But he already felt lumpy as he walked down the road out of the village, midge bites around his lips, eyebrows, inside his ears – anywhere the midge repellent wasn't applied fully.

He was on his way to meet the warden, just outside his house and field centre, a mile or two down the road at Anancaun. John MacKenzie was going to drive the two of them up a track some of the way, from the spot called Bridge of Grudie. There was no hanging about and they were in the Land Rover and away just as soon as Peter had said hello and put his rucksack on the seat. He hoped he hadn't kept the Warden waiting.

It was a short drive west along the main road towards Gairloch before they turned off to the left. It was a rough track and soon there was a ford across a shallow part of the river Grudie, about a mile or two after leaving the main road. John MacKenzie parked-up here and the rest of the way, Peter discovered, was on foot. It started as a steep, three mile long rising traverse across the western flanks of Peter's mountain. Initially across boulder and tussocky ground and then latterly becoming rocky and scree covered all the way to the broad inclined slope of Druim Ghrudaidh. They got there quickly, Peter thought, and he found it much quicker and less tiring than the longer approach from Kinlochewe and the Pony Track.

The Warden explained there was a third way of getting to this remote corner of the nature reserve. A stalkers road parallel to the river Grudie, and he pointed it to Peter. He explained it meant a very steep ascent the last half-mile, but it was safe enough if you knew the way, which he said he did. He suggested they might do that, if they ended-up coming up here again.

Having got their breath back, they took in the view around them. John MacKenzie continued speaking. 'As I said the other day, I don't get up here very often. The cloud base sitting on your mountain gives a sense of drama to the landscape don't you think? God I love it here – just look at it.'

Peter felt chuffed the Warden had said 'your mountain'. The two of them gazed around at the seemingly endless vista of mountains and lochans stretching away to the silvery edge of the sea that was visible, miles away at Gairloch. The cloud level weighed down on the landscape, compressing the view somehow. Peter thought it had the effect of widening the horizon and the image of the word cinemascope came into his head.

The Warden's reaction to the nearby metal outcrop was initially muted. To be fair, the glowering weather made the aluminium, if that's what it was, look very dull, with little lustre. All the colours had gone out of the landscape. Without sunlight, the scarlet of the sandstone looked like a damp dark maroon. The quartzite had lost its white shimmer and the metal was hardly that obvious. It would be easily overlooked in weather like this – the norm for the area really.

'Well, first inspection I would say it's bits of aeroplane. So, it's that bit up there above us and that other lot along there to our left? Is there more?', asked the Warden.

'I don't know yet.' admitted Peter. 'I have been up that groove and put my hand on the metal. I think there's more of it runs along the joint between those two strata layers of sandstone but it seems buried in it and there are bits of thick moss and lichen as you can see. The other bit down there is just what you can see.' He explained that he, Steve and Graham had scouted around and hadn't seen anything else obvious.

'The odd thing is John…' Peter started to say, then paused, again feeling hesitant using his first name. '…yeah, the odd thing is, this line, this crack I have climbed-up to reach that metal. Well, it's a fault.'

'Ah ha, I know what a fault is but I'm not sure I would always recognise one!'

'Sorry, I didn't mean to imply that.' Peter had slowed because he thought what he was saying was perhaps a bit silly. 'In fact, I didn't see it first. Steve pointed it out. But the fault means the layer of sandstone up there and the layer down here are the same layer. So it means all that rock was laid down at the same time, hundreds of millions of years ago.'

John MacKenzie had been following Peter's description, watching him pointing upwards, along and outwards. He could tell the young student was trying to find the right way to describe it.

'Well, it's just weird the metal being in both those bits and seemingly nowhere else. It's like the metal was in the sandstone when it formed. But that's just nuts of course,' Peter continued.

'There's a saying that goes something along the lines of when you have eliminated all the other improbables, you must be left with the correct answer, no matter how impossible,' replied the warden. To Peter, this made him feel a little bit like he was being tested and the

Warden reminded him of being at school.

'But,' said Peter 'the Torridonian sandstone is seven hundred million years old, some think maybe older than that too. Where would the metal have come from and would it have lasted to now?'

The Warden laughed. 'My Mother has some aluminium pots that date back to the war or even before that, but I see your point. Maybe the solution is to widen the search? We need more evidence don't we? It's a fieldwork job undoubtedly. You should include it in your thesis Pete. It might not be geology but it is taking up your time up here, quite rightly in my view. I think you need to sketch out a search plan for this cliff and work your way around for other bits of aircraft.'

Peter thought that sounded a good idea but wasn't sure Doc Griffiths would think it was a good use of his time. On the other hand, he was only doing fieldwork here at all by consent of John MacKenzie and the Nature Reserve and he didn't want to appear disrespectful. It felt a bit of a dilemma and once again Peter simply felt overwhelmed with the amount of work he still needed to do.

'So, you think it really is part of a wrecked plane then?'

'I can't imagine anything else. I'm starting to wonder if something came across the hillside here in bad weather and part, or all, of it whacked into the cliff here. There might have been a fire. That might account for the way the metal seems fused onto the rock. And, being in two bits of the cliff that look the same – just a coincidence.' Peter felt relief that was an interpretation that could yield a clear explanation.

The warden looked back west. 'There's a man in Gairloch, local historian chappie. He knows much of what's gone on here in the war. I'll have a chat with him. He's a pretty fit bugger and goes out all over the mountains hereabouts. I might be able to persuade him up here.' Seeing Peter become a bit crestfallen, he added, 'don't worry, I can show him, if you don't mind. You don't have to slog up here again. On the other hand, we can use the access road I just mentioned, and the Land Rover again – cuts down the time. You might like to hear first-hand what he has to say?'

John MacKenzie led the way down, having offered to a very grateful Peter, a lift back. Peter hadn't assumed it was a return trip and had half-expected to be left up here to do more fieldwork and the long descent to the village. It saved quite a few miles but the descent was quite hairy, compared to the climb up. John MacKenzie seemed to instinctively know which way to go but the slope steepened to about sixty degrees Peter thought, at the start. Approaching rock outcrops from above at such a steep angle meant you couldn't always tell if you were approaching a rock or a small cliff.

Tired now, Peter sat in the passenger seat as the Land Rover wove its way down to the main road. The warden took him all the way back to the campsite and thanked him for his discovery and for "sharing it" he had said. Peter loved that and felt very grown-up again. It was good to be taken seriously. It made him, when he came onto the campsite, ignore the tearoom and also encouraged him to refuse Graham's invitation to share a joint. He got into his tent, got out his notebook and put pen to paper for a while, and actually really enjoyed it.

Chapter 7

The dreary and slow-moving weather made all of them a bit despondent. The campsite was getting steadily busier too, subtly altering the feel of the place. Over the next couple of days, the arrival of more holidaymakers and continuation of the wet weather meant the tiny tearoom was often full to bursting. They had taken to lying around in their tents, reading, counting off the days left in Peter's case. Worrying about getting everything done and pining for Penny if he was being honest.

Sue or Julie had taken to running across the site to tell Graham and Peter when the tearoom was quiet, so they could get in. Peter thought this was so sweet and friendly of them, but whenever it was Sue, he also wished he found a way of inviting her to stay. Too embarrassing though with Graham nearby.

A brighter morning emerged soon enough and when Peter was coming back from a morning wash, thinking about a day of work ahead, he could see there was a bit of a commotion going on outside the campsite. Julie's uncle was speaking to the girls, clearly agitated about something and then left, went out of the gate of the campsite and started walking fast down the road. Peter went over to see what it was all about.

'What's up Julie, something going on?'

'Oh, hi Pete. Yes, Uncle Ben's in a real flap. The grocery van has gone in the ditch down the road somewhere.'

'God, is anyone hurt?' asked Peter.

'No! I don't think so anyway, it was all quite slow apparently, just some tourist or somebody wouldn't wait in the single-track laybys, and came on fast along the road, or something. Uncle Ben thinks the road is blocked now until they get it sorted, and he thinks he may be there a while!'

Peter decided to go and have a look, left his wash kit and towel with Julie and promptly jogged down the road after Ben. It was only a half-mile out of the village and Peter could see the van leaning over at an alarming angle. The front of the van, facing him, was more-or-less on the road and verge although the front nearside wheel was on a bit of a slope. But the back of the van was steeply slumped. When Peter got up to it, he could see the nearside rear wheels, a pair of them, were in a ditch. Ben was talking with the guy in dark blue overalls, who was obviously the driver.

'Hi,' said Peter. 'Julie said something about this and I thought I'd come and see if I could help.'

'That's grand lad. We're just figuring it out,' replied Ben.

'What happened then?'

'Some wee pillock came motoring down the road, ignoring the passing places and seemed to expect me to stop!' exclaimed the driver. 'I had just passed a bay. He was coming so quickly though, I had to swerve to avoid hitting him. As it was he went over the verge that side...' pointing across the road '...but there's no ditch there, so he was able to stay on to the road. Bloody wee sod though, hasn't even stopped!'

Ben explained, 'we can't get traction on both the back wheels, as they are hanging in air above the base of the ditch. So, we can't just drive out of the problem.'

The driver knew the solution, and Peter thought he must have experienced the same thing previously. 'We will have to fill the ditch in front of the nearside back wheels, to give it a surface to move over. It then needs a pull or enough of a push to get the wheel onto whatever we use as fill. Then we should be able to drive back onto the road itself'.

'Aye', said Ben, 'that sounds about right. The trick will be getting a compact enough surface with the ditch fill, for the wheels to get a purchase. We need to gather rocks and stones to fill part of the ditch.' As he spoke, he was scanning the adjacent fields and verges.

'If we can.'

'I'll go and get the other guys,' said Peter, thinking the ditch looked pretty deep and they were going to need a lot of rocks. He ran back to the campsite without waiting for any further comment. He noticed a couple of vehicles were now already queuing to get past the blocked road.

At the campsite, Steve was just getting ready to leave for some mapping, as was Nick. Graham sounded half asleep still. But Peter ran around quickly telling them what was going on and managed to get all three to come down the road to help. As he left the gate, he could see there now were four vehicles waiting this side of the obstruction. He, Nick and Steve ran down the road. Graham, he was surprised to see, wasn't far behind, running along and tucking his shirt into his jeans at the same time. They had all just slipped on trainers and came along, picking-up on Peter's sense of urgency.

Back at the van, Ben and the driver were scouting around for rocks or anything to fill the bit of ditch. The students joined in, Nick and Steve scouring the immediate area along with Ben and the driver but Graham and Peter going down the road, to where there was a small cutting. 'I've passed this bit of road most days heading-out,' said Peter. 'This cutting is a bit of moraine I think, alongside the valley bottom. Anyway, it's full of boulders and stones, which is what we want.' At the cutting, they each grabbed an armful, as much as they could hold, and walked back. It was disappointing to see how little difference they made to the depth of the ditch.

But, after three more trips like that, and with the efforts of the other four, there was soon enough material to roughly level the necessary bit of ditch with the roadside verge. They pushed and used their legs and feet, in turn, to squeeze the material as close to the wheels as possible and to compact the filling of rocks, stones and boulders.

'Right', said Ben. That looks fairly good. The danger is the wheel will just spin and send all our hard work flying but Bill will have a go. It's too awkward to get a tow or something to pull us now'. They all looked where he pointed, down the road to a now longer line of cars and vans waiting. 'They've effectively blocked the road access from the village. So, if we can't get a pull, we will just have to push!'

It looked a bit daunting. The van was about a four-tonner, with the groceries on the back, according to the driver Bill. He hopped into the driver's seat and the four students and Ben went to the back of the vehicle to push. Seeing what was happening, two or three men and a woman got out of cars – from the queue now lengthening slowly in both directions. So, about nine of them in the end managed to get a hand or shoulder onto the back of the van. The ones above the wheel and ditch had to perform a bit of an acrobatic manoeuvre to be able to give a push and to stay upright at the same time.

'Away you go then Bill', shouted Ben. The van started up, and slowly edged forward. As half-expected by the group, the stuck rear wheels initially held but then started to slip on top of the filling. For a moment it looked as if there might just be enough forward motion for the wheels to make it onto the verge and then more stones were spun-off and the wheel sunk down again.

The guys at the corner of the van over the ditch jumped back quickly as the corner of the van lurched downwards. There was a great variety of swearing and disappointed comments from the group of helpers.

The solution was felt to be more rocks in the ditch, to fill it for a longer stretch, putting more weight onto the stones under the wheel and hopefully stopping them from being spun off. The men had all now taken-off jumpers, some shirts too, and the search for more stones become more frantic and necessarily over a wider area. Peter and Graham were joined by further additional car occupants, and the little cutting was now being effectively being re-excavated by hand.

Peter was amazed at one point returning to the ditch, looking at the view before him. A van half in a ditch at a thirty-degree angle, about a dozen cars, a couple of motorbikes, another small van or two, lined-up in each direction. A scattering of men in fields around the van, with bare torsos or rolled-up shirt-sleeves. Some women too, in T-shirts, even in frocks. A line of maybe ten guys now, going back and forth along a line to the cutting. Everyone working-up a sweat and a sense of urgency setting in, as cars and vans one by one, gradually stretched the queues.

Everyone was also just starting to get a bit fed-up, the fun element that had been there briefly was now evaporating, when Ben called a halt. A length of ditch was now pretty well crammed with rocks, boulders and debris for much more than the length of the van. People were still treading it down.

So, it was then back to the original manoeuvre. The same moment of hesitation as Bill attempted to inch the van forward, and then suddenly the weight of the van was on the rear wheels, there was a bit of spin but the majority of rock filling stayed in place and then suddenly the van was back on the road. A cheer went up from those involved and some spontaneous clapping could be heard from all the other vehicle drivers and others, up and down the length of the road.

Someone had taken it on himself to organise the reversing of vehicles, steadily backwards into Kinlochewe, so that the traffic coming from the other direction could then flow past. The delivery van came first, only to have to pull into the village shop, its original destination. The line of cars behind all went past with a toot of appreciation from most. As the students and Ben got back into the campsite, walking, the vehicles heading down the valley were starting to get on their way too.

'You lads get yourselves a tea', said Ben. Tell Julie I said. I'm going to see Pam a minute and then I'll be over too'.

He then put his hand on Peter's shoulder. 'Thanks very much for that Pete. It was a big help.'

Peter was surprised how chuffed he felt with that remark.

In the tea cabin, Julie and Sue wanted to hear all about it and quickly organised teas and glasses of water. 'Well, that's the excitement of the day over then,' said Julie after hearing the story. They all laughed. Everyone felt in good spirits, until they remembered they needed to get out and work. For once, they all stuck to their fieldwork plans and the two women set-to, clearing-up and serving a sudden influx of drivers and passengers wanting refreshments.

CHAPTER 8

Some hours later, after being out on the hills a bit, by coincidence, the four geology students all found themselves chatting in Nick's frame tent. This was the first time they had all been in here. Nick didn't join in much so far anyway. Peter thought it was probably a question of money. Nick's family sounded close and helpful, but Peter had the impression of them all living pretty much on top of one another, maybe to make ends meet.

It seemed to Peter, that there was a clear order of wealth. Peter had felt the least well-off initially, maybe Graham, but now reckoned Nick had no money at all – never came to the tearoom and didn't stay long in the pub with the one exception of the whisky evening, and he ducked out of buying rounds. Steve was at the top end of the hierarchy, Peter sensed, his parents having paid for the static caravan as opposed to a tent, and, most of all, he had a car.

As it turned out Nick's work up here was shorter than the rest of them, just five weeks, and was more of a wide-scale interpretation of the geology, touching on all of the other three's areas. The discussion they were having became useful for all of them and Peter found himself discovering some facts and ideas he didn't know or hadn't thought about.

One other thing they all discovered, was that Nick had a decidedly hardcore porn mag with him. A gift from his brother apparently. It looked a bit well-thumbed and dog-eared. Nick offered it to the other three. Steve said maybe later, Graham declined it but Peter was intrigued and decided to take it back to his tent, and he flicked through it before the pub that evening.

To start with it looked like the few other magazines of its type that Peter had seen, although quite a bit thicker, but this one did not have the models with airbrushing. This magazine was much more photographically gynaecological Peter discovered. And became more so, page by page, soon becoming more like an anatomy book.

Peter found he wasn't being turned-on at all and thought of Graham more quickly deciding it wasn't for him. Once again Peter found himself seeing Graham with higher values and principles, or maybe simply more courage or self-confidence, than himself and he felt a little ashamed. Having flicked through a good half of it, Peter was about to put it in the end of his tent to give back to Nick, when he spotted there was an editorial on the inside page he had initially missed.

To call it an editorial was perhaps a grand word for the few lines that were there but what it said was *this edition of this magazine was breaking new ground for a high street magazine.* High street!? thought Peter. He felt shocked they might sell this in Smiths or the local newsagents. He had never seen it before. What it said though was that this magazine featured for the first time, on the high street, pictures with naked men with the women and *men featuring the state that anyone would expect to see in the pose you are looking at.* Peter hadn't seen any of that.

Flicking through again, he discovered in the later part of the magazine some of the images of women did have men alongside in some pose of other. They weren't exactly doing anything together, certainly not touching each other and their anatomy looked like anything Peter had seen in any changing room, or more recently down the shower.

But on three pages towards the end of the magazine, there were two images quite different from the others. Peter found himself held by these photographs as he looked at them. The first was most of a full page, of a man on his back, looking down the length of his body towards his feet. A young woman straddled his chest, posed above his face giving the man the sort of close-up that readers had seen on the other pages. Behind the woman though was the editorial reference point, standing proud and clear of his stomach.

Peter quickly looked over his shoulder, alone in his tent but momentarily fearful someone might be watching him. Peter found it hard to tear his eyes away from the first erection he had ever closely observed apart from his own, and he found it fascinating.

Eventually turning over the page, there was a double page spread. To the right was a close-up of a man, a different one, on his back again. This time the woman straddling his chest was facing down his body, lifting herself off his chest. Peter thought the angle and pose being held by the woman must have been uncomfortable.

But his attention was taken by the image on the left-hand page. On this page the woman's head and one of her hands were deliberately blurred out of focus but clearly her hand was around the man, and her mouth close to him, and he was thus proudly displaying the second example Peter had ever seen in close-up. And now Peter realised he was in the same state himself.

He felt as if he could hardly contain himself. Feeling giddy as well as aroused. He had hardly begun touching himself before a rush of pleasure engulfed him, too closely followed by a feeling of guilt. The memory came to him of a time in his first year at Uni when he had once inhaled so deeply on a joint, it gave him a tremendous hit but at the same time a wave of nausea and giddiness. This felt like that.

He lay on his back and couldn't move for a while. He felt he couldn't really think properly either. Then he had a cigarette, breaking his own rule not to smoke inside the end, rather than the doorway, of his tent. The smoke calmed him and he began to feel just tired and eventually, he thought, a bit dreamy.

Graham broke the spell, from nearby. 'Pete. Hey Pete, are you there? Do you fancy running for it down the pub?' Peter felt grateful for the interruption. He knew he would go right away to the pub, running to avoid the midges. He thought about it, but knew he wasn't going to take the magazine back to Nick after all, not just yet anyway.

CHAPTER 9

The weather didn't change much for a few days and all the students slowly got back into the reality of working in all weathers, sometimes it felt like "all four seasons in one day", as the locals described it.

Peter had worked on a rough plan to cover the geography, at least, of his mapping area, so that after about three weeks or so, halfway through the project, he had got a reasonable view of the surface geology. Compared to Steve's maps though, Peter felt his were really sparse. It was a better comparison with Graham, but at least Graham used Rotring pens all the time, which made his map look a bit more professional, Peter thought, even if the content was a bit lacking. Steve used the right drawing pens too, of course, but his mapping was full of content as well. It had arrows and symbols all over the place but Peter's map seemed to have just the odd one here and there. But that's how it was. Maybe Nick's was worse, but nobody had seen his fieldwork in detail yet.

Peter felt he was walking miles every day and taking compass and clinometer readings when he could, or maybe just when he could be bothered in the drizzle. He had gathered quite a few rock samples. But again nothing compared to the hoard of carefully labelled specimens that were accumulating in Steve's caravan. Peter found that thinking of Steve's approach to geology made him feel a bit useless.

There had been a time, playing cards in the caravan before going to the pub, they had chatted about this. Graham, Steve and Peter. Nick doing his own thing elsewhere. Steve felt his mapping area was just more compact. Graham's territory was huge but didn't have many outcrops. Peter's area on the other hand was both pretty large and had a lot of exposure – a lot of outcrops. 'And your geology is really complicated don't forget Pete', Steve said helpfully, but Peter felt it was just about trying to make him feel better. Still, that was a decent thing to say, thought Peter.

One afternoon, it was just Peter playing cards with Steve after a useful morning for each of them on the rocks. Really heavy rain had come though, forcing them, or persuading them, to retreat. But as it began to brighten up during a game of whist, Steve looked out of the window and suggested they might go down the showers. 'I just feel like the drive and getting out of the village for a bit really', he explained. 'It's too late for us to go back out mapping but now the sun's trying to come out again, I don't want to be in the caravan'.

Calling for the others, Steve and Peter discovered Nick wasn't in and Graham also out, or maybe asleep. Stoned too maybe, thought Peter. 'Think he just likes his own company', Peter said, thinking aloud. As soon as he said it, he realised this was the likely truth. Peter had learned Graham was quite content to be in his own space a lot of the time.

It had been one of those days that was to be the pattern for the rest of their time up there, so typical of the region in July and August. Rain one moment. Bright sun the next. And what went with the rapid changes was the wind blowing them through. They had all learned this was a very good thing, blowing away "the little biting critters" as Jock nicknamed them. The worst times, by a long way, were the still damp days, when the midges plagued everyone to death.

This was to be the third time going to Torridon but the first with just two of them. The first time had been the best so far – unplanned and a real trip out. Singing the shower song had become a bit of a legend for them all after just a fortnight. The second time to Torridon had really been a necessity and more of a functional trip. Steve hadn't taken any cash for petrol, saying 'just buy me a pint', but Peter wasn't sure the rounds had worked out like that. Peter considered now that although Steve was better off than the rest of them, he was nicely generous with it.

In fact Peter knew he had really warmed to Steve's friendliness but was still a bit in awe of his knowledge and instinct for geology. One evening, after a couple of pints, Peter had quietly said this to Steve in the pub. In return, Steve had told him that he admired his common-sense about the mountains and also said he had learned a lot from him about navigation and looking after yourself. Peter didn't think he did know much about those and couldn't think when they had talked about this sort of thing, but Steve had said that the day they all went up to the plane wreck had been an eye-opener.

So, the pair of them left the campsite in the car, with a quick wave to the girls, who seemed very preoccupied with some customers at that moment. This time, the road was deserted and they zipped along nicely. Steve took the opportunity to explain to Peter that he had confirmed on the phone the previous evening, that his tutor was on the point of coming up to do the halfway-through supervision visit.

He was excited by the prospect but also anxious about being prepared and ready. Peter tried to reassure him that the standard of his work ought to be good enough. Peter also talked about how a halfway visit might be more useful than an at-the-start visit like his had been. Maybe there's merit in both, he thought.

By the time they arrived at the Drumlin Viewpoint, as they had named it, the later afternoon sun shone through the gap between Liathach and Beinn Eighe and lit-up brightly the drumlin field itself and the river running out of it. They stopped for another look. Both of them were captivated by the view. The light and shadow highlighted and gave depth to the features in a way that made the view even more spectacular.

'Do you fancy a closer look Steve?' asked Peter.

'Have we got time?'

'Yeah, come on. Let's go over there. We can still get to the shower, but we might never get a better chance to see this.' Peter was surprised how enthusiastic he sounded.

Steve parked the car off the road and they were grateful they had come out with boots on. They hadn't thought about doing any walking or clambering but just hadn't wanted to get their trainers wet. Just as they were about to set off, Peter had a thought.

'Why not carry your towel too Steve? I've swum in this river and we could give it a go, if you fancy it?'

Steve seemed unsure but Peter just wrapped his own towel around his neck, along with a jumper and after a moment, Steve did the same thing. They headed off across the heather, both feeling good to be doing something different. Both of them enjoying the spontaneity.

They joined the track to the fishing hut and then on to the Ling Hut. The climbing hut didn't look occupied and seemed locked-up. Beyond there the tiny, intermittent path ran alongside the river and into the drumlin hillocks. They were all around forty or fifty feet high at the start and then became shallower, more jumbled up and overlapping further up. The image as viewed from afar, of a distinct group of hillocks, was much less clear when actually in amongst them.

However, it seemed a magical spot to them both. The river, near the hut they had passed was on a flood plain and the drumlins filled what was now clearly a shallow valley. So the river ran down from the mountains, through the drumlin field and then out on to the level flood plain. The river when in spate, had eroded the base of the bigger hillocks nearest the valley bottom and there was a lot of jumbled debris, boulders, rocks and pebbles.

Steve was impressed. 'I mean Pete, you read about this sort of thing, but to see it up close, well that's something else.' He dragged his hand through the out-washed moraine at the bottom of one of the drumlins, then held up a couple of cupped handfuls. 'Look at this Pete. This was the product of a glacier right here. What…? … just a few thousand years ago? Fresh as a daisy compared to what we're studying. I've seen pictures of glaciers in Iceland and the Alps, the moraine is the same as this, it's just the glacier that has gone!'

'I know what you mean Steve. The landscape here has the feel of being freshly made, doesn't it? Forged only yesterday' Said Peter. 'Pretty awe-inspiring really.'

They spent a while just wandering around the drumlins, with not a sign of any other people, imagining how it might have looked as a frozen landscape, with a glacier retreating back into the corries of the mountain behind, Beinn Damh, just a couple of miles away.

But Peter suggested they make the most of the sun while it was there. He had seen that cloud was blowing through a bit more again from the west, over the ridge of Beinn Eighe. The valley they were in was still in the sun, but it may not last he thought. They walked back out of the drumlins and back on the tiny track eventually leading back to the car, now a mile and half away.

'When I was here a few weeks ago now, staying in that climbing hut, this proved to be a good bit of the river to go in', said Peter shortly. 'Well, we did a couple of times anyway. It's broad here as you can see, that's shallower, easier to get in, but also slower and it's maybe a bit warmer. The sun gets into the riverbed a bit I suppose.'

Steve looked completely unconvinced as they both stood on the bank. Peter thought that if they hesitated any longer it would be like the time a fortnight earlier on his mapping area. Steve would never go in and a moment would have passed.

'What do we do then Pete, I haven't got any trunks with me. Just the towel you know. So, is this like you and Graham did that day?'

'I know Steve. Does it bother you? It's not so different to being in the shower block is it? I felt a bit shy when here with a mate a month ago, at first, but once in the water it's fantastic. You saw how much Graham and I liked the lochan up on the mountain didn't you?'

'It's just different Pete…' said Steve '…just not something I have done before.'

Peter decided he was going in anyway. 'Come on Steve. Give it a try'. He was already pulling off his shirt. 'It'll be cold but you'll love it. Hopefully! We can be in and out, dry off a bit with the last warmth of the sun, if it stays, and then jog back to the car or something. It will be fine'.

Peter felt Steve still looked resistant but suddenly seemed to make his mind up and got all his clothes off really quickly. Even before Peter finished stripping off himself. The river was a bit faster and deeper than before. Peter hadn't thought about all the recent rain and it raising the water level. The greater depth and flow also meant it was a bit colder but he thought it still felt fabulously clean and fresh.

They were in above their knees immediately, then to their waists and then they just went for it and plunged under. The cold numbed their feet and hands but their heads most of all. It was just deep enough to thrash about a bit and float over to the other side, where the river was a bit slower and they found it OK to lie back there for a few moments. Peter looked around, Beinn Eighe and Liathach to his left, Beinn Damh to his right, and the drumlins nearer at hand. Neither of them said anything, but Peter felt pleased that Steve had come in and did actually look as if he liked it.

Before too long though, the cold seemed to become more penetrating and they were back out again and drying off on the grassy bank. Peter saw the clouds blowing over from the west were now a darker grey but the mountains had split the cloud cover so at least they were still in sunshine at this spot.

What was it about doing this thought Peter, being in the cold water and warm sun, causing his body to have a response. He hoped it wasn't too obvious and looked over to Steve to check. Just at that moment he caught Steve staring at him, and he felt himself blushing immediately. Peter decided to just carry on drying himself and not to try and say anything. He distracted himself by thinking of the red deer he had could see on the slopes above them. After a few moments, he turned back to Steve and was relieved that Steve's gaze had dropped anyway.

Peter still felt a bit self-conscious as they got dressed. He hadn't meant that to happen and all his years in changing rooms, he had never really had an issue before of controlling himself. Just something about naked river swimming and sun, Peter thought to himself, just a physiological thing.

They did start off half-walking and half-trotting back to the car. It had now clouded over completely and the clouds were blackening further. The air temperature had dropped straight away too. Peter pointed out the curtain of rain that was quite obviously moving down the slopes of Beinn Eighe from the ridge. They thought they would make it in time, but the first drops hit them with a half-mile to go and then suddenly the curtain swept onto them, instantly soaking their clothes. There was nothing they could do but run on as fast as they could.

Reaching the car, Steve got the doors unlocked and they jumped-in. Looked at each other and laughed.

'Sod it. We won't think it so funny in a moment Steve. Bloody hell though, talk about changeable! Jesus, I'm soaked.'

'Me too' said Steve, swinging the car into a rapid three point turn on the narrow road.

The drive back was as fast as Steve could do, much faster than before, Peter thought. By the time they got into the campsite they were a little shivery and still a bit damp. Steve invited Peter in for a hot tea and as soon as they were in the caravan, he also put on the fan heater and the enveloping warm air made them both realise just how chilly they had become.

'It will soon get too hot', said Steve. 'And too expensive – it eats the electricity that thing.'

'Thanks very much Steve' said Peter gratefully, 'It would be really crap going back to my tent like this.'

'Don't worry, hopefully we can dry off a bit. Put your towel out somewhere, you don't want to be taking that back with you all damp and yukky".

'That's really nice of you. Sorry about all this, we would have been better off going to the showers in Torridon.'

'Bollocks to that! I know I was a bit unsure to start, but that swim was stunning and so was seeing the drumlins up close. We were just unlucky getting that cloud burst.'

They looked at themselves and around the tiny space of the caravan. The fan heater was doing an excellent job of making the air feel hot and the windows had steamed up. Steve drew the curtains and told Peter that he was going to hang out his clothes as best he could to dry and invited Peter to do the same. So, they were soon stripped off again, this time without any embarrassed feelings, to their underwear anyway, and damp clothes were being wrung out and hung around various points in the limited space. Steve suggested they might need to drink tea and play cards for an hour or two to get everything dried off enough.

Rooting around in the food cupboard, Peter was surprised to see Steve produce a half-bottle of whisky about half-full. Steve explained it was emergency rations, and this was just such an emergency. A decent sized shot was poured out and both of them sat back, still a bit damp, nearly naked and instantly cheered and relaxed by the spirit coursing through them.

'Think you were right about the fan heater Steve. I'm feeling a bit flushed. It's hot on my face. It's a bit like a sauna.'

'Have you been in one?' asked Steve.

'No, but I saw one on the telly. They didn't show everything, obviously, but it was in Finland. Everyone goes in saunas there, it said, all year round. Even in the snow of winter!' Peter remembered the programme. 'They were mixed sometimes too!'

'Really! I'd like one – to try one'. said Steve.

'Well, you were a teeny bit reluctant to strip off down the river Steve, so how do you reckon it will be at a sauna for you?' Peter asked.

That question stayed hanging in the air for a few minutes. They just sipped a bit more whisky and kept their thoughts to themselves.

It was a surprise to Peter when Steve suddenly said, 'Tell you what Pete. Let's make this a sauna then!' He jumped up and Peter noticed his face looked flushed – maybe the whisky Peter thought. 'my underwear's damp too and I'm going to take them off to dry. You have to as well! If you don't do the same thing, I will just feel a complete prat.' And with that, Steve firstly, and then Peter, took off their remaining garments and tried to find another spot to hang them to dry.

'Your pants hanging from the wall-light Steve –it's not a great look really', said Peter.

Steve laughed. 'I know, they look terrible like that don't they. There's nowhere else for them! Yours don't exactly look ornamental, draped over the door handle either!'

They sat then drinking their tea and the warming whisky. Gradually relaxing into each other's company and the initially strange feeling of being there naked evaporating. Peter felt a need to fill the silence though.

'So, do you reckon they do this in Finland? You know, heat up a caravan and get naked?'

'Don't know Pete. I thought saunas were all like log cabins – all wood and stuff like that. With pine benches to sit on.'

Peter decided to just lean back and just go with it. It was very still and quiet, just the whirring fan of the heater.

Something changed though. Almost imperceptibly at first. The afternoon whisky had made him a bit light-headed and he found himself looking across at Steve, at his face and then unashamedly at his naked body. He studied Steve's legs, the hair on them that, unlike his own, ran quite thickly all the way up to his groin. He found himself feeling envious as he slowly ran his eyes all over his anatomy. Suddenly becoming aware of the fact he was staring, he looked up. He felt taken aback to see Steve staring at him in return.

'What?' asked Peter, not really knowing what to say but just feeling caught-out and very self-conscious.

'Don't know. You tell me', said Steve. 'I was just thinking, you're very smooth bodied aren't you?'

'I don't have your hairy tummy, if that's what you mean.' said Peter. 'I don't know what happened there really, I started alright until I was about fourteen but it seems to have stopped from then on.'

'I like it' Said Steve. Peter felt himself getting flushed again. He didn't know why Steve had said that, but he also found himself intrigued and a little excited by the sudden turn in conversation.

Peter knew something was going to happen. He anticipated, and actually felt he could see, what Steve was going to do just before he came over and sat next to him. It was like everything went into incredibly slow motion. Peter giggled slightly, nervously. Even his voice seemed slowed-down when he spoke. 'What are you doing Steve?'

'I thought I would just come and sit next to you Pete.'

'This feels a bit weird. There's not a lot of space. Are you just having a closer look at my smoothness, as you put it?'

Steve didn't answer, nor look at Peter. They sat there naked with their knees now just touching. Peter's right knee and Steve's left. Peter coughed momentarily, looked away at the drawn curtains for a few seconds, turned back and found Steve looking straight into his eyes. Peter returned the gaze. Complete silence but for the continuing hum of the heater. Steve put his hands on Peter's shoulders. Peter put one hand on the back of Steve's neck. They leaned into each other until their foreheads touched, both looking down at the floor.

'You OK Pete?'

'Yeah'. Whispered. Foreheads touching still. They were looking into each other's laps like this, silently. To Peter, it was if time stood still and he had a sensation of hairs standing on the back of his neck.

At first, nothing happened. Neither of them moved again. Then Peter pulled his head back still with his hand on Steve's neck, Steve raised his and they looked at each other, faces just a few inches apart. In seeming incredibly slow motion, Peter closed the gap, inch by inch moving his head gently forward until their noses touched. It stayed like that a moment. Peter turned his face slightly and then his lips landed on Steve's. There was a moment where it almost felt like they were not actually touching and then Steve put a hand on Peter's neck and their lips pushed into each other's. It was one of those kisses that lasts a while, at first almost just brushing together but then developing and changing. Steve pulled back a little.

'Pete, I'm sorry. We shouldn't do this. It's just you are a lovely guy. I'm sorry …'

'Shh Steve. It's ok, I'm fine.' And Peter closed the gap again. And now the embrace and the kiss become full on and each of them was aware of their response and their arousal at what was happening.

For the next few minutes of time, they just had each other in that space and everything else became irrelevant. It felt much longer lasting to both of them. They found they were using their mouths and hands in ways that were new and strange to them both, but at the same time so easy to do. Apart from a rough feeling around his lips, to Peter this felt like some other situations he had been in, only this was with another man. At brief moments, very brief, he had that feeling of detachment from reality though, an out of body experience of looking at what's happening as if an observer, astonished at the scene he could see.

Eventually they reached a point where Peter became aware they were holding each other and the motions were such that there had been an unspoken agreement that they would finish this at the same time. It was a moment of trying to control the uncontrollable, in one way knowing so well what to do but at the same moment feeling on ground so utterly unfamiliar. They had one arm around each other's shoulders, heads side by side, breathily panting in each other's ears. When they finished, Peter felt a wave crash through him and a sense of falling, as if over a cliff.

They leaned heavily against each other, Still hugging with one arm, still holding each other in the other hand. The output of the encounter drying on the backs of their hands. Peter became aware they were both hot and covered in a film of perspiration. Neither of them spoke.

Eventually Steve coughed by way of breaking the silence again, and stillness, offered to get a tissue, maybe make another tea. From the little galley area he looked at Peter and they both gave a broad, smile at each other that they held for some moments. Still neither saying anything. Still both not knowing what to say really.

'I didn't think the day would go like this'. Steve said, speaking first.

Peter found himself just nodding. He looked around him, amazed they were both naked, and with a sense of disbelief at what had just happened. But, equally, he felt happy and at ease. It wasn't just the heater doing its job, he felt no need to put any clothes back on. And neither did Steve. They quietly drank the second tea, still looking at each other at moments and still smiling broadly. Steve looked at the clock. They knew they would be looked for soon, to see if they wanted to go to the pub. They just stayed like that, grinning, a little sheepishly. 'We can't be found like this Steve', said Peter, stating the obvious.

Eventually, without having to say anything, they got dressed. They were looking at each other as they pulled on their underwear. They stopped and studied each other at that point. 'That was bloody great', said Steve, finally summing up what they had both experienced.

Peter nodded, 'Yeah, it was. God, what have we just done though, eh?' He moved towards the door, then stopped himself and went back to Steve – gave him a big hug but somehow, now the desire had dissipated, he hesitated giving Steve a further kiss. But his mouth did find Steve's briefly and, this time, he really felt Steve's bristles. Nothing else was said.

He went off to his tent, other campers were doing the usual things campers do, all around him life was just carrying on normally. But to Peter it felt like he was in a dream and had landed on another planet. He shook his head and laughed to himself, but it was the sort of laugh he knew he would do when people might see him and he felt embarrassed.

CHAPTER 10

A whole day and night went past after that, and neither Peter nor Steve saw each other anywhere. Peter felt this wasn't deliberate but on the other hand what had happened did now feel a little unreal. Maybe, he thought, he was actually avoiding Steve, because he knew that would make it real again and also that he might not be able to prevent it happening again. On the other hand, he just wanted to see Steve again so much.

Out on his mapping area, Peter found he had been wandering around rock outcrops, working hard at thinking of Penny. Thinking really hard of Penny and not wanting to think of what he and Steve had done. And yet it constantly interrupted his thoughts. Sharp images, vivid even, of mouths especially, kissing and a lot more. Remembering these images, he found himself doing his fieldwork feeling quite sore and achy a lot of the time.

Another reason they hadn't met up had been the fact that Steve's supervisor Dr Smith was turning-up to ensure Steve was on the right track. All three other students knew of Don Smith, a renowned structural geologist and author of many research papers. There were good working relationships between him and Bristol's Doc Griffiths and Peter felt there might, therefore, be a bit of indirectly checking up on him and Graham, as well as on Steve.

Naturally enough, Steve had thrown himself into preparing for this visit. He didn't have to imagine this – he had seen that Steve was out before he walked past his caravan and was not yet back when Peter had returned. Peter wondered if Steve was also distracted, when trying to do his fieldwork, of the same images of what they had done together.

On the second morning after his encounter with Steve, it was a dry day and warmish, especially out of the wind. Supposedly another spell of sunny weather was arriving. Back at the hotel,

Jock or someone put a weather map up on the front door of the premises each morning. It was a Met Office chart, foolscap – all of the UK and the maritime shipping forecast areas. Someone keen was getting this at six o'clock every morning, thought Peter. But good for them, it helps me, he thought.

Julie and Sue came across to speak with him and Graham, just as he was loading up his field gear for the day ahead. He could immediately see they were in a cheery mood. He had heard and seen them chatting and laughing on the walk across. They were both lightly dressed – rolled-up cheese-cloth shirts and shorts. Perky was the word that came to Peter's mind.

'Hello Pete. And Graham, if you're in there.' said Julie, clearly pleased with herself. 'Glad we caught you. We're the laundry girls now.'

'You're the what?' said Graham from inside his tent, not yet emerged.

'We're on a special mission', said Sue, raising and deepening her voice. 'To boldly go where no man has gone before', she quipped. She nudged Julie, holding back a giggle.

'Oh yeah' said Julie, then more loudly 'To boldly go where no woman has gone before!', to proper giggles from Sue this time. 'We want your clothes off boys!'

'What the hell are you on about?' said Graham still not emerging. Peter looked at them quizzically but couldn't help smiling along, waiting until they would share the joke with him.

Julie sighed and then made a point of slowly explaining. 'Uncle Ben was really pleased with you all helping with the van in the ditch the other day. Auntie Pam said it might be nice to do something for you in return. They suspect, probably know actually, we are always giving you free teas and generally trying to seduce you into staying around. So, they wanted to do something else for you.'

'Steady on Jules!' said Sue, interrupting, 'I'm not trying to seduce anyone! Just looking after my friends,' she added with a feigned haughtiness. 'We're not trying to lure you onto the rocks, just to feed you', she said directly to Peter. This led quickly to more giggles from both of them. Peter laughing now too – it was funny the look Sue had put on, pretending to be aloof and detached.

'So, anyway', said Julie. 'We have been given the mission, should we choose to accept it,… yet more giggles from both the girls, Peter laughing along and Graham too, could be heard chuckling, still in his tent. 'You're bonkers you two.' He said from inside the canvas.

'This tape will self-destruct in ten seconds' said Sue, in a dalek-style voice for some reason.

'This is getting silly' said Julie, still laughing.

'Right. Let's have another go', she said. 'My lovely aunt has despatched us to gather up some washing from you four impoverished students.'

'Well, three impoverished students, and Steve as well' chipped-in Sue, to more giggling.

'Shh Sue, we'll never finish. So, to save you struggling with the washroom, this is the special offer of the day. Give us your washing and Sue and I, and Auntie, will get it done for you.' She smiled at Peter and Graham, who now had stuck his head out of his tent, at last.

'We are expecting dirty socks, shirts and we won't say anything about the smalls. Come on, hand them over,' said Sue, reaching out with upturned hands.

'Get them off and hand them over I say', said Julie, to more shared giggling. 'Right, we need to get on, it's a dry and breezy day, so we should have it all back to you tonight. Come on, hurry up. We have to get to Steve and Nick too.'

'Room service tips accepted', said Sue, smiling directly at Peter again and holding her gaze a little longer than he expected. 'In cash, or in kind.'

'Oh, Sue!' said Julie, feigning disapproval. 'I thought you just said we weren't doing the seduction thing!'

Peter found he liked the flirty turn of the conversation and played along. 'What sort of "in kind" are we talking about then?'

'Not the sort you might be thinking about Pete!' said Julie, jumping in. 'Ooo, you are naughty, but I like you' she added, trying to mimic yet another voice from the telly. 'No. Just because we are going to have our hands in your pants Pete; it's just pints down the pub we're after, isn't it Sue? Or fags too, in her case'. And they all laughed along together, Peter and Graham starting to grub around their tents for their washing.

That had a been a nice cheerful start to the day, thought Peter, later, having spent hours getting onto and around his territory, covering a wide area of outcrops and feeling a bit bushed. He felt good though. The overwhelming sensations and images of the previous day had lessened now and he was pleased he could concentrate on his work a bit more. He tried to avoid thinking about Steve by trying to think of Sue instead. He wondered if the short incident of flirtiness meant anything. Then he found he was feeling guilty about Penny again and tried to concentrate on the geology.

Sod it, he thought to himself, I need to just concentrate on getting this mapping done. He tried concentrating really hard on what the geology he had mapped on the surface might look at in cross-section. He felt he had earned a short rest though and lay down in a bit of a hollow by one of the many outcrops on the plateau. Putting his hands behind his head, he tried to visualise again the mile or two of strata immediately below him, trying to create a three-dimensional view of the plateau and mountain. Instead he found himself quickly drifting off and then, to his own surprise, he fell asleep more deeply.

Probably not for long though, he was thinking as he found himself coming round. The sun hadn't moved and everything seemed the same as just before except now four guys were coming over the rocks about a hundred yards away. Maybe their approaching steps had woken him. Peter leant up for a better look and one of the men spotted him and shouted a greeting. They paused and then they all came over towards him. Peter stood up.

'We thought we were the only ones up here'. The tall person in front spoke first. Peter thought he sounded very English, posh, in a BBC sort-of way.

'I think there's only me otherwise', said Peter. 'I usually have the place to myself too.'

'Mind if we join you then?' said the posh one again, 'just for a breather.' Peter just nodded and spread out his arms and hands.

The four men sat around on various rocks and someone offered round a packet of fags. John Player, Navy Cut, Peter noticed. All four lit up and he was offered one.

'Sorry, thanks but I can't do untipped ciggies. I'll have one of my own though.' Peter noticed they were all in a mix of fatigues and walking clothes. Their boots looked like army boots. Or what Peter thought of as army boots. He had bumped into the military on the hills sometimes in Snowdonia and especially the Brecon Beacons. This lot had a bit of a military look too, Peter thought, things like short back and sides. The taller one, who had first spoken, seemed to be in charge of whatever they were doing or wherever they were going.

'Fine scenery you have here old chap. You look as if you're studying it or something.'

Peter explained a bit about what he was doing. After a brief explanation, he asked them what they were doing too.

'Well, we are also studying, in a way. Actually, exploring is probably a better word.'

One of the other three men spoke for the first time. This one's voice was distinctly Scottish. 'We are looking for a crashed aircraft, if that doesn't sound too dramatic'.

Peter couldn't believe his ears, and he felt a shiver run down his spine.

'Really!?' he said. 'You're not anything to do with the Warden of this reserve are you? John MacKenzie?' Thinking that might be an explanation. 'Are you from Gairloch?'

The tall one looked quizzical and shrugged. 'Sorry, don't know him old chap. No, we know there's a crashed plane on Ben Ay, think that's how it's pronounced, but we seem to have got a bit off-course.'

'Well, this is sort-of Beinn Eighe' explained Peter. 'But where you need to go is over there about two miles in a straight line. I was there a few weeks ago myself and know there is a crashed plane there in the big corrie.' All four were looking at Peter, and seemingly hanging on his every word. He felt self-conscious about it and could feel he was going a bit rosy in the face. They seemed to want him to continue speaking.

'But, you're going to have to drop off this plateau area, and then contour around that hill and in towards that scree slope.' Pointing and gesticulating all the time he was speaking.

'Once you are finally in the Corrie, that's probably a good couple of hours, that fan of scree you can see, leads into a big cliff face and a plane did crash there and there is some wreckage. Corrie Mhic Fhearcair, the corrie's called. If I've said it right.'

He felt a bit embarrassed by their attention and hoped he had his facts straight and that the route suggestion was correct too. They didn't say anything, just looked at the landscape and the route Peter had defined. He found himself continuing to speak.

'It's strange, I was only talking with the warden I mentioned, about the same things, a few days ago. I thought you were something to do with it.' They were all gently shaking their heads at him but listening, seemingly intrigued. 'We think there's a crash site up here too, on the other side of this mountain from here.'

They seemed distracted by this news. 'No, I don't think that can be anything to do with us,' said the leader. 'I think you were right the first time.' 'We need to get up to that corrie. Looks a bit of a way.' Turning to the others, two of whom had said nothing. 'Come on lads, let's get on with it – make haste while the sun shines, eh!?' Then turning to Peter.

'Thanks very much…whatever your name is?'

'Peter'

'Peter then. Thank you, good to meet you. Thank you for kindly pointing the way!' He reached out his hand, which Peter realised with surprise, was gloved. 'I'm Wing Commander Wilson, by the way, and this is Carmichael, Williams and MacKay.' They all nodded in turn, shook hands and then they all headed off where Peter had suggested. After a hundred yards or so, they turned and all waved, and then they dropped off Peter's horizon and out of view.

Peter sat back down, then laid down and he turned over the discussion in his head. So they had been military after all, he noted first. It had been interesting speaking with these guys but also a little unsettling. With the whole incident with Steve and the goings on at the campsite, he had partially forgotten his crashed aircraft for a bit. Now they were gone, he would have liked to ask more questions. He would have to tell John MacKenzie about it. Thinking this, he laid back looking at the sky, wondering how good it would feel to be up there looking down.

He must have nodded off again and was suddenly surprised to see the sky had clouded over a little and the half-obscured sun was a bit further round the sky. Time to get on he thought. Looking south he could see no sign of the four men. He hoped they would be ok. They had looked fit but hadn't really been carrying much, if anything, now he thought about it.

Coming into the campsite that afternoon, hardly anyone was about but he noticed, sitting outside the little café, Julie and Sue were looking pleased with themselves. However busy they had been in the café, it appeared they had also managed to get the washing done, as promised. It was all hung out on lines, flapping around in the late afternoon breeze and sunshine. Talking with them, Peter discovered that after seeing him in the morning, the two women had gone to Steve's caravan, and to Nick's tent. Steve had been a bit coy apparently, but the girls had the impression that for Nick it was just like home! Completely normal for women in the house to run around after him they had imagined, collecting up his dirty washing wherever he dropped it.

Sue said she felt a bit sorry for him really, being away from home and having to fend for himself. She had seen inside the frame-tent canopy that Nick's diet clearly consisted mostly of stuff from tins. Julie had told her not to be so soft and that the fieldwork experience might help him grow up!

As the café had been steadily busy that day, it was Julie's aunt had done most of the washing and the girls had only hung it out on three long lines running between the café, reception and their caravan and the roadside fence. The shirts and socks were arranged randomly on the lines but the underwear was lined up in a way that made Peter think of a row of pennants, occupying an entire line.

'Do you like our flags then?' said Julie, seeing Peter had noticed, casting an eye backwards over her shoulder.

Peter just laughed a little. 'Yeah, I was just thinking. Very colourful!'

'More than colourful Pete,' chipped in Julie. 'Religious! It was your idea, wasn't it Sue?' But Sue was distracted by a customer needing attention and couldn't provide the explanation just then. 'Oh, well Sue said the variety of underwear we were starting to hang up made her think of a mountaineering image she had seen. I didn't know what she was on about!'

Peter couldn't figure out what either of them was on about.

'In the end we had to go over to Glen View and have a look at one of Uncle Ben's books', continued Julie. 'He likes mountains, but more from his armchair - Everest the Hard way it's called.'

'Oh yeah' said Peter, suddenly more engaged with the discussion. 'He came to Bristol to give a talk. Chris Bonnington. It was brilliant. We had a special Club trip to it.'

'Yes, Sue had seen him on his tour too,' she said. 'And Uncle Ben had the book. Sue remembered all the small flags outside the Nepalese monasteries on the approach to Everest. She's interested in that sort of stuff. I hadn't seen it myself, but sure enough, there was a good photo in the book.'

'Yes, I remembered it and thought it might give us all a smile to try and replicate it', said Sue, now coming over and joining into the chat.

'My aunt was a bit surprised by all your washing!' said Julie, seeing Peter's bemused look. 'She's still thinking all men have big, white jobs, I think coloured ones were a bit of a surprise!'

'So, there's this image in the book', said Sue. 'Outside a monastery on the approach path to Everest. Dozens of coloured pennants, fluttering in the wind. Almost horizontal in some of the shots.' Sue paused, clearly trying to remember something. 'It's their version of the elements of life. There's five colours to Buddhist flags and I can't remember all their meanings, something to do with earth, fire, water, air and sky. But they have to go in order, which seems to be blue, yellow, green, red and then white.' She said this last part, pointing to the long washing line of underwear.

'I can see your point I suppose – I can see the colour code now.' said Peter, shaking his head in disbelief. 'It does remind me of those Everest approach images I suppose, the books and the bits you see on the telly. Going through Nepal, there are lots of coloured flags and pennants aren't there? Never thought about them though. Hope the monks wouldn't mind their flags being imitated like this!'

'We struggled with green, to be honest. In the middle.' said Julie, ignoring Peter's last comment. 'You seem to have a pair of pale green, and that's it. So, we had to resort to socks at that point, putting that pair of dark green socks, also yours I believe, and a grey and green pair of Graham's, in the line to keep a balance.' She could see Peter still looked a little incredulous.

'Look' she continued, guiding Peter along the line by waving her right hand. 'Me, Sue, you and Graham all have shades of blue. We have put them in order, dark to light. Then, just Sue and me have some yellow knickers. Then there's the green section. Sue, me, and you two guys again, have various red colours, mostly Sue. Then you and Sue are the smaller white ones. Don't know what to say about that, to be honest.' She winked at Peter. 'The bigger white ones at the end, those are Steve and Nick.'

'Bloody hell' said Peter, and then he burst out laughing. 'Beats work doesn't it! Wish I had all day to think about stuff like this!'

'Cheek!' said both girls in unison. And then all of them were laughing a lot.

'Any more of that and you won't get them back' said Sue, still laughing along with Julie.

'You know,' continued Sue. 'Apparently, the idea of the Buddhist flags is spiritual? When they're fluttering in the air they are supposed to be sending out prayers. That's what we read anyway.'

'I could imagine what the blokes' pants' prayers would be' quipped Julie, causing more giggles from Sue.

'No' said Sue 'The flags have little prayers sewn or printed on them and when the wind blows, it carries the prayers off and spreads them around.'

'Well, one of my pink pairs has a '*no entry*' sign printed on them. Will that do?' said Julie. 'That's not a bad message for girls to spread around'. She and Sue now getting into a fit of giggles again, like the morning.

'And I have two white pairs up there. One with little flowers and the other with small robins. Maybe they will fly off.' Sue just managed to get this out between laughing, her and Julie propping-up each other a bit.

Peter couldn't believe he had been drawn into this conversation. He chipped in a contribution, saying 'Well I reckon the most significant prayers would come from Nick and Steve's by the size of them.'

After their giggling dried-up a bit, Julie said, 'Have you told him Sue?'

The two young women made a point of slowly giving Peter a deliberate up and down look. They were trying to hold back another laugh.

'You two have had a fun day haven't you?' said Peter, shaking his head in mock despair. 'Look, I need to get to the tent. Shall I take my stuff from the lines?'

'That's what Sue hadn't told you,' said Julie. Trying to speak between more giggles. 'We thought the four of you should collect your stuff but we want a modelling session first!'

'Oh yeah? Fuck off!' Said Peter, and they all laughed. He hadn't meant to say that, but it had just slipped out. It didn't seem to matter anyway, nobody had taken offence.

Peter left them to it. Walking off, he took a look at the white end of the flag line. He could recognise Steve's. He thought about that a moment. Remembering the afternoon in the caravan. He forced himself to look at Sue's. Concentrating on that, he thought he could imagine her. He could see the small robin motif she had mentioned and found it lodged in his mind for a while.

He had just got to his tent, when he noticed Julie had run up to him from behind. 'I forgot. There are some letters for you Peter', and she handed them over. 'Sue and I will drop-off the washing soon – don't forget the tip.' She winked at him again. 'Oh, by the way, a rather posh man has turned-up and has gone off after Steve. Don Smith. Doctor Smith, I should add', she said emphatically. 'He did!'

Peter wondered who had written to him. One letter he could see was from his Mum, now a regular treat, with a fiver in it no doubt, a small package from his sister-in-law containing a letter and a small tin of salmon. Another treat. His sister-in-law saw herself as a more experienced climber and walker and had taken it upon herself to send occasional treats – survival rations Peter thought she would think. Lovely idea though. The third item was a letter from Penny.

He scanned through it quickly. Missing him apparently. Enjoying her work at a department store in Manchester, staying at her uncle's place. She worked Saturdays but had Mondays off and had been to Hereford for a visit to Gordon and his mother. She actually wrote "don't worry, nothing happened". But it still felt like a punch. Peter asked himself why she felt the need to go and see this former boyfriend so often. There was other stuff, about her family, little incidents in the shop, tittle tattle about some friends from Uni. But all Peter could think about was the fact that she had been to see Gordon again. She had a relationship with him for nearly two years but it was like she couldn't leave it.

Graham was outside his tent, lying on his back, knees up, sun hat over his eyes. But not asleep as Peter had first assumed.

'You OK then Pete? '

'Yeah. Ta. You been out today?'

'Yep, not back long. Bored. You couldn't make one for me if you're doing a brew, could you?' Sitting-up and looking at Peter.

'Oh man, you look really pissed-off!' exclaimed Graham. 'What's on? I only just heard all this laughter in the distance just now. You and the girls sounded like you were having a laugh.'

'We were. About…, well you wouldn't believe me if I told you!'
Now Graham had the bemused look. 'I'll explain later. But I've
had a letter from Penny. Take a look if you like'. Half handing it
and half throwing it at Graham. 'Look at this though. A tin of
red salmon from my brother's Sarah. And a fiver from my Mum.'
Chucking his rucksack onto the ground, rattling the camping kettle
to see if there was enough water.

'It's a pisser Graham. I just had a good day on the hill, was having
a laugh with Julie and Sue and then this!' pointing at the letter.

By this time they were sitting across from each other. Peter got
the stove going and it hissed along in the background while Graham
read on. Eventually he gave a sigh and handed it back to Peter.

'Did you see she was suggesting coming up here?'

'What! Christ!' Peter hadn't taken in that bit of the letter and he
was surprised his first thought was about yet a further interruption
to his work. But she would do that for me? He mused. Come all the
way up here to see me? He felt a mix of emotions about it, starting
to feel pleased but also a bit put-out and bit suspicious.

'She cares for you enough to come up here Pete. That's a good
thing isn't it?'

'I don't know what to think. You saw that crap about going to
Hereford? That's the supposedly past relationship I was telling you
about.' Peter not knowing whether he felt angry or disappointed
or something else. 'I'm halfway through this project and have so,
so much still to do.'

'You shouldn't have spent some of those sunny days sitting round
here.' Graham trying to be light-hearted in tone.

'Yeah – getting stoned with you, you mean! Oh God. Fuck it.'
He lay back on the ground and stared at the sky. He wondered
again if he loved Penny. But what about what had just happened up
here? Maybe Penny coming up to see him might stop him making
another mistake with Steve. She would just assume that it was OK

for her to come. That's it, thought Peter, she just assumes I will be here, there or wherever. And whenever.

A lit cigarette was placed on his lips, and he inhaled it gratefully. 'Thanks Graham. Thought it might be a joint for a moment!'

'Got one if you want one Pete.'

Peter thought about it for a second, but the moment passed. The kettle boiled, they shared a tea and a further cigarette, pretty much without any further comment about anything.

Chapter 11

The next morning Peter was coming out of the washrooms, when he saw Steve wave at him. It was early. He was in the door of his caravan, one of those doors where you can open the top half separately and he was leaning on the top of the bottom half. Peter went over, he thought to have a conversation he knew he had been putting off.

'Hi Pete. I haven't really seen you, what with Doc Smith here too. I asked Julie and Sue to let you know. Everything OK? Wondered if you would you like to come in a moment?'

Peter could see that Steve really did want to speak with him, but he actually felt scared of what might happen. Concentrating on his map, chatting with the girls and Graham – it had all stopped him thinking about this really big thing that had happened. The big thing he realised he was trying to dismiss from his head as if it hadn't happened at all.

'Look Steve, I can't. I'm behind and need to get on'. Peter thought this sounded pathetic and he could see the disappointment in Steve's eyes. He thought he could see longing there too. 'So do you I imagine. Won't your supervisor be chomping at the bit to get out with you today?'

'We spent hours looking at my work last night, after he'd checked in the hotel. He invited me for dinner though and then we looked at all my notes and the maps in his room.'

'Well, there's posh!'

'Yeah, it was pretty comfortable,' said Steve. 'More comfortable than here', waving at the caravan 'or your tent come to that. We had whiskies too.'

'Well, when you're a lecturer yourself Steve, you can be like that too.'

'Oh, don't joke Pete.'

'I'm not! All of us reckon you're the bright one here. You know what you're doing. You're heading for a first and you know it. Research career to follow...' said Peter, speaking and thinking this sounded much more like a formal conversation rather than a chat with someone you had illicit sex with.

'I know. Maybe Pete!' He paused. 'But can't we have a chat? Please?'

Peter was trying to avoid looking at Steve directly, but could hear him needing to speak about what they did. He wanted to speak about it too, and yet wouldn't it be easier if he just buried it? He thought that if he walked away from this caravan now, it would all become history. Something that happened – once. He had decided, after all, that this thing was a one-off. It wasn't. Couldn't be. Mustn't be! Something that could ever happen again.

And yet the words that came out of Peter's mouth seemed to have their own volition. 'Alright Steve, I'll come in but can't stop long.'

Entering the caravan, Peter felt heavy-footed, reluctant, going against his will. Inside the door he could see Steve was still in his pyjamas. Typical that he would still wear pyjamas, thought Peter. Steve looked directly at Peter's eyes and, much as Peter struggled to avoid it, eventually the look had to be returned. Peter decided to say what he had been thinking while hesitating outside.

'Oh, no, come on!' Steve whined. 'Please Pete. I can't let that happen. What we did can't be a one-off that I can dump as if it didn't mean anything. I've thought of you; of what we did, all the time. The night after, out mapping, wandering around the hills. Doc Smith took all my brain out of me though. I hit that bed last night and went out like a light. But this morning, all I have wanted to happen is for you to walk over and come in. I've been watching and waiting.'

He looked and sounded slightly pleading, Peter thought. But sweet, and friendly, and nice too. To be truthful, he didn't sound or look as troubled as Peter had been feeling.

Steve said, as if reading Peter's mind. 'I know we're not queers Pete. I don't think of myself as that. But what we did. It was just really nice. Fun. Wasn't it?' And he hesitantly put his hand on Peter's arm. Peter glanced around the caravan. Steve had not yet folded up the stowaway bed, half covered with a neat looking duvet.

Peter sensed that something else was going on for Steve and now he felt it too. This was his last moment to back out of the caravan before something happened he might regret. But at the same instant he also felt desire rising in him. He lowered his eyes from Steve to try and turn-off that feeling. And then he noticed the front of Steve's pyjama bottoms betraying Steve's evident feelings. It would be so easy to just reach for that, thought Peter, and then he became aware of his own response.

'I had decided I could not do this again Steve', said Peter. 'I've got a girlfriend. I've had other girlfriends. This isn't me.' He thought he didn't sound convincing, more like a prepared script. Steve ignored him, said nothing – just used his eyes to compel.

And then they were up against each other. Peter didn't know if he had stepped forward or if Steve had pulled him forward, or what. But now they were just an inch or two apart. Close enough for Peter to feel, through his jeans, Steve prodding into his leg. He just reached down and caressed the pyjama fabric. They leaned into each other like the previous time, heads bowed, foreheads touching, resisting at first and yet the very action made the outcome more, not less inevitable.

It was like the previous time and yet not. They did the same things to and with each other, but now feeling strangely familiar with the actions that had seemed so novel just a couple of days previously. It wasn't so rushed, not quite so urgent, not as driven, Peter found he felt more relaxed, a relief that they were doing this, something that just felt natural.

Afterwards, lying back against Steve's naked body, both stretched out on the bed, Peter said quietly, 'What on earth do we do now.' There wasn't any fear in this question. Peter found himself anxiously thinking of the practical considerations. 'What the hell do I do about Penny?' Steve didn't answer and Peter let his mind wander.

Eventually Steve interrupted their reverie. Practical reality was intervening. 'Look, lovely as this is Pete. Lovely as that was. Doc Smith's going to be here before long...'

'Yeah, yeah, of course', said Peter. 'We can't be found like this. Obviously!' They hesitated a moment, looked at each other, stroked each other's tummies. They both sighed and then they sprang-up, and rapidly got dressed. This time, they kissed briefly on parting, but without any awkwardness, again it felt the appropriate thing to do.

As Peter left, he caught sight site of Steve's supervisor having a chat with Sue and Julie. They will waylay anyone they can, thought Peter. He set-off, thinking he knew for the first time what the expression 'walking with a spring in his step' actually meant.

After a hurried and tiring rest of the day on the hill, it was late afternoon when he returned to the campsite. Getting back to his tent, he found a note tucked into the tent's inner door. It was in a Kinlochewe Hotel branded envelope. At that moment, Graham, who was invisible but was evidently in his own tent, said 'I've had one of those too.'

'How do you know it's me and how do you know what I'm doing Graham!? And hello to you too! I didn't know you were back.'

'Just having a little puff or two, you know', said Graham lazily. 'That note's inviting us out!'

Peter read the note.

Hand-written and glancing to the bottom, saw it was from Steve.

Hi Pete.

Just a quick note. Doc Smith is inviting us all out for a drink and a bite to eat later. He gave me the paper and envelopes. I expect you think it's posh again. Hope you can make it? Please?

He's suggested taking us in his car, bigger than mine. Car that is! Don't know about anything else…

We're going up the road somewhere. He's ringing ahead to order some grub. We need to be round the front of the hotel about 6.45. Hope that's ok.

Steve xx

ps I have sent the same note to Graham and Nick, but excluding the joke.
pps And excluding the kisses.
ppps Please destroy this note after reading!!!

Peter looked at his watch. About an hour and a little bit to go. No dinner to cook. Better have a wash and a clean shirt though, he thought. 'What do you think about the invitation then Graham?'

After a hesitation, Peter imagining Graham inhaling and holding an intake of smoke, then letting it go. Sure enough, the slightly higher, slightly stretched voice. 'Sounds good mate!'

'Yeah, it does. Think we might need a starter drink though?', suggested Peter.

Graham agreed it was a good idea and the two of them went over the pub for a pint at about quarter past six. They both felt they had spruced themselves up a bit and had both put on clean shirts and tidiest jumpers.

'Couldn't do anything about my jeans though', said Graham.

'I know. Mine are the same. They will have to do. A few weeks grime and smoke can't be that noticeable can it!?'

They felt in a good mood and when they moved to the front of the hotel, found Nick and Steve waiting. The other two sounded upbeat too, so when the venerable geologist arrived from the car park in his car they were all already laughing and joshing with each other, mostly at Steve's expense, who had brought decent trousers with him, still neatly pressed, and smart shoes too!

Doctor Smith had a Vauxhall Cresta which seemed to Peter to be easily big enough for the three in the back, and Steve up front with Doc Smith.

'Steve, you could have borrowed this for your field work' Graham joked. 'Would have been better to take us down to Torridon for a shower!' Everyone laughed. 'Where are we off to by the way?'

Doc Smith explained they were going ten miles up the road to Achnasheen. Peter knew it as a station on the Kyle of Lochalsh line and the station he would return from when he left the fieldwork.

'There's a great place here, at Achnasheen.' And Peter heard he was actually Welsh, perhaps not posh as Julie had thought. 'The Ledgowan Hotel – a traditional Highland place. Thought it would be nice for us all to have a chat together.' Maybe his voice actually was quite posh after all, thought Peter, or at least deep and self-assured. Authoritative – that's the sound, he decided.

The hotel had rounded towers and turrets. It looked very grand to Peter, more like a small castle, tucked away in its own forest glade. It appeared at the end of a longish driveway. Inside, there were similar touches to the Kinlochewe hotel, such as large fish in glass tanks, memorabilia of fishing exploits, only the ones here were bigger. And there were a lot more of them.

The reception area was all polished wood and bits of brass, and a couple of large stag heads in a dominant position above the reception desk and facing the door. Peter found it all slightly intimidating and he definitely felt out of place in his dirty baggy jeans. He was pleased Graham was there and would be feeling the same. Nick too probably, he thought.

They were guided through to a bar area by the receptionist. Peter thought she had quite a superior air, but probably she was just being a bit formal as befitted the establishment. She looked the part, he thought, wearing a dark kilt, some sort of matching waistcoat and a crisp white, frilly blouse.

In the bar, the walls were festooned with even more stag heads and antlers. They had been given a nice round table though and, once sat down, it all felt a bit less overbearing. A nice chap, also with a crisp white shirt, and in his case a silky tartan waistcoat and black trousers, came and took an order of drinks. Doc Smith waved away offers and attempts by the students to start a kitty or to pay for a round. He made it clear that this was on his university. 'But you get nothing for nothing in life, so the deal is you spend the next couple of hours telling me what you have learned up here. See if I can crib any information for our research work up here'.

It should have been obvious to Peter but hadn't been until this point, that Bristol and Leeds were collaborating on research in the North West Highlands. That sort of thing tended to pass him by, and he could again see how different it was for Steve. Peter thought the people who are destined to get firsts are already part of the department by the time they get their degree. They integrate themselves, know what's going on, are invited to be involved with things.

The same thing was happening here. Steve was as much a part of his university's research work as the post-grad students and the lecturers. Yet for him, and he thought for Graham and Nick too, the fieldwork project this summer was a course exercise. It was something that had to be done, just part of the degree, and marked, but wasn't in itself likely to contribute to the research going on into the geology of the area.

So, as they tucked into thick broth and rolls, with accompanying bowls of chips, Peter felt it was great that Doc Smith was genuinely listening to each of them talk about their patch. Even so, he felt a bit slow and unstructured in his thoughts, compared to the conversation Don Smith had with Steve. But they held their own. It helped them all really, because they got, for the first time, an overview of the whole region. Doc Smith contextualised the Kinlochewe area into the wider geological framework running up from the Isle of Skye to Durness in the far north western corner of Britain.

And when they each talked about their own mapping areas, Peter saw for the first time really that Kinlochewe was near enough at the centre of a large square, divided into sections, that each of them was studying. But this was by chance, rather than by design. When this became apparent in the discussion, Doc Smith said he thought that universities could find a way of sharing fieldwork effort and findings in future years. This was, he said, something he would look into. Peter felt surprised that their rather haphazard map work, apart from Steve's, could have yielded something useful to this distinguished geologist. He felt good about that and found himself and Graham downing their pints, looking across at each other, knowing they were thinking the same thing.

When Peter went for a loo break, Steve shortly followed him. There was no one else in there and just room for two men to stand side by side at the urinal. They were big old-fashioned ones.

'Don't even think of trying to look over the top Steve. Someone might come in.'

'I wasn't going to.' said Steve. 'What do you take me for? A perv? The sort of guy who hangs around men's lavatories!?' he said in a mocking tone, finishing first and pulling up his zip. 'No...' and he made a half-hearted lunge at Peter's groin, '...I wasn't going to have a look, more a grope actually!'

'Get off, I'll splash myself, or you! Anyway, I'm finished now.'

'It's going alright though isn't it?' asked Steve, casting a look over his shoulder in the direction of the bar.

'Yeah, it's really nice of him to bring us all here. And nice of you too'. And he gave Steve a light touch on his arm. 'Funny old place though. I've never been anywhere with so many antlers', Peter said, going to open the door.

Steve pushed himself up against Peter, preventing him from opening the door further, and effectively preventing the door being opened from the other side. 'I don't know about antlers, but I'm horny anyway', he joked, and kissed Peter on the cheek. 'I hope to check out your antler later' and he put his hand on the front of Peter's jeans, trying to give him another kiss. 'Oh alright. Come on, better get back to the bar.'

'So, in summary' Doc Smith was saying when they all got settled down again. 'The thinking is that the Lewisian is of several periods of time and possibly much older than we currently think. Ditto the Torridonian sandstone. So instead of two and a bit billion years for the gneiss and several hundred million for the sandstone, they might be now three billion and a billion, respectively. More work to be done though, so if any of you still have a taste for it after this, there's plenty to do!' Steve looked enthusiastic and nodded vigorously. The other three looked as though they felt this was unlikely.

However, Peter spoke up. 'I don't know Doc. I'm not sure I can afford to do research and probably not good enough'.

'Don't underestimate yourself Peter. It's not everyone who can come up to a place like this and do what you're doing, what all you boys are doing actually'.

'Oh, I don't know Doc. We'll see, with the geology', said Peter, hoping to sound more positive than he thought. 'but the North West Highlands…they will always be part of me I think'. And that he did feel sure about. Peter looked across at Steve, who was watching him speak. Steve's look was so intense, Peter could feel it knock him off-balance.

'Me too', Steve said.

CHAPTER 12

It would have been easy, just from the point of view of physical enjoyment, for Steve and Peter to make it a daily event, but for a couple of days anyway, they managed to avoid it. One morning Steve came across to Peter's tent. The first time he had done that. Graham still asleep, or stirring maybe in his tent nearby. Steve asked if he could have a look at Peter's field map. He said that he wanted to check what was happening on the ground with what he could see from the other side of Loch Maree, looking back at Peter's area. He felt there was a geological alignment that he could infer from the physical geography, but needed to know more about the lithology, the actual rock type. Somehow, Steve managed to get his trainers off and get past Peter and into the tent, Peter having held all the cooking stuff, plates and pots out of the way.

As Peter backed into the tent, Steve grabbed him and pulled him backwards. 'Come here you, I need you. I really bloody need you, right now.' They didn't take their clothes off, just the bits that needed to be pushed out of the way. It was over in minutes and only then they noticed the door to the tent was still flapping, half-open. They started to laugh and had to put hands over each other's mouths to stop the growing fit from become noisy enough for anyone else to hear. Peter whispered, 'You know, I really like you Steve.' Steve looked at him, smiled and said, 'I really, really, really, like you too Pete'. They hugged, despite the flapping tent door.

During that particular day, Peter got a lot of mapping done, but he felt he was drifting around from outcrop to outcrop, forcing himself to take readings, examine the rock types, make notes, annotate the map. And really his mind was a torrent of thoughts. He had now done three times what he had previously only ever fantasised about. When he thought about those things, he just wanted to do them again and again.

He rationalised to himself, that Steve and he could carry on doing this. Up here anyway, miles from their normal, routine lives. It wasn't really him. Not his true self. Just something he had wanted to do and was now doing. He liked it. A lot! He could keep doing this, up here. But then what? He would be able to put it down and leave it now maybe. Maybe this would get it out of his system. Maybe it was just a phase. He could just put it down as a field-trip fling. Just different to others he knew about or had tried himself.

Things settled into a bit of rhythm after that. The imperative now for both Peter and Steve, was secrecy. This could not be known about by anyone else. They became adept very quickly, at going to the pub as normal, going to the washrooms as normal, sharing a tea or a chat as normal. But interspersed with moments of sexual intensity. Peter would go back to his tent, ostentatiously saying good night to Graham, only to silently re-emerge from his tent minutes later and nip across to Steve's caravan. Or once, arriving at the loos at the same time, they used one wash cubicle together, working very hard at washing each other, silently so other campers couldn't hear.

On another occasion Steve drove them both down to the far roadside end of Peter's mapping area and they had walked up the Glas Leitre Forest trail. This was theoretically the more popular part of the nature reserve, a delightful, steep forest walk through mixed woodland, stuffed-full of wildlife. In the early part of the day though, they had it to themselves and higher up, they stopped amongst a thick stand of giant Scots Pines, towards the upper edge of the forest. Peter took Steve behind a large rock outcrop. Large enough, and hidden enough, for two people to get behind, strip-off all their clothes and enjoy each other's bodies without fear of being observed.

On that occasion, they had both leant back against the rock

afterwards, completely naked. For a moment some sun filtered through the canopy of Scots Pines, warming them. Peter lit a cigarette and took a long draw on it, for a moment imagining himself in one of those TV cigarette ads - cool as a mountain stream came to mind. Steve asked for one too, as he did on rare occasions. They stayed there a while, Peter smoking with his left hand, holding hands with Steve on the other side.

But one evening, a week after the thing with Steve had started, Peter checked back into the campsite hut. 'There's been a call for you', Ben said. Peter hadn't often seen Julie's uncle, and he had forgotten how affable the man was. 'Lady called Penny. On train to Inverness tonight apparently. Coming over on the coach in the morning'. Peter was stunned. 'But she won't, because the bus doesn't get in here until about four', continued Ben. 'Shit' thought Peter. 'Shit, shit, shit!'. He got back to his tent. 'Graham! Are you there mate. Jesus! Can we have a chat please?' All the time, thinking to himself, what do I do now, what on Earth do I do now?

CHAPTER 13

Steve woke up after a dreadful night's sleep. He had to concentrate, there was lots of mapping to do. Waking up, he could think about that, focus on the geological work. He was well into his mapping project now and knew what he was doing, what he had to do, where he had to go in terms of location. But apart from doing geology, he felt completely adrift in an unknown sea.

In the pub last night, he had got there later than the others. Peter was there, chatting to Graham. Nick wasn't there, Julie and Sue were absent too. He nodded to a few locals. Hearing his voice, Peter had looked up, given him a nice smile. He got a pint and went and sat with them. Peter explained his girlfriend was turning up the next day. A surprise visit – out of the blue. Peter didn't seem over the moon about the idea and had been talking with Graham about how to fit in geological mapping with Penny here. As if that was the only problem, thought Steve.

Graham had been telling Peter that he needed to be nice to Penny though, as she had come such a long way for just a quick visit. They had all talked about why she was visiting. Peter had been dismissive of the idea it was out of love and had the assumption that she would be wanting to tell him something big in her life.

Steve felt it was simply disruptive to Peter, meaning he had to be here the next afternoon, needed to create some space in his tent, get some food in and so on. Just when he was making up for the earlier lost time, Peter seemed a bit peeved. On the other hand Steve could tell Peter felt a bit excited about the visit and Steve couldn't help himself feeling a little bit pushed aside.

This was the thing that had kept him awake. Thoughts about Peter having his long-term girlfriend here, making Steve feel distant from him. In the three o'clock in the morning phase, Steve had been tossing and turning thinking of Peter as if he were a married man. Feeling miffed, excluded. And yet, neither of them had felt a relationship would be possible with each other. They were having fun, was that all it could be? Steve yearned all the time, just to be alone with Peter, but a gay relationship? Neither of them had any knowledge or experience. How could they do that? Would they, even if they could? He knew Peter was going to settle down with a girl one day and presumably, he thought, he would too.

As the grey light of dawn emerged from the night, a thought came to him and Steve remembered someone who might help. Not help exactly. He just needed to talk with someone, other than Peter. It was at this low point of the night he thought of his piano teacher.

Steve felt he had so compartmentalised his life that he didn't see his piano teacher's world as relevant to his, except for playing the piano. But, he didn't know now, thinking about it this morning, why he hadn't thought about it since the whole thing with Peter had started.

Timothy was not only a highly qualified piano teacher, as his Dad had told him many times when talking about the fees, but lived with another man. Steve remembered now he had met Martin a couple of times. At Easter, he had been around for a lesson and Martin had brought tea in for them both. They both spoke in a slightly camp way to each other, or what Steve thought was meant by camp. He remembered feeling a little embarrassed as they called each other affectionate terms such as sweetheart, as in, he remembered clearly now the slightly lispy voice: "here's your tea sweetheart, and one for the nice young man. Hello, you must be Stephen, I'm Martin. I'm the one who tends to do everything round here while Timothy does the teaching…"

There had been some repartee between the two which Steve couldn't remember in any more detail. He assumed they were a couple but that didn't mean anything much in Steve's mind. Until now! And now, he realised, Timothy and Martin must do the sort of things to each other that he and Peter had started doing. He hadn't thought of them until now as a homosexual couple, but realised they probably were.

Everyone, his Dad and Mum included, just suggested Timothy was a bit odd. Referring to him was always in words like, 'flamboyant', 'theatre-type', 'luvvie type'. The words gay or homosexual were never used, but were these other words just synonyms? Were they code for something people didn't like to name, as if naming it crystallised the shameful or other negative feelings people had for people who were the dismissive phrase - one of them.

However, Steve really liked his teacher. Thought him attentive, helpful, friendly and generous. He had encouraged Steve and told him that he could be a really good piano player, but that he would need to give up rocks to do that. Steve and he had talked about studying, what it meant to apply yourself. Timothy had gone through music college in the sixties and had been kind to Steve about studying – helped him feel more confident about his own abilities. When Steve had come home from his first year, feeling broke, Timothy had twice told him to keep the cash his Dad had sent over with Steve to pay for the lessons. "You use it for books Steve", he had said. "Or maybe even beer or something more potent!"

Making himself some breakfast and getting ready to go out after the sleepless night, Steve decided to call Timothy that evening. Just the plan to do this immediately helped Steve feel better. He tried to put it out of his head the rest of the day, to not allow himself to be put off. He worked flat-out, came back to the caravan and was round at the village telephone box soon after six. This helped him keep from pining for Peter and, worse, looking across to his tent and presumably see him now with his girlfriend. Steve felt freaked-out by the possibility, a description of state of mind he hadn't properly understood until now.

It was six o'clock when the cheap call rate started. Someone else must have been waiting and had beaten him to it and another had turned up to wait, no sooner had Steve got in. He dialled and Timothy answered quite quickly. Steve heard himself take a deep breath, turning into the phone box, away from whoever was next in the queue outside. He needed to cut off the sight of everyone else to do this or he would lose his nerve. It was tempting to just say it was a wrong number and hang up. But he didn't.

'Hello Timothy. It's Steve – your piano pupil. One of your pupils anyway...'

There was a pause, to Steve it felt like minutes.

'Steve!? Well, that's a surprise. Goodness.'

'Sorry.' said Steve. *'Is it ok to speak just now? For a few minutes? Please?'*

'Yes, of course. It's me should be sorry. Bit rude. Let's start again, I was just taken aback. Right ...Steve! Hello dear boy, how are you? I thought you were in Scotland?'

'I am! I'm phoning you from a call box.'

'Good God. Is everything ok?'

'Yes, fine. I mean. Err...' Steve sighed.

'Steve, is everything alright, you're well, not injured, car OK, something happened to your parents? Anything wrong...?'

It was Steve who paused now. Again, it seemed like minutes. He could feel his throat going dry and his heart pounding.

'No. I'm fine Timothy. Oh, this is so difficult. I don't know where to start.'

'Steve, Take a breath darling. Breathe. Do it again. Breathe. That's good, I can hear you doing it. Breathe again. Take your time.'

'Thanks Timothy'. Steve felt himself taking another deeper breath.

'That's better, I can hear your voice has gone down an octave!'

'Timothy. Err. I'm calling you... I'm calling you because I don't know who else to call.' Steve could hear his voice rising again and he

could feel the words catching in his throat.

There was a very long pause this time. Steve found his eyes were misting over. And then Timothy said. *'OK Steve, look! You are phoning me from Scotland. Me of all the people you might call. You've said everything is OK with you, but it clearly isn't. I don't imagine you are phoning me about piano lessons!?'* And the tone was just light enough to encourage Steve to speak.

'No, though I miss it. It's something else entirely. Oh, this is so difficult.' Steve lowered his voice. *'There's now a little queue outside the box and this thing is eating all my change….'*

'I know, I can hear the pips going. Look Steve.' And afterwards, Steve remembered most the calm, even and friendly tone as much as the words themselves. *'Look, I can only guess why you would choose to ring me, from Scotland, sounding as if something big has happened to you, or is happening.'* A pause again and Timothy continued. *'Has this something to do with Martin? That is, has this something to do with the way Martin and I live together. That's just a guess I'm plucking out of the air.'*

'Yes'. And Steve bit his lip, wondered if Timothy could hear he had actually started to cry a bit.

'Oh Steve, I can hear how you are. You little sweetheart.' Tears really rolled down Steve's face now and he couldn't do anything to control them. *'When do you come home Steve?'*

'Just under three weeks Timothy.' He managed to say, snuffling and blowing his nose. *'Feels ages away.'*

'Whatever this is, and my guess sounds like it's on the right lines. You didn't contradict me anyway…'

Timothy waited for any reaction but Steve felt unable to speak and was just listening hard.

'…so, listen Steve. Steve - Don't feel alone! You're not! I can talk about anything you like next time you come round in August. Sounds much more interesting than even Mozart.' They both laughed – and

that broke the tension for Steve but he still found himself hanging onto every word Timothy said and he knew he was gripping the phone with some force.

'Er, Timothy, I'm going to have to go – people waiting and I can't say more here in this spot.'

'Of course you can't'. Another pause. *'Do you feel a bit more at ease now Steve?'*

'Yes, for the moment. Thank you. Thank you so much.' Another pause, and Steve found himself welling up again.

'Sometimes Steve, writing things down can help. You know this from your studies. You can't always see things clearly just in your head. It can get muddled. Write some thoughts down or just facts, whatever it is that's happened, just write it down.'

'Yeah, good idea. Good advice Timothy. Thank you.' Steve wasn't sure how he managed to get out the words.

'Steve. Oh dear Steve, I can hear you, I so want to give you a hug. Make it better if I can. If you like, if it helps, write to me. In confidence. I mean, it's not like I'm going to, wouldn't dream of, showing your Dad or anything!' Another bit of laughing, calming Steve again. *'Would you want to do that maybe?'*

'Erm – yes. Oh, Jesus, It's really personal though Timothy.'

'Of course it is darling boy, I can hear that for goodness' sake. Do you have my address? Do you have a pen? I can imagine you, you know, with your fieldwork jacket on, reaching for your notebook.'

Steve laughed lightly, tying to dab the tears with his handkerchief at the same time as getting poised to write, pips going again – the last of his change this time. *'Yes, I'm just like that right now.'*

'OK, here's the address if you want to write …I promise as well that I will send a letter back if you include your poste restante or whatever address!

Steve wasn't sure what poste restante meant but felt he liked the idea of writing to Timothy and maybe getting a letter back. He went straight back to the caravan, dropped the idea of going to the pub, remembered Penny would be there. Then he changed his mind and decided he would go, to be friendly, but then come right back and write the letter.

In the end, it had been the right thing to go over the pub. He would have felt miserable on his own. For once, Graham wasn't next to Peter, but Penny was. He couldn't help making a quick assessment of her looks. Short, curly hair, a different length and lighter colour than Julie's. Fair complexion. She wore jeans and a sweater, a bit like all of them. A bit slimmer than Julie but not as much as Sue.

Graham chatted away with Steve and it turned out Penny fitted right in. When Steve eventually said he wanted to leave, for an earlier night, Peter had followed him out. He had started asking Steve a geological question which Steve felt was odd until he realised he was being steered to the tucked-away area where the empty beer barrels were stored. They looked around quickly and Peter had given him quite a hard kiss on the lips. He went to sleep thinking of that kiss.

The next morning Steve posted his letter, done in his clearest hand-writing he hoped. He hadn't spent too long on it, underlined where he hoped it helped, tried to stick to facts and observations and got it done, like the phone call, before he changed his mind.

c/o static caravans
Kinlochewe camping
and caravanning site
Kinlochewe
Ross-shire
Scotland.

Monday 17th July 1977

Dear Timothy

It was nice speaking with you last night from the phone box. Thank you so much for speaking with me and not making me out to be stupid!

I feel stupid though!

Thank you for saying I could write to you. This seems a good idea. I hope when I get to the end of this letter, I actually get a stamp from the Post Office and then actually send it.

It's really difficult. It's not about piano, and it's not about rocks, and it's not even about the North West Highlands. But saying that, maybe it is.

Anyway, there are some other students here. Geology students, doing the same thing as me, but not exactly in the same area. Three of them are camping and I'm in a caravan. The weather has been brilliant at times, and wet other times. When it's been wet, or after the pub (we go most evenings), my caravan ends-up as the refuge. We've sometimes had whisky, sometimes play cards, sometimes sing songs! We could do with you as accompaniment!!

I decided writing this letter. That I need to stick to facts. It's OK so far. Now the tricky bit. Please, please, please, please, please promise you will never show this to anyone else. Well, maybe Martin, but you *know what I mean. You have been good to me Timothy and I am trusting you. I have to say something and have no one else I can say this to. <u>Please don't show this to anyone else.</u>*

One of the students is called Pete. The others are Graham and Nick. Pete's a bit taller than me, thinner than me. He's fitter than me, although he smokes. His geological mapping area is really complicated. He invited me to take a look and this included seeing what appears to be a wrecked plane from the war. Crashed onto the mountain! 'His mountain' he calls it. That's because the actual Gaelic name for the mountain, nobody is sure how to pronounce!

Anyway. I have a car and the others don't. I have taken us, the four guys, to the public shower ten miles away, because it's a case of doing a stand-up wash-down on the campsite. Ten miles for a shower, can you imagine!!

When we get to the shower it costs ten pence, which is fine, but the hot water can run out, so we double-up, which is a tight squeeze but OK. This is <u>NOT</u> the thing I need to tell you though.

About a week or so ago, (eight days to be precise), it was just me and Pete. I can't remember how this happened. Graham likes to smoke wacky-backy though and I think he may have been a bit stoned. Nick keeps himself to himself a bit. So, me and Pete. Oops, Pete and I!! We were driving to the shower and we decided to swim in the river instead. It was a couple of miles walk from the car. Pete's a real mountain sort of guy, although not in the rugged, tree-chopping way. Not a lumberjack!

Pete has done this before. He's swum in mountain lakes and streams. We didn't have trunks but did have towels. He went in naked and after some hesitation, so did I. Be brave, I thought, try anything once. More of that in a minute.

The swim was lovely. Cold but lovely. Really enlivening. Drying-off, I noticed Pete looked at me a couple of times. I don't know how to write this next bit – but he was... You will know what I mean. I hadn't seen another guy like that before. He hid it in his towel. I was a bit shocked. Then we had to run back to the car after we got dressed. It started to rain really hard and we got soaked.

We went back to the campsite and Pete came to my caravan for a tea to warm up. I got the fan heater going and it soon feels like a hot place with that going, but costs a fortune.

Our clothes were dampish and we hung them around to air. All of them! Pete says it was me suggested this but I don't remember. It was all a bit unreal after that. Things seemed to happen and both of us thought it was like acting in a play. But it did feel real. <u>Very</u> real!

I can't write what should be the easiest things to say – the easiest words to use. You will know, I hope Timothy, what I am getting at. We got to know each other <u>thoroughly</u>. And we have done that again since, a few times!

I don't know what this means about me. I don't know if I have to put a horrible name on myself? It doesn't feel like that. 'It' feels great!!!

Pete has a girlfriend, been together two years at Uni. Seems a bit on and off though, but she has come all the way up here from Manchester to see him, for a couple of days. Here now. I couldn't sleep last night thinking about this. I like him so much Timothy. When I go out doing my fieldwork I think of him all the time. I think of doing things with him, all the time.

You might remember me saying I've never had a girlfriend? Is Pete like a girlfriend? Can he be? Could we be like a girlfriend/boyfriend? We have talked about it but I could <u>NEVER</u> bring him home to my *house. Back in Bristol, where he's at Uni, he shares a house. How could he have me visit him. How could we be in the same room at night? But I want that, I think.*

There are two women students on the site too. They are good fun and run the campsite café. They look after us. One of them has become close to Pete too and I feel miffed about that as well.

He just seems like someone who has to have a girlfriend, will always have a girlfriend. But when he and I are together it is like we are living on another world. A world of our own. I know he feels the same at that moment.

Oh, Timothy, are you still reading this!? Sorry I have gone on. As you said, writing it helps.

I hope I have the courage to post it! So, if you are reading this I hope you understand something about me. If you have anything to say, please write.

I hope your summer is going OK and everything's fine with you and Martin. Hope you're not too busy and have had some holiday.

Cheers

STEVE

Chapter 14

The following Thursday, Peter and Graham got back from their trip in time for a tea at the tea-room. Penny had been here just two days. A fleeting visit but one that had left Peter's head spinning. He summarised it in his head. She had arrived on the Monday afternoon and it was now Thursday afternoon. She would be working the weekend in Manchester. The weather had been pretty damp but also quite windy, so not too midge-y.

Penny had fitted-in well down the pub, Peter thought. For someone who spends quite a bit of time in her own head, Penny can be very friendly and gregarious at times, he had reflected. It had made him proud of her in a way. Proud to have her as his girlfriend. She had insisted that while she was here that he did do some fieldwork. They had gone on the low-level ground. Useful really, as Peter hadn't spent very much time down at these lower levels of his mapping area at all, assuming the rocks were pretty uniform. It had been a surprise for him to find out otherwise.

The first day they had found a shelter to get out of some of the heaviest rain and Penny had immersed herself in a book. Peter had taken the cooking stove and kettle and they had a brew with some food. Penny had insisted on making bacon sandwiches at breakfast time, which tasted surprisingly good cold.

He got a fair bit of work done the next day too, in similar conditions, and felt a little less bad about then taking the third day off, going back to Inverness with her. Graham had been invited by Penny too. As it turned out, Peter felt so fed-up and disconsolate at the soggy Inverness bus station, that he was really pleased to have Graham's company for the three hour return trip. He realised that Penny must have anticipated this in extending the invitation to Graham.

Graham had been brilliant on that bus. Just being present,

friendly, knowing how Peter felt. Just being still and quiet. It was a while before Peter could speak about the visit. But they had a long chat. Graham talked about love. How he wasn't sure he and his girlfriend had that yet, but they both assumed they would. 'On the other hand,' Graham observed, 'you seem as if you're in love with Penny'. But, he went on to add more as a statement than a question, 'is it the same with her about you though?'

Peter looked at him, nodding and wanting him to say more, feeling a bit lost. He didn't know what to think at that moment, he decided. He was already missing someone he felt very close to. Graham speaking about it in a nice way like this, just quietly on the bus, really got Peter into a deeply reflective mood and he just couldn't say anything.

'Penny seems more like a mix of friend, sister but not so much a lover. That's how I see it anyway. It doesn't look like two lovers, more like friends who happen to share a bed sometimes. Or a tent', continued Graham.

Peter thought that this was probably close to the truth. Lovers? Penny had been good enough to give up a few days of work, come up four hundred miles to see him for forty-eight hours or so and then go back again. But, when Peter had asked her, cuddled and tried to encourage her, Penny had refused to have any other form of intimacy with him. So, they had been side-by-side in this small tent, closeness from a cuddle and a kiss, but that was it. Maybe "just friends" is true, Peter thought. On the other hand, trying to engage with Penny physically had felt a bit like something he felt he should do. Ought to do. The intensity of desire he had felt other times, just wasn't there. Was this because of what had happened with Steve, he couldn't say.

Peter gave the pub, and Steve, a miss that Thursday night. He lay in his tent and tried to gather his thoughts. He felt anxious about Penny, partly her travelling back and partly his future with her. He felt a bit anxious about Steve. He had been fine about not seeing him during Penny's visit. Peter hadn't had to explain or say anything. Steve had made it seem all normal, whereas what they had been doing with each other felt anything but. How had Steve been about it though really? Thinking of it all made him feel anxious.

But the next night, everyone was back in the pub. They were all packed around the little table in the corner near the bar, their favourite spot. They felt like locals, and Jock treated them as such. The oil workers hadn't arrived yet, but there were a fair few campers and people passing by the village, stopping off for a drink or a bite, or both. Peter found himself sitting, as usually happened now, with Steve on one side and Sue on the other, looking out into the room. Julie sat opposite Sue, with Graham alongside her. Nick then to Graham's right. Looking around, Peter couldn't remember when the pub seating arrangement had changed. He seemed to remember most of the first few weeks, he had been habitually sitting next to Graham.

John MacKenzie came in, looked around the public bar and Peter could see a nod in his direction and the Warden made a made a bee-line to him. At this moment, Peter had just got himself into a bit of a conversation with Sue. She was asking about the fieldwork. She told him that she had realised that although she had heard him and the others talk about it often, the last four weeks or so, she didn't really know what they actually did in the field. She said she wanted to know while she still had the chance to find out, before they all went off back home from Kinlochewe.

'Sorry to interrupt,' said the warden 'but the man from Gairloch that I mentioned, Donald Fraser, is really interested in having a look at your plane. I know it's short notice, but any chance the day after tomorrow? The weather is looking sound and I can pick you up as before, go up the stalkers' track and then up to the wreck from there. We only need an hour or so maybe up there and then I can take him back down and to Gairloch again, and you can get yourself down I know. Or you can come back with me, of course.' He said all this without drawing breath.

'Yeah, sure', said Peter, unhesitatingly. There really wasn't any other possible answer. Also, he thought that he would pretty well do anything the Warden requested, simply out of respect. In any event, it wasn't really a problem to postpone what he would otherwise have done and he thought it would be good to get back to the plane, if that's what it was. It had been preoccupying to him such a short while ago, before the whole thing with Steve that is.

'I can come back down the Pony Track', Peter continued. 'I wouldn't want to put you out again for my benefit.'

'Well, whatever. It's no bother Pete really. But, you must know it nearly as well as me up there by now'. Peter thought the conversation over but then the Warden said, 'what about the lass?' John MacKenzie nodded to Sue. 'What about it Sue, would you like to join us? You said you were wanting to get on the hill. Has young Pete told you all about his plane wreck?'

'Yes, he has!' said Sue, 'he's spoken about it and some of the other boys here have been up there too. But, yes please.' She paused and looked at Peter as if to check his agreement. 'If it's alright with Pete, I would love to come along. As you say Mr MacKenzie, I'm itching to get out on these mountains.'

'Well, that's settled then. You come along too then'. John MacKenzie winked at Peter. Does he think he's helping me, thought Peter. 'The Land Rover will get us up two thirds of the way and Peter will get you back down safely I have no doubt, but there's the shorter option back if you prefer.' He got up to go. Looking at Sue. 'Just tell Ben I asked you - and insisted. Mind you tell him that. He'll give you the time off I'm sure.' Finishing the pint he had brought with him and standing up.

'OK then, see you two the morning after tomorrow. Nine sharp, mind.' Another wink to Peter and he was gone.

Chapter 15

Sue found she had settled into a nice way of life now, some weeks into the stay. Mostly, the work hadn't been too demanding. Serving some breakfasts and some lunches, the odd tea or coffee at other times. She and Julie had been able to sit outside in between customers, when it was warm and sunny, which it had been a fair bit, unusually according to Julie's uncle and auntie. The deck-chairs they had dug-out had got more use than they initially imagined.

It had been a bit more boring when it was grey or rainy but they had taken to reading quite a lot. They found, as at university, they were comfortable in each other's company and there wasn't ever a situation where either of them felt they had to fill a silence. She thought it so nice to have such a good friend.

They had known each other only less than two years, having met in the first year at Swansea. They had been assigned a shared room in the Student Village at Hendrefoilan, which could have been a disaster, but they had enough in common, and enough difference, to hit it off. The following year they had their own rooms, but in the same house as each other, still in the Village.

When Julie had asked her, back around Easter, about coming up to Kinlochewe, Sue had been immediately taken with the idea. Her first year summer holiday period had been spent doing some work now and then in the local shop. Being near the coast in Devon, it had been a bit hit and miss, but weekends and the school holiday period had been steadier and she had earned some money. Her Mum and Dad were not especially well-off but happy enough to support her during the long holiday, but they had been pleased when she was able to handover some housekeeping cash too.

It had been an effort getting here. She had travelled from Exeter to Birmingham New Street station. She had met Julie there, who had travelled up from home in Oxford. They had got the train to

Edinburgh. Stopped a night in the youth hostel and then gone up to Inverness the next day. Julie's Uncle Ben had met them there. The drive back to Kinlochewe had been absolutely spectacular. The weather had been a bit heavy and the glowering skies had only added awe to the feelings she had. The last twenty minutes down the glen to Kinlochewe had been like entering another world.

The work meant about ten or eleven weeks in the Highlands, a region fairly unknown to her. It was a long way from Devon but she had been on the Uni mountaineering club trip to Skye after exams at the end of her first year. That had been a long drive too and then a stay in the Glen Brittle Hut. She had loved the scenery and it was a tight group of ten of them, fairly mixed. She hadn't been able to do much in the hills though. Too rocky mostly and she didn't have the scrambling or climbing experience. She thought the hills around Kinlochewe looked pretty tough too, but definitely not as jagged. She yearned to get out for walks on them.

In the evenings they had got into the habit of going over the pub quite often. They didn't want to go every night and they didn't really have the money to do that. But the Hotel really was the heart and soul of the Village. The public bar at the back was popular with everyone it seemed. Campers from the site went there, although some went in the posher bit at the front, for meals. That was more of a restaurant really.

In addition to campers, some climbers and walkers passed through, stopping for a drink or something. It had been really odd to find about a dozen blokey men in there. Not all of them every night, but sometimes. They were working on the oil production platforms being built down at Loch Kishorn. Apparently hundreds of men were working there, all in accommodation here and there, like the little bunk house just down the road from the campsite. She had seen that their coach picked them up early in the morning and she knew they got back no earlier than seven-thirty in the evening.

They were all pretty knackered most of the time, Sue thought. A couple of times she had been chatted-up, but nobody had tried it on or become too annoying. So far anyway.

And now she had been invited out for a day's geology with Pete. As it turned out, she happened to be chatting with Peter in the bar when the nature reserve warden had come in and talked to him about a wartime expert from Gairloch. She hadn't tuned into the whole conversation, but Peter and Mr MacKenzie seemed enthusiastic about whatever it was and then suddenly she was being brought into the conversation.

She knew from a previous chat over a tea, that there was some wartime relic on the mountain where Peter was doing his geological mapping. Steve and Graham had already been up there, soon after Peter felt he had made a discovery. This person from Gairloch was going to shed more light on it. It was all set for two days' time. Apparently there was a road of some sort for a fair part of the way and then some steep walking to the site. She could come back the same way or stop with Peter if he didn't mind.

Sue had felt this was Mr MacKenzie being nice really, remembering a talk he'd had with her a couple of weeks back, about getting onto the local mountains. She had looked to Peter for confirmation though, as it was his work she felt, but he had seemed really happy about the idea of her joining in. She only hoped her walks in and around the village after work most days, had kept up her fitness enough for what she imagined would be a big mountain day.

She didn't stay through to pub closing, for a change, and when she got back to the caravan, with Julie, they had a chat.

'So, what do you think Jules? I've been invited out for a trip up the mountains.'

'Yes, I heard that bit of natter. You all seemed enthusiastic but I was chatting to Graham and Steve and didn't catch it all. What's it about then?'

'Well. Apparently, Peter has found some bits of an old aircraft or something, as you may remember, and there's a bloke coming from Gairloch to have a look.'

'So they really think it is some sort of plane?' asked Julie.

'Some sort of wartime thing. There are a few bits of wreckage around the Highlands apparently. I didn't know either!'

Sue explained to Julie what she knew, the fact the reserve Warden had, technically, invited her. She explained they would all be going up in a Land Rover for a good way. But, could she have the day off please?

Julie and Sue had agreed with her uncle and auntie that they both didn't need to be in the tearoom the whole time and could take some time off sometimes. But, unfortunately, time off together might be tricky. Julie's aunt had volunteered to cover for the two of them one day though, so they could go out together somewhere. The gardens at Poolewe had been suggested. But Julie knew Sue was itching to get up one these magnificent mountains, so she happily agreed to help Sue get out on this trip.

'It's really up to my uncle though Sue.'

'Of course Jules, I know. I wouldn't do it if he wanted me working instead. '

'I know that pet,' said Julie slowly. 'This means you get a whole day out with Peter too doesn't it?'

'Oh Jules, I know you would like that.'

'Yeah, I would but it's not going to happen is it? Anyway, to be fair, I think he has eyes for you, as I've said before.'

'Maybe. I don't see that though Jules. Don't think I'm tuned-in to boys really.'

The following day, Julie's uncle came over to see them mid-morning, when they were just clearing-up some things from some breakfast orders.

'So, I have just had my orders from John MacKenzie of the

Nature Reserve', said Ben, pretending to be annoyed and looking at Sue. 'I don't know what you've done to deserve it, but you've been summoned to an expedition up that mountain', pointing to the bit of Meall a Ghiubhais visible from the tea shop window.

'Uncle, don't be mean!! Sue's been working hard here since we arrived – harder than me to be honest.' said Julie.

'I know well enough Julie. Just teasing. It's tomorrow apparently. I'm happy about it. Looks a fair day, bit cloudy and a bit windy, especially up there. Should be good though Sue. You have to be ready for nine pick-up here, outside reception. And nine means nine with John MacKenzie, as I know to my cost.' And with that rather enigmatic statement hanging in the air, Ben had cleared-off.

That evening, after shutting up the tearoom, Julie had been out for a stroll to the shop and phone box. When she came back she found Sue walking around the caravan in her sleeping T-shirt, a bit like a floppy mini-dress.

'I can't think what to wear out on the hills Jules!'

'Well, I suggest more than that!' Said Julie briefly looking Sue up and down and raising her eyebrows. They both giggled.

'My aunt thinks you're too thin and need feeding-up, by the way.' Julie continued, giving Sue another quick, deliberate up and down look and a mock frown. 'I told her you eat all the leftover cakes but you never put on weight, but she doesn't believe me. You can expect a blow-out meal one of these days I reckon.'

'Your aunt's lovely Jules. I'd eat anything she put in from of me.' Sue said.

'What's the choices then?' asked Julie.

Sue ran through the options, even though they were limited as they hadn't brought a lot. Julie had asked what sort of mood Sue was in, and she had replied, a bit surprisingly, Scottish! The way Sue elaborated on it, made Julie think of Culloden and claymores. This thought put another into Julie's head and she went off to Glen View leaving Sue to it, pondering her hold-all and the tiny wardrobe.

Sue decided it would be walking boots and socks of course, but instead of stretch climbing breeches, she had decided her tartan mini-skirt and fair isle jumper would be a good start, and having put them on felt good about the choice, even though the skirt was probably a bit too short. She added a T-shirt to go under the jumper – good to have layers. She would put on thicker tights, take an additional woolly, simpler than the first, in the rucksack and also a waterproof.

Julie returned and Sue presented herself, arms outstretched, did a little twirl.

'Bloody hell girl! You look Scottish alright! Really nice look. I think it's your natural look, that you can get away with those boots. Bit weird maybe though!' But she smiled too.

'Aw, thanks Jules. It feels right anyway. I wanted a tartan number, and this mini-skirt is it really. This Fair Isle is pretty new, from Mum and Dad. I love it, but it's too hot in it in here.' Sue slipped off the jumper, pausing for Julie's opinion.

'Yeah – that skirt sits on you nicely. But it wouldn't take much of a blow up there for you to be doing a bit of a Marilyn Monroe though!' They giggled again. 'Especially when you have three men with you!'

'I had a thought though', continued Julie. 'My aunt used to be about your size, apparently. Not so different now really. My uncle says she needs fattening-up, a bit like she then talks of you! Anyway, I knew she had a box full of old stuff from when I was here last year and…' Julie paused until she got Sue's attention and at that point, there was a light knock at the door and it opened. Sue hadn't seen Pam coming across from the house, although Julie had been looking out, wanting it to be a surprise.

'Hi girls', said Pam, a bit breathlessly coming up the step and into the small space. 'I heard you wanted to be a bit Scottish Sue?

What about this?' She held up with both hands a kilt, quite a strong broad check pattern but with soft shades of maroon predominantly, bluey green squares, dark blue edges to the squares of pattern. All of the colours fairly muted in themselves but the overall effect was rich and distinctive.

Sue was taken aback, trying to sort out what was happening but found herself admiring Pam's offering. 'Oh, wow Pam, that's gorgeous. What is it?'

'It's a kilt, of course!' said Pam.

'Yes, I can see that! Sorry, I meant...' said Sue, 'er, where's it from? I mean, what is it?'

'Well it is mine' said Pam. I used to be a bit of a sylph, like you, and Julie just reminded me of it. If you would like to go out in it on the hills, you would be very welcome. More than welcome. A good blow through will do it good. Otherwise it's likely to become just a home for moths'.

'Oh I can't Pam, I wouldn't want to get it dirty or anything.'

'Don't be daft. It's been stuck in the box for years and years. Go on, it will be fun for you. Different anyway,' said Pam.

'Well, OK then' said Sue, feeling quite taken aback by the whole thing. 'What can I say? Can I try it on?' Sue was out of her skirt in moments and pulled on the kilt, thinking there was probably a bit of learning needed here that she didn't have yet.

Julie's aunt launched into a brief discussion and fussed around a moment. The main thing seemed to be getting the kilt to hang right. There was a waist adjustment with a shiny leather strap and buckle and another strap and buckle on the same side of the kilt, that was just about mid-hip. This was where it needed to be according to the Pam. There was a bit too much material apparently, but Pam made some movements with her fingers to gather material along the waistline. She also gathered some material at the hem and secured it with the giant silver pin that seemed to have the job of keeping the whole front looking like it did. After a few moments, it was all adjusted and Sue did a turn. Both Pam and Julie clapped and told her it was a good fit.

'I love the colour Pam. Is this your tartan?' asked Sue, touched by the appreciation of the other two.

'Yes, it is. It's my maiden name – Lindsay. A much-loved tartan in Scotland, for obvious reasons. It suits you Sue. It really does. You will look good out on the hills in it.'

Sue felt quite ecstatic. Looking in the narrow wardrobe mirror in the caravan, she could see the length of the kilt was the right look for the day, coming down to just above her knees. It was clearly traditional but also felt surprisingly modern to her. The predominantly dusky plum colour would go perfectly with her Fair Isle sweater. With the other two still watching her, she went over to her bag, found and pulled-on the sweater again.

It had a light-grey, shaped body and a traditional, patterned band across her chest and shoulders of dark and light brown horizontal stitches, woven into a pattern with creamy shades and some small, dark blue zig-zags. It had been a present from her Mum and Dad, especially for the Scottish summer job.

Pam told her she had the figure for it and said that Sue reminded her of herself. 'When I was your age, I occasionally had that feeling you have right now. Wanting to be on the hills, looking the part, feeling natural, alive. Go for it girl. Enjoy yourself!'

Sue felt she couldn't wait to get out the next day. She gave her friend Jules and her aunt a hug each. 'I promise to take good care of it Pam. Thank you so, so much.'

CHAPTER 16

Just after nine the next morning, Sue found herself next to Peter in the back of the Land Rover, Mr Mackenzie driving and Donald Fraser from Gairloch up front. Everyone seemed cheerful and there was a bit of banter as they set off down the road west out of Kinlochewe. Sue felt proud of herself to be in this company and in a vehicle with the official National Nature Reserve marking on the side. The two older men up front seemed very at ease with each other, chatting away knowledgeably about anything and everything – she thought they just had that air about them. Peter, next to her, looked relaxed in brown checked shirt and the black jumper he wore most days she saw him with one. It looked a bit worse for wear. All three men were in heavy boots, long socks and tweed breeches.

She had started the morning wondering whether she was dressed properly and a bit of self-consciousness about this was the only thing bothering her about the whole day. However, meeting-up and getting in the vehicle, all three men had been very complimentary about her outfit and she felt well made-up about that. The two older men had said that it was rare to see a woman on the hills in a kilt these days, but that she could easily start a new trend looking the way she did. They had certainly run their eyes over her she felt and was pleased when they just stopped short of making her feel uncomfortable.

Peter hadn't added to that, just nodded along, a bit deferentially she thought. But she had been aware how he couldn't seem to stop looking at her either when she first turned up. Driving along, she decided to relax about it and to concentrate on just feeling good in herself. Sitting back at that point, it struck Sue she couldn't remember ever feeling so right about a day out in the mountains.

Sue hadn't really been out of the village west that far yet and was amazed at the extent of Loch Maree. The view opening up was spectacular, particularly the bulk of Slioch which looked even more majestic from a bit of distance. After about four miles, the loch widened still further and she was pleased she was in a vehicle with a bit of height, to see out better. The view just seemed to become bigger and bigger. It was at this point though, that they left the tarmac road and joined onto a rough and stony track, with boulders in places. It immediately became very bouncy.

The Warden was explaining about the track and the occasional stalkers who used it. There were few people out here at any time according to him. There might sometimes be other estate workers from the big house and the buildings they had passed when they left the loch. It was incredibly steep in places and after about three miles, they pulled over into a scoop of land, an obvious stopping area. It was clear this is where they would be getting out.

Sue was astounded by the scenery when she looked around. It was quite high cloud and breezy, as predicted, and she felt it was just as well it wasn't hot. She suddenly felt an increased respect for Peter working in this environment and having to go out most days, whatever the weather. To be honest, Sue felt in awe at the size and extent of the landscape and even slightly intimidated.

To her west was the steeply rising flanks of Beinn a Chearcaill, so she was told, and to the south the main spur of Beinn Eighe and a slightly smaller spur by its side. To the east was their objective, Meall a Ghiubhais, vast and brooding, with steep flanks looming over them and on to the south. Everywhere was littered with boulders of all sizes and all the mountain slopes were covered in steep scree. The main colour of the hillsides, she noticed, was deep maroon.

She hadn't been aware of Peter coming around and now standing by her. He said, 'your sweater and kilt blend in Sue. If you wandered off on your own, we would soon lose sight of you.'

Sue thought she liked that and took it as another compliment. Peter went on to tell her the dark reddish colour was the Torridonian Sandstone, which formed the body of all the mountains they could see. The grey and hummocky, rocky ground beneath the sandstone was, apparently, gneiss. Peter had told her the spelling and the pronunciation. 'Nice – and easy to remember', he had joked.

It stretched away from them in all directions, covered with bog and watery pools and lochans, as far as the eye could see to the west and south. Peter pointed out the whiter scree and the crest of Beinn Eighe south of the spot. 'That's quartzite! You'll have heard of quartz, and this is like a massive version. And there you have it really – quartzite on top of sandstone, on top of gneiss. That's the first geology lesson.' And he smiled, a bit sheepishly Sue thought.

'And that will have to be the last for a bit', intervened the Warden. 'We need to crack on.'

Sue knew she had some knowledge of mountains and landscapes but couldn't help feeling astonished when Peter added in the ages of the rocks, as they got their packs on their backs. Two billon years or more for the gneiss, several hundred million for the sandstone and five hundred million years for the quartzite. Sue found the figures so large she found it hard to contemplate that degree of antiquity. While she was still trying to get her head around it, they set off.

Mr Mackenzie led the way, explaining and describing landscape features, plants, and occasional birds as he went. Being questioned, it seemed, all the time by the man from Gairloch. Sue thought it was a little like an act. The duo knew so much, all the questions and answers were really confirmations of what they already knew. It sounded like they were testing each other but Sue also thought it was the two of them just sharing the love and knowledge of this amazing place.

A lot of the discussion was about the boggy ground. She and Peter seemed to spend all their time watching where they were walking, trying to avoid getting wet feet. The trip already was an eye-opener to her, having previously mostly thought of peat bog as something to be avoided or endured on walks in the hills, like now. She was also seeing it all in a different light. From what was being said at the front, she was starting to become aware of it being something alive and integral to the landscape. Listening but not saying much either, Peter fell in behind her as the ground dropped away on the approach to a river.

The ground became even wetter and boggier near the fast-flowing river. The Grudie, she was informed. Sue could see no way across and she and Peter exchanged a concerned look about it. Peter had said there was nothing this fast or wide on the area he had mapped so far. Both of them agreed it was quite a bit different to the things they both had more familiarity with, in the Lakes or Snowdonia. Unlike those English and Welsh areas, Sue thought it was the scale and emptiness of the landscape around them that made everything feel more committing.

The two men in front kept on walking towards the river and seemed confident of what they were doing. After crossing a couple of outlying streams, a large step over one and a jump over the other, they were on the bank of the Grudie itself, and Sue could see now they were opposite a very low lying islet, hardly rising above the water level, about a hundred feet long. It emerged they were on a shallow, broader section of the river here, which allowed access to the island via some stepping stones, one or two a bit submerged but not enough to get a boot full. They all concentrated on staying upright and not slipping into the water.

Once on the islet, they walked the entire length of it northwards to where they encountered a similar bit of broad shallows, much as they had just crossed. This again involved walking and hopping from one boulder to another and Sue felt grateful to be following someone else leading the way. After that they were now over the river and it was boggy ground again for ten minutes or so, as they walked up towards the increasingly daunting steep slope of Peter's mountain.

'Right', said Mr Mackenzie. 'This is the tough bit coming up. Bit more demanding than the previous time Pete.' For the others, the Warden pointed out the route he and Peter had taken before, coming across from the north at a longer, slightly gentler angle.

'For us though, it's about a thousand feet up to the broad grassy ridge, which is our objective. I've been up this way, so don't worry. As you can see, there's a hell of a lot of rock, scree and many small cliffs. We'll weave a path through, don't worry. It just takes a bit of vertical navigation.' He laughed and winked at the man from Gairloch.

Peter again brought up the rear of the group as they broke into a line, going relentlessly upwards. Sue felt great though, a bit out of condition but familiar enough with the steps, although the relentless steepness was a surprise. By the time they reached the broad ridge, nearly an hour later, the views around now revealed thousands more lochans and water courses, not visible from below. But still everywhere, the dark reds of the rock, and its weathered scattering of scree and boulders over the whole prospect.

Sue was surprised to find there really was a broad platform here. She had thought they meant perhaps a couple of feet, but quite hidden from below, the ridge was really a platform of rock, ten to twenty feet across at this point, sloping up from the north and thinning noticeably around the end of the mountain to the south.

Reaching the top, Mr MacKenzie had brought out a couple of flasks and some small cups, and set-about distributing tea to everyone, followed by chocolate digestives. They sat round in a small semi-circle, on rocks, looking out across the endless vista to the west. Donald Fraser pointed out a few things but mostly they all sat quietly. Sue realised she hadn't thought or known there was anywhere like this in Britain. She liked the fact that Peter was just sitting beside her, drinking in the view even though he was familiar with it.

After that they went across to the sandstone cliff behind them, just a few yards really. This was a vertical band of cliffs that reminded Sue a little bit of sea cliffs down on the East Devon coast, both in terms of scale and colour. But here, instead of sea, was a thousand feet drop of steep ground and more cliffs, onto the boggy moorland, now looking so far below them.

Peter led the next bit, outlining to all of them the structure of the cliff which Sue could see was in layers of strata, each several feet thick, and fractured by vertical cracks here and there, some a few inches wide and others a few feet. Peter actually started climbing one of these, much to her surprise but not, seemingly, to the other two. He was high enough off the ground, Sue thought, to break an arm or his neck if he fell, when he started pointing out something to his right.

He was indicating the strange outcrops of metallic objects that he had found previously. Everyone strained to look and to Sue there really wasn't much to see. The grey metal looked undistinctive although Peter was saying it was more impressive with the sun on it. What they all commented upon was the compacted nature of the metal, looking like it had been jammed into the strata. Once they had taken in the fact there was several feet, in length, of the metal, Peter climbed back down.

Walking north a bit, they encountered more strata, and more hidden this time, another line of jammed, grey metal. Sue thought there was even less to be excited about. There was a lot of discussion about a fault and how the two areas of metal must be connected and it was peculiar to be separated in the way they were. Sue made a mental note to talk with Peter about this again as she thought there was more to the whole discovery than she could get clear right now.

The man from Gairloch thought the metal was definitely aluminium and imagined a crash of some sort where there had been a fire. Hot, melting metal, he felt, accounted for the odd nature of the find. All three of them seemed to find this a rational explanation but she wondered from Peter's slightly subdued input to the discussion, whether he was happy about this or not. Sue thought perhaps he wanted people to be more excited or maybe, for him, the gloss had come off now he had been here so often.

Donald Fraser took some photos and there was some talk about getting a reporter to pick up the story as a local interest item. Sue was surprised to hear how significant the whole area had been during the war and she wondered what life must have been like for people then. She tried to imagine the insecurity of war against the sense of freedom she felt most of the time, and so strongly and personally right at this moment.

'What was it like for women up here during those times Mr Fraser?' she asked.

'Oh, do call me Donald please Sue. Well, women folk just got on with their lives back then, same as the men. For everyone it was about keeping your head down, keeping your nose out. Hear all, see all, say nothing. But some lasses and older women too had work in the camps up here.'

'Camps?' asked Peter.

'Oh aye,' continued Donald Fraser. 'there were hundreds of military stationed around here. They all needed catering for. Lots of support roles, Secretarial stuff too. Some women got the chance to do jobs they would never have been able to do normally.'

Sue tried to imagine what it must have looked like up here. She couldn't visualise the scene and found it equally hard to think of the way people's lives had changed so quickly. She was pleased to see Peter looking thoughtful too and wondered if he was thinking the same things.

The two older men had soon found they had seen and heard enough of the plane debris and were thanking Peter for his time and effort, and congratulating him for spotting something new. They seemed pretty convinced it would be parts of a crashed wartime plane. Maybe connected with the crashed plane on Beinn Eighe itself, nearby. Then Sue was surprised as the attention of all three had turned onto her. Mr MacKenzie asked if she was coming back with them, him and Donald Fraser, reversing the way they had come up, or did she want to stay up here and make the return leg with Peter?

Peter was asked to explain what that would mean and he duly described what he said was a steep but safe route, he had already done before, around the southern end of the mountain above them, crossing more boulders and scree and down to what he called a plateau. He said eventually they would pick up the path called the Pony Track which would come out near Kinlochewe village, a half-mile or so from the campsite. This would be about six miles in total and would take up to three hours. Going back via the Land Rover would be half the time.

John MacKenzie followed what Peter had said on the map and considered his own knowledge of the mountain 'Well, Pete, that sounds fine. If you feel it's OK and you're happy about it, but you know the first couple of miles will be steep. Both of you seem happy enough with the rock, like you came-up just now. That was a good test I think. But both of you need to make sure every step. That end of Meall a Ghiubhais, pointing south, is remote. If you have a tumble there, you are a long way from home!' He turned to Sue. 'Well lass, it's really up to you, of course.'

Sue felt like the previous few minutes had been about her but with nobody actually saying so. She felt slightly put-out but didn't want to comment on that. She said instead, 'I would love to stay up and see round the other side. I've loved coming up here and it's too soon to go back.'

Then, thinking of what she had said and how it might sound abrupt, she added, 'Oh, Mr MacKenzie, I hope you don't mind. It was brilliant coming by the Land Rover and crossing the river and coming up here...' Sue found herself feeling slightly embarrassed. 'It was great and I'm grateful. But it just sounds like a complete round trip to go back with Pete like he's said. I'm not tired yet and really feel like doing it.'

John MacKenzie nodded and smiled at her. 'Well, that's grand lass. You stay up here. You don't want to be spending any more time listening to us banging on about the wonder of peat bogs anyway. It's fine. I expected you would go back with Pete.' Then turning to Peter. 'You just make sure we see the two of you back at the campsite later.'

Sue found herself thinking what Peter needed to do right now was pull his feet together, put his shoulders back, salute and say, "yes sir!". But she also felt touched with the concern, which again she felt was primarily about her.

'I'm fine with it Mr Mackenzie,' was what Peter actually said, picking up the formality from Sue. 'Sue's easily as good a walker as me and I will make sure we are both safe.'

'I know you will be safe. Enjoy it too. I'll pop into the campsite and make sure Ben knows to look out for you about, shall we say, five o'clock? No need for you to rush it.'

And with handshakes and a few words, they were gone off down the slope, moving quicker than Sue would have cared for. She turned to Peter, suddenly feeling the remoteness around her more keenly, now it was just two of them and the older men departed. Peter had his rucksack on and was ready to go.

They continued south to start with on the rising ramp of rock and then the ground became steeper and the platform of rock narrower as they reached the southern nose of the mountain. Peter told her that from here they would be contouring around the mountain and the ground dropping away from them would get much steeper and they would be walking across scree. Above them the whole time would be a cliff of red sandstone called Creag Bhan, Peter told her.

Sue was surprised how quickly they gained height until at one point she looked back and could see they were now a few hundred feet higher than the metal outcrop and the breeze was sharper. Sue felt the cold of the air on her legs but felt happy to be in the kilt. She could feel the wind blowing out her hair and she suddenly felt a great sense of being alive. Peter led the way and took it slowly, checking all the time that she was comfortable with what they were doing. After twenty minutes or so, she was aware that going on was the only choice, as turning around and going back now felt much harder.

She had been on scree before, but nothing like this – nothing that felt so steep and open, so exposed, nor so remote. There was nobody else around, not for miles maybe, Sue thought – and no roads, no pylons, nothing! Peter was keeping a few yards ahead of her and when they reached a solid rock outcrop in the slope, he turned to check she was OK.

'Sue, I know you've done scree before but this is really steep and nobody comes here, so you will find it feels untrodden and it slips away with you, all the time, moving down under your feet.' Sue thought she hadn't seen him look so serious before. 'Traversing it goes on a way yet', he continued, 'so it's best to lean your left side into the hill just a bit. If you find a foot starts to slide with the stones, just let it. Don't try and out-run it. We don't want to go sliding here – it's a long way down. The stones will build up under your boot if it starts to slide, and that should stop further downhill movement. Then you can go forward again. We're just going to keep a nice, even pace – not too fast, but not too slow either.'

Peter then laughed a little and said, 'Sorry Sue. It feels like my mountain and I'm sorry if I sound like I am being over-protective. Must sound like an old fart!'.

Sue had been grateful for the long explanation though and had really listened to him. 'Pete' she said, 'it's fine. I've done scree before, but it's good to have a reminder. It does feel different, it's just we are so out on our own here.'

She loved the way Peter was being calm but also attentive to her. She was really enjoying it and didn't want to think of anything bad happening. She would have been pretty nervous to do this on her own though and wondered how Peter had felt doing just that, and, in fact, how he felt now. She hoped he was enjoying it and wasn't being anxious.

'I'm fine Pete. It's going like you say.' She paused. 'It just feels great and I'm knocked-out by the views. Let's just carry on.'

She meant it about the views. Now the full range of Beinn Eighe was visible to her south. She didn't want to lift her eyes too much, for fear of slipping, but when she did the extraordinary landscape of rock, mountains, scree and boulders amazed her.

After another twenty minutes or so the ground soon became less angled, grassier and she could see easy, but still rocky, slopes stretching down to the path that Peter was pointing out. They were heading down to a large rocky outcrop above a lochan. Peter had got a little ahead and was waiting for her. He was smiling and Sue later recalled how wonderful it felt when he had said she looked so good coming across the slopes in her tartan and Fair Isle with hair blowing around. That just was a perfect thing to say, because he had seen what she could feel she was experiencing. It was a great end to an exhilarating hour of climbing and walking like she had never felt so strongly before.

Sue wanted to hug Peter and felt so pleased when she realised they now had a long, unhurried descent to Kinlochewe ahead of them.

CHAPTER 17

Sitting in his tent after demolishing tinned haggis, oatcakes and an apple, Peter reflected on the day. He had told Graham he might not go to the pub as it had been a long day and he needed to catch-up with himself a bit. Graham had looked sceptical and told Peter he did just look tired and it was fine not to go to the pub sometimes. But Graham had also made clear he wanted to hear how the day went at some point, being friendly, not nosey.

Peter lit a cigarette, looked out at the view across the campsite, quite busy at this time in the early evening now. He needed to recapture the day. He mulled-over how it had gone, and started to run through the whole experience in his head…

Before nine Peter had been over at the café caravan, just to help Sue be ready. He needn't have bothered. He could see straight away that she was more than used to packing a rucksack and, indeed, had hers ready. She really looked the part. Peter saw her in a different light, looking like a keen mountain walker – good boots, well loaded pack. He hadn't expected the Scottish look though and thought it was really striking. She had been wearing a kilt, beautifully coloured he thought, and an island sweater of some sort. He wondered if it was from the Hebrides or something. She had dark red socks and well-worn boots on, her hair tied back a bit, a broad grin and Peter felt really chuffed to be with her like that.

He didn't exactly feel like it was a date, not that sort of feeling, but it did feel really special and nice. He wouldn't have asked her himself, or thought of it really, but looking at her now Peter was pleased John MacKenzie had precipitated the situation. It would be the first time he and Sue had been together any length of time, without others, and he had realised how much he was looking forward to her company.

John MacKenzie was bang on time and with him in the Land

Rover was the guy from Gairloch, Donald Fraser. Introductions all round, everyone seemed in good spirits. They set off up the road, past all the usual points of departure for Peter's mapping, and turning off the road to go up the stalkers track. Peter was amazed and could hardly recognise it from this way round. It had seemed steep and rough enough coming down this way a week or two ago now, but going up looked incredible.

But, by soon after ten, they had been parked up and looking up at Peter's mountain above. The warden and his friend were in breeches and Peter was pleased he had worn the same thing himself. He did feel self-consciously young though, with Sue beside him in her Scottish outfit. But off they set, still all being amiable.

The warden's friend was naturally charming and inquisitive and Peter felt flattered he was getting them to divulge their life-histories, breathlessly at times, on the steepening ascent. But for the most part, he and the warden had kept up a steady commentary on the insects, wildflowers and plants they encountered in and around the bogs and rock.

By the time they reached the level area where the wreck was located, they all needed a sit down. 'We came up there at a fair old rate', said the warden. 'I should have warned you, if you give this man an inch he will take a mile. He's like a sponge with information, a walking encyclopaedia, and you two now have your entries too I imagine.'

John MacKenzie had brought a couple of flasks and some flask cups, which was brilliant, Peter thought. So, after a tea and look at the immense view, they went over to the nearby cliff exposure to examine the wreck.

It had all felt very familiar to Peter and he had quickly pointed-out the two exposures they knew about, including shimmying up the rock and pointing the length of the rock joints. Knowing the holds now, he traversed south a little further, along the bedding plane and established for certain that the metal object did indeed run along for a few yards.

Peter was exchanging comments and the short history of the discovery to the other two men. Sue was sitting on a rock listening. She had let her hair down and had her head back a bit, so the surprisingly thick, long expanse of hair blew outwards in the breeze. Strands blew into her face and she gently moved them away with her hand or a flick of her head, all the time squinting up at Peter, with the hazy sun in her eyes. Peter found himself drawn towards keeping looking at her.

There wasn't, in the end, that much more to say when they had come to share their thoughts. The man from Gairloch thought it couldn't be anything but a plane wreck. He thought the dulled and pitted surface of the metal was like pieces he had seen elsewhere. It was a new discovery though. He said he knew folk in the forces and he would delve around and see what he could discover. It was hard, he said, not to link it in some way to the wreck in the cliffs so nearby, as a plane flies, on Beinn Eighe. But they didn't find any more of it and Peter still thought it was bizarre that the two exposures were separated by a fault, the line of which was a half-billion years old.

Sue had asked a question about life during the War, especially for women. He had felt really moved by the short description given by Donald Fraser and thought he could see Sue feeling affected too.

When it came to concluding the morning, Peter had started to think he really was a lucky guy. Here he was, saying cheerio to the Nature Reserve warden, a retired academic and with the whole of the next few hours to spend in Sue's company in scenery that he felt a part of. He had decided to take her round the south end of Meall a Ghiubhais, even though it was decidedly tricky. He was sure of the best line to take through the rocky bit and across the scree, before descending onto the quartzite plateau. He felt Sue had been at least as steady and confident as him on the way up. Anyway, once they started, they would have to finish.

The two older men had, Peter thought, been checking-up on him, getting him to describe the way he intended to go with Sue. But he also thought they maybe just felt responsible, particularly the warden, and certainly about anything that might go wrong.

In the end, it had worked out OK. The traverse across the scree felt a bit hairy at times, but Peter thought Sue looked exhilarated by it rather than perturbed. In the occasional sun going round the mountain, her hair was blowing all over the place and Peter thought he could discern hints of red in it. Maybe she has some Celtic blood, he wondered. He certainly felt she looked the part right then, a slightly wild looking woman in a kilt scrambling down a Scottish mountain. With the backdrop of the Torridon mountains Peter felt the whole image was unique and something that would stay with him for a long time.

Conversation with Sue had properly re-started as they levelled out and stopped for a breather by a large boulder of sandstone. An erratic, deposited on the quartzite terrain by a retreating glacier, Peter thought.

'You looked good coming over that lot, did you enjoy it? Looked as if you did.'

'Aw, that was just brilliant… 'Just brilliant.' She reached across and gave a little squeeze to his arm. He smiled at her and they looked at each other for a few seconds. 'I thought it was brilliant too' he had said.

They sat down, using rucksacks as padding to lean back onto. Peter produced a packet of cigarettes, looked at Sue enquiringly.

'Oh, yes please, I'd love one.' She took it from Peter and she cupped the end of it as he flicked his lighter.

They both sat there together, knees up, looking north, taking in the scenery, smoking unhurriedly. Peter recalled the conversation exactly.

'I can see why you study geology.' Sue said after a bit. 'You obviously love being in the mountains, you were like a bit of a goat coming round the hill there. Who wouldn't want to study something that got you out here doing this?'

'I know. You're right', sighed Peter. 'But you love your studies too, from what you've said down the pub?'

'Yes, that's true. I, and Jules also, do like what we're doing. Other people call it the "liquorice all-sorts degree" but I like the way it gets you exploring related things like, psychology, philosophy, politics...' She had been thoughtful again then. 'But it doesn't get you out on the mountains much!'

Peter had thought that was funny but seeing the landscape through Sue's eyes had the same effect on him as with Steve and Graham. 'Being here right now', he had said, 'just reminds me how much I have to do still. I've taken too much time out and I'm over half-way through the time.'

'Oh but this plane thing is important, surely your supervisor will see that, won't he?' Sue had asked. 'You could end up with your name in the papers too! Well, the local one anyway.'

'You thought they were serious about that?' asked Peter.

'Yeah, the two of them were saying it was a potentially interesting local news story. They're going to get a reporter & photographer out and get the three of you in a picture, is what I heard'.

'Oh, I don't know Sue. Maybe, yeah, let's see.' Peter wasn't sure now it was as exciting as he had first thought. It had seemed more magical when he first discovered it but now it felt more mundane.

'I think it's quite a big thing for them Pete. The war's not so long ago for those guys and the memory of everything must be very strong. Up here, so far from London and from the main battles and stuff. And yet, by the sound of it, they were really involved with the war effort up here. I can't imagine that view out west being full of battleships!'

Peter looked at her, then to the distant sea, then back to her. 'You know Sue, I hadn't thought of it like that. Then there was that experience with those people looking for the Beinn Eighe plane.'

'Was there?' said Sue. 'Don't know that bit Pete.'

'Oh, I don't know either Sue, it was a bit weird. These guys appeared out of nowhere one day recently, not far from here. There were four of them. They seemed a bit lost. It was odd, but I was a bit odd that day myself I think.'

Sue waited for more information but none was forthcoming. She decided to say something encouraging.

'Well, never mind Pete, let's hope they do get a reporter out quickly and you can take a copy of the local paper back with you. Maybe send one to your Mum. Or to your girlfriend.'

Penny, thought Peter, might be interested a little. His Mum would definitely love it, would be proud as punch in fact. His supervisor though? He didn't know if the university might view the whole thing as a waste of time.

'Did she enjoy her visit by the way, if you don't mind me asking?' Sue asked. And before Peter had replied, added 'She wasn't here long, must think you're pretty special to come up here like that. Or missing you maybe?'

There were at least a dozen points of discussion in that short set of questions, Peter mused. He didn't know how to begin to answer. He felt good just now, in this place, the two of them, like this, and now Sue had brought up the subject, he realised he was keen to talk about it. It was like she was giving him permission to do that. But he didn't want to bang on about himself all afternoon. So, he didn't respond.

Sue filled the gap, having turned to him enquiringly, cigarette in one hand resting on her knee, the other hand holding up her chin and elbow on her other knee. She wanted him to say something.

'How long have you known each other then?'

So, Peter had felt able to stay on safe ground for a few moments, giving a short history of how he and Penny had met. With Sue looking at him like that, he found he could neither bluff or gloss over bits and found himself revealing something of the visits by Penny to her ex.

Sue looked out to the mountains and blew out smoke from the second cigarette they had lit-up. She hadn't puffed it much, preferring to just listen to Peter. Staring out though, allowing the silence to settle on them. Just a breeze riffling through bits of grass and rocks. She replied to Peter. 'You know, it's tricky sometimes to know what you want. I'm not hugely experienced but I just think at this age we have a lot just going on don't we? I don't know, I've had a couple of boyfriends, nothing serious really. I just feel I haven't the time really – some friends at Uni seem to spend all their time wrapped-up in relationships with this or that person. It's not me, not just now anyway.'

'But you must have loads of guys interested!?' Peter couldn't keep the surprise out of his question.

'Oh, get away. But thanks for the compliment Pete. Julie says that about me actually, but I don't really notice it'. She laughed a little and Peter found he had broken into a smile himself. She continued, 'The blokes I'm aware of being interested in me, well it seems to be they're just on the prowl the whole time anyway. It's not just me…anyone will do for some of them. Do you know what I mean?'

'Yeah, there is a guy in our club, the mountaineering club I mean, who has that as his actual philosophy!' Peter thought of recent club meets and social events, drinks down the union bar. 'This guy right. He literally says, "if I ask enough women to sleep with me, then a certain number of them will". Paul's his name. He's notorious!'

'Yes, that's the type. I know that type very well.'

'You know though Sue'. Peter found he wanted to just say something nice to her again. 'You do look great – just like that. Your hair blowing, that kilt, your easy-going manner, just getting on with stuff, like coming over the mountain just now. Most guys I know in my Club would die to have you as a girlfriend, and I don't mean the Paul types.'

'Oh, gosh!' Sue was taken aback, put her hand on her chest, 'Thanks Pete, that's really nice.' She leaned over and gave him a kiss on the cheek. She hadn't moved back much though, and then they had both kissed, quite a long kiss, on the lips. 'That's for being sweet', she said, still holding his shoulders and faces still close. 'Shall we head off again?'

It was easier to walk side-by-side for the next mile or two, across to the top of the Pony track that would take them back down to Kinlochewe and the campsite. Sue wasn't going to let the subject die, and Peter was grateful. It would have been easy to spend the rest of their trip just chatting but he had thought such a lot was unsaid and left hanging in the air.

'I think you and Penny have to decide what you want from each other, if you want my opinion. In a year's time, you will both be heading-off to work. Not a shop like she's doing now, or you working in the pub like you were saying you do between terms. But you will be starting careers. Proper jobs! And you will probably be moving to do that.'

Peter felt, again, there was so much truth in this and Sue again had opened up another line of conversation, but he wasn't sure what he wanted to say.

They carried on walking along the track. The two of them remained silent for a while. Looking north into the wilderness, and just slightly to the east, a bit of Kinlochewe coming into view.

'You love her don't you?' Sue asked.

'I say that to her Sue.' Peter paused. 'She doesn't say it back. I'm just thinking it's a habit maybe. Being with Penny is familiar and I like that.' He had hesitated before going on, but found he couldn't hold this back. 'Don't tell Graham this! I had a bit of counselling at Uni last year, I was feeling a bit depressed to be honest. The counsellor said that he thought I was a "nest builder" and really wanted a "mate" to share it with.'

'And that's right isn't it?' Sue asked gently.

'Yeah,' he shrugged, 'probably.'

'OK, but maybe Penny doesn't want to be a mate in a nest. She likes you or she wouldn't have come up here but she goes off to see this other guy and so on, as a way of not getting too entangled with you.'

'You sound a bit like my counsellor did!' Peter replied. 'He said this was probably down to what happened when I was younger. My Dad died when I was a young teenager. This bloke said security of a steady nest and partner was important to me; perhaps because of that. Sorry, this is your sort of stuff – stuff you study I mean…'

'Oh Pete. That must have been awful. Losing your Dad at that age. I can see why you're close to your Mum.'

'Am I?' Peter didn't remember saying that much about her.

'You don't say that much about her but Julie and I were saying you must have a great Mum. Sending you money now and then. You queueing up at that phone box, phoning her. We've seen you! You've mentioned her in the tearoom, more than you think maybe.'

Peter looked sceptical.

'I don't mean like a Mummy's Boy or anything like that' Sue qualified. 'There's nothing like that about you! So…?' Sue continued and left it hanging in the air.

Peter was thinking about all she said. It was as if Sue had got inside his head and opened a lot of drawers, revealing things he had forgotten, not thought about. He felt a bit pressured and dizzy, running things around and trying to think what thing was most important to say next. In the end, he decided to ask her about herself again.

'Have you liked being up here then?'

'Oh Peter!...', suddenly using the longer name, '...talk about changing the subject!' She half-shouted at him, then laughed. 'Yes, well, maybe it was getting a bit heavy. But listen Pete...' She turned to him, put her hands on his shoulders and looked straight in his eyes. For the first time for a few hours he thought of Steve – the self-same action and movement. How long ago had that been? He couldn't think about Steve now, wanted to, started to think about the remoteness of where Steve was working, right at this moment, probably just a few miles in a straight line. But Sue's face was right in front of his own. How could he be thinking of Steve?

'Pete. Thank you for saying what you have. I didn't want to interrogate you. You're a lovely guy.' And she moved up to kiss him again, and they kissed briefly once more. 'That's for being sweet again', went to pull away, but Peter put his hand round her waist, pulled her towards him, thinking how small she felt, thinking of Steve so much bigger. Do all men feel big to women, compared to themselves? Peter wondered. That was all in flash. Their lips connected again and they kissed again. Peter said, 'and that's for you being sweet too. It so nice to talk with you Sue'. And then they kissed a third time, and it went on a while. Sue moved away a little, only to speak really, and she sighed. 'Are we going to do this all afternoon Pete?'

'I don't know Sue. You started it', he said, as if about to push her away again. They looked at each other. Peter felt unsure what to do, or what he wanted to do. Then they had both giggled, then laughed and the tension and passion of the moment dissolved.

She turned her head and leant against his chest, giving him a big hug. He felt turned-on by that, then felt guilty about it and hoped she hadn't noticed. Whether she did or not, they stayed still like that for a while and then Sue pulled away.

'Come on you. We'll end-up getting benighted if we're not careful'. She had put her hand on his arm and gave him a tug and they nearly fell-over starting off again on their trail.

Peter had wanted to get away from the previous discussion and to stop thinking about wanting to kiss her again. 'What about you Sue? Your Mum and Dad sound important to you too, you've mentioned them a bit I mean.'

'They've always done their best for me, is what I feel most.' Sue said, without any hesitation.

Peter thought that was a big thing to say, just like that – off the cuff.

'I have an elder brother and an elder sister.' Sue continued. 'You don't want the whole history. Not that there's much. We used to live in Twickenham. Dad was a teacher. Once my brother and sister started to settle down, Mum and Dad wanted to move to the country. He got a decent enough job, down in East Devon, change of lifestyle for them. So, we moved when I was about thirteen.'

'So your brother and sister are quite a bit older than you?'

'Yeah, thirty and twenty-seven. Huh! Think I was a bit of an afterthought!' She laughed quickly. 'Or maybe a mistake!'

They carried on walking, on good solid ground but with the downhill bit steepening now.

'It's not the same as what you experienced Pete, but I think a big change when you're thirteen is a bit of thing that you have to get used to. Starting new friendships in Devon took a while. Getting to Uni actually felt like starting again with friends. People like Jules. Or Jules particularly actually.'

Peter found he wasn't sure what to say again, but he thought Sue seemed quite happy walking along with him. He felt as if he had known her a lot more than just a few weeks. After a while, Sue brought up a new subject.

'Tell you what Pete. Tell me about your swimming in the river. That sounds nice'. And Peter again found his mind jolted back to images of Steve.

'Well, it's dependent on Steve really. He's the only one with a car. He's taken us to the shower down in Torridon a couple of times.'

'I know. Julie asked her uncle about you all using one of the ones in the house. But he just said "you must be joking! We'd end up with the whole campsite coming in", so that died a death'.

'Blimey. Thanks for that thought though Sue'. It had never occurred to him to ask about showers in the owner's house. 'Julie's aunt doing the washing…well, all three of you really… that was nice. Helped me a lot anyway.' Then they both just laughed, remembering the array on the washing line.

They walked along a bit more and Peter could see they would soon enter the fenced area, protecting the newly planted trees from the deer. He thought of Steve again. Remembered the swim and what that led to afterwards.

'Anyway, this one time', he continued, 'it was just Steve and I and we parked-up and went over for a swim in the river by where I was when I first came up here a month ago now. It's a great location. Incredibly fresh water but it runs fairly shallow in places there and has some little patches where the sun warms up the water if there is any sun.'

'You took your trunks with you then?'

'Oh come on Sue, you know the answer to that. You're just teasing me. We just jumped in. Left our clothes on the bank. I had done this just once before this summer, but now seem to be doing it a fair bit.' He explained briefly the river swims and the mountain lochan, but leaving out the effect it could have on him, although it was in the forefront of memory he found, while speaking.

'So, it's all boys together then is it?' She said, tilting her head to one side and giving him a suggestive look.

'I'm sure I don't know what you mean Sue!'

'Well I've always thought it strange blokes having communal baths and stuff, after rugby and football.'

'I was always crap at those Sue. Never did them'. Peter said quite quickly, keen to get out of that conversation.

'Well anyway', Sue went on, 'Jules keeps threatening to take me over to the river flowing into Loch Maree. Apparently there's a spot a half-mile or so from the site. You can find a place to change amongst some gorse bushes and like you said, there's a shallow area with pools you can swim in. Jules made the same sort of comment about it as you just now.'

'Come with us Pete.' Sue continued, after a minute. Peter found he immediately loved the idea, but just nodded. 'You've made me feel we should do it. We will be wearing swimming cossies though, Jules and me. You do what you want!' Then Sue added as an afterthought. 'Bring Steve along too perhaps?'

Peter felt a further distraction from fieldwork coming and hoped the next day would be gloomy. If Sue went back now and told Julie she wanted to go to the river now after all, Julie would do it as soon as possible – probably before or after the next day's work in the café. We need a wind though, thought Peter, or we will get bitten to death down there at the big river…

Having recalled the day, Peter was shocked how vividly it appeared in his mind. It was as if he could literally feel the memory being laid down in his brain.

CHAPTER 18

The rest of the descent to Kinlochewe on her day on Peter's mountain was something that Sue felt she would never forget. She loved describing it to Julie when she eventually returned to the caravan. Julie's aunt had brought over a stew and dumplings for them and Julie had got in a bottle of red wine from their drinks kitty. 'I thought you might prefer an evening in, to going down the pub tonight Sue. And you can tell me all your adventures.' Julie had said.

Sue managed to hold-off most of the discussion until they had eaten their food, cleared-up and settled down for a good natter. As it turned out Julie had been fairly busy at the café, "steady" she had described it as. Just enough customers to keep busy but not so many that she couldn't handle comfortably. Julie had described some of the couples and others, but mostly pairings of different ages, who had been through that day for teas and so on.

They settled on one of the caravan couches, Julie in the corner between the side and front windows, Sue facing her at the other end, propped-up with cushions. Sue managed to get her legs up and crossed comfortably. Julie found that harder to do and had her feet on the table instead. The bottle of wine was open and two glasses poured and started. Sue had, so far, managed to fill her in with the story as far as the end of the dodgy scree slope.

'So, go on then', said Julie. 'What happened next, after Pete flattered you!? Do you think he really liked your Scottish look?'

'Oh, I don't know Jules. 'The thing is... I felt really good. I just felt free up there, Light and airy. Any blowier and I would have been chilly but we kept going. It just felt really physical, tiring in a good way. I could feel my nerve-ends tingling at the end of that slope.'

'The kilt was warm enough then.'

'Fab Jules. I've been walking in a skirt before but not in proper mountains. Definitely felt different to those stretchy breeches I usually would have worn. I'd do the kilt again. Must tell your aunt.'

'No Marilyn Monroe scenes then?'

Sue laughed, shook her head.

'That slope though', continued Julie, 'was it actually dangerous then?'

'If one of us had slid and couldn't stop, it was a long way down at times. But really once you got used to the scary feel of motion of the stones all the time, it was OK.' Sue tossed her head back a bit and shook her head. 'Just thinking about it – it was just a brilliant feeling.'

'I can see that Sue. You look really made-up about it! Sooo…' asked Julie. 'I'm still all ears'

'Oh yeah. Well, what happened next', continued Sue 'was also really, really interesting but not the same thing. It was boulders everywhere and a bit of clambering around at first, but most of coming down was easy enough and eventually it's a good track.'

Julie looking at her now over the top of her glasses.

'OK I know. So, what you really want to know Jules, is we had a really good and long talk, nearly all the way down.'

'Just talked?' Julie asked, doubtfully.

Sue wanted to tell Julie everything. But it wasn't just what happened that she wanted to convey, but how she felt about it too.

'Pete told me quite a bit about his girlfriend, you know, Penny.'

'Did he start that conversation then?' Asked Julie.

'No, of course not! Well, he may have done for all I know, later or sometime, but, no, I asked him. We were chatting and he was easy to talk to.' Sue wondered how much to say really. She didn't think Peter had put a boundary around it like "please don't repeat this to anyone", other than the bit about counselling, but she did feel it had been personal. So, she gave Julie the gist of what he had said and how she had reacted.

They were on to the second glass of wine now and Julie was less lying back and more upright now, wanting to hear Sue's story. She asked, 'So, basically you told him you thought Penny was being put on a bit of pedestal and that was an uncomfortable place to be?'

'That's a good way of putting it Jules. That's what I actually think too.' Said Sue.

'How did he seem then, after that?' Julie wondered.

'He seemed alright, listening, thinking really. He looked a bit sad though, so I gave him a hug and then I found I had kissed him!'

'What!! Oh, wow Sue, talk about spinning it out, you minx. What happened? Exactly.' Julie said, excitedly.

'Like I said, he had been so… open, that's the word. And then after I said a bit, he looked a little down, so I told him he's a nice guy and gave him a kiss. Only a quickie. He asked what it was for and I told him it was because he was sweet.'

'And…?' Said Julie. Sue hesitating. 'Come on, and what then?'

'Jules, he kissed me back! A bit longer that one.'

Julie took a bit intake of breath and, rather exaggeratedly Sue thought, put her hand to her mouth. Really it was pretend shock horror.

'And…?' Julie now edging forward on her seat.

'He said that kiss was for me being nice to him!'

'Well fair enough Sue, one each. That's nice.'

'And then, after a bit, we kissed again.' Sue said, excited now in retelling it.

'You are a little devil Sue, spinning this out like this.' Julie said in more mock outrage. 'Come on then, get on with it!'

'That is it though Jules. Well, actually, that last kiss was really in three parts. It stopped there though. But, oh my God, that last kiss felt really something!'

Sue explained there had been a bit more conversation and more uncovering about each other but Sue also thought that essentially the afternoon's long talk was in good part defined by those kisses. At first they had been a sort of thank you to each other. But the last had been about something else.

'I can't stop thinking about it now Jules, it went on what seemed a long time. It wasn't, you know, it wasn't tongues and that. But he held me really tight and I wrapped myself around him, it felt like…like we sank into a bath together. I had just this amazing sensation of warmth enveloping me and moving through my entire body!' Sue, who had been holding herself quite tight during this statement, released and her shoulders and body relaxed down.

'Bloody hell Sue. That sounds a kiss and a half. That was it though? Nothing more you are keeping stored up for another glass of wine!?'

'No Jules. Nothing else to say. Yes please, might as well pour it out! I feel a bit squiffy now though, drinking too quickly…'

'Blimey. Well, thinking of it now, what happens next?' asked Julie.

'Yeah, that's the question. You know what? I don't really know.' Sue said.

Julie looked at Sue, chose to keep her mouth shut and waited. To both of them it was clear the jokiness had turned into something more serious.

'Well, I haven't kissed many guys, honestly. Just silly snogs at parties and down the pub at Christmas. That sort of thing. I've had a couple of romances at uni, as you know.' Sue felt uncertain – was it the wine or did she really not know her feelings. She felt unclear about what she wanted to say.

'Go on pet.' Julie now moved up to Sue for a cuddle side by side.

'Oh Jules. He was so nice to me up there today – making sure

I was safe on the rocks. Complimentary. All that openness. Then the kissing. But, sometimes I saw him as a really good friend, then as like a brother and then like something else.'

'Yes indeed Sue – I think that would probably be known as a lover!' Said Julie emphatically.

'Yeah, I guess Jules. You know it was sexy, the last kiss. But I didn't feel any urge from him to want to take it further or even have another one.'

'I reckon Sue. In my own limited experience, I have to say.' Said Julie making a joke of things. 'In my experience, a kiss to feel like that. Any emotion that, intense! Anything like that must be two-way. He must have felt that impact too. Don't you reckon?'

'Hmmm. Thanks Jules, you're a real pal. I can't reach my glass with you leaning on my arm.' The girls gave each other a hug, giggled and snuggled in towards each other a bit more. They both sighed simultaneously, giggled again and sipped their wine.

CHAPTER 19

A couple of days after Sue and his visit to the plane wreck, and their big chat, as Peter saw it, he found himself getting ready to go for a swim with Sue and Julie. He was pleased he had been able to get out on the hill first thing, had completed some good work, he thought, and now was looking forward to a good end to an afternoon. They still had the long summer daylight, cloud was coming and going and a good breeze was blowing from the west. It seemed perfect.

Steve had said he would come down to join them after he got down from his mapping area too. Peter wondered if that would happen though as Steve was piling in the time on fieldwork now as the sense of time running out became stronger. They would all be going down to the south side of the river, about a mile, to the recommended swimming spot. There was a short walk along the main road then the Field Station track, past where John MacKenzie lived and worked, and then through some trees to the riverbank. Julie's Uncle Ben had shown her, the previous year, this place on the Kinlochewe River where there was a copse of alder trees and a wide bend in the river.

Peter didn't bother to change from his field work clothes, just dumping off his rucksack, map and notebook and grabbing a towel and his trunks. He met up with Sue and Julie and they headed off. They were all surprised to find Steve waiting on the field station road. Ever prepared, he had taken his kit with him and had come straight round to here from where he had been mapping, just across the river. There was no usable fording place and he had hurried along a bit of a detour.

When they arrived at the chosen spot, it turned out to be quite shrubby near the trees and they changed in separate areas of the wild gorse bushes. Steve and Peter changed together and Steve kept grabbing at Peter's body, tapping his bottom, trying to touch him as they were getting into their swimwear.

'Stop it Steve, we'll be seen.' Whispered Peter.

Steve ignored him, grabbed and pulled Peter to him, by putting both hands on his backside. He whispered into Peter's ear: 'I can't wait to get you back to my caravan after this Pete. It's been a couple of days at least and I could really do with you. I'm going to …' He couldn't complete the sentence, as Julie shouted, from quite close by, that they were ready.

So, after another minute or two, they all emerged. A strange sight in some ways. The two guys had very brown arms and legs, but the latter only between the lines of their shorts and their socks. This left white feet and ankles, whiter areas around their tummies and chests and over much of their bodies. The look was topped-off by sun-tanned and wind-blown faces and necks.

The two women laughed at this sight. They looked much more evenly tanned, having had the chance to sunbathe around the café at times. Sue was in a simple dark red bikini and Julie a dark blue swimming costume. Julie's kit was Speedo, the same as Peter's and Steve's striped trunks. They decided to run to the water's edge, where there was a bit of a gravel beach, and then into the water as fast as possible, so as not to lose their courage.

It was the usual approach, Peter thought, of running in bravely and then warmth rapidly running out of them as the water came up their thighs and then to their waists. There was a lot of shivers, shouts, and sharp intakes of breath. Half-tripping, half plunging into the bits that were about deep enough, sitting in them and plunging heads back or forwards into the water.

There was some joshing and flicking water around at each other. They were close together in the water and Peter felt it one of the happiest moments he could ever remember. The words "halcyon days" came to him from somewhere he couldn't remember. Something he'd read or been taught maybe, that sounded appropriate in his head. It was a totally absorbing, joyous moment.

'Well, this is more like it,' said Julie. 'A bit of an adventure, more like I thought would happen up here. Hoped anyway.'

They stayed there for a half-hour or so in the end, fooling around a bit, chatting about nothing much in particular. Bits of stories of the tea shop customers from the women, with brief descriptions of deer and eagles seen, chats about some rock structures, from the two men. It felt longer for all of them. Sue stated at one point that if everyone just stayed still, they would be all right, the water would warm slightly around them. Steve laughed, unconvinced but being friendly. 'It's just if you move at all, a new bit of your body gets hit by the cold water and it feels a shock.' He said. But they all tried it anyway, keeping motionless as long as possible.

'My feet have gone completely numb. I'm getting out.' Sue was the first to give up and they all promptly followed, a bit off balance on the stony riverbed, hard stones digging into soft soles. Rather ungainly exits onto the river bank. Peter found himself gazing at Sue and the way her wet swimwear stuck to her. In the gorse bushes though, Steve grabbed him as he was trying to take off his kit, and kissed him hard on the mouth. Neither of them said anything. Peter found he was thinking of Sue as well as Steve, but responded by putting his hand onto Steve's stripes.

But when they had dried-off and were all set to go, Peter was pleased there was a short walk before they got back to the campsite. He wasn't sure he wanted to dive onto Steve's bed as soon as they got to his caravan, but he knew that was what Steve would want, and probably now expected. Peter wasn't at all sure what he felt. Two young blokes and two young women swimming together in the river, felt both natural and normal. Felt safe. Being in Steve's caravan, naked together on the bed or the floor, still didn't feel normal to him, yet it did feel very natural.

Peter realised he was hungry. He was pleased when Steve said he was ravenous. The need for food trumped the desire for anything else.

Back at the site, the swimming party broke up with happy words and friendly hugs and kisses on cheeks. Steve invited Peter to share cooking something in his caravan. 'Look Steve, I get really hungry sometimes and it makes me bad tempered or tetchy. I really am going to have to eat. You know. Before anything else.'

'I know Pete. I promise not to molest you before dinner.'

Graham was outside his tent stirring something in a pot on his Primus stove. Peter felt he wanted to be here at this moment. It would be nice to just sit down now outside his tent, chatting with Graham. He turned on his heels to go back to Steve with a change of mind, and there was Steve coming towards him with a couple of tins, as if psychic.

'Thought I would join you here. It'll be a tin of macaroni and a tin of baked beans. Quick and filling.'

The three of them eating there felt good to Peter. He felt sort-of back on track. A good day on the mapping area had been knackering, doing so much so quickly, and he had loved the swim but felt just empty of fuel. Just getting some food inside had been the right thing to do, and the company of both Graham and Steve felt good. Natural and normal were the words that came uppermost in his mind again.

CHAPTER 20

Peter found life on the campsite was changing. He had been here nearly five weeks, well over half-way. Steve was on the run-down to his departure. There was usually a queue at the washrooms now and the midges were often terrible. Peter would queue there with a T-shirt over his head, smoking a cigarette. He didn't like a smoke so early but just drawing on a fag and blowing out as much smoke as possible kept him from being too badly plagued.

One particular morning, on the way out, he caught sight of Sue waving at him from the tearoom and he ran over. 'Quick. Inside. Quickly. Shut the door. God, it's awful out there this morning', said Peter, as Sue let him in.

'I know. I can see everyone coming and going across the site from in here, people flapping arms, running, some trying to be serene – or maybe they just have good insect repellent.'

'Nobody in today then?' he said, looking around at the empty space.

'No, we are shut 'til lunchtime today. Julie's gone with her uncle to get supplies. They made an early start to get to the cash-and-carry at Inverness. Then they're hoping to get back in time for us to serve some snacks at lunchtime. Hopefully! Were you wanting something then?'

'No, its fine, I just came over cos you waved! The best thing to do today, for me, is to get as high as possible as quickly as possible. There's always a breeze up my mountain, as you know!'

'Well, call in for a cup on the way out if you like?'

'Yes please. But not if it's awkward in here with just me if you're trying to keep campers out.'

'No, silly, I meant at our caravan.'

Peter liked that thought. A cup of tea would be nice, just another chat with Sue on her own. He didn't want to delay getting more work done, still worrying about running out of time. 'I'll just run and get myself together and come straight back. If that's OK with you?'

When he returned, Peter couldn't think why he hadn't been in the caravan behind the reception hut before. His immediate reaction was the girls had got it looking really nice. Very different entrance than Steve's. A bit bigger of course, which made a difference. There were some flowers, from the site warden's garden, he assumed, lace curtains. Tidy, clean, nice smelling. He liked it.

Sue sat Peter down in the sitting area, a bit like Steve's, just more spacious. 'Do you have a bed fold down from the wall here then Sue?'

'Well there is one, but I just use the seating area as a bed, its good enough for me. I can't deal with all that fuss every evening and morning, folding up and folding down, for the best part of three months. Julie has a bed in this bit at the end, here just past the kitchen. That little door leads into a room with two bunks in it. A bit narrow but nice enough. Gives us both a bit of space from each other.'

'You two get on fine though, don't you?'

'Yeah, but you know how it is if you're together with someone all day. You just need to get away from one another a bit.' Peter thought that made a lot of sense, didn't think he would like sharing a confined space for a few weeks – better on his own any day.

Sue finished making two mugs of tea, carried them over and they sat down and looked out of the window.

'Thanks Sue. I'm sure I can see clouds of midges out there, just lurking. Waiting!'

'You're welcome to stay here Pete, but I know you're wanting to get on. Budge up, I'll sit next to you'.

Peter felt like a scruff. His tweed breeches, long woolly socks, gaiters, tattered old jumper and his field jacket. All getting a bit smelly after a month in the field, he thought. It was too awkward to wash anything but underwear, socks and shirts. The rest would have to do another two or three weeks.

Sue, on the other hand, thought Peter, looked relaxed, clean and happy. Jeans and jumper – a look that she had most days and one that just suited her so well.

'Sorry, I'm probably a bit stale smelling. It's these breeches mostly, the wool just gets a bit manky if you wear them a lot. I've only these or my shorts for on the hill though'.

'No bother Pete. You're fine'. She was studying Peter when she spoke. The caravan was very quiet.

'Come on then, a penny for them.' Said Peter.

'What?'

'A penny for your thoughts! A favourite expression of my Mum's.'

'I was just thinking we haven't spoken much since the day on your mountain and the swim. I loved both of those.'

Peter had liked them too. He had thought a lot about both. He had particularly gone over and over the discussion with Sue up the mountain. He had fantasised about the swim. Would like to do it again. Steve came into his mind then, thinking of him swimming and not wearing much. Thinking of him naked. But then thinking of how Sue looked going swimming too. A torrent of thoughts again, mostly of flesh and minimal clothing!

'Thanks again for that day out, it was really great you know. For me. I felt special. The way you looked after me.' Sue said, and now Peter felt taken aback.

'It was no trouble Sue honestly.' He paused, thinking about what to say back to Sue's comment. 'I should be thanking you really. All that stuff we talked about was helpful.'

Peter had thought about that a lot too. One consequence had been with Steve. Since the swim, he and Steve had been together just once. The two of them crowding into the tiny washing space again one morning, trying not to make any noise that gave themselves away.

Here with Sue, Peter again had a strange sense of living in two worlds at once.

'You thanked me already Pete.'

'Did I?' He couldn't think that he had.

'The kisses I would say.'

'Oh, yeah – the kisses.' He felt himself starting to get anxious about how this conversation might develop. He remembered kissing Sue well enough. After the chat they'd had, Peter remembered feeling he could have fallen comfortably into Sue's arms all afternoon, just cuddling her.

Sue was looking at him. There was nothing else to say. He leaned towards her and she met him halfway. They held a long kiss. A bit like he had been thinking. He felt he would be happy to stay just like that the rest of the morning. She didn't say anything and he wasn't sure what he should say. If should was the right word. Was she wanting him to stay, was she inviting him for more? If this went further now, would he, could he?

The usual anxieties started running faster. Contraception was the first. Being able to do it properly enough. To please her. Really please her, like he felt he should. Stuff he didn't think about at all with Steve.

Mostly, he didn't want to disappoint Sue but this meant he was no more certain what to do next, nor if it was up to him. He decided he couldn't take the lead but would go along with whatever happened.

As it turned out the moment passed and the intensity that had been about to ignite, damped down again. Instead Sue talked about the swim, the odd sun tans of him and Steve, how she also hoped they could do it again. How she would like to try the river by the drumlins and how to persuade Steve to drive them there. Peter didn't think this would happen. Steve would want him to himself.

Peter felt that letting that moment pass had maybe left Sue feeling disappointed. Maybe she had set-up the whole morning and he had let her down. He felt he had to offer something, so he said:

'You know, if you get another day off and fancy coming out on the hill with me again… well, I'd be really pleased to have your company.'

Sue looked back at him. It was that look Sue could do. Gave him the sensation again of her browsing through his mind, searching.

'Aw, thanks Pete'. She said after a moment and touched his arm. 'That would be great.' She looked away, clearly thinking something. 'This coming Sunday might be the next chance. Whatever the weather, I'll do that.'

'Well look, it might be a bit boring for you. I will have to work. I can't just show you stuff. By then, I think I will be going out on the ridge from that viewpoint pointed-out the other day, you might remember.' He thought about the practicalities.

'We will go down to the Mountain Trail car park, a couple of miles walk from here before we start a slog uphill – unless you persuade Julie's uncle to do it maybe…?' She was nodding. 'From there we go up the high point, about 1,800 feet up, the Reserve's viewpoint. But we will go north from there, back towards the valley, working downhill a bit. We can contour round then to the pony track again and back. Sound alright?'

Sue hunched her shoulders slightly, looking at him attentively. 'Whatever you say Pete. I can't visualise all that, I don't know it like you. Sounds fine though. It's a Sunday, will it be busy?'

'Busy? You must be joking, it's never going to be crowded, not like, I don't know, er, places we both know like Helvellyn or Snowdon or something. Nothing like that. On the trail itself, as it's a Sunday, there might be some visitors. Anywhere off the path though, we will have the place to ourselves.'

Sue beamed and clapped her hands excitedly. Leant forward and they had another, briefer, kiss on the lips.

CHAPTER 21

In Steve's caravan later the same day, both tired after a fairly hard day's work, battling weather, midges and high ground. Friendly but not yet passionate. Chatting, but, Peter thought, maybe not as a prelude to anything else.

'You know I only have a week and bit left Pete?'

'I know Steve. It seems like we have been up here so long.' He paused. 'You know, I will miss you.'

'Will you?' Steve looked at Peter, wanting him to say more. Willing him.

'Of course. I don't know…we didn't expect any of this did we? I think I have become fond of your company. Fond of you I suppose…' Peter looked at Steve, wondering where this conversation might go next.

'Fond of getting your end away, you mean!' joked Steve.

'As if it's just me! You're the one who's always up for it. Literally!'

That loosened what was otherwise starting to become a tense discussion.

'Will you really miss me though Pete?' Steve moved across from where he had been sitting and snuggled in beside Peter.

'Yeah, I really will. This whole thing…' Trying to find the right words, trying to be clear about how he felt. 'I never expected to do this. Ever. Let alone up here. I'll never forget what we have done. Meeting you…'

'Nor me you.' And all of a sudden Steve's face crumpled a bit and a tear slowly appeared and started to run down his cheeks. Peter found himself having the same reaction to that, biting his lower lip, trying to stop it. They leant into each other and hugged.

'I don't know what to do Steve. I'm very fond of you. I love what we've discovered together.'

They held the hug for what seemed ages. Peter's mind was

running fast through a whole load of things he felt anxious about. Steve's head was spinning too.

'You know we could be arrested!?' he eventually blurted-out. 'Neither of us is twenty-one.'

'It's not that though is it Steve. I know we have to think about that but it's about us being queer isn't it. It's saying you're queer. Being a queer! I hate the word. I just don't think of myself like that. It's just something that's happened.'

'Well, you have Penny to go back to.'

'That's not the same thing Steve. When I came here I was thinking about her all the time and now I spend half the time thinking about you.'

'And the other half, Penny still? Or is it Sue maybe?'

Peter sighed, his shoulders dropped and he turned to look out of the window. Looking to collect his thoughts. 'What I like about being around Sue is it makes me feel normal. It makes what we do, you and I, feel like a dream or something. Oh, I don't know how to talk about it Steve.' Peter reached for cigarettes and his lighter, which meant disconnecting from Steve, but he put his right arm back over Steve's shoulder and smoked with the left. 'Look, what we do feels natural on a physical level, doesn't it?' Steve nodded, listening. 'In fact, I love it! But. But it isn't normal is it? I can't tell Graham for instance, or anyone at Uni, or my Mum, or Penny, least of all Penny. Can you talk about this to anyone back home do you think?'

Steve confessed he couldn't. He hadn't been with girls much but nothing with other boys either. This had really been his first, full, sexual experience with anyone other than himself. Like Pete, long-held fantasies had become real in each other's hands and mouths.

Steve told Peter about his telephone call with Timothy. It was emotional for both of them, as Steve recounted the conversation. Peter found himself trembling. It was an incredible feeling knowing their secret had been shared with someone and the world hadn't crashed in on them.

The tears dried-up but they went on hugging for some while. Neither said anything and it felt tranquil and peaceful. Detached from the real world Peter thought. Neither of them felt in a hurry to break away from the hug nor from their reverie.

CHAPTER 22

The next morning, with the weather heavy and wet, everyone was hanging around inside the shelter of their tents. Around mid-way through the dreary morning, Graham had shouted over and offered a joint to share. Peter invited him in. The two of them sitting either end of the long yellow foam mat, heads slightly bowed because of the low inner height of the tent, the ridge just grazing the top of their heads as they sat cross-legged.

Graham was nearer the door, rolling the joint, carefully heating a corner of the resin with his lighter, and then crumbling it along the tobacco. Even Peter could tell it was good quality and it felt hot when they started to smoke it. The roach barely enough to keep the smoke cool. A small red-hot piece fell off the lit end and landed on the foam mat, melting a tiny crater for itself.

Graham was not saying much, letting it flow over him, not enough of a hit to be weird but enough to feel drifty – drifting towards a happy, untroubled state. After a chat about friends in common, the campsite and the people on it, generally talking about nothing in particular, there was a gap in the conversation until Graham suddenly said:

'Pete, are you and Sue sleeping together?' Peter wasn't surprised Graham thought he was up to something, maybe noting Peter's absences and late returns to his tent. Peter was just pleased Graham hadn't suggested it was Steve.

'No. I thought you spotted me going into her caravan the other morning though.'

'And she coming onto your mapping area the other day.'

'She's doing that again at the weekend.'

'Really!? You see Pete! No smoke without fire.'

'She's really sweet Graham. Think she could be a good friend.'

'You don't want to have your wicked way with her then?'

'I don't think so.' Peter said too quickly. But having been asked, he didn't know really if that was true.

'Pete…' Graham took a long draw on the joint, passed it across to Peter. Lifting his head to look straight into Pete's eyes, blowing out a cloud of thick smoke. His voice now tightened a little, '…do you think you could be gay?'

So, there it was. A simple question from Graham. Peter had an immediate sensation of falling, felt he had no place to hide in the cramped tent space. It felt too intimate and somewhere hard to lie. Peter found he just couldn't be, and didn't want to be, dishonest to his friend.

'Why do you say that? Because of the night I asked you for a hug?'

'Yeah, of course, that's part of it. You see, I've never asked to have a night-time cuddle with another guy. Not in the way you asked me!' He said this in a very matter-of-fact voice, no drama.

Silence followed and another to and fro of the joint, now nearly finished. 'I'm not bothered, by the way', continued Graham. 'If you are I mean. It makes no difference to me. I'm not. But I wondered if you might be?'

Graham turned around and stubbed out the joint in the ground in front of Peter's tent.

'That was a great joint Graham. Thank you.'

'Ta. What about Steve then, do you think he could be gay?'

Peter felt himself blush. He couldn't control it and wondered if this was a conversation in the abstract or Graham being perceptive, maybe having planned this all along. Peter felt his defences were completely down. He had always thought of Graham as being quietly observant. Seeing everything, saying little – or keeping his observations to himself. He felt for a moment he couldn't breathe and the air in the little tent had been sucked-out somehow. Then he started to feel embarrassed, conscious of how much he must be blushing, making it worse.

Graham just had his head to one side, knees drawn up, arm and elbow on one knee and that hand holding the side of his head.

After what seemed an eternity. 'I don't think so Graham. Why do you say that! No. I mean. Oh, I don't know I suppose.'

Graham responded quickly. 'You see Pete. I think you are. I also think Steve is. And I think you two know this well enough'.

Peter found himself feeling completely exposed, as if he was naked. He also found his hands were shaking. He assumed Graham knew exactly what had been happening between him and Steve.

Graham continued, 'Do you think Penny knows?'

'Look Graham. I'm not sure what you are on about really. I don't think it would occur to her to think about anything like that. None of us knows anyone gay, do we? It just doesn't happen, does it? I'm not sure what being gay means.'

Graham continued looking, more gently now at Peter, still in the same position, being very still. Unmoving.

'Pete. Come on man. It's just me here, Graham. And you.' And Graham said this very quietly, no fuss. 'Pete, don't beat yourself up.' He continued. 'You are who you are I reckon. You're not going to get a second shot at it. Life, I mean. You need to be yourself'.

And suddenly Peter felt overwhelmed. "You are who you are" he thought. Peter felt an uncontrollable need to bite his lower lip. The power of having to confront truth in this way, this surprisingly gentle way he felt completely unprepared for. He couldn't stop a tear forming and rolling down his cheek and he turned away. Graham leant forward and wrapped his arms round him.

'Hey man, whoa – there's no need for that. Jesus, I didn't want you to do that.'

Peter sighed and allowed himself to just fall forward and be supported by Graham's arms, that felt surprisingly strong. Reassuring really. Eventually he pulled away again, snuffling a little.

'Sorry Graham…I'm just being a prat.'

'Shh. Shut up Pete, you don't need to say anything. Take it easy man. Relax. Come on. It's a beautiful world and all that! All those things people are supposed to say to one another when they a bit stoned.'

'So, you know Graham, don't you? You've seen Steve and me or something? We thought we were being so careful.'

'Pete, what I've seen or not, it doesn't matter. I like you as a mate. Come on, shall we change the subject? Have another puff maybe… or what?'

Peter sighed. 'Do you fancy a little walk or something Graham?'

'Pub?'

'Yeah,' said Peter, suddenly finding himself cheering-up. 'Now there's a good idea!'

Jock was surprised to see them. Although they had been in the pub pretty well every evening for more than a month, this was the first daytime visit. The pub had only just opened at midday and there was no one else in there. They were rewarded by the affable barman with two pints of Seventy-Shilling, on the house. Peter took a gulp and found the effect relaxing and calming. The three of them chatted at the bar for a bit. Talked about the oil platform workers. According to Jock the guys were raking it in but they were getting fed-up. It was hard work, three weeks on and a week off.

'Jock,' Peter asked when there was a dip in the conversation. 'Is it quiet round the other side just now? Can I take Graham through for a quick look? I'd like to show him some of those photos on the wall, if you don't mind, please?"

'It's no bother lads. You're not exactly barred from the lounge bar you know. But you know how it is if we have folks staying in the hotel and wanting a bit more peace and quiet. I doubt there's anyone there right now. Go on, help yourselves.' And he shook his thumb in the direction of the door from the bar into the main body of the hotel.

'Come on Graham. It seems a while since I was in here with the Warden and Steve, but there's something you might find interesting'.

They wandered into what was the back of the hotel's reception area, a staircase leading up to the rooms, with a heavy dark wooden bannister rail. The reception desk was in the same wood and either side were doors to the lounge bar and to the guests' lounge, which was where the photographs were located. There was nobody around at all, neither staff nor residents.

Graham had only been in the lounge bar and so was surprised at the feel of the guest area. He thought it was quite baronial. Peter was explaining a bit more about the supposed plane wreck, the man from Gairloch and so on. They were looking at the photos. Graham was interested in the reaction of the wartime expert and both of them talked about how the discovery of the plane seemed so long ago, yet was only a few weeks.

'I think the whole experience up here has been very different to what I expected', commented Graham. 'The geology isn't as interesting, on my bit anyway, but it's been OK, doing it. But all the other things, you know…This pub, the girls, this plane thing, the van in the ditch. It's not been boring!'

Peter was surprised at this as he had thought Graham had actually seemed bored quite often. Again, it made Peter realise how much he had come to understand with Graham as a guy simply content with his own company and spending hours on the campsite.

Peter talked about the day with John MacKenzie and Donald Fraser and the way in which he, and Sue too, had been really surprised at how impactful the war had been up here, even though it was far removed physically from the main areas of wartime action. He told Graham about her questions and what it had revealed.

While chatting, the two of them were also browsing the photographs. Peter felt himself drawn in to the photo of the crew of the plane that crashed on Beinn Eighe – the wreck in Corrie Mhic Fhercair. The four crew looked more familiar than the other pictures, more connected with him somehow. It seemed to him as if a lot had happened since he last stood here. He looked at the faces of the air crew and peered at the faint writing underneath. He could see better now in daylight, not really remembering being able to read the names properly on that first evening. The names on the print were given as Wilson, Carmichael, Williams and McKay. Peter felt his blood run cold and a shiver run down his backbone. He thought for a second he was going to fall into the photograph and the wall.

'You OK Pete?', said Graham, grabbing his friend's arm. Thought you were fainting or something there for a second. You OK mate? You look like you've just seen a ghost!'

Peter shook his head, looked around him, around the room and then back to Graham. 'Yeah, I think I have Graham. Exactly that!'

Chapter 23

The Sunday arrived, Peter's last weekend but one. Not that the weekends or weekdays had been that distinct, for the fieldwork anyway. It was more just remembering the village shop would be closed and the pub had different times. Life for the geologists, and indeed for most of the campers, seemed the same one day to the next.

Sue's second visit brought with it a much better day, thought Peter. It was sunny on and off and the gentle southerly wind was warm again. He was pleased he could be in his cord shorts. Tattered as they were, they felt fresher than the musty breeches. When he met with her at their caravan, he found Sue had got shorts on today too. Cut-off denim and a pink T-shirt with a red dragon on it, replacing the kilt and wool of the first time.

Best of all, Julie's uncle gave them a lift down the road. Julie too, but she stayed in the car with her uncle as they returned to Kinlochewe. When they got out of the car though, Peter was thanking Ben, when he overheard quite clearly Julie whisper, good humouredly, to Sue, "Don't do anything I wouldn't do!" Sue had just laughed and shrugged it off.

There were some other people out walking on the trail. It was a friendly sort-of start to the day. Everyone saying "hi" and "good morning" to everyone else. Peter again was surprised at how fit Sue was, and the two of them passed people at various points all the way up to the viewpoint, both of them enjoying going at a pace and feeling good about it.

An hour later and Peter and Sue were finally on the viewpoint itself. The fastest he had got to this point and he had Sue to thank for that. She was just taking in the view, especially north to the looming mass of Slioch. 'We will have that in front of us the rest of the day,' said Peter. 'I never get bored with it. Also the eagles hunt sometimes over the bit where we will be, so fingers crossed'.

'That sounds great Pete. Just coming up here was pretty spectacular – all those Scots Pines and that red squirrel. We're lucky aren't we!?'

'What? To see the squirrel, yes I agree. It'll be disappointing if we don't get the eagles over. It's happened most days and when I first saw them I was knocked-out by it but now they are daily company.' Peter thought he was talking too much, but was aware he was a bit on edge about the day. He'd been looking forward to it but wondered how the two of them would get on this time.

'That's what I really meant by being lucky,' said Sue. 'Just having this experience. Having this summer. So very different...for me anyway.'

They headed off across the rocks, heading east. Sue commented on the amount of rock and Peter explained that the degree of exposure around this part had been the main issue for him. There had been so many outcrops to examine, he explained, that it took a lot of time.

'When we get to one I haven't done yet, I'll show you what we do, if you like. It's not compulsory though!'

'Well, what is this rock Pete – it looks really hard and whiteish, sort of shiny at times. Is it the quartzite?'

'It's all quartzite. It's about five hundred million years old', he answered. 'Would you like geology lesson one!? Just the one maybe – the first and last lesson of the day?'

'Go on then', said Sue. And while heading out and slightly downhill Peter explained the sequence of rocks and their ages. They had gone a good half-mile or more before he finished.

'And if it's really going to be a lesson, you now have to give me a summary back!' Peter said.

'And if I don't, will you put me in detention or something? I wouldn't mind being stuck up here for an hour after school any time.' They both laughed.

'Go on then Sue'

'Oh bloody hell, are you serious!? Ah, alright then. I can't remember all the names but roughly. OK? First there were some rocks formed billions of years ago and there might have been mountains then too. Billions is right isn't it!? Jesus, billions! That's the rocks we see over the other side, where your plane and the fault is. All those lochans we walked past with Mr MacKenzie and his friend. All those wet bogs, are on the oldest stuff'. She got a nod and broad smile from Peter and so she continued.

'Can't get my head round it. The concept of deep time. Anyway, then, just several hundreds of millions of years ago, there was a huge mountain range out to the east. All this sandstone was washed off those mountains. Then more millions of years, it was all under the sea. Another big mountain range was formed across Scotland, Greenland, North America? The formation of those mountains pushed huge parts of the Earth's crust on top of other bits. Then more millions and millions of years it was all above ground and the Ice Age shaped it into the landscape we see now. How's that?"

'Brilliant Sue.' Peter beamed at her and clapped. 'You go to the top of the class without a doubt.' And they both laughed again. 'Sorry, I didn't mean to be like teacher,' added Peter.

'You're not like any teacher I've had Pete.'

'Good, I didn't want to be coming over like that.'

'I just meant you're better looking than them Pete!' And Sue looked at him. He turned to her, studied her face a moment and decided not to say anything. He changed the subject back to rocks.

'Here's something interesting to see Sue. This rock here in front of us, the other side of this dip we're heading down. Can you see how the side of the hill is bright green? Different plants and vegetation to the rest of the slope give it that distinct bright colour.' They'd stopped to look at what Peter was pointing-out. Sue nodded.

'Well, that's because its limestone under there. There's not much of it around here, but I can tell where it is by these bright green swards. And that, which I found out in my first days up here, has saved me a lot of leg work! I can thank my supervisor for that actually – he told me.'

'I love the way you talk Pete', Sue said after a moment. 'You see things I wouldn't notice. You're not show-offy about it, you just like sharing what you know. I like that.'

'Anyway.' Said Peter, not really knowing what to say back to Sue. 'We're heading off across this bright green bit and then all the area to our right as we look, to the east, from this level down to about fourteen hundred feet, is the bit I have to examine most today. It's the last real gap on my map.'

'So what will you do? Exactly?'

'I'll just go from one outcrop of rock to another. Identify the rock, see what it is, if I can, and measure the angle of it and any structure. That sort of thing. I make an entry on the map then, and in the notebook. Then move onto the next. To start with, there are loads, as you can see, and I don't know after that. We can't go too far north, below fourteen hundred feet there's cliffs and then the forested part of the reserve.' Peter remembered being at that part of the forest with Steve one day, behind a massive boulder, with no clothes on. He tried to dismiss the memory, but it lingered.

They set-off and for a couple of hours they worked in a progressive way, moving from one rock location to another. Peter worked as fast as he had ever done, worrying about Sue getting bored. Working east though, they reached an area with an even greater concentration of outcrops and Peter decided the best thing was to set-up Sue somewhere she could read, snooze or whatever she wanted to do, while he worked round in a quadrant to cover all the outcrops. Peter realised it would be helpful having Sue at the centre, a point he could return to and use as a fulcrum. He also thought to himself that it would be a bonus to be able to catch views of her while he worked.

Really, he just would have preferred to sit with her and enjoy the place, the views, the sun, her company. This had been a good day so far and he felt his initial nervousness had now been replaced by a great sense of calm just being in her company. He couldn't help thinking she looked good too, particularly when she clambered over boulders and rocks with him.

Sue said she was really happy with the idea of staying-put in one place for a while though, just enjoying a book and the intermittent sun. She told Peter she was reading Narziss and Goldmund by Herman Hesse, something he had read too. They shared some nuts, cheese and water and chatted about the two main characters in the book. They both liked it and agreed there was something really thought-provoking about the idea of two lives being so close initially and then diverging over time.

Peter reminded her of the story of the four guys coming by when he had been near here previously. She listened and told him she felt intrigued by the story. Especially the fact the men had used the same names as the photo in the hotel. When he finished the story he went to get some more water.

'Pete,' Sue said when he returned. 'It's like your aircraft, isn't it? It's not myth and magic! You don't believe in superstition and the supernatural do you? And neither do I.'

Peter waited, wondering what Sue was going to say next.

'I think the first time you went in the hotel you must have seen those names, even if you think you didn't. Your eyes saw the words and they slipped into your mind. Then up here that day you fell asleep and had a dream. A very lucid one, that felt very real.'

Peter considered this and thought there was a probable truth in it. They both sat quietly for a few minutes.

'It's that sort of place though isn't it.' Peter said finally. 'It feels like a dream today, being here. Right now.'

'Look', Sue said, 'From the way you said that, I can tell you want to just hang about here but if you do that, I will feel really bad. The deal was, I would come with you today but you would definitely get some work done.' She had her hands on her knees, hair down and over her shoulders, a nice smile on her face. 'Go on. Shoo. Do your quadrant thing. Please.'

'Do you know?' Peter said, in a teasing way, 'You have really picked up a tan the last few weeks, since I first saw you?'

'Pete! Bugger off.' She gave him a playful shove. 'Go on, stop prevaricating.'

So, he went around. The resting spot was in the centre of the quadrant, so he could return to it every half-hour or so as he worked systematically round the outcrops, working as quickly as possible. He wanted to get it over with but there was a lot of it. He would have much preferred chatting to Sue than doing clinometer readings, he thought, each time he measured a dip, but he had to do this now as he wouldn't have time to come to this part again.

And he knew in himself, how it would be good to have completed the geographical range of his work – the bits he could reach anyway. In between thoughts about the rocks, he thought again how it felt today, to be with Sue. And then each time he looked north, he thought of Steve, just a few miles away as the crow flies. Time was running out for Steve up here, thought Peter. What's going to happen to us? He found it hard to connect his thoughts.

When he was nearly done, he sat on a small boulder to complete some notes in his book. He looked-up and saw Sue, lying back a bit in the lee of the large rock they had selected as the resting point. Looking at her, it felt like he used to feel in the sixth form at school, and in his first year at university, before getting involved with Penny. He used to hang around with a mix of male and female friends, people just being comfortable together.

A memory came to him of a concert at that time at the Kursaal in Southend, 10CC. It had been a daytrip leading into the night. He could see in his mind a group of them swaying along to 'I'm Not in Love', with his arms around Bobbie and Tony's arm on his shoulder. Chris there, arms around Sarah. Yes, he thought, that's me. This memory was suddenly so clear to him and he wondered what had happened to those friends and to that easy feeling of those days. The recent chats with Steve and Graham had left him feeling a bit lost. Today just felt so normal again, it was nice. He thought if people had watched them today, they would have assumed that Sue and he were girlfriend and boyfriend.

That prompted the thought, was Sue becoming his girlfriend? Was she interested in that idea? He looked across at her. I have no idea where this friendship is going, he thought. That made him think of Steve again. He knew that later on, Steve would ask him about today. Steve would want to know how it went. He would be sure to want to know if 'anything happened' with Sue. Nothing had, but he felt drawn to the idea of talking with Steve about it, whatever happened.

Just thinking this, he imagined the discussion with Steve, propped up close together on the narrow caravan sofa. Naked, probably. He should be thinking of the geology, which was not making any sense at all. Instead he was thinking of sex, and it wasn't making much sense either.

The resting area was sheltered, warm and occasionally sunny. There was some shade though, from the size of the rock. When Peter had finished his rapid piece of work he was thirsty and ran back the last few hundred yards to sit there with Sue drinking the fresh water from the nearby spring. She had rolled her eyes at his attempt to explain the reason for the springs along the line of one rock on top of another type.

She had taken off her T-shirt and was now wearing just a vest and her shorts. And great boots too he noticed. They were an Alpine brand, she told him. He felt envious of them and wondered how much they would cost and whether he could afford some. He thought he probably could as he didn't have Sue down as particularly well-off. He thought she was more like him and Graham in that respect.

All in all, Peter thought Sue just looked really good like that. Outdoorsy, fit, slim, attractive. She was half-lying back, relaxed, legs stretched out. A look Peter had seen, and admired, at the tearoom area more than once.

'It's alright for some isn't it!?'

'You've said that before! It is a day off you know!' Sue said.

'Nothing to do with me Sue. You do what you want! You look good like that. Distracts me from my work though, every time I look back this way I could see you relaxing.' he laughed. He got out a packet of cigarettes, offered her one.

She turned on her side, towards him. 'That's nice Pete.' Then after a pause, while he was drinking more water, 'I have been watching you too, you're a bit like a goat again – hopping around from rock to rock. Nice watching you too.' She took a cigarette, let him light it for her. 'It's nice you were looking back at me'. She took a drag on the cigarette, puffed it out in a big cloud. 'I thought you maybe weren't so interested?'

He paused now, drinking some water. Her comment made him think this was another one of those moments where something could happen, but he wasn't sure what. He wasn't sure what he wanted to think. He thought of Sue back on the campsite a few days back.

'You mean when I had tea with you the other morning.'

'Yes. Then. I've been thinking about it when I dozed-off and lost track of what Goldmund was up to!' And she smiled. 'I thought maybe you thought I was trying to get you to stay with me that morning.'

'Well. Were you?' Peter studied her, shielding his eyes as he looked at her. He had thought exactly that, at the time. 'I thought you might have been disappointed with me, that I didn't stay'.

'Maybe Pete. I didn't mind that though. I'm not sure what I wanted that morning particularly, it was odd being there without Jules around. I wanted to chat to you that day though, wanted to figure you out a bit more. Know a bit more about you.' She looked at Peter who now had his hand over his mouth, looking straight at her and looking like he was concentrating hard. She continued, 'I actually can understand you a bit now I think, but I don't know if you want to …I don't know. Look, I think you wonder if I'm trying to make you a boyfriend and you are already involved with someone else?'

Peter had wondered exactly that. 'Well, is that what you would like?'

Sue didn't answer directly. 'Like we've talked about. I'm not involved with anyone. But, you are. I don't want to try and be a girlfriend to someone who already has one, but you have given me signals of interest! And I've probably done the same back, to be honest.' She was sitting up now and Peter sat down on an adjacent rock, so he could see her more clearly. His legs just felt a bit weary too. 'Like when?' He asked.

'Like…when we kissed!?' She looked to Peter for confirmation and he nodded, now looking at the ground but listening. A pose Sue found familiar.

'So, when we did that. I should say, when we do that. Well, then, I feel something special with you. The first time, up here when you were telling me about your life.'

'Oh God, sorry, did it feel like that! Didn't mean it to be like an episode of This Is Your Life.' He looked up now to check she wasn't looking fed-up with him or something. But she just laughed a bit.

'That's a dreadful programme isn't it! No, it wasn't like that. You weren't like that. I wasn't bored, I was really interested. I hadn't really ever had a talk like that with a boy before.'

'A boy?' Peter asked.

'Just a figure of speech. Man then. But I think of myself as a girl still you know. We're not exactly grown-ups are we?' She looked at Peter, reached across and touched his face.

'Oh, you mean me not needing to shave much!' Peter said.

'Oo, who's being sensitive today then!?' And she deliberately touched and stroked his chin. He smiled.

'Only joking. I don't know why I'm not hairier. Would like to be.'

'Oh no, you look nice smooth! Jules says that all the time'

'Do you two spend all day discussing the men on the campsite then!' Peter said in a tone of mock outrage.

'Well, now you ask'. Sue said, sitting up straight and acting assertively. 'Pretty much, Yes!' Sue laughed a bit then and Peter joined in.

'Some of the blokes on the campsite maybe don't get a lot of attention from you two, I guess?'

'No, you're dead right there. Jules gives marks out of ten! A lot get pretty low marks.' And she giggled. 'Not you though.' She paused. 'Anyway, I meant, we are still kids aren't we? I feel like that anyway.'

She drew her legs up, wrapped her arms round them and rested her head on her knees. Peter thought she did look a bit like a younger girl then, sitting like that. Sue continued, 'I mean, we are not like our parents, or teachers or the lecturers at uni, are we?' She then looked a bit wistful, Peter thought, as she looked out to the northern horizon. 'Maybe you become older when you start work!'

'Well, we do work don't we!' Peter said. 'A bit anyway. You and me, Graham, we have to work or we'd be broke. I'm going back to work in the pub after this, and you're working up here.'

'Maybe. When I'm not up here interfering with your studies though eh?' Said Sue.

'Don't be daft. It's been good today – I've really liked it.' He paused, thinking of how the day had gone and how the rest of it might still go. 'Anyway, what I meant is, there's some people at my uni have never done anything, just live off their parents.' He knew he sounded resentful, but at that moment, he was feeling that. 'I feel older than them – so, yeah, that is what work does maybe.'

'Yeah, me too Pete – we have those types too, still tied to Mummy and Daddy and their cheques!'

They looked out then, something had caught their attention at the same time. Rising into view, loftily soaring across the rocks, not a beat to its wings, was a golden eagle. 'Wow,' Sue said softly. They watched it move across their field of view from the hollow they were sat in and it disappeared somewhere behind them.

'As I said'. Peter remarked. 'They're up here all the time. It's incredible really – something else I never ever expected.' They were lost in thoughts then for a moment.

Sue broke the silence. 'I kissed you that day because you were so honest Peter, and you seemed…I don't know, like you needed a cuddle.' She was looking at Peter now but his attention was turned to the ground again now, thinking and listening. 'Deserved one.' She smiled at Peter, which he didn't see, and gave a slight sigh.

'That day though, when we kissed a couple more times, that felt pretty special. I've not kissed many boys. Sorry, men! You know, in the sixth form, it's like a game…see how many people you can snog down the pub at Christmas. Did you do that?'

'Yeah, of course. It was a thing at the time. Haven't done that since being at Uni though'. Said Peter.

'Each time we've kissed Pete, I think it ends when it does because it has to. I don't know if it's you or me stops it? I'm having this

208

moment with you and suddenly it's on the point of running out of control, but you won't let it. Or I won't!' Sue looked at Peter for confirmation but he was still looking at the ground, clearly concentrating and just nodding a couple of times.

That was true Peter thought and he didn't know the answer to Sue's question either.

'Well, there's two of us doing the kiss Sue, it's not just me. And not just you.' Right now though, Peter thought, right now, Sue is offering an escape from the discussions with Steve and Graham. He had felt exactly what Sue described. He could feel that kissing her had been on the point of becoming overwhelming and now he knew he wanted, and needed, that feeling again.

So, when he lifted his head this time, looked across at Sue, it felt like the unstoppable was already underway. He leaned forward now, and she leaned to him, across the rock to kiss. This time, he knew he wouldn't be able to stop it, unless she did.

She didn't.

They kissed at first awkwardly, the conversation they had been having still getting in the way a bit. Plus they both were aware of suddenly finding themselves perched on the edge of rocks leaning across to each other at an awkward angle, and the rock was hard.

'Come on'. Pete said gently. 'Let's just edge down onto the grass a bit. The ground's softer than this boulder.' And that's where the second, longer kiss took place, alongside an outcrop of tightly folded quartzite, on ground of shallow heather and small tussocks of grass. This time, they laid down, Sue on her back with her arms round Peter and his right arm around her upper body, his left behind her head. Their lips moved over and around each other's mouths. Peter leaned back, to see her face, there was the briefest hesitations as their gaze held on each other. 'OK Sue?' he asked.

In answer, she put her hand around his head and pulled his face back on to hers. By the third kiss they were entering that moment of oblivion they both knew was there, and that they had previously held back from.

Their tongues met, their arms around each other tightened and they both felt a huge rush, like a tremendous high, a surge of energy flowing from their lips throughout their bodies, and especially to the areas which both of them now fondled earnestly.

In moments, still lips sealed on each other, they were undoing the buttons and zips of their shorts simultaneously, hands delving inside. Peter fought hard to not let himself go immediately. That moment passed and was replaced by a strength of desire, an urgency he needed to sort quickly. They were exploring each other in fast-forward and it felt overwhelming to both of them.

'Pete...'

'I know, I just realised we need to get our boots off too!' said Peter.

This wasn't what Sue had meant and she didn't know how to say something really important to her. Peter was almost tearing at his boots to get them off, and she decided she wanted to do that too. Both were leaning forward now, naked from the waist up, other clothes in a bit of disarray. They were both tugging at their bootlaces, pulling at their socks. They paused and looked at each other, Sue had her hand over her mouth trying to suppress her giggles. Peter saw this and they both let out a laugh and held each other gently. Another quick kiss.

'Sodding boots' said Peter. 'Not the easiest things to get off in a hurry are they?'

They were both now side by side, boots and socks scattered on the ground at their feet. They looked at each other again, Peter with his hands on the top of his shorts and underpants. Then he pushed his shorts down and off, onto the ground near his boots. He felt a bit embarrassed. Sue did the same and he thought she looked a little embarrassed too.

'We're both in red pants Sue. What did that stand for?' He could have kicked himself for feeling the need to say something, just to cover his nervousness.

'Ahh, now that would be fire I think.' Sue said. 'Oh, but you liked the ones with robins on didn't you, I should have worn those… well?'

'I think you look good like that Sue. I think we're both hesitating, talking about them, when they actually just need to come off, yeah?'

'Come on then', she said, hooking her thumbs in the fabric. He did the same, and then they were naked. Peter found himself needing to say something else, but realising it might be better just shutting-up, but nerves still getting the better of him.

'Your hair. Down there. It looks like fur a bit.' He said.

'You say some funny things Pete…it's sweet.' Sue put her hand on his cheek, looking at him expectantly, then becoming very, very still as he moved his hand down over the flat of her abdomen.

They both settled, and Sue put her arms round his shoulders.

'Pete I need to tell you something.' She whispered.

'It's OK Sue, I can guess.'

'I've never got on the pill' Sue confirmed. 'What about you and your rucksack full of so many useful things?' She was asking, but also slightly teasing him he could see.

'No Sue! Didn't think about that. It ought to be in my first aid kit next time!' They both smiled, he hoped it didn't look like a smirk. She gently bit her lip, searching his eyes, checking all was well. He was actually happy about it. He didn't want to disappoint her. That was the main thing he was feeling. Some concerns evaporated and he felt the better for it.

'It doesn't matter Sue'. And it really didn't to him. He wasn't uncomfortable, felt that it helped him. He was on new ground with Sue and wanted to do whatever he could with her, but at the moment it didn't matter what. And to prove that, he fondled and kissed her intimately. Kissed her and held his mouth and tongue to her.

'Sue – just slip your legs over my shoulders'.

After what seemed a short time to Peter, Sue just arched her back, making a shallow bow out of her body as if in a spasm, but she stayed there quite a long time and then slowly let her back drop down to the ground. She was nearly silent although he could hear her deep and steady breathing, even with the wind riffling across the rocks and through the grass.

Still gently caressing her with his right hand, he brought his head up to kiss her. Another kiss that went on a long time.

Putting her head back to see him, Sue smiled. Their mouths wet and glistening a little. He didn't say anything, just kissed her again. Their arms enveloped each other strongly again.

'What should I do with this then?' said Sue teasingly, moving her arm. She had him in her hand and he was already feeling lost to the world. He gave into the moment, the feeling of so easily being transported to another place. Felt like he was uplifted, soaring. She pushed him onto his back, and she put her mouth over him. He had a thought of saying something, asking a question, a question he felt he should ask. Didn't know how to, didn't really want to. But then it was too late anyway. For a few intense seconds, he was absolutely certain he had blacked-out. She stayed there a few moments and then eventually brought her face back to his.

They looked at each other for a long time. Peter felt a tinge of guilt as well as happiness. Wasn't sure if the guilt was about Steve or just what he had let happen. Still thinking a little that he should have asked first.

'I've never done that before.' Sue said. 'Not right to the conclusion! Didn't know what to expect.' And she gave Pete a slightly questioning grin.

Peter didn't know what to say, so he just looked back at her.

There was a peaceful silence again, just the light wind still blowing now and then across the rocks and grasses. Eventually he just said, 'Thank you.' And they smiled back at each other.

Sue rolled onto her back. 'Jesus Pete'. She let out a sigh, more a blow of air, as if clearing-out her lungs. Peter, on his back, was just looking at some clouds drifting over. Just the pure, physical delight was like a high, difficult to come down from. He was now thinking of the same feeling he had with Steve so recently. First time a woman had done that to him, right to the end. First time a guy had done anything to him at all. Peter just wondered about the physicality of it all. Here he was in the remote Highlands having experiences, bringing fantasies into reality, that just all felt natural and good.

'So...'

'What? I don't think I'm ready to move Pete.'

'Nor me Sue. We don't have to.' And Pete felt happy to be beside her. They reached out and felt for each other's hand. To be naked on the mountainside. He had a feeling of calm. Of completeness. After some minutes, he had a thought and made a suggestion.

'Well, I wondered... Just when I was doing my quadrant, I saw there was a tiny lochan, about a hundred yards away. What do you reckon?'

'Can we go there like this?'

'Of course! Don't see why not.'

In the end, after a bit of faffing about, they decided the easiest thing was to ram everything in their sacks, slip on the boots and socks loosely and walk like that. Peter thought it looked and felt a bit ridiculous, but he didn't really care and it didn't look to him as if Sue cared much either.

It was a little further than he said. Peter thought that in bad visibility, one could get completely lost here. They were in the middle of a huge rock encrusted hillside, gently but steadily dropping down to the road, eventually, some distance away. There were no trees, just hundreds of hummocky outcrops of rock, small bands of low cliffs, boulders. Peter wondered if anyone out on the mountain could see them. He doubted anyone was around – couldn't imagine anyone wanting to stray from the obvious path, which was some way from them.

They headed south a little towards the Allt-an Leacach stream. On the way they kept glancing at each other and giggling at their stark nakedness except for big boots. Just to the east of the stream suddenly emerged a more level area and the lochan Peter had spotted earlier.

One side was a bit boggy but the other had a bit of a sandy edge to it. It was definitely breezy here and there didn't seem to be any insects to trouble them. Much more at ease with each other now, the palaver of taking-off boots felt easy. They walked into the quickly deepening water, holding hands at first until Peter slipped and almost fell in backwards. 'Might as well do that anyway' he said, and allowed himself to plunge backwards. Sue followed suit. They lay back long enough to feel the silky feel of the water and soon after, to feel the penetrating cold.

'Your theory Sue! Not working, again!'

'No, it is Pete, you just have to keep very still. It is cold, but it has that wow feeling doesn't it. It's what I imagined.'

Peter nodded. He just felt pleased she wasn't disappointed, with the swim, with the whole day, with everything they have done. Not disappointed with him, he hoped. Neither of them said much, just allowed themselves to be there.

Sue scrambled out first. Ran to her rucksack and produced a towel with a flourish. 'Look what I brought! Good girl guide and all that.'

They shared the towel and dried each other. It felt arousing for them both and they kissed and fondled each other, standing up in the wide open landscape. By unspoken agreement, they stopped themselves repeating what they did earlier and got dressed again, taking their time.

'That book I'm reading' said Sue, 'you've read it too you said.' Peter nodded at her. 'Well, Goldmund's like us, like you? I could imagine him doing this in the wilds with a woman he's come across.'

'I know the stuff you mean. I liked that book a lot. But he's a bit crazy, does things, you know, a bit recklessly? Anyway, you're not a woman I happened to come across, for instance!?'

'I know Pete. You have bits of both the characters, me too although I'm a girl. I guess that's what it's about? Come on, we can chat about that more on the way back.'

Setting off for the return walk, Peter decided he had pretty well finished the mapping he could do, and the whole surface geology. He felt pleased that after a lot of worry, he had covered the ground. Now all he had to do was decipher it, figure out the three-dimensional picture. It had been a good day for him he felt, in so many different ways.

He took Sue's hand when they walked away from the lochan and they stayed like that all the way down the Pony Track. They passed only two other people, the only ones they had seen for hours. They were a middle-aged couple and they all stopped for a brief chat. While they were doing that, Peter found himself feeling inexplicably proud of Sue being beside him, hand-in-hand.

Later, on the road and nearly back to the campsite, Peter asked if Sue was going to tell Julie what they had done. As soon as he asked, he wondered why he had said it? Was it a daft question? Why did it matter to him? What answer would he prefer?

'Jules is amazed something didn't happen between us the other morning. I told her not to judge people by her own standards!' Laughing. 'Joking really. In truth, she's not so different to me. She reminded me we are all together up here, thrown together by chance and it might be what they call a holiday romance. Even though I, we actually, you included, are not really on holiday.'

'Felt like it up there though Sue. I could happily spend the rest of the field trip having days like this one'.

'Could you?' she asked. 'Do I get a say in it?' Joshing with him now. 'Anyway, what about you? Are you going to tell the boys all about it?'

'Do you think I would?' Peter found himself sounding more serious than he intended.

'No, not really Pete. Think you're much more likely to keep it to yourself. But...' turning to him in the road, just a hundred yards from the village now, no traffic to concern them, '...I hope it means something to you. Something special. It does to me anyway.' And she took him into her arms and they held another long kiss, right there, in the middle of the road.

Chapter 24

Peter was aware that in Steve's last week, everything to do with his fieldwork became full on. He knew Steve was working fast now to cover the remaining parts of the mapping area and to revisit and check locations and make sure he understood connections between the various parts of geology. The evenings were spent with maps out in the caravan and several sheets of paper held together by sticky tape containing long sketchy maps and cross sections of the geography and geology that Steve was determining from several different transects.

In fact, all the geologists were rushing now to complete their field assignments before the deer culls got under way in early August, and many of the mountains would become inaccessible to them. Even near the nature reserve, there would be shooting in some parts, affecting Peter's freedom to roam that he enjoyed for the last five and a half weeks.

The sense of everything coming to an end was felt in a variety of different ways. For one, Peter had run out of money. With just under a fortnight left, he didn't have enough to cover food or the train fare home, let alone drink and cigarettes. Having written a rather obsequious, he considered, letter to the bank manager, practically begging for some cash, he received a reply one morning.

Lloyds Bank Ltd.
The Triangle
Bristol, Avon.

Dear Peter.

I hope you don't mind the informality of using your Christian name.

I have received your letter of 24th July, and I will be pleased to help you. I don't get many letters from hard-pressed students outside of term time but please be assured you are not the first!

There is no problem providing an extension to your overdraft until your grant arrives at the start of next term. The sum of £25 (twenty-five pounds) is available to you at the counter of the nearest bank to you by presenting this letter to the cashier at the counter.

This bank is a branch of The Bank of Scotland and is located in Gairloch. I hope it is not too far for you to travel – we had to look it up on a map in the office here! We found Kinlochewe too. It all seems a long way from here.

Good luck with your studies.

Yours sincerely

Signed by the manager too, noticed Peter. Relieved he had been given five quid more than he asked for. It was a worry out of the way. He went straight over the shop. Pam wasn't there but the Postmaster was on duty. He had just opened and nobody else was in. Peter always found him to be a bit dour but he had come to like the little shop and he had become very familiar with their stock of tinned, dried and occasional fresh food. Recently he had started to wonder what he would have done if it hadn't been there.

The postmaster advised about the postbus and gave Peter the

times, and he didn't make Peter feel foolish when he had asked where to catch the bus.

Peter had invited Graham to come to Gairloch the next day and he had known the offer would be accepted. "Anything to avoid another day traipsing through bog and heather", as he put it. So, the two of them were outside the Post Office and Shop the next morning. They had their first cigarettes of the day waiting there and chatting to a couple from the Netherlands who were working their way around Scotland. The bus took ages but cost virtually nothing and they all learned a lot from each about the obvious differences in landscape of the two countries.

As it turned-out, the Bank was on the edge of the town, which itself was in two or three parts, or settlements, gathered together here and there it appeared, around a wide bay. So after getting his money and Peter feeling flush again, the two of them walked around the little cliffs and beaches into what seemed to be the centre.

The beach along the way and the views out to sea looked amazing to both of them. Having spent so many weeks in the mountains and deep glens around Kinlochewe, everything suddenly felt very level and expansive. The horizon stretched before them, out across the sea. Peter could see houses, singular ones and others clumped together, scattered over the land to the north and west. He wondered where Donald Fraser lived and what it would be like for anyone to live here and to have been brought-up here. What would it have felt like being here in the War?

They found a tearoom and decided to have a cup of tea and another cigarette before returning. They were sitting at a little table beside the main door, placed there for days good enough to sit outside, like now.

A family passed by and, hearing them talking, stopped for a moment.

'You two don't sound local.' The father, as Peter assumed, spoke to them. Friendly.

'No, we are from down south, as they say round here.' Said Graham.

'Wales too by the sound of it?' Said the man, nodding to both of them.

'He is! I'm not'. Said Peter. 'What about you? You don't sound you're from round here either.'

'We're from down south too. Come here once a year. My wife's relatives come from here. This is Katherine, Kate generally, and I'm Ray.' They all shook hands.

'I'm Graham and this is Pete. We're staying down the road in Kinlochewe.'

'Goodness me. What are you doing there? Walking I suppose. Not fishing?' asked Ray.

'No, we are doing fieldwork – geology.' Graham said. The man clearly didn't know what to say to that at first.

'Well, that's different. This is my nephew Mike.' Nods to each other. He's interested in geography. More or less the same thing I suppose? He's hoping to go to University in a few years.' Mike looked a bit sheepish. Just smiled. And this is Jane, my daughter.' More nods. Jane didn't speak either.

'You camping then?' asked Graham.

'Good Lord, no! You are? Well, rather you than me. We're in a place just up the road a bit.' Conversation seemed to run-out then.

'Well, we will get on.' Continued Ray. 'Just heard your voices. We come up here most summers, voices like yours are still unusual up here!' Then they all parted, with a warm cheerio from the family.

'It's funny' said Peter, when they were alone again. 'Do you ever get that feeling of time compressed?'

'Sorry, what are you on about now?' asked Graham. Being friendly, not dismissive.

'You know, do you get that feeling like you've been somewhere or met someone before, even though you haven't?'

'Like déjà vu, you mean'?

'Yeah, I suppose so. "Someone walking on your grave" my stepfather says.' Said Peter.

'You've just had that feeling then have you?'

'Yeah, sort-of. Like I'd met them before, not in another place, but like in a different time or something.'

Graham gave him a look, as if to say he must be dreaming, but actually said, 'Dunno Pete. In physics, there's a lot of theory about time and space being the same thing isn't there?' Which made both of them quietly concentrate a minute.

They had known they would have to hitch back to Kinlochewe but hadn't thought people might not stop for the two of them together. As soon as they split-up though, lifts came along quickly and it felt a bit of a race. Peter had got in a car with a couple of people on holiday. The man driving had a lot to say for himself and Peter wished he would just concentrate on the road instead. It made him think about Steve's driving and he had the realisation, not for the first time that day, that his and Steve's time together was nearly up.

Chapter 25

Steve had been so busy and his caravan so littered with paper, that the time he and Peter had been able to be together had been constrained. Peter was in two minds about this. After the day with Sue on his mountain, he had felt very unsettled. He and Steve found moments in passing to hug and grab a bit of intimacy together, but they hadn't had a proper talk together alone, nor spent a decent amount of time with each other. Peter wondered if the fire had gone out of it now. He didn't know if this was due to Steve or to himself. When he thought about it he could see the passion dissipated when they didn't spend time together, but he knew it could be rekindled quickly when they were.

Peter knew he was confused about what he wanted. Sue, Penny, Steve? He had seen the former since their walk, but not alone. They had talked down the pub and he felt Sue wanted him to take things further, invite her to his tent maybe, but she hadn't actually said that. He knew he felt a very strong attraction to her and sometimes thought that if they were in his tent together, they would never re-emerge. He could feel like that in Steve's caravan too. Why did the thought of Sue seem more reassuring?

One of the most down moments for him had been taking a long call with Penny. She was on her uncle's phone, presumably in nice, quiet dry surroundings. Meanwhile, he was speaking with her in the pouring rain, in the public phone box of the village. She knew there was something upsetting him but he couldn't express his feelings without talking about Sue, which would get a prickly reaction at best. Of course, he couldn't imagine how he could even begin to say anything about Steve. A longish queue of campers and others, in cagoules or with umbrellas, had formed and in the end he had to just end the call in mid conversation. He knew another letter would be on its way.

He had come away from that call and stood outside Steve's caravan for some while. He just looked through the window and watched Steve working on his maps and diagrams. It was raining so hard, it was almost dark and Steve was in the light inside. Peter hadn't known whether to go in or not. Right at the moment, looking at Steve, watching him move about, seeing a body he now knew so well.

He thought Penny would think it was about Sue, would have made that assumption. If it was just about Sue and Penny, that was bad enough to untangle his feelings. But, here, watching Steve, he felt the same emotional tug towards him. Was he falling in love with Steve? In the end he went back to his tent, shook off as much water as possible and managed to get inside in a fairly dry state. He had tucked himself into his sleeping bag and just tried to sleep.

The following afternoon, both Peter and Steve arrived back at a similar time, late afternoon. Steady drizzle the whole time, Peter was invited into Steve's caravan. There was just one place now, amongst all Steve's work, where it was possible for two people to hug each other. It was also a spot which could not be seen, they thought, through any of the windows. Steve and Peter properly greeted each other there.

They just cuddled and hugged for some while. Peter felt surprised that Steve didn't push it further but went and made tea instead. Steve then asked if he and Peter could talk about a couple of key locations where they had been. He asked Peter to describe the rock types and structure of the slopes of Cadh a Mheanbh–Chruidh – an area of significance to Peter geologically but it was also where he had been with Sue. This was directly opposite the cliffs of Meallan Gobhar, a precipitous part of Steve's mapping area. Neither of them could pronounce the names properly, they knew.

Looking at the maps, it was astounding to the two of them, how the geology that was so physically dramatic on both sides, was also

223

different from each other. The landscape looked continuous but structurally was very different. The effects of a large fault running down the valley where Loch Maree lay.

'Faults have a huge significance for us this trip, don't they Pete.' As soon as Steve said this, Peter realised this conversation had been thought about in advance. It was Steve's way of opening-up a talk that had to happen sooner or later.

'Yeah, they certainly do', Peter said. 'I hope this has helped you a bit anyway?' Hoping that sticking to geology would stop having to talk about something else.

'Brilliant Pete. Thanks. The key thing is just how the two sides are so different aren't they. Most of the people here looking at the scenery would have no idea. It all looks the same to them, steep rocky mountains and hills. And yet the one thing, that one landscape perspective, has completely different interpretations one side to the other.'

It was then that Steve asked about Sue.

After a bit of a preamble, Peter said: 'The day out with me was something special to her. That's literally what she said.'

'Didn't she get in your way?'

'No.' Peter smiled, remembering Sue lying against the rock, reading a book. 'It was sort of helpful at first. I had to describe things and I found that a good thing. Then there was a point where I went off all around this bit', he pointed at the map, 'while she sunbathed.'

'Bet she looked good doing that. I'm surprised you could concentrate.'

Peter looked at him, wondering why they hadn't had this discussion sooner. Had he been avoiding it? Thought he probably had. At that moment he didn't want to be asked too many questions, but neither did he want to lie to Steve. But that thought died as Peter realised what he wanted to do more than anything was pour it all out to Steve. But he didn't know if he could.

'She looked great Steve. Well, you know that, don't you? Come on, you've seen her here on those warm days.' Peter found now he had started he needed to get it all out. 'She's a nice girl. Woman. Reckon she could be a good friend if we were at the same uni.'

Peter paused. Steve just looked at him and Peter couldn't tell what he was thinking, but he had to go on.

'We had a swim in a lochan, if that's what you want to know. That tiny one there.' Pete's finger on the map again. Remembering the swim and its prelude, Peter felt guilty and started to feel like he was going to blush. Trying to stop it, he knew he already was going red.

'Yeah Pete, I knew you would. Or would do something like that. I don't mind, I would have done too maybe. If I had known what to do.' Steve gave a shrug and a light laugh.

They hugged.

'And was this a swim with trunks or without?'

'Steve, you know the answer! No, no trunks and no bikini either. She had brought a towel though. I had told her a bit about our trip to the drumlins. She wanted to do that, as you know. Think Julie would have done too, but wouldn't want to walk halfway up a mountain to do it!' Peter sucked the corner of his lip and looked around, conscious he was making small talk instead of sticking to the main thing.'

'That was the start of it Pete.'

'Our swim in the drumlins you mean...? I know. I'm glad it happened.'

'Are you Pete? Did it feel different getting-off with Sue?'

Peter didn't know how to speak about that, he just felt embarrassed. He wanted to say but just couldn't get it out.

'Pete. You have a girlfriend. Graham talked about the Easter field trip and another girl – Clare. You've talked before. I know you like girls and they like you, some of them. What you and I do is different to that.' Steve had said this, sitting alongside but now had his arm round Peter's shoulders and pulled Peter around to face him, and to kiss him. 'So, come on, just tell me!'

'OK then. Look, the first time Sue came up, with John MacKenzie and the other guy, yeah?'

Steve nodded. 'It was a couple of weeks ago now wasn't it?'

'Yeah' said Peter. 'Well that day, I did think Sue looked good. I mean, I was really taken with her. She was in that kilt and comfy woolie. She's not a big girl up top and those clothes just fitted her so well and suited her. You could see she was looking as she wanted to feel. I have never seen that so clearly in someone before. The way she came across the scree slope in that get-up with her hair blowing out behind her. I was transfixed.'

'Go on'. Said Steve, after Peter paused.

'She said she loved it. I could see that.' Continued Peter.

'Is she the sort of girl you would like Penny to be then?' Steve asked. 'Maybe Sue's the sort of girl you should marry?'

'Hmm. I don't know Steve. I haven't thought of anything like that. Nor with Penny, you might be surprised to know.' He suddenly rummaged around in his pockets. 'Sorry Steve, need a fag.'

Pete took in a long draught of smoke, exhaled, he put his shoulders back and he felt relaxed again. 'I used to think I wanted to settle down with Penny I suppose. Bit like Graham and his girlfriend, just something that happens? Sorry Steve, where's the ash tray gone?'

While Steve found the ash tray and brought it over, Peter tried to gather his thoughts.

'Just being here has changed that Steve. Everything has changed now hasn't it?' He looked at Steve, put his cigarette down, reached out and squeezed Steve's shoulders.

'Sue is special to me I feel. I seem to be able to talk with her in

226

a way…In an honest way. I can't do that the same with Penny I don't think. I can talk easily with you too Steve – and God knows, we have! With Penny I'm always trying to tell her what I think she wants to hear.' He took another long drag of the cigarette.

'So, up there, before the swim. Sue and I did get pretty passionate. I mean we didn't take our clothes off just to have a swim. Not at first anyway. We didn't go the whole way. No contraception, or we would have, I think. But we did go pretty far.'

'I knew you would Pete. I'm not surprised. Will you do that again? Or will you do everything next time?'

'Well, nothing else has happened since then. Honestly, nothing.'

'Give us a drag of your fag Pete. I need a puff. No, not a whole one, thanks'.

But Steve kept the cigarette though. Neither of them spoke for a couple of minutes.

Steve broke the silence first. 'I think you are always going to want to do that with girls like Sue. Attractive, natural-looking women. And they are going to want to do it with you. That's what I think. But. What about us then Pete? Do you think you will do what we've done with anyone else?' asked Steve.

'It's always going to be there isn't it? I've had these feelings towards other boys and now men, since I was twelve probably. We've talked about this before. You have been the same. It's not going to go away.'

'Shall we have a nip of whiskey?' Steve went over and poured out a small amount of the dwindling whiskey supply in one glass. They each took a sip. Peter found he could feel his body uncoiling as they both leant back into the cushioning.

'This all sounds a bit final Steve. We haven't finished yet though, have we?' And as Peter said that, he realised it could have two interpretations.

'I think I should draw the curtains and we should check...' and

Steve leaned over to Peter again, kissed him and put his hand in Peter's groin. Peter offered no resistance but his mind was distracted. Steve was here and he felt a bit horny being next to him, knowing any minute they were likely to take some or all their clothes off again, but not sure the talking was finished yet.

'I would like to see you again Steve. After this. You feel the same don't you? I mean, after the fieldwork, not after this moment!'

'Of course I bloody do' Steve said, now grabbing and pulling Peter into a horizontal position. 'Every time I toss myself off, I will think of you!' They were groping each other, more fumbling of zips and belts. Peter took Steve's forearms, lifted them up and brought a halt to the moment.

'Is that all I will be Steve? Just a centrefold memory for your hand-jobs!?' Peter found the question was important in his head but hoped it hadn't sounded too blunt.

'You cheeky bugger.' Said Steve, taking the comment lightly and pulling away a little from Peter's arms. Thinking of you doing that stuff with Sue has got me going.' But just as they started, Steve leapt up. 'Damn, I had better close the curtains don't you think!?'

Chapter 26

That night in the pub, Sue and Julie weren't there. Just Graham had come over with Peter, who knew Steve wasn't likely to be coming either, before his intended "last big day" on the hills. The bar was quite busy though and they had to stand at one end of the counter, next to an older guy they hadn't seen before. He was just sitting quietly, smoking a pipe and looking very solid in that situation, Peter thought. Like he had been there always, like part of the fittings. He wore a certain, smarter, style of tweed breeches, a thick green shirt, tie and a pullover.

Peter nodded to him and got a nod back but that was all. To get another drink in though, Peter had to lean across the man a bit to reach the bar counter.

'Sorry' said Peter apologetically. 'It's a bit crowded tonight.'

'Aye, always is this time of year.' Said the stranger. Strong local accent.

'You a regular visitor then?' Peter asked.

The man took his pipe out of his mouth and it seemed he had made a decision to speak with the two students, but gave the impression that was a concession. He explained he was there to shoot deer. Principally on the nature reserve. Peter was shocked at that, having thought all wildlife was safe. He knew he must have looked shocked.

'I can see you are a wee bit surprised about that?' Asked the man, half statement and half question.

'Yes, sorry I didn't know they shot deer on the Nature Reserve.' Said Peter.

'Well they have to. Same as any other estate hereabouts. The deer wander freely and don't respect anyone's borders!' The man went on to explain that the deer numbers had to be managed and the only way of doing that was to cull them. If they weren't culled,

229

the population would rise, making getting new trees growing really difficult, amongst other things.

Peter thought about that. He had learned about the reserve's tree planting schemes but hadn't thought of them being browsed by deer so much that they wouldn't develop. Then he thought of the deer fences and felt stupid for not putting it together better in his brain.

'How do you do it then?' asked Graham.

The man was on home ground now, had an audience and took a gentle pleasure in sharing his world with the two students. He told them how he needed first to count the deer, which meant a while wandering around the nature reserve and the surrounding estates on this side of the valley. He established what herds existed, what numbers, which were the dominant stags and where they tended to be from day to day and at different times of the day.

'Do you use binoculars then?' asked Peter.

'Yes, a bit.' The man replied. 'But a telescope more. I need the 'scope to recognise the individual stags. You can tell them apart quite clearly when you know what you're looking for. By the time I'm done, I think of them as my animals really.'

'But then you shoot some of them?' asked Graham.

'Yes, then I indeed shoot some of them. That happens next and after I know all the numbers.'

'Do you do it all on your own?' asked Peter.

'Mostly. I agree with Mr. Mackenzie. You ken him I imagine? Yes, good. Well he agrees the numbers and I go out and take them. The estates and the reserve help recover the deer for venison. We leave the gralloch for the eagles and buzzards.'

'That's the innards' said Graham, surprising the other two with his knowledge of the word.

'How do you avoid shooting walkers?' asked Peter.

'Or geologists!' Quipped Graham.

The man laughed. 'I ken what you're doing up here lads. Don't worry. We put signs up to stop people getting too near shooting areas on the days we are doing it. We haven't shot anyone yet.'

'That's a relief' quipped Graham again, to more brief laughter.

The man explained that by the time of the shoot he has been quietly working his way around the ground and knows where everything is. Knows the deer habits and locations. 'Like you boys', he said, 'I spend a lot of time in one place, moving slowly from one rock to another.'

'You might have seen me out on the mountain already then, if you've been here a few days?' asked Peter.

'Aye maybe.' The man looked at Peter from under his bushy eyebrows, relighting his pipe. 'You would be surprised what I can see in my telescope scanning the hillsides up there!'

Peter felt himself blush. Graham noticed this, put two and two together, but graciously didn't say anything. After a moment or two, he changed the subject by asking the man how long he had been doing it and how he got started. Peter still felt hot and bothered as he ordered a round for them. He was surprised to learn that the shooter got free drinks. Jock just gave one of his enigmatic shrugs and a wink.

CHAPTER 27

That same evening Sue had decided she was running short of cash too and needed to save a bit before going home at the end of the next month. In fact, it was nearly August now. Where had July gone? And yet, Sue thought, it hasn't gone by quickly really. There's been so much going on. In all sorts of ways.

However, the mood had changed the last few days. Everyone had become aware that the group of people thrown together for a few weeks, was about to break up. Sue knew Steve was rushing to get his work completed and Peter was fretting about his too, still feeling he had "wasted time on other things" and she hoped he didn't see her in that away. She didn't know much about Nick, and Graham seemed sublimely calm the whole time – serene even. Sue had no idea if his work was finished or if he cared really. But the earnestness of Steve and Peter was palpable.

She and Julie were having a night in. Trying not to drink for a change and not eating too much either. Instead of both, Sue was treating herself to a cigarette. She had bought a packet of ten, not wanting to be too serious about it and wanting to pay-back Peter for some of the ones she had cadged. Julie was half in her book and half looking out of the window. One of the things Sue was thinking about was the invitation to go out for a walk with the Mountain Rescue team. Last Sunday with Peter on his own and this Sunday with a small army of men, she imagined.

'Are you thinking of your next Sunday walk then Sue?'

'Yes, I was a bit. It will be great to get up Slioch. Can't believe Mr MacKenzie invited me really.'

'What did he say then?'

'Oh, just that he knew "all the lads were busy with their maps and rocks" so would I like to get out and up another mountain! It was so nice he thought of me.'

'Are you a bit intimidated though Sue, going out with that lot?'

'I was at first Jules. But Jock is going too and he told me down the bar that I didn't need to worry about it, nobody would be going any slower than him!' and she laughed briefly. 'He was quite reassuring about it. Said there would be at least one other woman coming, from Gairloch, bit older than me he thought.'

'One other!' said Julie. 'Blimey, it's a man's world up here isn't it!?'

'I know Jules. I had been hoping I would get to go up that mountain with Pete maybe. I think he wishes now they hadn't dossed about at the start of their fieldwork here, now that times running away.'

Julie nodded. 'We'll leave the boys to it tonight then though, eh Sue?'

'That thought just came to me Jules. We will miss them when they're gone. You know, they will be all gone within a fortnight.'

Julie was quiet then. Sue knew her friend always prefaced an important discussion with a long silence. It was a bit of a hallmark from someone who would otherwise normally be chatty. 'Come on then Jules, what is it?'

'Hmmm . Well, You know we have said before how Steve and your Pete are very close…?'

'Jules, he is not "my Pete"!'

'Well alright. Just Pete then. Reckon you will really miss him though eh?'

Sue let it go. Lit another cigarette, thinking it might have been better just to get a bottle of wine, wondering where Julie was going next with this chat.

'I was going over the washrooms the other day. Well, late afternoon. I had seen Pete go into Steve's caravan. Yeah?'

'Yeah. So what?' asked Sue.

'Well. There was a bit of a queue. I chatted with a couple of women campers. I could see Steve walk across the window of his caravan, with no shirt or anything.'

'Well, they were doing work together. Maybe it was warm and stuffy in there.' Said Sue, shrugging.

'Yeah, but then I saw Peter also without a shirt or anything. They seemed to be speaking closely with each other.' Continued Julie.

'And so?' asked Sue.

'Then when I came out of the loo, I looked across again and saw Steve at that moment draw the curtains of the caravan. And he must have knelt on the sofa-bed or something, to draw the end curtains. I saw him – everything'.

'You what!?' said Sue, a bit incredulous.

'Look. I mean he drew the curtain to the side, then when he drew the end-curtain facing this direction a bit more, he must have had to kneel up to reach the wire or something to pull it closed. He had nothing on. I saw his, you know, everything'. Julie threw her arms open as if to ask a question. Sue replied in the same way, as if to say so what.

They were quiet for a while. Then Sue took a drag and stubbed out the cigarette. Feeling she really shouldn't have had two.

'Jules…they just spend a lot of time together. Like us! I walk round here with so little on sometimes that you say things like "God Sue, the whole world can see what you're made of" - we're just relaxed in each other's company. The two boys are the same.'

Julie looked like she had more to say but didn't speak. It made Sue think a bit more of things she'd seen, things she had heard Peter and Steve say to one another. Ways they had been with each other, little touches of arms, very comfy in each other's space.

'Hmm, maybe I've seen a couple of odd things Jules, if it makes you happy! I got up around dawn one morning and saw Pete leaving Steve's caravan. He must have been there all night. He was carrying some clothes and a book or something. Basically he was just in his shirt-tails and trainers. No one was around. He hurried across to his tent.'

'Perhaps he had just been asleep in Steve's caravan. Maybe after some drinks of something?'

Sue just nodded, didn't know what else to say. Except... 'I saw something similar another time too. Back a while maybe. It was their early days and mine. Didn't take much notice. But...' Sue paused. 'What are we talking about Jules? Are you thinking they are being more than just good friends?' Even saying it, Sue thought the idea sounded ridiculous.

'Sue, what you told me about up on the mountain. You and him. Pete can't be a bit queer or anything can he? If that's what we are getting at.'

'You would think not Jules. Bloody hell, I hate the bluntness of that word though, don't you? Do we actually know any gay people at Uni?'

They talked a while, speculated about people they knew. People who they were aware of in the GaySoc and things like that. They couldn't associate any of these people with Steve or Peter though.

'Don't know what to think of that Jules. It's odd though, after what Pete and I did on the mountain, I expected him to want more. You know, get something to use with me.'

'And you would have been happy with that?' asked Julie.

'With him? Yes, I would.' confirmed Sue. 'I don't know what he and Penny use? Then when he went to Gairloch,' she continued. 'I know there's a chemist there from what your uncle and auntie have said. I wondered if he might get a packet, you know. I thought he might be back wanting to finish things off or something. But no.... Not yet anyway.'

Another long moment of silence prevailed.

'Sue. You reckon you have this big open thing with him. Why don't you ask him?'

'Don't be stupid Jules, I can't go up to him and say "hey Pete! How about it? Are you a bit gay or am I going to get laid by you"!?' They both chuckled at that.

But actually, Sue thought, Jules had a point. She could talk with him. Maybe needed to, in fact, and time was running out. 'No, hold that Julie. Sorry.' She went over to her friend. 'Can we have a girly cuddle please? I think maybe I do need to find a way of asking him about it. But how? And when?' They gave each other a little hug and left the subject there.

Chapter 28

The next day was fair – set for the day. Steve knew he had to go for it today. He and Peter hadn't spent the night together. He felt refreshed and made an early start. He had explained to Peter where he was going and had his note to hand-in to the site hut on the way out. Sue gave him a wave from the tea cabin. She's always up early too thought Steve. Julie, being less of a morning person, he saw more rarely.

He stopped and Sue came over, jeans today and the Fair Isle jumper that Peter liked. He could see she was attractive but he couldn't imagine going out with her, or even having the courage to chat her up, let alone doing what she and Peter had done. He had an image of her and Peter naked on the hillside, could visualise it easily, and suddenly felt a bit down and sad.

'Hi Steve. I see your note there. Shall I take it for you?' He found Sue looking at him, looking a bit concerned. 'You OK Steve? Cheer up! This is going to be your last big day today I gather.'

'Yeah, did Pete tell you that?' The thought of Peter wanting to tell Sue what he was doing, made him feel momentarily more cheerful. 'I need to go for it today, but I will be back at five. Nine hours' time. It's really just a bit I need to get to and then back, but it's way over in the corner of my patch. Pete knows and it's on this note.' He noticed Sue was still giving him the same look. She looked concerned.

'Thanks for asking Sue'.

She reached out and touched his arm. It was a gesture that made him purse his lips. He felt he could easily have stopped and talked with her. He had to be focused. 'Right, sorry, got to go.' He went down the short bit of road, turned and saw Sue was still watching him, she gave a quick wave, blew him a kiss and he blew one back. It made him feel a bit calmer.

The day started with a walk to the village cemetery and car park area. He had thought of bringing the car to save a bit of time, especially if he was back later than intended, but it seemed too much faff now. He headed east on the stalkers' road, nipping behind the sheepfold as two Land Rovers came down the track. He didn't want any arguments with the estate about where he was going – just needed to get on with it. So, he was pleased when he met the stream, Alltan na Coise, coming steeply down the slopes to the track. He headed straight up the right bank of the stream – a way of accessing the upland ground he had already used on other days.

Then he knew it was four or five miles of rocky ground, boggy in places, to the furthest corner of his mapping area, and until now unvisited by him. But it was the only gap. He felt pleased with himself as he walked and sometimes scrambled past outcrop after outcrop that he had previously visited and logged. It was steadily uphill most of the way that meant, in theory, the ground should be draining and becoming drier, but it didn't feel like that and he found the going slow until at last he arrived at the deer fence near the waterfall of Cadh a Ghobhainn in the north-west corner of his mapping area.

The view into what he had learned was called 'the great wilderness', was astounding and the immensity of Lochan Fada lay before him, in the middle of scree covered Torridonian sandstone mountains.

'Such a privilege' he said to himself. Six weeks or more of being in this scenery. He didn't know the names of all the mountains but thought that one day he would have to come back and explore them. Although the landscape in front of him was immense, he knew that geologically it was simple compared to the place where he stood. He was not only on the edge of his map but on the edge of the zone of geological complexity that had brought him and Peter to this area.

From this lonely spot, he had planned to use the line of the deer fence to descend into Gleann Biannasdail. But first, he needed to study several remaining unmapped outcrops around the numerous lochans just here. He wondered why these small areas of water were called lochans when the same diminutive prefix was given to the huge expanse of water opposite.

It was nearly half past one by the time he was ready to descend into the Glen, with the vast mass of Slioch ahead the whole time. Taking stock of what he had done and had still to do, he admitted to himself that he had been over optimistic. However, he had just days left and this excursion was the last major foray into the wilds. In addition to then tidying-up notes and sketches, of which there was a lot still to do, he also wanted to reserve some time just to be with Peter.

The walk across to this point in the morning had been a slog and apart from avoiding rocks and water, his mind had been preoccupied with Peter. He thought of the talk the previous day. He had needed it. Getting him talking about Sue had been important. He wasn't sure what he felt about it. Peter stripping off and going "pretty far" with Sue was only what he had known would happen, but he felt disappointed about it. Fundamentally he would have liked it to be him with Peter, not Sue.

He supposed he felt jealous that Peter and Sue could be girlfriend and boyfriend. Now there were just a few days left, he liked the idea of Peter being his boyfriend, if such a thing was possible. The worst bit had been hearing they walked hand-in-hand off the mountain, down the Pony Track. The image haunted him, wanting to put himself in that picture.

He knew he wanted to see Peter after the field trip was over, because he wanted to keep doing those things they had enjoyed. He realised he had quickly got used to the passion and really enjoyed the physical nature of it all. But he also just wanted to see Peter, to chat with him, to share tea with him, to wake-up or go to sleep with him – to just have a simple, daily routine together.

He couldn't see himself joining the University Gay Club and meeting and doing stuff with other guys. It was all back to the uniqueness of the time and place up here, miles away from routine life.

But could he and Peter keep in touch? Was it practical? And what did he want more than the physical stuff. He knew he had become fond of Peter. But he didn't see himself like his piano teacher Tim and his apparent boyfriend Martin. He couldn't see himself sharing a house with another man. He would hate the idea of people talking about him, about them.

And what did Peter want anyway? He seemed to attract girls quite easily and was turned-on by them. He was in a relationship, but Steve thought from the little he knew, that the thing with Penny would end along with university life and the start of work.

Steve also wondered what Peter would do with the relationship with Sue. Steve thought it was odd – odder than other relationships he saw mates having at Uni. Peter seemed at ease with Sue, and vice versa, like he felt about himself and his sister. Friendly. Like close friends, like family. And yet, of course, they had done something sexual together too. Peter didn't seem in a hurry to develop that though.

Maybe he and Peter should meet anyway next term? Just see how it goes. Maybe he could go to Bristol? If Pete came to Leeds, he could hardly bring him home to his parents' house. But if he went to Bristol, how could he and Peter sleep together with Penny and others around? Even if they otherwise pretended that there was nothing between them!

The descent to Gleann Biannasdhail was steep and all other thoughts had to leave him then, in order to concentrate on the ground. It all felt a bit committing and after a few hundred feet down, Steve realised he had simply been ploughing on and wished he could go back and start again or retrace his steps across the rocky high moor. But that was out of the question and yet, it appeared, so was going forward. The abrupt change in the steepness and rockiness had happened so quickly! For a moment Steve was flummoxed. The ground below him clearly was becoming a cliff. It might be passable but if he went any further he wouldn't be able to come back if it didn't work out.

For the first time on the entire trip, he felt a panic, and it was rising quickly. 'Sit down' he told himself, take a deep breath. The slope was so steep, Steve was suddenly having to edge every step and just sitting there felt precarious. Getting his sack off felt destabilising but he had to get something to eat. A Mars bar might help. He could see in his mind, the ruck sack slipping from his grasp and hurtling down the slope and bouncing over a cliff. He could see himself going the same way. The intense sugar rush calmed him though and brought things back into focus.

It was a predicament but he had got this far without tripping or stumbling and a little bit further should be sufficient. It probably was the most exposed position of the descent but really there was no choice, so he just had to concentrate and keep his nerve.

In the end he traversed south-westwards along a narrow layer of sandstone strata sticking out from the ground, and the ground eased a bit to the west after a while and eventually he dropped down into the valley via another steep, but grassier slope. He took stock as it was now three o'clock. It was at least two and a half hours from here back to Kinlochewe. That didn't leave him long to log a last cliff outcrop to the north, but he felt a need to do it. In fact, he realised, he would be late back and people might start to be concerned. Peter would be concerned.

As soon as he started towards the outcrop, it felt like going against the grain. It felt the wrong direction to be heading north up towards Lochan Fada, when the village was reached by going south. Steve knew he was tired. He needed to keep this simple. No going overboard. Fortunately the distinct outcrop of cliff behind and within the wooded east slope of the valley was straightforward. It would help him complete the picture, but getting to the rocks was tricky, through boulders and tussocky ground, mostly covered by bracken. He saw a pine marten though at one point and that cheered him.

At the last outcrop he found it was what he expected and it meant he could confidently have the whole vertical sequence of rocks and their structure complete in his head. It would have bothered him to have left it undone. That blank on the map would have irked.

But, heading back, he knew he needed to hurry or he would be getting back to the campsite somewhere between half-six and seven. Peter had chatted over the day's plan with him and had told Steve he needed to be focused and attentive – to keep safe, not overdo it and to get back on time. Steve remembered he had held Steve's hand then and got him to promise. That last descent had shown Peter had been absolutely right to be concerned.

So, it was a bitter blow when Steve encountered the river which, coming down the Glen, was much higher and faster than he expected. He had to cross it though to get to the small track on the other side. He knew that path was then distinct enough back down to Loch Maree, where he would be on safer ground, on the flatter and much more used loch-side path back to the village. He wandered up and down the riverbank, feeling he was losing time and recognising he may have to wade across, but would need to find somewhere slower and shallower.

At one point, the river went through a bit of a meander, close to the track opposite but it would necessitate a short scramble up mud and moraine to get to it, once he had crossed the river. Steve knew things could look different if you were patient, so he waited and stayed in one spot, concentrating.

As he stood there, he could see now that the meander did become shallow enough here and there to reveal slabby blocks of sandstone just below the surface. He decided to go for it. Hopping and balancing from rock to rock. They weren't particularly slippery. He tested each one before transferring his full weight, but some gaps were a stretch and he had to commit to the move once started. All was going OK until there were just three or four yards to go. It had been a long stretch but the block of sandstone he was stepping onto looked especially big and solid. But as his weight transferred beyond the moment to pull back, the rock wobbled.

Unable to keep his balance, Steve's legs buckled and he found himself falling backwards into the cold water. Instinctively his hands went to the back of his head and he didn't feel any collisions with rocks anywhere, which was good. But not so good was the fact that he had fallen backwards into a deeper bit of water, deep enough to just cover him completely.

Steve swore out loud and he tried to stand up and now, where the rocks were permanently wet, it was more slippery and he found himself falling forward. He ended up in a position like an angled press-up, with his arms just keeping his shoulders and head out of the water that was running fast all over him.

Steve felt so angry and annoyed with himself and the situation, he scrambled out of the water, up the bank and was on the track and starting to head down before he stopped to think, striding along on a surge of adrenaline. Then he felt his brain recovering. Was he really alright? Had he cut himself or twisted anything? Had he got everything, was his rucksack soaked inside? He hoped his notes and maps, in plastic inside, would be OK. He retraced his steps and forced himself to be assured nothing was lost or fallen out. He went back to the river and checked around.

Doing this also cleared his head further and he stopped and took stock of the situation. He was soaked and now he also felt cold.

He had a cagoule, spare jumper, some woollen mittens and a wool hat inside the bin liner in his sack, but that was all. Everything else he was already wearing and it was all saturated. Standing there, weighing it all up, he could feel his boots were full of water and everything was just wet. He was literally soaked to the skin.

Once again, he forced himself to stand still and think. Standing there on the bank of the river he decided to strip off everything and wring it out. He moved quickly. Being naked in the wilderness with nobody about for miles and a long way back home, he felt fear creeping up for the second time that day. He remembered the chocolate effect and knew he had a bit left, so he could do that again. But first he twisted and squeezed as much water as he could out of the clothes he had been wearing.

He dried his body and head with the mittens as best he could until they were also soaked. He put back on the damp underpants, breeches and socks. He put the spare, dry, jumper directly on his skin and the cagoule over that. The hat felt good but his lower body felt horrible and he could feel himself shivering standing there.

Looking at his watch he realised at best he would now be back in Kinlochewe at eight. If it was any longer than that it would be virtually dark – dusky at least. He took a deep breath and set-off.

CHAPTER 29

Five days before Steve had to leave the site and just a week or so more left for Peter, there was a window of weather. In what had been damp and murky days with low cloud, a lot of the time, a high had come in from the north, bringing colder but clearer and drier conditions. Peter used the morning to fill-in some lower-level geology nearby, before returning to the campsite at lunchtime.

By the afternoon of that day, Steve's last big day on his territory, he was late returning. Almost without exception, the four geologists had worked in common to look after each other's interest by reminding and insisting each of them left a route note each day and the time by which they would be back. Steve had become a stickler for this and Peter was troubled immediately when he found Steve late. Particularly as they had gone through the walk together on paper, the previous afternoon.

It was immediately disturbing, because Peter knew that Steve had gone this day to the furthest north part of Meallan Gobhar, to very remote country with precipitous cliffs after miles of rugged and boggy ground.

He went to the site hut and Ben was there as he was expecting some campers and a caravan that evening. Peter asked to check Steve's route notes for the day, and knew Steve would have been diligent doing these in some detail. The notes confirmed where Steve would have headed. The note stated clearly the return time of five-thirty at the latest.

At seven, feeling fretful, Peter decided to go to the pub and speak to Jock, John MacKenzie or whoever was there. He just had a bad feeling about it all. Most of these men were involved with the mountain rescue team locally, and Peter had previously said to them that he would in fact be happy to be seen as an extra pair of hands if ever needed. However, in respect of rescues and people losing their way, they had all had a quiet summer so far.

As it happened, both Jock and the Warden were chatting to each other in the Lounge Bar and they quickly picked-up on Peter's concern.

'None of us have over-run the return time until now. That's five weeks. Six in Steve's case. He knows what he's doing and I hope he's just been determined to complete work, rather than come a cropper in any way, but I thought you should know.'

John MacKenzie decided to take Peter out to the Land Rover and they did a quick drive down to the furthest point they could on a road. The warden was speaking to him 'This is as far as we can go. The landowner here won't allow anyone to drive up his stalker roads without written permission. Two hundred thousand acres! You'd think they would find space for us all now and then.'

They jumped out of the car and John MacKenzie scanned the hillside with binoculars, passing a spare pair to Peter, who said 'Steve was working in the furthest bit from here today, he wouldn't have time other than to come back by the obvious path from alongside Loch Maree. That's what his notes said and that's what I would do. By the time you've messed around in the wilds for several hours, you just want to get down and back asap.'

'No sign of him though is there?' replied the Warden. 'Hmm. It will be pretty dark in a couple of hours. Think I need to get back and maybe just get Jock to start to get things on standby, just in case.'

Peter felt himself gulp at that. He felt this was all now feeling a bit too real. He would have preferred it if the Warden had just reassured him and said there was nothing to worry about. John MacKenzie put his arm on Peter's shoulder. 'Come on lad, hop in.'

In the car, Peter needed to know what might happen next.

'Right, well, with something like this and that country, there is no point wandering around in the night. We could easily miss him. It will be getting light again at five-thirty ish and we need to be gathering the team here at that time.' Peter heard himself gulp again. 'If he doesn't turn up shortly that is Pete!' And the Warden gave him a more reassuring look. 'Here we are then.' They pulled-up outside the hotel door and went inside.

Jock had already started alerting a few members of the team and he said that some people were getting themselves ready for a potentially short night and a dawn start. It was nearly eight and Peter was convinced now that something had gone wrong. It wasn't a short delay, anymore, not to him anyway. It meant something had definitely happened to Steve.

Peter offered to go back to the campsite to see if Steve had come back. He found himself feeling quite panicky and he effectively passed this on to Julie's Uncle Ben, who he encountered first, then Sue, Julie, Nick, and then Graham. The latter, who had earlier been telling Peter not to worry, and Nick, wanted to know what they could do and wanted to come back to the pub with Peter. Peter spent a few minutes organising his pack, putting his boots on.

'You just told me John MacKenzie said there was nothing they could do tonight.' Graham said, concern clear in his tone.

'I know Graham but I've been thinking we could get on down the main path, the obvious one, go down there for a couple of miles until it forks and steepens. If he's made it down the glen beside Slioch, he may just be knackered or maybe he's sprained an ankle and hobbling along? Anyway, we can't get lost on the path and can try it at least. If the warden will run us down there again. He just took me that way an hour ago.

By the time they got back to the pub, it was eight-thirty. Three hours beyond the expected return time. John MacKenzie, surprisingly to the geologists, agreed to Peter's suggestion. In truth he was presented with three young men who he felt were likely going to walk anyway, and he would be better saving them some time. The warden had spent enough time now with Peter to know that he wasn't going to do anything stupid.

The rescue team's gear was stored in an old garage in the centre of the village. While Peter had been at the campsite, Jock and the warden had set-up walkie-talkies for themselves and put some others on charge. The Warden took one. Peter felt an odd mix of excitement and fear. He realised his body must be pumped full of adrenaline. He hadn't thought about the radios and they made everything feel more serious. And it was all about Steve! Peter found himself biting his lower lip.

Parking-up at the furthest point on the road again, now at a quarter to nine, John MacKenzie said he was going to accompany Nick, Graham and Peter, with the walkie talkie. They had three head torches between them, Nick didn't own one, and it was agreed they would walk an hour. Three miles maybe. They would come back to the car and should be back at the pub by eleven.

Despite pleading, particularly from Peter, John MacKenzie resisted the offer of the geologists joining the rescue squad in the early morning. 'They know what they're doing and they know each other. We will go out in a search pattern we have done in practice. I know you're safe Pete, but I can't have anyone in the team diverting any time to you, and you would be a distraction – an unknown quantity. If, God forbid, we have to widen the search area after that, there will be a need for your help then.'

Peter found himself feeling close to tears now. Again, the reality of the situation hit home. "Widening the search area". That phrase meant Steve would not have just turned up, would not have returned to his caravan, would not have been found, would still be on the mountain somewhere. And that would mean he wasn't just lost, he would be injured, ill or worse. They walked along quickly and silently. The concern washing around in Peter meant he walked very fast and the others, including the Warden, picked up on the anxiety and fell in with that pace.

It was getting pretty dusky, cooler and Peter could only see images of Steve in a ravine, at the foot of a cliff or lost, disorientated and exhausted. These visual thoughts were becoming overwhelming.

It was John MacKenzie who spotted a light ahead first. Gone nine thirty, in the gathering gloom, a very faint dot of light was spotted, or so it seemed. At first, John MacKenzie thought it was a possible flashing light, a distress call. Then he decided it was possibly a steady light, moving in and out of view behind trees and rock outcrops. Then they lost it.

'Do you think it was someone coming down, a long way ahead?'

'Maybe. It looked like it was on the level – the lochside path. It's maybe not so far either, you wouldn't see a head torch from miles off, not in the gloaming'.

After another ten minutes of fast walking, the shadowy faint and distant image of someone walking towards them with a light on their head, became more distinct. Peter had to resist the urge to run along the path, but the pace upped tempo immediately anyway.

Around a twist in the path, a rise in the ground and then the figure was just yards ahead.

'Hi Guys, is it you? Have you come here to meet me?' Steve sounded very tired, a bit scared and trying to make light of the situation and put a brave face on it.

John MacKenzie was very much in charge, at the front now. 'Are you all right laddie? We were hoping to come across you and pleased we have, I can tell you.'

'You've got half the village getting ready to come and find you, you silly bugger.' Graham said.

'And Pete's got the entire campsite on alert now too.' Nick added.

Peter couldn't speak, just grabbed hold of Steve, threw his arms round him and just said. 'Thank fuck Steve. I was getting freaked-out. Are you OK? What's happened? Jesus, you're soaked.'

'Is he?' The warden again. 'Steve, are you wet? I can see now, yes. Are you cold?' John MacKenzie felt over Steve's clothes. 'Christ, you really are wet. You must be cold! What happened?' and then without waiting for an answer. 'Never mind now. Just get walking – all of us.'

'I am really cold actually. I've just had some chocolate, just back there – was beginning to wonder how I would make the last couple of miles.' And then Steve just sat down on the path, which was a bit worrying for everyone.

With the headlights of Peter and Graham shining on Steve, John MacKenzie gave Steve a quick once over, asking questions the whole time… any injuries? Are you sure? Do you hurt anywhere? Do you know if you hit your head? Did you fall in a river?' He thrust his hands under Steve's clothes to feel his chest and back.

'Right, well you sound and seem OK but you are pretty cold. So we are going to get you back up and we're all going to walk back to my vehicle at a steady pace. Not slow but not fast enough to trip-up. It's virtually night now and we have a half-hour walk to go. Pete, you're behind Steve the whole way.' And additionally he whispered into Pete's ear 'If he starts to stumble at all, call out.'

And off they went. The Warden leading, then Graham, Nick, Steve and Peter bringing-up the rear. They were not to get separated and had to always have each other in sight. And so it worked. There was a crowd in the Land Rover and a fast drive back to the pub. John MacKenzie had been on the walkie-talkie to Jock on the way back, but Peter had been out of hearing range and was also trying to keep up a conversation with Steve the whole way. He didn't know what the radio conversation had been about.

Peter had got Steve to describe what he had been doing all day, where he started, what he discovered and eventually, what happened. Peter knew it had been a case of being too ambitious. Hurrying to get back, knowing he had been out too long, Steve had just done one thing too many. It had been boggy and the bouldery heather was deep and then he had to ford a fast-flowing stream. Steve had just lost his balance and fallen horizontally into a stream. Enough to soak him through. He had stumbled across the rest of that ground onto what he knew was the return track, eventually leading to the one they were on now.

Arriving at the hotel, the students were amazed to discover Jock had arranged for them to go straight to one of the guest rooms. Peter was unprepared for everything happening so quickly now. The hotel had a couple of unoccupied rooms and this was one. Graham and Nick had been thanked by John MacKenzie, and Steve, and free pints and whisky chasers had been lined up for them in the lounge bar. Peter, though, had been instructed to accompany them to the room.

Inside the room, which was on the upstairs floor of the Hotel, Steve was asked to take off most of his clothes. Jock was running a hot bath. In a completely un-embarrassing way for everybody, John MacKenzie gave Steve a quick check-over. Getting him to lift arms, legs, move his head around, turn around, lie back, have his legs, arms and back felt.

'Don't think you're injured Steve. But you are very cold. We need to get your core temperature back up. You're staying here tonight.'

Steve in the bath now, quite hot, but not scorching. Told to stay there for a half-hour. The warden addressed Peter. 'So, your job is to make sure he's OK. He seems sound, but he may have hit his head when he went in the stream. The bath should restore his body temperature but you need to make sure he stays warm and monitor him for anything odd. So, any concerns - go and get Jock. He's in the staff cottage next door, you know? Having said all that, I think he will be fine by morning.' Peter nodded all the time, grateful to be given the tasks, pleased to be trusted, desperate just to give Steve another hug. 'We just can't have him going back to a cold caravan' concluded the Warden.

Jock said 'You two lads, just stay here, like John has been saying. I have got Maggie in the kitchen sorting some soup, coming up soon. There's a pot of tea too. You've both missed your suppers and you need to eat this when Steve's out of the bath. Maggie's got some pyjamas for the two of you too. In the morning you, Pete, can go back to the campsite and get changes of clothing. Sorry you're going to have to double-up lads,' he gave a heavy shrug, 'but it's all we have.'

Peter didn't disagree with any of that! He had only just realised that they meant him to stay with Steve the night, as his minder. He was taking this all in and realised that he and Steve would be in a double bed together all night. It suddenly felt like a nightmare was turning into something like a dream. Just as long as Steve was really alright.

John MacKenzie was speaking again. 'There's also some soup and that being given to Nick and Graham downstairs. So, don't fret about them.'

Maggie came in. Peter introduced himself properly as they had only seen each other briefly before. Peter thought she might be Jock's wife. He didn't know, but she was friendly and attentive. Putting the food and tea out on the little table in the room, putting two sets of pyjamas on the bed. Peter wondered who they belonged to, or did hotels have them for guests who forgot to bring any? He didn't know. She whispered to Peter, there's also two miniatures of scotch on that tray, but you're not to have them until Steven has finished his bath and you've eaten and you're both sure he feels steady.

Peter was left then. Almost. The door had been closed, then knocked on again. Maggie said ' Oh boys, I forgot to say, I will bring-up some tea at about eight o'clock.' Peter started to thank her, knowing he looked overwhelmed and she touched him on the arm and said 'Shh now. You don't need to say anything. Just get yourselves a good sleep.' Peter checked his watch and was shocked to see it was way past eleven.

He knocked on the bathroom door. 'Are you alright in there Steve?' And he opened the door and went in anyway. They talked together, with Peter on the edge of the bath. Peter now trying to make a joke of it, Steve looking really done-in but sounding OK otherwise. 'When John MacKenzie was checking you over I was getting jealous! The only thing he didn't check was your knob.'

'I think that's OK Pete. Jesus, I feel such a prat putting everyone to this trouble. I can't believe all this has happened. People have been so nice.'

'So, you're sure you are OK Steve? Warmed up again? There's food out here and instructions for us to eat it'.

Steve couldn't stop running over the eventful day, again and again. Seeing it from different angles, speculating how it could have been avoided, what, worse, could have happened, what he did wrong.

'Don't say all that Steve. Stuff happens. You did what you could and you're here now.' Peter found he was dead-beat and didn't want to keep re-running the drama and the anxiety it had provoked.

Eventually, they were in the double bed, and in the pyjamas they felt obliged to wear. It was gone half past midnight and they quickly slipped into sleep, side by side with the light on. After a couple of hours, Peter got up for a pee and came back to bed, turning the light out and giving Steve a cuddle, spoons, somebody had once said this was. Cuddling a lover, your front to their back. Steve didn't stir.

The dawn light woke them. A bit disorienting, especially for Steve, who had slept very deeply. They turned to each other, cuddled front to front now. They kissed and felt the desire in each other. Afterwards they fell back to sleep again until there was a knock at the door.

'Hello' Peter shouted, coming round from sleep and forgetting for a moment where he was. Maggie's voice. 'You two boys alright?'

'Yes, thanks Maggie. Just coming'. And Peter was half out of the bed.

'No bother, as long as you are alright and Steve too. The tea and some bacon's on a tray here.' Her voice tailed-off and Peter could hear her going down the corridor.

Coming back from the door, he saw Steve starting to sit-up. They looked at each other and smiled.

'How are you feeling Steve?'

They talked over the tea and bacon sandwiches. Peter took Steve's caravan key, went back to the campsite, got fresh clothes for them both. Had brief conversations with Nick, Sue, Julie, Ben. Everyone had been concerned. Everyone was relieved.

Back in the hotel, they got dressed and went down to reception. Maggie came and spoke with them, remarked on how good Steve looked. Peter told her the pyjamas were piled in the room, hoping they wouldn't be examined before washing. He couldn't imagine they would be.

Maggie told them that she would let John MacKenzie and Jock know all was well and she also said a reporter from Gairloch was on his way down later that morning. He had heard something about a crashed plane from the War, thought some sort of story might be created. John MacKenzie had also left word that both Steve and Peter should stay down today, and not go on the hill.

Peter tried to thank Maggie for the room, the food and everything else, but she wouldn't let him say any of it. Just kept telling him to "Shh – none of it was any trouble".

Peter and Steve walked back into the campsite. For the first time, to Peter it felt like they were a couple. Wanting, in fact, to hold Steve's hand, like he had with Sue. He would feel so proud doing that this morning, but of course he knew it was impossible.

CHAPTER 30

It was late enough for others to have set-off for the day, but early enough for Ben to greet them. Sue and Julie came out of the tearoom and hugged them, practically dragging them back in. The whole story was told over mugs of tea until Julie's uncle ushered in Andy – the reporter from the Ross-shire Journal. A man in his late thirties, it seemed, quite thick-set, wearing a tweed jacket and a green tie with some sort of emblem on it.

The reporter had to just fit in, so there were five of them round a table. Andy asked questions and made notes for some while, enjoying the tea and the banter between, and with, the four young people. It went on for an hour or so and Peter thought he and Steve were still running on left-over adrenaline from the previous evening, talking a lot, gabbling at times. However, Peter noticed Andy always gave far more attention to anything the girls said.

'OK, look, I need to get back but it's been great.' said Andy. He had been mostly quiet, taking in the stories of the students, but now he was leaving he became surprisingly fulsome. 'I'm just going to get some photos of you outside. There's a nice wee story here. A little feature really. I don't think folks appreciate what's on their doorstep. Locally they're all wound-up about the oil platform work. Those who are employed on it love the money. The others don't like it at all. Think it's brought in too many outsiders, just getting blotto down the pubs, spoiling it for the locals and taking all their money away with them after.'

'But you are doing something different.' He continued. 'I had no idea personally that our little bit of the world caused a stir in academic circles and that students come here from all over Britain to study our rocks. Think that's a surprising story actually.' Everyone nodding. 'Then there's some more students, you two lovely girls, working up here for the summer, helping visitors and folks have a good time.' And turning to Peter and winking, 'and maybe helping the geology lads have a good time too, I'm thinking.'

'You might think that,' said Julie. 'They just give us a hard time actually, just treat us as tea-ladies and none of them has any bloody money to spend.' Laughter from all of them at that.

'So, our readers don't know about any of that, and it's nice. Your photos will light-up a page I reckon – especially you two girls.' At this point Peter thought Andy was in danger of becoming a bit over-attentive to Julie and Sue.

Instead though, the reporter turned to Steve. 'We have a bit of real-life drama too. Didn't know any of this before this morning of course. But now we have someone just maybe overdoing it a little, letting enthusiasm take them into danger.' Peter wasn't sure if Steve would like this or not. 'But getting safely back under his own devices – but only just. His friends and our local rescuers on the verge of pulling out all the stops to save his life.' He paused. Everyone now looked slightly sceptical.

'OK, I know. As I say, a bit of drama! I can pep it up a little. Doesn't need much actually. People will like it. Right, come on, I need you to pose a bit outside – the tearoom will be a nice backdrop. We'll get the name of the tearoom and the campsite in the shot. Girls up front and the lads behind'

And that was that. Steve wanted to go back to his caravan, to sort himself out. Peter left him for a while to sort out his own stuff too, but went back later. They felt obliged to accept the instruction to stay-put for the day, even though the weather was settled fair. They spent a chunk of the afternoon looking at maps, helping each other figure out what to do in the remaining days. Creating a final plan. Peter wished, for the umpteenth time, how he should have done this more often.

After the night before, the two of them felt very safe and comfortable in each other's arms again at one point in the day.

Back on the narrow bench seats of the caravan, they realised just how much a luxury, and treat, the double bed had been. The compactness of the caravan made Peter feel cocooned, cut-off from the rest of the world, not worrying about a thing, just enjoying the here and now reality of Steve's body pressed against his.

Chapter 31

The final days of Steve's assignment passed in a blur for him. Finishing the fieldwork, getting maps and notes together, labelling rock specimens, loading stuff into the car. Eventually packing up his personal stuff for the final departure in the morning. It was the latter that made both him and Peter feel quite dejected. They had made the promises to keep in touch, to write, phone, meet.

But both of them felt that parting at Kinlochewe was really an end to the whole affair. They would keep in touch, but for how long would it last? If they met, where and in what circumstances? Where would they find a place to be together properly? They both lived in shared houses at uni, and otherwise with their parents. They were sure Steve's Dad and Peter's step-father would be shocked at any revelation. Would reject them probably, they thought. They could both quote the hateful remarks they knew so well, directed at anyone deemed to be a homosexual.

On one of the last mornings, Steve received a reply letter from Timothy, in beautiful, polished handwriting.

Higher House
Holme Bank
Leeds
West Yorkshire

23 July 1977

Dear Steve.

Thank you so much for writing as you did. I was incredibly moved by everything your letter said and by the things that were unsaid too.

One of the nicest things I have learned in life is the value of being trusted by others. Your letter is so full of trust I only hope I can respond adequately.

We can, and indeed must, speak more of all this when you are back home. We can compress some piano practice later but what is going on for you is far more important. This is a point of your life that probably feels so overwhelming that it is difficult to comprehend, so hard for you to accept what is happening and how you feel about it.

But please be aware and know, Steve, that what you are experiencing is something shared with many, many, many other men, including myself and Martin. You are not alone, although you will be feeling like you are!

Where this moment happens, differs for everyone and I have heard many stories of the self-discovery you have made and are still in the process of making. Choosing to have this revelation in the far northwest highlands is a first but it sounds a suitably intoxicating and beautiful part of the world – magical even. As good a place as any and better than most maybe?

You didn't use the words, but I knew what you were describing, both physically and emotionally, so do not worry about being misunderstood.

One of the things to realise and remember is that what you and Peter have done with each other is a really nice thing. It is about joy Steve, so take the time to enjoy it.

Peter will be as confused and as shocked by this self-discovery as you are. Maybe he is a bit more experienced with girls, and maybe not. What appears on the surface may not be what is going on beneath. From what you have told me about geology, this is a metaphor you might like!

Peter will be in the same position as you but will be having to work out whether the feeling and joy he has previously felt with young women is the same as that experienced with you. On one level, it is all physical, but inside it is not. The fact is, Steve, that some men like men, like to enjoy men in the way we are referring to, and to also love men. Yes, love! Martin and I very much love each other. What you are experiencing is a love for Peter I think. From what you have said, he is maybe thinking that about you too.

The world about us doesn't equip anyone to see two men together in the same way as a man and a woman. Men and women couples are everywhere, but men as couples are not. But there are a lot more than you think right now.

'They' all think they are normal and we are not. This is not so Steve. We are as normal as them, you, me, Martin and countless others like us. So, don't think anything bad about yourself or beat yourself up too much. What you are discovering is simply who you are. It's your underlying bedrock*

Be good. Come and see me when you are back. Enjoy this special time and special place. I'm sure you will remember Kinlochewe for a long time, and in a good way.

Take care.

Timothy.

* I had to research that geological reference! Hope it fits!

So, the last evening together, after the pub, in the caravan together, they did a lot of soft talking together. Steve shared Timothy's letter with Peter. They kept reading it, over and over. Just the realisation that other guys felt like they did about each other. That guys could feel an emotional bond to one another, not just a physical attraction. All of that felt new to them both and it was comforting.

But in a way, Peter felt that now he had been allowed to acknowledge what he felt about Steve, it made their parting much harder. They didn't use the word love, but Peter told Steve how fond he was of him and Steve talked in the same vein. There was a lot of cuddling and some crying. They tried to get this all out of the way before going to the pub. Steve couldn't really have much of a drink as he was getting away early.

They stayed together the night and then at first light, Steve was gone.

Chapter 32

Now it was Peter's last week too. In all that was happening, Peter had tried to maintain normality. Tried to pretend someone he knew he really cared about, with whom he had shared everything, intimately, was leaving his life as abruptly as he had entered it. And yet it had been essential that the rest of the world didn't know it. So, the turmoil was all internal, to be hidden, for the shame of revealing it, even from Graham, who surely knew, and certainly from Sue, who he worried might also have started to figure it out. Confirming their suspicions was not something Peter felt he could do.

Sue and Peter hadn't returned from their time together on the mountain to act as an item in any way at the campsite. They had got on with their stuff without becoming like a couple. Even if it had been likely, the 'rescue' of Steve had interrupted it. It was odd, Peter thought. He felt that what he ought to do, after something like they had done with each other, after what they experienced, was that they should behave as a couple. After all, weren't they now, effectively, girlfriend and boyfriend?

Peter felt this could have happened at one point immediately afterwards. Steve's adventure and the lead-up to his departure had crowded out the possibility of developing a relationship with Sue. He knew he had used the excuse of the fieldwork nearing completion, as a reason to exclude himself from contact with others. Except for time with Steve. He had been close, ish, and friendly with Sue, he hoped, had found time for a hug and kiss here and there, but always keeping it to that, not allowing it to go deeper.

Then one morning, warm and sunny again, actually pretty hot and humid in the canvas of the tent, Peter was lying flat-out on his sleeping mat, working on his notes and using the morning to catch-up with himself work-wise. He would then use the last two or three days to go up and check anything uncertain or fill in any gaps. There was lots of the former and a fair bit of the second, but it would have to do. Graham had gone out, so no dope-smoking distraction likely. He realised he was concentrating heavily because Sue came into view right in front of him before he looked out and noticed.

'Oh, hi Sue, gosh I was buried in my notes then. Trying to make out the stuff I have marked on this map. Think it's crap if the truth be known!'

'I'm sure it isn't Pete' said Sue, looking a little disconsolate, 'Thought I would come and see you again'. She sat herself down outside the tent, as she had done sometimes before. 'Chance for someone nice to make a tea for me for a change, I hoped.' She was wearing her tartan miniskirt and the pink T-shirt with the dragon again. That fitted her quite tightly and Peter found himself distracted and cheered-up simultaneously.

'You're good at it! You and Julie always have people wanting your tea.' Peter set-to to get the stove going, leaning into the flysheet area.

'Are you naked in there?' Sue noticed Peter's upper body, at least, unclothed.

'Not completely. No'. He felt himself blushing, feeling like he had been caught-out, thinking this was silly given what he and Sue had done with each other. 'But it's quite hot under canvas, but a bit breezy out there. It would blow all these maps and papers about, so, it's just easier here inside, even if it is very warm.'

Sue leaned over, gave Peter a kiss and looked past him into the tent. 'Ooo, you really haven't much on have you? I remember washing those for you.'

'What?'

'Those white pants of yours. When we did all that washing for you guys, Julie thought some of yours were a bit skimpy. Not sure what she meant but she said she thought it a sign of someone being confident with themselves.'

'That's nice. Never thought of any of that really. Just like them.' Peter felt a bit nonplussed.

'I'd agree with her, in your case. Move that kettle then, I'm coming in.' And Peter had to hurry to turn off the gas, move things quickly to enable her to clamber in. He thought it was nice that Sue would just squeeze herself into his tent like that - not at all worried about the invasion of the small space. He did feel a bit exposed in his undressed state, but worried more about being a bit smelly and smoky.

'It's a bit tight in here, part of the reason I've never invited you in before I suppose.' He hoped that didn't sound too lame. 'I hope I'm not too sweaty!'

'Is that the reason?' Sue said. 'Yes, it is a bit bijou, but I like it. These foam mats are a sort of carpet really. They're warm too aren't they'

She managed to get down to the middle of the tent, settling to sit cross-legged with enough head-clearance for her to sit up. 'You aren't, by the way.' Then, 'I like it Pete! Cosy. It is a bit hot though.'

Peter got the kettle going again, felt Sue's hand on his backside. It made him turn around. Sue said, 'The dimple here in your bottom, it's a good look on a guy. I like to see that and yours is nice.' Peter started to feel he could be getting turned-on by this but at the same time feeling frustrated that the planned work of the day was about to get postponed. And then he was concerned this could easily become a conversation about him and Sue that he wasn't sure he could manage.

'I thought you said you hadn't seen many men, you know, with not much on?' asked Peter.

'Well,' Sue said, 'you do see men with not much on, at swimming pools, on meets on climbing trips and so on, staying in climbing huts. This is the first time I have been alongside one in broad daylight, in a small tent though!'

'Sorry you haven't been here before Sue', said Peter, feeling he needed to excuse the lack of previous invitation, 'but you can see it's not very spacious, to say the least.'

'Don't worry. I just wanted some time with you though'. She had stopped stroking him now and was looking straight at him. 'You'll be gone soon and you have been busy. I wanted to spend some more time with you.'

'You're very welcome. I'm pretty tired of the fieldwork now. This stuff I'm doing this morning – there's just too much left to do, bits I haven't recorded properly, bits I should go back to. I'd happily spend the last few days being distracted by you though.' Saying this, he realised he meant it. Then he felt bad about thinking that, with Steve gone just a few days. However, he really did feel close to her now she was here. 'I haven't had time to ask you about Slioch.'

'Ahh, Slioch. That was great Pete. Not such great weather, but we did get a view at the top. The Great Wilderness area looked fantastic.'

'You didn't get burned-off by the team then?'

'No, not at all. I was surprised. In the middle most of the time. I felt a bit spoilt and looked-after to be honest.'

'Yeah, well, all those hairy blokes would want to look after you Sue! Was it the kilt too?'

'Nope – my breeches this time. There was one other woman in the end, not much different to me in many ways. Daughter of a lady who runs a tea-shop in Gairloch. Really loves the mountains. We felt like good mates right-away.'

'I'm pleased you got out on another decent mountain day Sue.' And Peter felt sad it hadn't been with him.

'God Pete, look at all those sketches.' Said Sue, changing the subject. 'Didn't know you had to do drawing.'

'Well, they're not art are they!? They're just my attempts to sketch

out some of the features I've found. Some attempts at cross-sections
– you know, a way of interpreting what's going on underneath the
surface'.

'Have you one of the crashed plane site we went to?' Sue asked.

Peter produced a blank page of foolscap paper. 'Not yet, but I'll
draw it for you.'

So, he was now crouched down, knees tucked under him, the
better to be able to draw on the paper. His head close to the page
and pencil in hand poised to draw. Sue stretched out lengthways
beside him, leaning her head on her arms, hands cupping her face.
Attentive.

'I'm all ears' she said.

'Well, you need eyes for this bit too.'

'I've eyes only for you Pete.'

'Oh, stop it. You'll really distract me. I thought you wanted to
see ...?'

She just nodded and pushed her head forward exaggerating the
movement. He chuckled.

'OK, here we go then.' He drew several lines across the page,
explaining this was the cliff containing the airplane metal. Above it
he drew an outline of the main mountain, explaining that, keeping
proportions, the top of the hill would be way out of sight. He
pointed at the cliff.

'These lines indicate the, roughly, horizontal bedding of the
sandstone. Layer after layer stacked on top of one another. At first I
thought the rocks, like these lines, just ran along consistently. It was
Steve spotted this wasn't the case.'

He filled in with heavy shading two horizontal areas, one a bit
above the other. 'These are the two locations of the metal – the
plane. So, this whole cliff is about sixty feet high. This first location
here, that's where I first saw the metal, about fifteen feet off the
ground. It runs along horizontally, really like it's part of the rock

266

fabric, for at least ten feet.'

'But the second location of the metal is near the base of the cliff, about twenty feet along to the left, looking at this drawing. So they're about twenty feet apart horizontally and, say, fifteen feet apart vertically.'

'So' Sue said. 'If it was a plane wreck, bits of it broke-up and embedded themselves in the cliff. Like the man from Gairloch said, the force of the impact and all that?'

'That's correct Sue.' A truck or something went up the road behind his tent, suddenly revving an engine and Pete looked back. 'Blimey, that was loud.' In so doing, he saw the length of Sue's body right alongside him. 'God, are you OK there. I've got all my clothes, food, junk down that side of the tent – you've got no space at all.'

'It's not me distracting you Pete, it's you distracting yourself. Come on, concentrate on what you were saying – I like listening to you.' She put her left arm around him, adjusting the position so she was more on her side, and still able to study what Peter was drawing and explaining.

Peter continued: 'But the thing is these two outcrops of metal are separated by this line.' He drew a vertical line on the cliff, between the two shared metal locations. 'This is the faultline. Steve discovered it by closely looking at the rock, which is made up of tiny bits of sand grains and bigger pieces of red stone and sometimes pebbles. I've a piece here, just a second.' He rummaged at the back of the tent, refusing to allow himself another lingering glance at Sue lying there, found a lump of rock and came back to his sketch.

'This is a piece of the rock by the lower area of metal. If you look at it close-up, you can see it has a line of small, tiny even, red pebbles running across it?' Sue nodded, holding the rock in her hand.

'Well that line on the cliff is horizontal, so it's a feature of the time of deposition. So, water was running over finer sand at the time this rock was laid down, made if you like, by depositing these small pebbles. Steve spotted that this distinct pebbly line was on both these shaded sections on my sketch. In other words, the fault has caused the rocks to separate by fifteen feet. That happened millions of years after the sandstone was made.'

'So, looking at the cliff, straight on, if you can remember, visualise it, these horizontal rocks all look the same.' Peter thought this was turning into a lecture and he speeded-up to get through it, hoping Sue was as interested as she looked. 'Layers of horizontal, near enough, sandstone fractured here and there and weathered so it looks sort-of 'blocky'. But this line of blockiness, if that is a word, is a fault. So, first appearances are deceiving. It looks consistent across the cliff, but on close examination, it isn't.'

'I get that Pete. And I remember the talk up there that day. The four of us looking at the cliff. You, me, Mr MacKenzie, Mr Fraser. Because the metal looks so much a part of the rock, you would swear it is! I remember you saying it is like the metal was on the sand before it consolidated into rock. But that would be hundreds of millions of years ago. Can't remember how many!?' She laughed slightly.

'Seven or eight probably', said Peter.

'So it's impossible then, because there wasn't any metal lying around at that time. Unless an alien dropped it. That's right isn't it?'

'Yep, you've got it. So, those two guys said, as that idea is ridiculous, then it has to be just a weird occurrence, that two bits of metal got fused into the cliff here and here', indicating on the sketch. 'And a coincidence that it is the same rock. It wouldn't have become so pre-occupying if Steve hadn't uncovered the fault. Steve made an important discovery.'

'Thanks Pete. I've got all that now. The reporter didn't really pick up on the alien idea did he?'

'No. I think people up here are just fairly straightforward. No-

nonsense types, as my Mum would say. Also, the war and its happenings is a big thing for people who lived up here then and they know of a few wrecks already, and so on.'

Sue sighed. 'Wouldn't it be great though if it was aliens!' Imagine them dropping by the Earth all that time ago.'

'Yeah, don't know why they would have bothered Sue. It was mostly just desert then, the oceans might have had some jelly fish but otherwise just the rocks and the weather.'

'Like your mapping area Pete!'

'Yeah' he laughed. 'There would have been no lochans to swim in though!'

'That would be a shame.' She turned her face away from the sketch to look at Peter. 'That was a nice day wasn't it.' Statement, not a question. 'Pete'. She said. 'I loved that day and I don't know I've thanked you enough. It wasn't the obvious, but everything of that day was ... just, oh, just really nice. Two great days I've had on your mountain, in fact.'

Sue looked at the drawing Peter had just produced. 'When you talk about it I can see you love this subject. Like when you were hopping around on the rocks up there. It's so different to an arts subject. To any subject maybe.' She let out a long sigh. 'Pretty perfect for someone who loves the mountains too. Maybe I should have done geology.'

'You're interested in it though, that's something at least.'

'Aw Pete, you're just a good teacher. Seriously.'

'Hmm – maybe. We've got our careers to think about when we get back to the final year. Someone else said I should consider teaching.'

'Was that Penny?'

'No, it was another geology student. A mate really. Mate of Graham's too.'

'Do you think you and Penny will try and work near each other?'

'I doubt it. We all might just have to go to where the work is. I don't mind really.'

'Maybe you could get a job up here? I could come and visit you maybe. We could go walking in the mountains, I'd like that.' Said Sue.

They were both lost in thought then. A mix of daydreaming and thinking of the reality of final year and getting work afterwards.

'Do you think we will keep in touch Pete?'

'Of course!' Peter answered within a split second. 'I'd like to write to you Sue. When I get back to Mum's, I will send a postcard or something to say I'm there, as a starter. Just so you know. It would be good to write properly though.'

'I'd like that.' A pause. 'Do you think we could meet?'

'I'd like to, very much. Need to think how. Maybe I could come across from Bristol.'

'Would you? What about Penny? Not sure she would be too keen on you doing that.'

'I don't know. I would like to see you again though.' And Peter realised how much he meant it.

'What about the others here Pete?' asked Sue.

'Well, Graham's a mate already. I imagine we will try and keep in touch after uni, but that's a way off yet.'

'What about Steve though?' Sue was giving him that look again. The one where he could almost feel her rummaging around in his head. It suddenly dawned on him that the conversation might have been steered in this direction. He felt he was in a situation now where he would tell Sue anything, if she asked. They were together in a cramped tent, him semi naked, warm, comfortable and enjoying sharing each other's company. But also, effectively trapped, as he had been in a talk with Graham.

'You and Steve seemed to have a lot to do together after his near-accident.' Peter heard an alarm bell starting to ring in his head.

Knew Sue was definitely exploring something with him now.

'You like him, don't you? Miss him I imagine?'

Hesitating, feeling he was being drawn into a discussion that he couldn't control. Peter just said, 'Yeah, he's a really nice guy.'

'The two of you, nice guys I'd say.' Said Sue.

Peter poured the tea looking out across the campsite, just pulling the flysheet zip closed a little. Felt like the need for privacy, but still keeping contact with the outside air.

Turning round, Sue was taking off her mini-skirt. 'It is hot in here Pete. Thought I would join you.' She took off her T-shirt too. White bra and pants, small robin motif on both.

Peter smiled. 'When you did all that washing, I loved the look of those, as you know. They are kind-of cute.' And he had the idea Sue might have put them on specially, meaning this whole talk they were having, had been planned by Sue. He felt humbled at the thought. Then he realised it was true and he had been set-up, but in the loveliest way he could imagine.

'Thanks.' She said. 'I've had them a while, don't think I've grown much, in any direction.' She paused and looked up and down Peter's body so close to hers. 'I can see you have just grown a bit in yours', she teased.

They sipped some tea, cross legged, in just their underwear, at ease with each other like that. Peter felt a desperate need to do or say something, but couldn't think what. He had fantasised about seeing Sue like this, in his tent and yet now, it all felt too late. The thought of Steve intruded into what would have previously been a dream-like situation.

Tea finished, they stretched-out. Facing each other, lying on their sides, heads propped up on their arms, elbows digging into the foam mats. Comfortable for both of them. Looking into each other's eyes. Peter felt he had known her for so much longer than seven weeks. He could feel his arousal had gone and was struck now by how much he just liked Sue and her company.

'Pete...'

His eyes dropped then, he bit his lip, he knew in the one word that Sue was going to ask him more about Steve. Knew he would have to tell her. The irony of that struck him forcefully. The first woman he felt really comfortable with, when intimate, either naked embracing each other and kissing, or having a deep conversation together in just your pants. This woman was going to ask him the profoundest thing and he was not going to be able to deny it.

'... that faultline. It's interesting isn't it? You look at something, like that cliff of rocks, but what you're seeing isn't the whole story. There's something else, hidden unless you really look hard.' Just like that, said calmly, still friendly, reaching out to him with her eyes. Imploring him.

They looked at each other, she was wanting him to say something and he understood for certain that she knew.

'How do you know?'

'I didn't for sure. Not until this discussion maybe.' Peter saw Sue's eyes become moist and he could feel he was starting to well-up too. He realised he was biting his lip again, really hard.

'I've seen you going into Steve's caravan, coming out again in the morning. I thought it was just like me and Jules – a change for you from your tent. Steve just being nice and friendly'

'I'm not a queer Sue.' Peter needed to declare it quickly and emphatically.

Sue paused before speaking. 'I hate that word too.'

'I can't be though can I? Look what we did together just a week or so ago.' Peter felt like his fingers were slipping as he clutched at normality.

'Yeah, it was lovely. But you know I can feel that part of you is compelled to do it, you wanted to do that with me to be what you see as normal?' To Peter, it was like she really had been inside his head. 'It's small things. You have been attentive, friendly, open, kind. You did something with me I haven't had any other guy do – not like that. Not with the same result. I knew you wanted to please me and I found that a huge turn-on. I trusted you and I loved being up on your mountain that day, with and without clothes.'

'I just wanted to please you. So much.' Peter bit his lip so hard it hurt.

'I know. You did. You do! But Pete...You need to live to please yourself too.'

Peter supped his tea, then drained the rest. He wasn't sure what to say. Felt a mix of things, relief probably most strongly. Being honest felt good too. He reached for the packet of cigarettes and took two of them out and lit them both. He passed one to Sue. He needed her to join him right at this moment.

'When did you first know?' Sue asked.

'I had feelings for other boys at school, classmates. Thought everyone did, but soon realised that wasn't so. The changing rooms I suppose. My Mum's shopping catalogues!' He laughed, breaking the tension a bit. Sue laughed along with him, saying she hadn't realised teenage boys used their Mum's shopping catalogues in quite that way.

'But knowing? I don't know, probably just right now too. Here in my little tent. With you.'

Sue moved closer to him, wrapped an arm round him. They kissed. The tang of smoke didn't bother either of them. She leant her head against his chest as he lay on his back. Peter felt lost in his thoughts as Sue rolled over on to her back too. The tent was so warm and filled with the orange glow he had come to love. It felt safe again. They finished the cigarettes. There was something about the conversation and the warmth – Peter found himself drifting-off and noticed a change in Sue's breathing. For a few minutes they were both asleep.

Stirring, then fully coming round, Sue sat up with a start, waking Peter. 'Oh God! I'm really sorry Pete. I promised Julie I wouldn't be too long. I've been a couple of hours. Sorry.' Putting T-shirt and skirt back on. 'Must get back. Sorry'

Stopping in the tent doorway and looking at Peter now sitting-up, running a hand through his hair, rubbing his eyes, Sue asked: 'Can I come back later?'

'Sure.' He said, looking at her, feeling a little befuddled. 'Er, yeah, of course.' Then, shaking his head and ruffling his hair again, more brightly… 'Sue I'd like that. Come over whenever you like. Please'. She smiled and ran off across the site towards the tea room.

CHAPTER 33

Peter didn't see her again that day until after the tearoom had closed. Graham, who had been out on his mapping area, had returned. They'd shared a fag and a natter. Peter found himself feeling closer to Graham now too. They had been neighbours and companions for nearly seven weeks.

Graham had offered to take Peter's rock samples back to Bristol and bring them in at the start of term. Peter thought this was so thoughtful and helpful. Graham's parents had brought him here and were collecting him. He didn't feel envious of that. In fact, in a way he was looking forward to the long train journey home on Saturday morning. Just two more days in the field, two more days here. Mixed feelings and mixed emotions.

'One of your looks going on there Pete. Penny for them?' asked Graham, throwing back at Peter one of his own phrases...

'Hmmm, sorry, I was just miles away there, mulling over the whole thing. Thinking about getting back.'

'I could see you were deep in thought then. Your brow was really furrowed.'

'Really? Well, a lot's happened it feels! Thought it was just fieldwork – didn't know all the other stuff would happen.'

Graham laughed, 'I know one thing. I'm really looking forward to a proper bath and shower.'

Laughing together then. 'Yeah. Stand-up washes get a pain in the end. How many times did we go to Torridon in the end? Four times?'

'Probably' Then we all had a swim in your mountain lake and then there was the river. Then you had I don't know how many more swims with Sue!'

'Well you could have joined in Graham. There was that time by the river just over the other side of the village, me, Steve, Sue and

Julie - that was all I think you missed-out on.'

'Plus you and Sue had a swim you said. Up there somewhere'. Pointing towards Peter's mountain.

'Yeah, that too.'

'Talk of the devil!'

Sue was coming across to them again. She and Julie had just cleared-up and she wondered if she could have a quick word with Peter. Graham took the opportunity to go and have a wash, and leave them to it, just saying 'If you're fixing a time to go to the pub, count me in and let me know.'

Sue sat down cross-legged in front of Peter. 'Pete, I've been thinking. I wonder if I can ask a big favour?'

'Anything Sue.' Peter knew he really would go along with anything she suggested.

'These last three nights of yours'. He wasn't sure what she was going to say. 'Can I come and share your tent? Please?' He hadn't expected that. He immediately felt a bit tearful again, just the idea of her warm company. He fought against showing it.

'If you would like to do that...of course. Sue, that would be great.' Another new experience.

'Do I need to bring anything?'

'Well, are you moving in!?' He smiled at her, thinking, trying to be practical. 'erm, maybe, a pillow would be good.'

'I've two, I'll bring both – nice for you too, for a few last nights.'

'Sleeping bag. Of course. Toothbrush? Depends if you're going back to your and Julie's caravan? Guess you will'

'Yeah, I guess it's really just the nights. I want your company. I will miss you like mad when you go.'

Graham was back, when Sue came over with two pillows. He just flicked his eyes from Sue to Peter, raised his eyebrows, more in question than comment. Didn't say anything.

So, that evening, the nightly visit to the pub was relaxed, friendly and cheerful. Peter was conscious how much he would really miss all this. The reality of finishing was becoming very real. He had thought he and Sue would leave early to go back to the tent that evening, but it felt a bit embarrassing in the end. Sue seemed to think the same, at least he hoped that's what it was.

They said the usual good nights, people going their own way. Graham said to Peter. 'Change of plan then? Thought Sue was moving in!'

'Think she is. Just gone to clean her teeth I suppose. I don't know.'

As it turned out, this first night Sue had hung back in the shadows, feeling a bit awkward, until Graham had shut up his tent, and then she came over to Peter's. With her sleeping bag.

'Get yourself settled Sue, while I do my teeth. Won't be a few mins.'

In the wash block, he realised he had the head torch that he used in the tent, hoped he hadn't left Sue in the dark but thought maybe he had. Getting back he was relieved to see his tent showing a welcome orange glow. Inside, she had arranged the two sleeping bags next to each other. With the notebooks, clothes, rocks and everything else, it meant the sleeping space was even narrower than it would normally be for him.

'So, what do you keep on in your bag Pete?'

'What do you do?'

'I asked first.'

'OK, well normally I wear nothing if I'm on my own. If I'm on a Club trip or something, sharing, then I would keep my underpants on.'

'Let's do that then' Sue said. 'I was thinking though. Will you make a nice cup of tea for me in the morning?'

'Of course, anything' said Peter, just so happy to do things to please her.

'I might have breakfast here one morning, haven't brought anything for tomorrow though. Better go back to Jules. Maybe do a meal together though, one evening? I'd really like that.'

'Ok with any or all of that Sue.'

Going off to sleep, Peter felt so comfortable. He could feel Sue in her sleeping bag, close against him. There was no escaping each other in the space. He felt as if he was…what? Home?

The next evening they did do a meal together and it was OK to sit outside. Peter had completed his last day of map work. Graham joined in a bit. Jules brought some stuff over, including wine and glasses. Peter felt like other people on the site. He had gone from being a solo camper, student, to what would seem to others like another young couple with friends. Normal again, he thought.

As a break from beer and because the evening damp and the midges were too misery inducing, everyone dropped the idea of the pub for a change. Peter felt just as happy lying in the tent, reading a book, sharing a quiet moment with Sue. Happy! They had hardly spoken for a couple of hours and decided to sleep once it became really dark. Peter found he hadn't smoked that evening. A first! He realised he hadn't even thought about it.

They were just quietly lying there. Light gone out. Sue said, 'Pete, can we do this differently.'

'Whatever Sue. What do you want?'

So, they put the torch light on. Sue opened up the two sleeping bags, used one underneath and the other on top. No sooner had they got in the new sleeping arrangement and the light off, that they embraced each other. Sue whispered 'If I kiss you now, we will not get any sleep.'

'Let's see'.

They kissed. Sue whispering in his ear. 'Is it alright if…?'

'I know Sue. I just like hugging you tight like this too. Kissing you makes me feel like, I don't know, like falling into a pile of velvet cushions, or something.'

'It just feels the nicest thing Pete. I feel so snug like this.' They kissed again, neither wanting to let it go. Eventually sleeping.

Pete's last day was partially spent on writing and drawing and partially tidying-up seven weeks' worth of papers, notes, maps. Leaving rock specimens with Graham. Speaking to Nick, Julie, the campsite warden. Also taking time to talk with Jock, the village shop staff and lastly John MacKenzie.

'Well you've had some experiences Peter. I don't think you will be forgetting us in a hurry.'

Peter thought to himself how true this was and whether the Warden would sound so happy about it if he knew more of those experiences. 'I don't think I will ever forget this time up here. I can't believe the seven weeks stint is up already and yet I also feel like I've been here for months.'

John MacKenzie had shaken his hand then. 'Peter, you will be welcome back here any time. It's been a pleasure knowing you a wee while and I really do wish you all the best for your future. Whatever you do, I hope it works-out well.'

Then he continued, 'a lot of people your age, come on something like this, have an adventure, do their work and move on to the next experience. I don't think that's you. You've struck me as someone who thinks a lot about what you're doing, but more than that, the people you meet.'

'Do you think so?' Peter was really surprised by what felt like a speech from the warden.

'I know so! I never had any concerns about you up there on the mountain on your own, not like I would for others. The way you dealt with the wee drama with your friend Steve. And other things. The gang of you have been noticed in the village you know. Mostly in a good way.'

Peter was quite taken aback by this and didn't think he deserved it. Felt embarrassed a bit. It made him feel a little sad too. Even so, what the warden had said made Peter feel like he had at least done something with the summer and his fieldwork. Something important to him. Something… what word was he searching for? Yeah, that was it! Valid.

A letter arrived from Steve on his last day. It was all steady handwriting, he noticed, very straight lines, even on plain paper.

31st July 1977

Dear Pete.

I hope this letter gets to you before you leave Kinlochewe. Think it will, but I meant to post it earlier. By the time you read this, I guess you will only have a day or two left?

Well, I made it back OK. Took hours! Made me think of your journey up from Bristol. It must have taken your mates days to get over the drive.

I have been unpacking all my stuff. My Mum was amazed at the mound of dirty washing! I think she was a bit appalled too. I told her how difficult it was to wash stuff, and dry it, but I don't think she believed me. I started to tell her about the girls washing some stuff for us all. She looked really shocked, so I cut it short.

She said she was worried about me getting under their feet for the whole of August and September (most of it anyway). So, I was shooed off to get a job. I've managed to get some shelf-stacking at the local Morrisons, covering staff holidays. Just done my first day. I quite like it and it gives me some cash for a few beers when I get back to uni!

I got permission from my supervisor, Dr Smith, to go into the department at the Uni. I dropped-off my rock samples and he's arranged to get them cut into thin sections for the start of term. This will give me a head start on writing up the thesis. There's so much of it! I had worried I had got distracted by things. By you, mainly! But there's more than I can deal with really. Doc Smith seemed impressed. He said my rough maps were 'excellent'. Can't be bad can it?

He also said how nice it was to meet you, Graham and Nick. He thought I would have been lonely up there if there hadn't been some other geology students around. He thought you and Graham seemed like decent guys. I told him about the 'rescue', and your part in it. He was pretty silent when I described it to him. He said it made him wonder if he should pair-up students going into wild country. A postgrad I bumped into in town has asked me about that since, so I think my nearly getting trapped on the mountain has given me notoriety already!

I also mentioned to the Doc that you had helped me with information about your mapping area and we had discussed it all together. I didn't tell anyone in the Department what else you and I did! I feel I shouldn't put everything in a letter either!!!

I am going to see Timothy though. By the time you get this, I should have met him for a piano lesson. I'm nervous about it but I am also just desperate to talk with him. After the phone call and the letter, I can trust him. I need to tell him everything. Hope he won't be bored or think I'm a prat.

It's been pretty difficult getting back to life here and I wish I was still up there. Wish I was still with you! I haven't been able to stop thinking about you Pete. Not only during the day, but every night I lie awake. Sometimes you can probably imagine how I help myself remember you!!

I thought I was going on a field project, to discover some geology. But I ended up discovering a lot more than that. I will never forget it.

Thank you for all your help with my map. Thank you, especially, for nearly rescuing me! I don't know what else to write!

I hope you have a good return. I expect you have been very busy. I hope Graham hasn't distracted you with too many joints! I expect Sue and Julie have been fussing over you. Especially Sue. She has a soft spot for you I reckon.

So do I!

Please promise you will write to me when you get home.

All the best.

Cheers

Steve. xxx

Peter was glad he had read this in his tent, because his hands were shaking and tears making traces down his face by the time he finished. He quietly snuffled, for quite a while.

After some persuasion that afternoon, Peter had eventually shown the letter to Sue. She had been concerned for him, seeing him quiet and bit withdrawn.

'Pete, that's a really nice letter. I would be made-up if someone wrote to me like that.' This made Peter feel upset again. Sue hugged him and used a tissue to dab his eyes. Seeing him like that made her well-up too.

'God, we're a right pair aren't we! Blubbing away here like this. And you with just one more night left.'

That very last night, of course, was down the pub. More cheerios. A pint 'on the house'. An early finish.

The last sleep in the tent, with Sue. The two of them locked together, finding it hard to get closer, but trying anyway, not wanting to let each other go. And then finally, the last morning arrived. Ben was taking him to the station at Achnasheen in his van. It had all been a bit of a rush. The tent had to be taken down and packed away and added to the enormous pack Peter had assembled the previous evening.

The last items to pack had really just been his sleeping bag and his tent. Julie was making an early morning tea and some toast for him. Sue rolled up her sleeping bag. There was only room in the van for one passenger, so it had meant the farewell had to be at the campsite. It was just as well because Peter was completely at sea. Before he took the tent down, as the last act, he and Sue sat cross-legged inside it, facing each other. The tops of their heads touching and the rest of their bodies just very still as they whispered their goodbyes.

Peter was simply unable to find any words he could say that would make sense, just couldn't speak really. Sue went off to join Julie and he rolled up and attached the tent to the rucksack frame. Took a deep breath. Blew his nose, took another deep breath. Walked over to the campsite hut.

Getting into the car and driving away, he noticed and read for the first, and last time, the small sign at car-driver eye-level, staked in the ground by the gate. Thanks for visiting us. Please come again.

Part Two

Aultbea, 2017

CHAPTER 34

Peter brought Mike a mug of tea and used it as an excuse to wake him. 'Oh, hi. What time is it then?' Drowsy, rubbing his eyes, stretching. Peter always thought he still looked boyish doing that.

'About nine.' Said Peter. 'Not too bad considering.'

'You look as if you're going out for a run or something.'

'No, just woke up feeling a bit bad about eating and drinking so much, so you know me, if I put these leggings on I just feel fitter.'

Mike thought that Peter was always wanting to look fit, was fit really! 'Pete, you don't need to worry about it… even if you are over sixty now!' He smiled.

'Ha bloody ha. It's only a day over.'

Peter changed his mind and decided to take off most of his clothes again and sit in bed for a chat, now Mike was waking up. They talked about the night before, how it had all worked out. Four couples in four chalets, each providing a course for the meal. It had saved a lot of preparation and a lot of clearing-up.

'John and Tina did a nice starter didn't they?'

'It was all good Pete. Think they got that salmon at that place in Shieldaig? You know, the woman who has converted her shed into a smoker – we stayed near there once.'

'Yes, reckon that's right. Our main course was good. Slow roast lamb, never fails.'

'Not the way you do it Pete. Sue and Ian's pud was nice. Two puds even!' added Mike.

'Yes, typical of them,' said Peter. 'Thoughtful. A rich one and a light one. She had both too, but it never shows on her, does it?'

'No, it doesn't. Think we're all doing alright actually, considering. Then there was the cheese and stuff from Philip and Alan'.

'Do you think they've got onto the local Grindr yet?' Peter joked.

'Don't know, but think they were a bit taken aback with the remoteness up here, but they seem pretty knocked out by it too.'

Mike thought that would have pleased Peter a lot. He always wanted people to share his enthusiasms and especially for the really important stuff like the far north west. He didn't need Peter to be too enthusiastic just now though, as he was still waking up. He knew Peter had picked-up on this and had immersed himself in his notebook, still sitting beside him though in bed, but being quiet.

It had been a really nice evening Mike thought. Peter's sixtieth had gone through a few planning iterations before deciding on a small group of close friends, so it could be up here. Location being the main thing in the end. He and Peter had wanted to pay for everything, the accommodation, the food and drink. So, the original plan to do this for lots of friends just would have been ridiculously expensive. No point in starting retirement by blowing a huge hole in the budget.

These chosen friends were mostly known to both of them for decades, Philip and Alan a little less. In terms of age, John and Tina were older than Peter, Sue the same age, and everyone else, including Mike, a bit younger. It all helped Peter feel comfortable about the big number birthday.

After a while Peter went off to set breakfast and drove down the beach road to the village shop to get newspapers. It would be full of Brexit and the forthcoming election. It felt really good, Mike thought, to be away from all that. And it did feel very away from it up here. Increasingly like a foreign country, in fact, but in a good way. Almost like going away to Iceland, a recent holiday, wild and remote, a similar feel. He mulled on that a bit.

The morning passed by with breakfast, coffee and chats with their friends popping in and out. Nobody seemed to want to do anything much and that suited Mike too. He really just wanted to spend the day reading and enjoying the light coming into the big picture window, and seeing all the birds on the seed feeders the site owners had provided. He knew Peter would not be satisfied with being still though, and hoped he would go out, enjoy himself and make the most of it while here.

So, he stretched out and made himself comfortable. Trying to settle into the book he was reading. He did keep thinking about this area too. It had been important to him, as well as Peter, since he was a teenager, or even a bit before. Once the two of them started to go on holiday together, he had found his way to Wester Ross again, and it had been nice. He was feeling drowsy in the warm sun from the big window.

Coming back some while later, with another mug of tea, Peter thought Mike looked very peaceful, stretched out on the couch, book fallen open on this chest, his drink untouched on the coffee table. Bluetooth speaker playing a favourite playlist from his phone. Reluctant to wake him but not wanting to fester the whole day himself, he knelt down and whispered in his ear. 'Mike, I'm going for a walk up the hill with Sue. Would you like to come?' Mike just smiled, turned a little, didn't open his eyes and curled-up a bit more.

'That's what I thought! I'll be back about four, maybe five, depends on how far we get. I don't know if it will be dry enough to get…'

'Just go Pete!' Stirring enough to give a kiss. 'Be careful. Come back if it starts to rain.'

As expected, Sue was outside her chalet, waiting. 'Ian not coming then Sue?'

'Nope. Neither Mike then?'

'Nope.' He copied Sue and gave her a smile. 'Curled up for the rest of the afternoon I should think'.

They set off over the cattle grid and up the track across the rough pasture, past a couple of houses. Both in trekking trainers, running tights and fleeces – dark red top for Sue, light grey for Peter.

The level section near the hillside oil bunkers always surprised him. This was his third time here and the extent of the NATO fuel site was greater than he remembered.

'Maybe they have built more of it then?' Sue asked.

'Don't think so Sue. It's just getting my eye in. They don't exactly label it, but there's a hell of a lot of oil stored here. Look at all those bunkers buried into the slopes.'

'I thought it was amazing that new exhibition place they have tacked-on to the end of the village.' said Sue. 'When you look back over the loch now it's incredible to be able to visualise, from those photos, just how many ships were here during the war.'

'The most amazing thing is no one was allowed out of the area and most of the rest of country had no idea. In fact, most still don't. This oil dump though; it's current, not history. Again, all the time I've been coming up here I had no idea there was a Naval refuelling station until recently.'

'There's a lot we don't know Pete.'

'Yeah it used to bother me. That sort of thing. All the military stuff and the secrecy. But now, well it's like Philip was saying last night "whose finger do you want on the button? Ours or the other side!?" I know what he means. How you think about the world changes doesn't it? When I was twenty I thought I wouldn't change in that way'

'Well, I'm not sure you have changed much really. And yes, we did all cover a lot of ground talking last night!' Then, changing the subject, 'God I needed to get out this afternoon, no matter what weather. It's a good spot Pete. Nice place to celebrate a sixtieth.'

'I just feel at home here Sue. I've loved it up this way for decades, as you know.'

He couldn't be anywhere else. Just him, his partner, a handful of close friends. The small chalet park only had a dozen cabins and he had taken over four of them. Last night they had all piled into the one for drinks and supper. Today's poor weather forecast had given everyone an excuse to lie-in and fester away the afternoon.

'You've been up this path before then, obvs?' asked Sue.

'Yeah, it's good for a stretch, you'll see in a mo' that it's really quite wild up here, once you get past the military thing.' He paused, reflecting on previous excursions right here, with Mike and on his own.

'The first time we came here, three years ago, was just when I was trying to get my head around the idea of future retirement. Loads going on. It was a good break. Near to the Torridon Hills, but with other mountains around and some between here and there too.'

'Ann seems friendly.' Said Sue, referring to the site owner. 'Happy to help us but keeping out of the way.'

'She and her partner grew up here apparently but moved away. They came back when tourism started taking-off. Their house was her parents' and they had a small holding, but the chalet park is a steadier income I guess.'

'Wow, that's a great view looking back.' Said Sue, taking a breather and looking out across Loch Ewe towards the North Atlantic.

'Yeah it is! We will head up that hill to the north there a bit, where it's even better. You can see down to Torridon. It's a couple of hundred meters up from here and it's about a mile of tussocks and rocks. Ankle straining stuff.'

At the hill-top the view to the east and north was broad and clear. The rain had blown away and the cloud base was lifting steadily. To the far north, the Coigach hills and even Suilven were visible in the clear air. Snow still capping the summits. They had the place to themselves.

'The last time I came up here it was a bit warmer, it was late May that time, just a little later than this trip.' Said Peter.

'Still pre midges then.'

'Yeah it was. I stripped off when I left the path and came up here like that, dressed like that. Well, undressed like that.'

Sue laughed. 'You don't change do you? Still taking opportunities to take off your clothes in the mountains.'

'Winding up my work was doing my head in and I got up here and just felt so free. Just so liberated. I just needed to throw-off everything, including all the worries and little anxieties.'

'I know you've been up this way many times but I never understand why Ian and I have never made it at the same time.'

'Just busy lives I suppose. Nice we're all together now though. With the party done last night, I'm hoping the weather will clear a bit to get back to Beinn Eighe, 'my mountain' and whatever else we can fit in.'

'It's all a long time ago isn't it!?'

Rather out of the blue, Peter said 'I contacted Steve on Linked-in. Did I say before?'

'I remember you had lost touch with him, but, no, what's that about then?'

'The wonder of modern technology I suppose. Looked up his name, university, the word geologist and up came his profile. No pic though, so don't know what he looks like now. I sent him one, or rather there's one on my profile anyway.'

'Did he reply?'

'I was hoping you would ask that Sue. Let's sit down a moment.' Peter smiled at her and pulled a sheet of paper from his pocket. 'Here's one I produced earlier', he said with a slight flourish.

'This is the only correspondence for very many years. The first part is my message to him and the second bit is his reply. Would you like to read it?'

'May I?' Sue looking for her glasses case in the top of her rucksack. Peter nodded, feeling very focused on her right now. Whenever they sat together closely, he marvelled how little she had changed in his eyes. Like himself, a few lines and wrinkles maybe, but her hair still long and bronzy – even if topped-up with a tint. His was very silvery, he knew.

'That's better' she said, 'I can see it properly now'.

Hi Steve. I have found you on Linked-in. This is Pete from the fieldwork in Kinlochewe! A test of memory maybe! But, hopefully you will remember…

How are you?

Gosh, it's hard to know what to write after so long. Firstly, I was pleased to see your profile says you are a professional geologist. I knew you would be! Of the geologists doing fieldwork that summer (1977!!) you were easily the brightest and best.

The last time we were in touch, we were still trying to find a way of meeting up again. You were well stuck-in to your research and I was working in the road transport industry. Looking back on it now, it was all-consuming. I eventually left the transport industry though, partly, a big part actually, because I couldn't be open about my identity there.

I have travelled an interesting career path, others tell me, but have never stopped collecting rocks and in fact I now volunteer as a guide in the nearby nature reserves, where I live. I never lost interest, and have often reflected on, and remembered, your natural enthusiasm for the subject.

There were other things I never lost interest in either and you might be interested to know I got married – civil partnership anyway. My partner is called Mike and we have been together for years. He

saved me from myself and from the possibility of forever living a lie!
Although I had no girlfriend at that time, I had tried very hard to not
be like this. To not be who I am. He was in a similar position really,
so we sort-of saved each other really, which was lovely.

Do you remember the others that summer? Do you remember Sue, at
the tearoom? You may remember we were close! I'm pleased to say she
is still a great friend – the first person I came out to. This happened
twice in fact! A long story…

It would be great to know how you're getting on Steve. And maybe a
little about your life now, if you feel like it.

I remember you with great fondness and it seems a shame we
lost touch. Probably inevitable though. However, I have always
remembered you, your caravan, your car (!), the trips to Torridon for a
shower, and so much more.

It would be great to hear from you if you feel like writing back.
Maybe a photo? Your profile doesn't seem to have one, or maybe it's my
(lack of) IT skill. I'm in Aultbea, north of Kinlochewe, in May. Bit
of a long shot, but wondered if you might be around?

Best wishes.

Pete

26 March 2017

Dear Pete.

It was a nice surprise to get your note out of the blue! Despite being a geologist, I am still amazed by the sense of passing of time. Your message took me back a lot.

As you say, I have become a 'proper' geologist over the years. I think that's what my boss would say.

After Leeds, I decided I had enough of academia and went into oil, as you might remember, and then mining. The money has been a lot better than Uni for sure. I have spent most of my life travelling though and for the last few years have been split between the UK and Australia.

I have stayed single. Probably the best thing with all the travel. Relationships never seemed to work-out for me, though I tried a few times along the way. It has always been like we were, if you take my meaning.

I remember Kinlochewe and those things you mentioned. I also remember the swims in the river, being buzzed by the RAF, nearly scaring the crap out of us. I remember that tatty old caravan and can't believe I survived several weeks in it. And you were in that tiny tent!

I will never forget coming off the mountain, soaking wet and cold and being met by you and a rescue party.

I'm glad things have worked out for you and you have found someone to share 'your nest'. I thought it might have been Sue at one time. It's nice you have remained friends all this time.

I remember you well, of course.

*I can't be in Scotland the date you mention, but if you want to try
and find another time, I would love to go walking in the hills above
Kinlochewe again with you.*

Keep in touch.

STEVE

Sue studied the paper for a long time. 'What did you think?'

'At first, it's like he mentions in there. I think that I understand time. Reading that though, the sense of time completely overwhelmed me at first.' He shook his head. 'I don't know Sue. It was all a bit intense then, I think.' He looked to Sue for confirmation. 'It's nice to be remembered. I'm sorry he didn't find someone to share his life with.'

'But perhaps he's happy Pete? Maybe he wasn't so emotionally insecure as you!' She laughed.

'Oh, thanks a bunch Sue!' and he gave her a playful shove.

'What's that bit about the RAF? I don't remember that story.'

'I didn't either! Shows my memory is not infallible. Which was a shock in itself! In the end I had to imagine where that would have been. Had to think of the noise of those Phantom jets or whatever they were, suddenly ripping the sky above our heads. It came back to me then – the river by the drumlin field. They still do that down the valley actually, over Torridon.'

'It's nice he remembered me too.' Sue said.

'He probably just remembers the free teas and greasy pizzas.'

'Bugger off, you cheeky devil.' She gave him a light push this time. 'They weren't that greasy!'

They both felt wistful then.

'He was a nice guy Pete. Must still be, I imagine. None of us knew anything then did we? About the future I mean, we had no idea where it was all leading. I look back on being twenty, back there that summer…'

They were both lost in their thoughts then, just looking out at the distant mountains and the sea.

Chapter 35

The next day, they had all decided they wanted to go to Gairloch first by car, and then walk through the village together, out the other side and on the road to Badachro. They were dressed for all weathers, boots of various styles, jeans or something more outdoorsy, jumpers and various brightly coloured cagoule jackets – all zipped open at the moment.

Mike told Peter that he didn't want him reminiscing again about Gairloch forty years ago and how they may have met outside a café! It was too late though, to avoid raising the interest of the others who had overheard the remark.

Mike said 'You know what Pete is like, he's always reminiscing.'

'It's not true Mike. I just think that particular story is interesting and I know you have heard me go on about it before.'

'Only every time we come up here!'

'Get off Mike, that's just not true.' Peter ruffled up Mike's hair and gave him a hug.

'Get off yourself.' Mike replied, laughing.

'Well, if you've heard it so often, you tell it then!' said Peter.

They had all stopped now. No traffic on the tiny road by the loch under the trees. Sue stood back a bit, knowing the story, probably as well as Mike did.

'OK' said Mike. 'Years and years ago, I used to come up here with my aunt and uncle and cousin Jane. You've met her.' Nodding at everyone. 'We used to come here for a series of summers, not sure how many. My aunt had a relative here and there was a house that was a holiday let – to friends and family anyway.'

'How old were you then?' asked John.

'I think it was between about eleven or twelve, and fifteen. And it was around that age, the last holiday up here, Peter thinks he met me!'

Peter took up the story. 'I had come into Gairloch with a mate from the campsite where I was doing my geology project. I had done about three-quarters of it and had run out of money. My bank, back in Bristol, had arranged some cash for me to be obtained at that bank branch we just passed on the corner back there.'

'Crikey, has it been there in the same space, all that time?' John again.

'Yeah – hasn't changed. Don't think so anyway. Anyway, my mate Graham and I wandered into the main part of the village for a look around, where we have all just parked the cars, before hitching back. We had a nice little walk along the beaches and little cliffs – like we've just done. So, I remember clearly we found a tearoom. I can't recognise it now. It was about fifteen pence a cup! Mike, his uncle and aunt, and Jane came along and we all had a brief chat. No kidding!'

'None of us remember it though' said Mike. 'Except Pete.'

'It sounds pretty unlikely' said Ian, typically. He was always the one to be rational, thinking things through, suspicious of anything that even approached mystical.

'Yes, but I remember it...' continued Peter. '... because, a, getting the money was really, really important to me and, b, I couldn't believe I would get it.'

'How much was it again?' Sue asked, giving Peter a knowing, teasing look.

'Twenty-five pounds!'

They all laughed at that.

John said, 'Yes but fair enough, if a cup of tea was really fifteen pence, I can see twenty-five quid was quite a bit.'

'Enough for food and drink for a week and half, and a train home', Peter stated.

'And cigarettes. They were the main thing then!' Sue said. More laughter from everyone.

'Yes, and fags!' said Peter. 'And look, I've nearly lost the thread now. The point is, it was a significant moment and I know it was…' emphasising the word know, '…because I had one of those feelings like time was compressed or something. I remember it but it's hard to describe the feeling – a sense of being in the same physical space but in a different time? Weird.'

They walked on. To Peter, none of the others looked very convinced.

'Think everyone else thinks the same as me with that story Pete.' Said Mike, after a moment.

'Well, I don't care! It is true!' said Peter, 'it's my party and I'll believe it if I want to!' he half-sang. They all laughed with him.

They gathered together under the trees by the signposted path to The Fairy Lochs. After a comfort break and some sharing of cakes, they set off.

It was somewhere that Peter had wanted to visit for a while. The track was boggy, wet and bouldery but the brief description in their pocket-guide was accurate enough to follow easily. They were all in a line with Pete at the back, Mike and Sue up front.

At one point they stopped and Sue read out an extract: '*In a particularly wet area, the path fades, bear right rather than continuing towards a point where the burn cascades down. A cairn marks the high point on the path, with great views of the Torridon mountains ahead, as well as back over Gairloch.* Well, that's all true. This view is stunning' she said. And they spent some time trying to interpret which mountains they were looking at from this angle, which ones were hidden. Could they see Pete's mountain, he was asked. They spent some time looking. John, Ian and Peter all had binoculars but the bulky mountains all nestled in with each other from a distance and even those that knew them found it hard to separate and name the peaks. Philip and Alan seemed quite awe stuck by the scale of the landscape.

Sue continued then: '*The path descends towards a lochan, where the wreckage from a Second World War air crash can be seen. The bomber was returning troops to the USA in 1945, when it became lost and hit the top of Slioch, above Loch Maree. The aircraft was damaged and the crew may have been looking to land on the water by Gairloch, when it hit the rocky spurs around the Fairy Lochs, killing all fifteen on board, most of them in their twenties. The site is now a war memorial and it is forbidden to collect or move any of the debris.*'

'I remember this story from nineteen seventy-seven, believe it or not, or, at least, the outline of it.' Continued Sue.

'Sue went up Slioch back then, didn't you?' added Peter. He described the nature of the mountain to the others, Sue chipping in too. Then they approached the site of the tragedy and all of them became more sombre.

When they reached the actual site they were astonished to see, amongst other bits of plane, a large propeller half emerging from the water. There seemed to be much more wreckage than they were expecting. Bits of aluminium and maybe other metals, mostly dull but some astonishingly shiny. There was a plaque on the rocks, saying much the same as the guidebook, but with the added poignancy of the names of those who had died and their very young ages, save one who had been a few years older.

They were all silent and moved, just reading all the names to themselves. It seemed a long list like that – quite overwhelming. Without anyone asking, all eight of them looked out to the propeller and stayed quiet for several minutes. When people finally started speaking again, Sue asked Peter about the remains of the plane.

'I know what you're thinking Sue. Do you remember? What gets me is the colour and look of the metal. It looks like the stuff on Meall a Ghiubhais, doesn't it?'

'Yes, it does. This all looks more obviously like bits of something constructed though doesn't it? What I remember about your site was that the metal looked non-descript, abstract, fused onto the rock.'

'I know, but the colour and look – the reflectivity, it is all very reminiscent.'

None of them wanted to leave the spot quickly, wanting to be respectful to the individuals who had died and thinking of the significance of the whole event. Tina, Philip and Alan were actually all a bit moist-eyed.

'When you invited us Pete', said Alan, I didn't really know what it would be like. I didn't know what anything north of Glasgow looked like. And now, in addition to the scenery, we come across this. I'm pretty overwhelmed to be honest.'

After a while they quietly moved away and took the path round, to complete the looped trail, and back to the starting point. It was only on the path nearing Gairloch that anyone spoke again, so thoroughly lost were they all in their thoughts.

Chapter 36

The next day, Mike decided he had previously been up the Beinn Eighe nature trail and accompanied Peter onto his mountain, so declined to come again this time. In the end it was just Sue and Peter who went up on their own. The others opted for the chance of staying in the Gairloch café and bookshop for the morning instead, to let the weather clear. 'Clear enough to find a way to the pub I reckon', said Peter as they waved them away.

In truth, Mike, Ian, and the others had maybe cottoned-on to fact that the trip back to the mountain area above Kinlochewe was a bit of a private moment for Sue and Peter. Too heavily steeped in memory and nostalgia for others to join in comfortably.

Tina said she would have found it a bit tough-going as well and John wouldn't leave her for the day. Philip and Alan said they would have liked giving it a go, but they would enjoy Gairloch as much. They might be disappointed if they were on the prowl though, Peter thought. Although, he admitted to himself, 'I haven't a clue really'. There will be guys up here wanting to meet other men. Just because he had never explored it, didn't mean it didn't happen.

He and Sue parked up in what was now a much bigger car park than had been there in 1977. They headed up the more organised and signed path, noticing it was also now a quite entrenched and well-worn trail. There was a likelihood of more rain that day, but it had kept off so far and they hoped it would stay away for their little trip. They wore pretty much the same as the day out by the Aultbea oil bunkers, both comfy in fleeces and stretchy leggings. Both feeling fit and just glad to be outdoors.

However, the going was tough for both of them. 'Thank God we don't smoke any more Pete.' Said Sue, halfway up, stopping for a breather by some rocks where people could sit and look down Loch Maree. They both had noticed what hard work the path was, being so abruptly and unexpectedly steep compared to their memory.

'Well, you never did fags much anyway, did you? Just cadging them off me and others happy to share their evil habit with you.'

'I'm sure I bought some to give back to you guys.'

'Nope, not that I remember.' He looked at her, tying to give a stern and reproachful look, but unable to hold it. They both laughed. 'I don't recall this trail in detail either, do you?'

'Well, I only came up it the once.' Sue said. 'I remember it more generally than specifically I suppose. The feel of the place has come back to me very strongly though.'

At the highpoint, the plateau before them was vast and felt a bit unfamiliar at first. Like the previous time here, twenty years earlier, which had been with Mike, Peter was disappointed that what he considered to be an intact memory, was not so perfectly preserved. It was hard to point out landmarks even though at one time he believed he had known nearly every square metre. They decided not to try the summit of Meall a Ghiubhais. 'It's not going to go away' Peter had said. And Sue had replied, 'Yes, but how many more years will you be able to get up it?'

Peter looked to the north and directed Sue off the trail a little way. 'If we go across and down a bit, half a kilometre or so, we should get to a rise to see another view.'

The terrain was mostly a mix of rock outcrops and boggy dips, some drier, sandier areas of ground around pools and small lochans. The going was a bit slippery and after a couple of hundred metres they passed a particular area of water that was hidden from above, but marked on the map. Then on a rising outcrop, Peter stopped and pointed ahead and down. 'Look Sue, I was hoping we could get a glimpse of that lochan. Can you see it? Do you know what it is?'

'Where we had a swim that day? I do remember some bits of detail Pete.' Sue had known all morning where they were heading.

'Yep. Where we had that swim. That day. Christ, it's so long ago

Sue.'

'Yeah, I'm not going to say anything daft like "Oh Peter, it feels like only yesterday", she said. 'But, yes, I can make it out. So, just this side of that is where we spent some time one warm afternoon?'

'Indeed'.

'I expect you remember it as well as me. We seem blessed, if that's the right word, with great memory…'. They carried on walking, sometimes using their hands for balance on some of the slippery rock, '…of events anyway, not all these damn rocks!' They soon arrived at what now seemed like a decidedly small shallow area of ground with a large boulder beside it. A light breeze seemed to be steadily blowing across.

'Do you reckon this is it Pete?'

'I'd like to think so Sue. Unless my mind is filling-in the gaps for me. Standing here though, I can feel how I felt that day, not just my emotional feelings, I mean I can see the twenty year old me standing about here!' He looked around, trying to find anything that would give further certainty. He thought it was a good enough fit. 'You know, to me Sue, my memory is always somewhere I can go to if I want to escape or struggling to sleep or something.'

'And is it often here Pete?'

'To this area and that summer, more than anywhere else or any other time. I mean the whole area! Not just this one tiny spot!'

'Yes, it is small. If I was trying to be romantic, it would be spoilt a bit. It seems so damp around here, rocky and scruffy. It's a fond memory for me though. For us!' She reached for and held Peter's hand a moment.

'You know, I have been coming up here, to the mountains, since those field trips in the seventies.' Peter said. 'We didn't know how lucky we were. That summer was exceptional. I wore shorts loads of days here, mapping. You did too. On the campsite anyway. But I reckon I can practically count on one hand the number of shorts-days in the north-west highlands since then!'

Sue laughed. 'Me too. I liked those knackered shorts of yours, they were really tight on you and half a leg was ripped I remember.'

'And yours were pretty tight too Sue. But you had the figure for it...' seeing Sue's mouth turn down, '… and still do of course!'

'Don't be silly Pete'. Then she sighed. 'It was an important time for me too.'

'Let's have some of that flask of tea.' Said Peter. 'I've something to show you.'

They sat on one of the rocks, the driest they could find. Peter looked at it, grey, damp and covered in lichen. He couldn't recognise the rock, but knew it would be quartzite. Wondered how on earth he had managed rock identification all that time ago.

They both checked their mobiles. It hadn't occurred to them until now and they weren't sure they had much of a signal anyway.

'Message from Ian…' Sue said, '…In the pub, no need to rush back, followed by a smiley and that kiss emoji.'

'Yeah, pretty much the same for me too. I got a heart emoji though. Mike says they are having a good time and will be getting some fresh fish for tea; from Loch Ewe he says!'

'So, they are all fine then. Let's leave them to it for now, eh?'

Peter produced a notebook. A paperback-sized, black Moleskine one with a soft cover, that seemed to fit snuggly into his jacket map-pocket.

'I've kept occasional notebooks since the fieldwork, as you know. But I'm not going to do any geological sketches just now! Do you remember them Sue?'

Sue nodded, giving him a broad smile.

'But I still write down important things that happen. I was on a workshop recently, one of the organisations I was doing some work with, and the idea of a life timeline came up. You know the idea? This is mine, it's the peaks and troughs of life.'

'God Pete, I suddenly had a vision of one of your sections...
cross-sections! You drew some for me.'

Peter sighed then. 'It's sweet you remember that Sue. Mind you,
I don't know if anything I said or did then made sense – about
geology I mean. Or maybe anything else. When I look back, I feel
my twenty-year old self knew so little.'

Sue put her hand on his arm this time. Squeezed it tightly for a
moment. He looked at her face and gave a smile that he held for a
few moments.

Peter showed Sue the wiggly line going across several pages,
explaining the far, left-hand side of the first page was sort-of
childhood and the farthest right-hand side, more or less right now.

'The ups and downs of the line are the key life moments for the
author of the chart. Me!' Peter explained the idea was to draw it,
reflect on it, identify what was happening in your life at a particular
time and then to consider the whole thing. To identify patterns
that emerged. To ask what did it reveal for you across your history?
And, finally, and most importantly, what did it mean for you now?
He said it was a tool to ground someone, to expose their roots and
their inner core. Peter said that although he was actually pushed
back by some of that language, it had actually worked pretty well
for him.

'There's an obvious trough for me near the beginning with Dad
and everything, it's vague before then. I think that moment was
so significant it started my memory working the way it does now.
When I look back, it was like pressing record and it's still doing it.'

'Hmm, Pete. That's a pretty profound thing. I wonder if memory
is just more significant for those who like reflecting on things? If
someone doesn't think the past is important, they probably don't
remember much of it. That's definitely not you though! Or me.'

'I know Sue. The first time I drew this it was all events – new
job here, moved house there, nearly went bankrupt at this point,

salvaged by a decent job here, etc.' he zipped his finger across the pages while saying this.

'But the second and third time, think that's what this is, I understood the nature of drilling down and down, further and further. Getting to the moments in life that are most critical in leading to who you are today. I mean, to who I am today! If you follow?'

'Ah ha, I think I see where you're going with this. I wouldn't mind drawing one myself. Maybe not today though!' she joked.

'No, you're right. Sorry it's too self-indulgent Sue.' He moved, to put the book away.

'No Pete, I didn't mean like that. Come on, tell me. I didn't mean to put you off. I would like to, want to, hear it.'

'OK, well, in a nutshell.' Peter took a deep breath. Then pointing at a mark on a page, 'This is here, geographically here, that summer of '77, a high. There's rubbing-out on these pages as you see, cos I put in quite a bit about work, home and so on. Rubbed them out. All that's left is the moments that are fundamental to who I am. So, it's an identity chart really. It's probably what they do in psychotherapy!'

'You might pay someone a lot of money to do it for you though.' Quipped Sue.

'Don't mock Sue. I might just do that before long. Anyway, as I say, in a nutshell.' Running his finger slowly along the graph. 'From here, four decades ago, where it's about Steve…and also about you, of course. That point where I was trying to find the right way to go, looking back on it. Sue, doing this, I realised…. I'll come on to that.' He moved his finger to the right. 'Then there's a period of working really hard at being straight!'

'Trying to forget Steve, you mean?'

'Trying to forget what Steve and I did together, at first, yeah, as you well know. It was just too awkward to keep in touch with him across the country and I was trying so hard not to be like that.'

'So you never did.' Sue said. 'Keep in touch. And presumably he felt the same.'

'No, I never did meet him as such, and letters soon seemed difficult. Yeah, I guess he did feel the same. It was tricky then back in the seventies. Neither of us knew anyone who was homosexual who was a positive role model. Steve's piano teacher popped-up as a possibility, but he meant nothing to me. I think he helped Steve though. But other people who might be gay - It was all people you didn't really want to be like, so better to not be.' Peter continued, still moving his finger to the right.

'Then there's the intense period of trying to settle into work. Soon into that, Penny dropped out of my life and into that of someone else, which was the best thing to happen to her.'

Sue smiled at him. 'That was a very good thing for you too Pete!'

'Yeah, that's true.' Peter shrugged. 'It just would have been wrong.'

They took some sips of tea, pulled their fleeces a bit tighter as they turned to look down at the glen and towards the distant village. Peter found his eye following the line of the river flowing west towards Loch Maree.

'And during that time I lost contact with you a bit too'. Peter continued. 'Busy lives, too much distance, apart from anything else. Everything else!' Peter looked at Sue, studying her, could see her thinking, eyes at one moment closing slowly and then re-opening as she concentrated.

'So, to continue and speed up. Can you pour some more tea please? It's about here I got off with a bus driver in Portsmouth.'

Sue nearly spilt her tea. Laughing. 'You're joking, I don't remember you mentioning that before!'

'Well, it was a singular, but significant experience. That's why it's here on this page. I had contacted gay switchboard, gone to a meeting of a group called Adonis or some such. I liked this guy, who drove buses, and phoned the organiser of the group and got him to get the bus driver to make contact with me, if he wished. That was how it was done then, I think. I didn't get into it as a habit.'

'What happened then, did you meet on a bus then?' Sue teased him.

'Ha ha. No, at a pub. I was trying to not smoke then, and he didn't, which was unusual for gay men in the eighties. But I remembered smoking a packet of fags by the time we got back to his place though and, after a lot of encouragement, into his bedroom.'

'You the one having to be encouraged?' Sue said gently.

'Correct'.

Peter continued. 'He was nice, wanted to do what everyone thinks is the only thing gay men do, but the whole AIDS thing had kicked-off and I was nervous. We had a niceish time, but when I got home I couldn't wait to have a shower. Felt so guilty Sue, tried to wash it away, now I look back at it.' He paused a moment, then continued, 'I could have done more of that. You know – casual encounters. That was a real moment in time. That's what a lot of gay men do after all. Philip and Alan for instance, it's a way of life for many.'

'But you didn't. So, it was back to trying to make a success of being straight? Passing it off as just a phase you were going through?' Sue asked, knowing the answer already though. She paused briefly. 'And then came the Alps?'

'The Alps.' Long pause from Peter this time. 'Don't you reckon Sue, it was pretty uncanny to bump into each other in Chamonix that time?'

They both did a deep sigh, simultaneously. That made them laugh and they hugged again and looked up and around at the distant hills and mountains, both of them searching their memories.

'Yes, and no.' said Sue, picking up Peter's question. 'A surprise yes. But back then any Brit interested in climbing would end up in Chamonix and the Bar Nash, or fortuitously in our case, The Alpenstock bar.'

'The dear old Alpenstock!' A big high on Peter's graph, as he indicated. They both laughed together. Peter was pleased this wasn't becoming a heavy thing. He added 'But you see Sue, that's why I can't dismiss the idea of meeting Mike in Gairloch decades ago – the story everyone else poo-pooed yesterday!'

'Hmm, I know Pete. Sometimes things happen because it feels they are meant to be. I can't completely dismiss the idea of fate. Back in Cham' though. Two different climbing club groups in the same place'. said Sue. 'You were on some sort of Club meet with your mate Simon. I thought the two of you were so close, I was suspicious.'

'Simon and I were close. I think climbing partners become like that. He wasn't interested in girls or women at the time. But he wasn't into blokes either. I didn't think he was interested in sex at all, but a year after that trip he was married with a kid on the way!' They took another sip of tea. Peter looked at Sue, asking really if it was ok to carry on and he saw consent.

'So, we know this bit of the story well don't we? Before the Alps, I had known you had got married and was surprised at the speed.'

'I felt terrible not inviting you. I knew about Penny by then. You had written and told me at some point, but I was completely absorbed with my true love.' She shrugged. 'I knew you were probably on your own, but…'

'Come on! It would have been difficult me being there, I would have been in a sulk or something the whole time.'

'I know Pete' She gave him a hug across his shoulders. 'This is a great memory check, I'm enjoying it.' Have some more tea and carry on. Drink tea and carry on!' They laughed together.

'Yes, thanks. Lovely. So, back to 1985 and Chamonix, it had all come crashing down for you by then. That bastard you had discovered was still shagging his old girlfriend from before you and, on top of that, wanted you running around looking after him like his own mother.' He paused. 'And you had found out what else he could be like too.'

'Yes, all of that', said Sue, shaking her head a bit. 'it was a total mistake.'

'He swept you off your feet and straight into his bed.' Said Peter, nudging her to ensure she knew he was trying to keep it light.

'Yes, I had never had a boyfriend who was so self-confident. He was up for that sort of thing the whole time, he was successful in his job, into cars… he just was also still tied to apron strings.' Now she paused a second or two. 'Like you say though, a bastard…let's forget him and move on.' Sue snuggled a bit closer to Peter.

'I'm glad we're doing this Sue, thought it would be hard to share really. You joked about *This Is Your Life* once, do you remember?'

'Actually Pete, think that was you!'

'Oh, right. OK. Anyway, back to Chamonix again. Let's keep focused. It was like fate Sue wasn't it? Our paths crossed and there was a week or so's overlap, and we spent a lot of time in your tent, cuddling and kissing like we had done down there.' Pointing at the distant glimpse of Kinlochewe.

'Except we went a bit further.' Sue said.

'Except we went a bit further.' Peter repeated. 'It was all nice Sue. Really nice.'

'So, this bit of the graph is our affair?' Sue asked, pointing at the upward curve on the line Peter had drawn.

'Indeed it is. And your divorce.'

'Hooray!' said Sue. 'That was the right thing to do. Chamonix had been an escape from the grimy reality of that divorce. It was nearly over at that point and you turned up at the point I needed someone.'

'So, I was just your rebound shag then?' Peter said, pretending to be hurt.

'Yeah, it had to be someone! You would do!' She gave him another hug, 'Only joking. Yes, I needed something, or someone. Though, for a while I thought we might become more.' She sighed and Peter squeezed her arm this time.

'Then work took off for me and I had to travel a lot and had to move.' Peter found himself taking a deep breath, made him slightly dizzy.

'I knew when you changed jobs, that it would be the end of our thing Pete.'

'I know. I was back in the same old quandary again. But I look back on that time with great fondness Sue. We had some good times didn't we?' She leaned into him and they kissed lightly.

'We still do Pete. Really good friends … you have to be something to stay friends for so long. It was lovely and what we have now means so much.' They sighed again at exactly the same moment, which made them chuckle briefly.

Sue stretched out her legs, stood up and gave herself a little shake. Peter joined her and they took a few moments out of the conversation to look through Pete's binoculars at the landscape around. Looking for wildlife but just spotting a few other walkers on the trail. Peter mimed taking out a packet of cigarettes, lighting a pretend one for each of them. Sue giggled.

'Love and friendship, a bit of sex, that's what this chart is about, isn't it? Said Peter, as they resumed their seated positions. 'Different things done and said with different people at different times. One thing that surprises me about this chart, doing it for me, was the paucity of characters in it! Just a few central actors…'

Sue leant back and looked at Peter for a while at that. Peter suddenly recalled something he hadn't experienced with Sue for some while – that intense feeling she was rifling through his head, raiding his mind. He wasn't uncomfortable with it and in fact it was as if he had just given her permission. The moment felt a bit dizzying and then passed.

'Come on. You'd better keep going, it's getting chilly. I can see there's this short, flat bit and then this peak, and that's Mike of course?'

'Yep – Mike. Before him, trying to find my way again. But I felt free then too. I was in no relationship, had a nice little home, a good job, getting to the mountains a lot, and could please myself what to do.'

'And into your life walked Mike!'

'When you're open to it, things can happen. Though I resisted that too at first! It was whisky that did it in the end!' said Peter, smiling, looking up across the landscape.

'Whisky again see!' exclaimed Sue. 'Bit of a connection with up here really. Those whisky-fuelled evenings at Steve's caravan and then years later a whisky session with Mike and that was it.'

'About the same time you got involved with Ian.' Peter said. 'A guy you knew as a friend. He was there in Chamonix even. There's a pattern here isn't there?' He was nudging Sue gently, both of them smiling. She realised something she wanted to say then.

'What happened with you and Mike…well, you know, I think it released me from something too.' She paused, thinking, looking at Peter for corroboration. They both looked out across to the mountains in the north.

'Maybe we were a brake on each other Pete.'

Peter thought she had just nailed a forty year old truth. He gulped and fought hard, but unsuccessfully, against welling-up a bit.

'It's about nests and mates.' Sue continued, unhurriedly taking out a tissue and dabbing Peter's eyes. 'I remember you telling me those words, down there,' pointing over his shoulder, 'on that path over there – far away and long ago.'

The wind was getting up. A stronger gust blew across the spot where they were sitting so hard, they actually both ducked momentarily. It reminded them of time passing.

'Time to get going Pete?'

'You know Sue…' He sighed, nodded and got up, starting to pack the rucksack again '…that summer here was the pivotal moment of my life. Everything else spins off it.' He shrugged, his shoulders dropping a little. Sue remembered the same movements, here, in the past.

'Yeah' he continued, as if talking to himself for a moment. 'The significance of memory, the need for a nest, a mate to share it with – it all evolves from this starting point.'

'It had to be another male bird in the nest though Pete.'

'I know Sue, but now at this age…this point in my life.' He felt he was in danger of rambling. Found himself suddenly faltering, like when he was younger. 'Don't get my hesitation wrong.' He turned to Sue, standing upright, as if declaring something. 'I love Mike to bits. It's not about that. I would defend him to the end of the Earth, and more. Would literally lay down my life for him. He is my mate. For sure'. Now it was his turn to shake his head. 'Oh, I don't know what else I'm trying to say…'

'…but seeing yourself as gay or straight isn't the main thing for you, is that it?' said Sue. 'We've talked a bit about this before.' They hugged again.

'We have Sue. Needing stability and finding it has been wonderful. Sharing a life with someone. Caring for someone and being cared-for in return. We are so fortunate. That's it really. So much has worked out. But, you know, that afternoon up here, right here in fact. When I think of that time…it's all about the faultline…'

'Come on, the cloud's thickening and you're in danger of getting philosophical.' Sue adjusted her pack and got ready to move off.

Peter tugged Sue's arm and stopped her from immediately heading back the way they had just come, back across the outcrops up to the ridge to rejoin the trail. 'Can we stay here another minute, for old time's sake?'

Both of them now held each other in a gaze. The moment, to both of them felt giddying as the years fell away. Peter gently took her arm then and turned them together on the spot, slowly, through a three-sixty degree circle. They lifted their heads and looked out. The cloud was just hovering above what had once been Steve's mapping area, gathering around the dramatic tops of Slioch in the north and more so on the expanse of Peter's mountain behind. The landscape spilled-out before them, rising and falling in all directions, with a myriad outcrops of rock scattered everywhere.

They stopped rotating, comfortably and easily fell into each other's arms and hugged closely, feeling the warmth, allowing the sense of themselves to permeate through each other, finally bringing their lips together and allowing themselves a long, long kiss. Eventually, Peter moved his face back enough to say something he realised was a simple and fundamental feeling. 'Thanks for being there all these years Sue. You know, I do love you.'

'Stop it, you old softie.' She said. 'You've made me cry now.' And they continued to hug closely, small tears emerging and rolling down their faces.

Afterword and acknowledgments

Firstly, I want to thank a number of people for their outstanding support to me in the writing of this novel.

Sheena Duncan and Pat Stephens helped me considerably with editing and proofing. Their insights as well as their eyes have been vital to me. Nik Crane was interested in this novel from early on and I am eternally grateful to her for listening to me verbally downloading pieces of dialogue and characterisations over masked and socially distanced coffees in the hospital.

In addition, the following people were kind enough to be readers of drafts of the novel and provided many helpful comments and views. In no particular order: Angie Avis, Bob Kenney, Polly Parker, Lucy Payne, John Windsor, Diana Bevan, Mair Graham, John Graham, Lisa Merrell, Liz Pearcy, Lou Keedwell-Wirtz, Alison Begley, Hannah Painter, Michelle Dolling, Helen Walters, Bill Walters, Katie Madge.

And Dave – what can I say but thank you for being there.

Very many elements of this story are true! As an example, the river by the drumlin field, the one flowing into Loch Maree and the lochans on the mountainside really do exist and are still, hopefully, great places to do wild swimming. By Loch Maree these days, you might well be joined by an osprey!

A large vehicle really did go off the narrow road and took all that effort to get it going again. There was a mountain rescue team alert in Kinlochewe that summer, involving a geology student lost on Meallan Gobhar, which ended happily. There actually was a small café on the village campsite, in 1977 at least. A washing line of 'pennants' truly was hung out in the way described! And more…

In the mid to late seventies, over three thousand men were employed on contracts to build oil production platforms in the deep-water loch at Kishorn and a small group of them were housed in a bunkhouse in Kinlochewe during that time.

The Highlands have a number of sites of plane wrecks from the Second World War and other times. All the ones I have seen are poignant and invoke strong feelings in everyone who visits them. They are often still and sobering memorials to mostly young men who gave their lives on behalf of their countries. The site on Beinn Eighe is one such example but is very difficult to access. The Fairy Lochs wreck is much easier to visit and is a moving and affecting place, as described in this book.

In Aultbea there is now the Russian Arctic Convoy Museum, which reveals more information about these incidents and the incredibly extensive wartime activity in North West Scotland, and how it all impacted on local men and women. It is well worth a visit.

The Beinn Eighe National Nature Reserve was the first such reserve established in the UK, in 1957, by the Nature Conservancy Council, partly in recognition of its astonishing geology. It is now managed by Scottish Natural Heritage/NatureScot. The Glas Leitre Forest Tail and the Mountain Trail have been in existence since 1973 and give fantastic reward for the effort involved walking them, as does the Pony Track.

The Reserve is crowned by the beautiful and lovely mountain Meall a Ghiubhais. Golden Eagles really do nest on its cliffs and from there they soar over the ancient and spectacular rocks and scenery.

John McLellan, November 2021.